P9-BZJ-164

LAURA GRIFFIN

TWISTED

POCKET STAR BOOKS

New York London Toronto Sydney New Delhi

Pocket Star Books
A Division of Simon & Schuster, Inc.
1230 Avenue of the Americas
New York, NY 10020

This book is a work of fiction. Names, characters, places, and incidents either are products of the author's imagination or are used fictitiously. Any resemblance to actual events or locales or persons, living or dead, is entirely coincidental.

First Pocket Star Books paperback edition May 2012

POCKET STAR BOOKS and colophon are registered trademarks of Simon & Schuster, Inc.

For information about special discounts for bulk purchases, please contact Simon & Schuster Special Sales at 1-866-506-1949 or business@simonandschuster.com.

The Simon & Schuster Speakers Bureau can bring authors to your live event. For more information or to book an event contact the Simon & Schuster Speakers Bureau at 1-866-248-3049 or visit our website at www.simonspeakers.com.

Manufactured in the United States of America

10 9 8 7 6 5 4 3 2 1

ISBN 978-1-4516-1737-5
ISBN 978-1-4516-1743-6 (ebook)

For Kathy

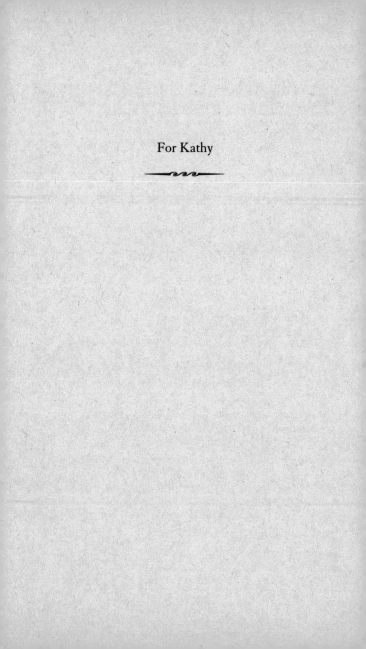

ACKNOWLEDGMENTS

One of the many joys of writing the Tracers series has been meeting and interviewing so many dedicated professionals in the fields of law enforcement and forensic science. I'd like to thank Kyra Stull, Ruben Vasquez, Jennifer Rice, and Mike Snow. Thank you also to the numerous other experts who shared their knowledge through fascinating books or workshops, including Kathy Bennett, Robert Genna, Rob Preece, D. P. Lyle, and Gavin de Becker.

I appreciate the hard work of everyone at Pocket, including Abby Zidle, Lisa Litwack, Ayelet Gruenspecht, Renee Huff, and Parisa Zolfaghari. Thanks, also, to my amazing agent, Kevan Lyon.

And a special thank-you to my family, for their patience and support as I wrote this story.

TWISTED

CHAPTER 1

The day Jordan Wheatley last ran free was clear and bright, like her sixteenth birthday. Like her wedding day. Like 9/11.

She'd overdressed that afternoon in sweatpants and a long-sleeved T-shirt, and she came off the trail with her face dripping and her ponytail saturated. She reached into her car for a tall bottle of water, guzzled most of it down, and poured the few remaining ounces over her head. Jordan checked the timer on her watch. Ninety-seven minutes. That extra two miles was going to make her late getting home, and Ethan would be in a sulk. She needed to hurry.

First, though, she tipped her head back to gaze at the sky and took a moment to just *be*. The late-afternoon sun touched her cheeks. She inhaled the crisp fall breeze, tinged with cedar. The runner's high thrummed in her veins and her muscles felt loose. She could do anything. Everything. She could run the whole course all over again, right this minute if she wanted to.

But Ethan was waiting. She checked her watch again and tossed the empty bottle into the car.

"Hey, you wouldn't happen to have a phone, would you?"

Jordan turned around and saw a young man standing beside a green minivan several spaces away. She glanced over her shoulder to see if he was talking to someone else.

"It's the battery again." He smiled. "My wife's going to kill me this time—she told me to get it changed." When Jordan hesitated, his expression turned wary. "But looks like you're in a hurry. You probably don't have time to play Good Samaritan, do you?"

She stepped forward. "No, it's all right." Then she remembered what he'd asked for and reached back into her car. Her cell phone was locked in the glove compartment, and she dug it out.

"You want me to call Triple A or . . . ?"

He sauntered over. "Thanks, but I'll do it."

She surveyed him more carefully now, feeling odd about handing over her phone to a complete stranger, even a nice-looking one. He was tall, dark-haired, and had wire-rimmed glasses. He wore faded jeans and a Rice University sweatshirt with the familiar blue crest on the front.

Jordan passed him the phone.

"I've actually got a favorite mechanic, if you can believe it. He specializes in German cars, but he owes me a favor, so . . ." He dialed a number with his thumb and pressed the phone to his ear, and Jordan turned around, pretending not to eavesdrop. She wiped the sweat from her brow with the back of her arm. In the distance she heard a pair of high-pitched barks as some dogs encountered each other on the trail.

"No answer. Damn. You have any jumper cables?" He smiled hopefully.

"'Fraid not."

He sighed and looked around at the surrounding scenery—canyons, hills, and scrub brush as far as the eye could see. "So, what do you think the odds are we'll be able to get a tow truck out here by sundown?" He glanced at the sky. "Not good, I'm guessing. I probably better call the wife."

Relieved for some reason, she turned away to give him privacy as he made the call.

A weight slammed into her. Air exploded from her lungs with an *oomf!* and her face plowed into the gravel. She shrieked. The sound was cut off as her head was yanked back and then smashed forward. Pain lanced through her skull.

"Don't make a sound," he growled in her ear.

Jordan's pulse pounded. Her mind reeled. She squirmed and struggled to breathe as his knee dug into her spine.

"You hear me?" He yanked her ponytail again, and her head snapped back. She gazed up at the blue sky and smelled her own terror, ripe and pungent.

This isn't happening. But it was. Tears burned her eyes and her neck arched painfully. Her heart thundered inside her too-tight chest. For the first time in her life, she felt a fear so complete it replaced every sensation in her body.

Jordan bucked. She kicked and twisted, throwing elbows and knees. The weight slipped off and she scrambled to her feet. Fire shot down her leg as he clawed her skin.

She lunged for her car. He was right behind. He tackled her and she was on the ground again. A fist smashed into her cheek and a bright burst of pain exploded behind her eyes. Blood filled her mouth. She felt a tooth sliding around on her tongue.

He yanked her head back, and through the daze she felt him shift on top of her. She tried to scream, but his weight was on her and it came out like a wisp of air. A hand clamped hard over her mouth. He hauled her to her feet and dragged her across the gravel, and through tear-blurred vision she saw her car.

This isn't happening. No, no, no!

Jordan writhed and struggled. Pain radiated down her right arm, but she used it anyway, reaching back, desperately trying to gouge his eyes. He gripped her harder. In the corner of her eye, she saw the side of the van. She kicked viciously, trying to break his hold. A muffled curse. He flung her against something hard, making her brain rattle against her skull. Nausea washed over her as his arms tightened once more. The pain was consuming. She felt it taking over, swallowing up her will to resist. All of her limbs quivered.

"There's no point in fighting." His breath was hot against her neck. "Just be quiet and I won't have to hurt you."

Jordan knew he was lying. From deep inside her came a primal scream.

CHAPTER 2

Detective Allison Doyle knew better than to expect the whole night off. The way things were going, she figured she had a nine-out-of-ten chance of being back on the job before her pizza even came out of the oven. But she was an optimist at heart—and she was hungry—so she pulled into the parking lot of Sal's Quick Stop savoring the idea of a hot Meat Lover's Supreme. Before she even cut the engine, her phone buzzed. She heaved a sigh.

"Doyle."

"Where's the Borman file?"

Ric Santos. At least it wasn't her boss calling her back in.

"No idea. Why?"

"You remember who posted his bail?"

"I want to say his girlfriend, but I couldn't swear to it." Allison got out of her truck and headed into the store. "Might have been his sister. She had a different last name."

"You remember it?"

She made a beeline for the freezer section. It was six months ago, but Allison never forgot a name. "Trautman,

Leslie. It's in the computer. What do you need the file for?"

"Our system's down again." His voice echoed, and she pictured him in the stairwell at the station house. He was on his way out, and he sounded in a hurry.

"You need a hand with something?"

"Nah, got it covered. Enjoy your night off."

First in weeks, she wanted to remind him, but he already knew. Everyone in the department had been working round the clock. Allison's reward was going to be a junk-food dinner and a mindless night in front of the tube. She pulled open the freezer and selected a sausage-and-double-pepperoni pizza with extra-thick crust. She made a quick detour through the dry-goods section for cat food, and approached the register.

The store owner's gaze darted to her. His tense expression morphed into relief.

Allison's skin prickled. Her attention snapped to the customer at the counter with his back to her. Greasy brown hair, oversize leather jacket, shoulders hunched up around his ears. His body moved back and forth with the agitated tic of a tweeker.

Holdup.

The news flash was accompanied by a kick of dread as she realized that both her hands were full.

Always keep your gun hand free. Allison knew that. She'd had it drilled into her by every firearms instructor she'd ever met, and yet here she stood with an armed assailant, encumbered by a frozen pizza and a bag of kitten chow, her service weapon tucked neatly beneath her jacket. Panic threatened, but she tamped it down as she scrounged for a plan. If she dropped her groceries, she'd startle him—

The man whirled around, and she cursed her hesitation. She looked at his pistol and widened her eyes in fake surprise.

"*Step back!*" He jabbed the gun at her with a shaking hand, then spun back to Sal.

Allison scanned her surroundings. No other customers, thank God. Two cars in front, including hers. No getaway driver in the other vehicle, but the headlights glowed, hinting at a running engine. Why hadn't she noticed it? She was 0-for-3 here, and her marathon workweek had now culminated in a string of potentially deadly mistakes.

The situation worsened as another car turned into the lot, pulling up to a gas pump. She hoped they were paying outside.

The perp spun toward her, panicked. White male, five-ten, one-forty. Dilated pupils. The tremor in his gun hand extended to his whole body; he was clearly jacked up. Bad news for everyone. So was the fact that he'd made no effort to disguise himself and seemed oblivious to the security camera mounted behind the cash register. Even from ten feet away, Allison could smell the desperation on him.

"I said *back*, bitch!"

She stepped back obediently and tried to look meek.

He turned to the register. "The *money*!"

Sal reached for the cash drawer. It slid open with a *ping,* and Allison watched the store owner, noting all the details she'd missed at first glance. He didn't just look tense, he looked frightened. But it was a fierce frightened, like a cornered animal. Sweat beaded at his temples as he glared at the man aiming the gun at him.

Allison eased forward. Sal glanced at her, and his defiant look had her pulse racing. She knew exactly what he thought of this two-bit meth fiend trying to rip off his business, and she hoped he wasn't rash enough to do anything stupid before she got this under control.

Allison slid a glance at the gunman. His attention bounced nervously between Sal and her, and she prayed he wouldn't notice the bulge beneath her blazer. She needed to get her hands free.

Sal took out another stack of bills, his eyes imploring her to do something. The perp caught the look and thrust his gun at her.

"You! Over there!" He waved the pistol at the soft-drink station.

Damn it, she needed to get closer, not farther away. Her best chance was to disarm him at close range.

"Now, bitch!"

She took a baby step back.

"Now!" A burst of spittle accompanied the command.

Allison took several steps back, looking deep into those desperate eyes. It was the desperation that concerned her. Those wild eyes told her he'd shoot her as soon as look at her, and the knowledge made her chest squeeze. She'd thought about being shot in the line of duty, but she'd never envisioned having her life ended by some tweeker with rotten teeth.

He turned and grabbed the bills with his free hand as Sal stacked them on the counter.

"Faster!"

A flutter of movement in the convex mirror near the ceiling caught her eye. She tried not to call attention to it, but she glanced up to see someone slipping from the corridor at the back of the store into the aisle closest to the door, which led straight to the register. Tall and dark-haired, the man wore a charcoal suit and looked remarkably like the defense attorney Allison had gone to war with in court just last week. But it wasn't the attorney. This man was leaner and broad-shouldered and made a lot less noise.

"That's *it*? That's all you *got*?" Meth Man snatched up the pile of twenties and waved them at Sal. *"I want all of it!"*

Sal grumbled a response as Allison cut a glance to her left. The businessman hunched low now behind a beer display. His gaze locked with hers, and his hard expression commanded her to stay put.

Crap, just her luck. *Don't try to be a hero,* she tried to tell him with her eyes, but his focus was on the confrontation now.

"Hand it over!" The perp was bobbing up and down on the balls of his feet—shrill and angry, but distracted.

Now was her chance.

She flung the pizza away like a Frisbee. In the next instant of confusion, she whipped out her gun and lunged for the man's weapon.

His pistol tracked her far too closely. She registered the black barrel pointed at her face as a shoe came up and the gun cartwheeled out of the perp's hand.

Allison thrust a heel into the side of his knee. He howled and crumpled to the floor. The man who'd kicked the gun away shoved Allison aside and flipped the robber onto his stomach. A Glock appeared from no-where, and he jabbed it against the perp's neck.

"Don't move!"

Allison's mouth fell open. The man turned and gave her a blistering look.

"Who the hell are you?" she demanded.

"You plan to arrest this guy?"

Her shock lasted maybe a second, and then she sprang into action, jerking a pair of handcuffs from her belt and elbowing the suit out of the way. "I got it," she said, taking control of the prisoner with her knee on his back.

The robber squirmed and spewed obscenities as she yanked his wrists behind him and slapped on the cuffs. Allison's back felt damp. She took a steadying breath and tried to regain her composure as she conducted the pat-down.

"You're under arrest," she said, with much more bravado than she felt at the moment. Her lips were dry, her hands clammy. She glanced up at Sal, who was on the phone with the 911 dispatcher. "Tell them to send a cage car," she told him.

Sal nodded.

"You got any other weapons on you?" she asked the perp. "Knives, needles, drug paraphernalia?"

He didn't answer and she checked his pockets. When she was satisfied, she started to climb off him.

He exploded in a blur of movement. Pain stung her cheek as she caught an elbow, and she had to sit on his butt to make him stop thrashing. The man in the suit pressed a shiny black wing tip between the prisoner's shoulders as Allison struggled with his legs. At eye level was a shelf of fishing supplies, and she grabbed a roll of twine. She ripped open the package with her teeth and lashed the binding around his ankles. The prisoner cursed and squirmed for a while, but eventually the fight went out of him. He was trussed like a turkey now, and she knew she was going to catch all kinds of S&M jokes from the guys at work.

Allison glanced up at the man now leaning against the checkout counter. His palms rested casually on the Formica, and the Glock had disappeared beneath his suit jacket. He hadn't even broken a sweat.

He lifted a brow at her. "Not bad, Officer."

Okay, he was definitely a cop. DEA? Immigration? FBI? And suddenly it hit her. She knew exactly who he was and why he was here.

The corner of his mouth curved up, and she felt a surge of annoyance.

"You have a permit to carry a concealed handgun?" she asked, although she knew the answer.

He sighed and reached into his jacket. He pulled out a leather folio and flipped it open.

"Special Agent Mark Wolfe, FBI."

Allison sat in the interview room, running through the surveillance video for the fourth time. It didn't get any less embarrassing with each viewing.

Distracted police detective walks into a store, failing to notice the car parked out front with its engine running. Detective shops for groceries. Detective interrupts robbery-in-progress armed with kitten chow instead of a gun.

She watched the surveillance cam bird's-eye view once again, as Mark Wolfe burst out from behind the beer display to kick the gun from the perp's hand the instant before it could have gone off.

She shuddered. A fraction of a second later and she might not be sitting here, all because she'd neglected to follow her most basic training. She watched herself cuff the perp, and even the grainy recording didn't hide her shaking hands.

Disgusted, Allison ejected the disk from the player and slipped it into an evidence bag. She dropped it into a brown accordion file already fat with paperwork. She'd spent two tedious hours booking Steven P. Irby, thirty-three, for aggravated robbery and resisting arrest, and another two completing the reports. Now she was exhausted, cranky, and in dire need of a hot shower.

Allison went back to her desk, where she locked her case file in a drawer for tomorrow. The bullpen was empty, but she spotted a fellow detective from the Crimes Against Persons squad coming out of the break room.

"Heard about Sal's," Jonah Macon said. "You all right?"

"Fine."

He glanced at her cheek, and his frown told her she had a bruise where Irby's elbow had landed. "The fed already left, I take it?"

"Slipped out right after Sean took his statement," she told him.

"That was fast."

"Said he had a plane to catch."

"Bet he missed it."

Allison pictured Mark Wolfe leaning against the patrol car as he gave his statement. Cool. Composed. He'd watched her from across the parking lot with those brown-black eyes, and she hadn't been able to read his opinion of her. But she could guess. He had an arrogance about him that indicated what he thought about their small-town police department.

Jonah was still staring at her. He had something on his mind.

"What?" she asked.

"Nothing."

"No, really. What's your take on him?"

"Don't have one. He talked to Reynolds." Jonah moved for the door, and she knew she was getting the brush-off. "Go home, Doyle. Get some sleep. Looks like you need it."

Allison watched him leave, unsettled by what he'd told her. *Not your case,* she reminded herself. And anyway, she had enough to worry about. She made her way downstairs and once again took off for the night. She hitched herself behind the wheel of her dinged Chevy pickup and coaxed the engine to life. Then she pulled out of the parking lot and headed for home.

Alone in her truck, she took what felt like her first deep breath in hours. She tugged the elastic band from her ponytail and buzzed the windows down to let the cold air whip through her hair. But her mind wouldn't clear. She kept picturing that gun.

All those years, all that training, and still she'd ended up on the wrong side of a loaded weapon. It was a blow to her reputation, and worse, her confidence. And although no one had said anything directly, she knew her sloppiness hadn't gone unnoticed by her coworkers.

The night was blustery. Discarded candy wrappers tumbled down the street and huddled together against curbs and tree trunks. Sagging jack-o'-lanterns sat in doorways, gazing out with empty eyes. The costumed kids who had scampered up and down the sidewalk only a few nights before were now safely in bed where they belonged.

The street's small brick houses gave way to cookie-cutter apartment buildings where young professionals enjoyed workout rooms and greenbelt views. At least some of them did. Allison hardly ever opened her blinds. And when she had time to work out—which she hadn't lately—she either went for a run or hit the no-frills gym at the YMCA near the police station.

Allison parked and gathered the pet food off the seat, along with the frozen pizza Sal had given her as a thank-you when she'd left his store. She collected her mail before unlocking her door. Silence greeted her. She stood still for a moment and listened to it. It sounded different tonight. Lonelier.

Or maybe she was just in a mood.

She dumped the mail on the counter and shrugged out of her blazer. Then she removed her holster and boots. She filled a cereal bowl with cat food and stepped onto her patio, where a striped tabby was waiting impatiently beside the railing. She set the food down for him and scratched his ears.

The air outside smelled of burning wood. The temperature had dipped, and it was the first night cold enough for fireplaces. Allison leaned against the railing and gazed out at the trees. The thicket looked dark and foreboding—probably because a woman had been killed there recently. The discovery of her remains had sent a shock wave through town and put the entire San

Marcos police force on high alert. And though everyone was working to maintain a calm front, the department was reeling. Crimes like that just didn't happen in this community. Drug busts, yes. Convenience store robberies, yes. Last summer they'd even had a school shooting.

But women being murdered and left to rot in the woods? That sort of thing didn't happen here.

Except it had.

Allison wasn't even on the case—yet—but still she felt connected to it. It wasn't just the brutal nature of the crime or that it had happened only steps away from her home. As one of the few female cops in this town, Allison felt particularly responsible for the women here, and she was determined to see justice done.

Back inside, she turned the shower to scalding and tossed her wilted shirt onto the floor. She thought of that gun barrel again and suddenly she really, really didn't want to be alone tonight.

She showered and pulled on jeans and a fresh top, then stood before the mirror in the hallway—critiquing, debating, and critiquing some more.

Don't be a wuss, she told herself.

She took a deep breath and reached for her keys.

Mark prowled the chat room, searching for any trace of Death Raven or one of his aliases. He hadn't found him yet, but it was still early, and many of these men were nocturnal.

Mark surfed. He analyzed. He scrolled through page after page of blather, scanning for a familiar handle or turn of phrase. As he entered his second hour of searching, the sites started to blend together and the words became a blur.

Only this and nothing more. The phrase echoed through his head. *Tapping at my chamber door.* His brain spooled. His temples throbbed. He rubbed his eyes. *Tap-tap.*

Mark looked up.

Tap-tap-tap.

He crossed the room and checked the peephole, even though he already had a good idea who he'd see standing on the other side.

He paused for a moment. Then he pulled open the door.

"Detective Doyle."

She nodded. "Special Agent."

For a few seconds they stared at each other.

"You need something?" It came out harsher than he'd intended, but she didn't seem put off.

"I do, actually. You busy?"

"Yes."

She leaned a palm against the door frame and looked him squarely in the eye. She wasn't intimidated by his federal badge or his height or the hard stare he used on vicious criminals. His being busy didn't seem to matter much, either, and he knew why she'd come to see him.

She stepped past him into the room and glanced around. His laptop sat open on the rumpled bedspread, and he'd forgotten to clear the screen.

She turned and folded her arms over her chest. With the leather jacket and the attitude, she looked more like a biker chick than an officer of the law.

Mark steeled himself. "What can I do for you, Detective?"

"You can talk," she said. "I want to hear about Stephanie Snow."

CHAPTER 3

———— ❧ ————

They went to Randy's Pool Hall, which she claimed had lousy food but was one of the few hangouts in town not overrun with college students. The bar was dim and crowded. Doyle drew looks from some of the cowboys and truckers as she made her way to a small table in the corner, as far away from the noise as it was possible to get.

Mark eyed her tiny waist as she draped her jacket over the back of a chair and sank into it. He glanced around the bar and felt himself being scrutinized from beneath the brims of baseball caps. The women were much less subtle.

"I'm starving," Doyle said as he pulled out the chair across from her. "You hungry?"

"Had a sandwich in my room."

A waitress came over. She surveyed his Brooks Brothers shirt with suspicion, and he was glad he'd left the coat and tie behind.

After they'd given their orders, Mark leaned back and looked at the woman who'd brought him here. She'd left her dark hair loose around her shoulders and added makeup to her hazel eyes—nothing flashy, but enough to announce her femininity to anyone who might be wondering. Female cops took a lot of crap.

"How'd you know where I was staying?"

"Small town." She shrugged. "Not a lot of options."

True, but he could have found something near the airport. That was in Austin, though, and he'd wanted to spend the night here, closer to the crime scene. Any extra time in a place gave him more data points to work with.

"You ever been here before?" she asked.

"Not until today."

"And what do you think of our fine little town?" She glanced toward the bar, then back at him. She had the cop habit of scanning the room while she talked, checking out faces, looking for trouble.

"It's not so little, really."

"Depends how long you stay," she said. "You stick around awhile, it feels small."

The waitress delivered their beers and moved on to another table to clear empties. She had that efficiency of motion of people who worked on their feet all day.

"You know, you don't look like a profiler." Allison picked up her beer.

"What does a profiler look like?"

"I don't know. Thin. Nerdy. Maybe wire-rimmed spectacles."

"You're describing Scott Glenn in *Silence of the Lambs.*"

"You look more like a jock."

He couldn't suppress a wry smile. It had been years since anyone had accused him of being a jock.

"At my age, I'll take that as a compliment."

"What age is that, exactly?" She looked him over as she tipped back the bottle. Her tone was neutral, but he sensed an agenda behind the question.

"Forty-three."

If the number bothered her, she didn't show it. It bothered him—considering he was sitting in a bar with a twenty-seven year old.

Mark had looked up Allison Doyle. She'd joined the San Marcos police force right out of college and made detective at the tender age of twenty-five. Small-town politics? Token woman? He didn't know, but he had a feeling he'd get his balls handed to him if he suggested either.

Her beef-vegetable soup arrived, and she dug in. He watched her eat, enjoying her gusto.

"Sure you don't want anything?" she asked between spoonfuls. "It's actually not half bad."

"I'm good."

"So, you were here meeting with Lieutenant Reynolds, I take it. How did it go?"

"Probably how you'd expect."

She lifted an eyebrow. "You mean he didn't welcome you with open arms and thank you for your thoughtful insights?"

"Not so much."

"He doesn't like outsiders butting in. Particularly federal ones."

"I caught that."

"And he likes our suspect—Joshua Bender."

"Stephanie Snow's ex-boyfriend."

She nodded. "He's got a sheet and she called the cops on him a few months ago, said he was harassing her."

This was news to Mark. In typical small-town fashion, Lieutenant Reynolds had been territorial, defensive, and stingy with information.

"Define *harassing*," Mark said.

"Showing up at her house. Following her out on dates. Calling her cell phone at all hours."

"The ex who won't let go," Mark said. "We see it a lot."

"But in this case you think there's more."

"I know there is."

She pushed her bowl away and leaned back. "I'm listening."

He studied her face. She was the only female detective on her squad, one of only four women on the entire police force. Just the fact that she was here said she didn't mind going against the grain.

"This crime's different," he said.

"How?"

He weighed how much to tell her. It wasn't her case, yet she was interested—interested enough to come looking for him after an unusually difficult day in order to pump him for information. He could tell she was smart. Plus, she was young, which could mean open-minded. Maybe she'd listen.

Or maybe talking to her was going to put the freeze on his already cool relationship with the local police lieutenant overseeing the case—a guy who probably didn't want one of his people talking to the FBI behind his back.

But what the hell did he care about politics? He'd be on a plane in the morning, and he hadn't managed to convince anyone who mattered to consider his theory.

Mark took a sip of his beer. He looked at her for a long moment.

"I work for the Bureau's Behavioral Analysis Unit—BAU. You know what that does?"

"Profiling?"

"That's what gets the most attention. We cover a lot of bases—counterterrorism, white-color crime, crimes against children, kidnappings. Sometimes we get pulled in on homicide cases if the local police think they're dealing with a serial killer."

She looked at him expectantly.

"In the fall of 2000, I got a call about a murder out in Shasta County, California."

"That's north of Sacramento, right?"

He nodded. "This was near Redding. The year before, a woman went hiking in a park on October thirtieth, never came home. Her boyfriend reported her missing that same night. Her remains were discovered in a shallow creek east of the park a week later."

"Cause of death?"

"Sharp force trauma—her throat had been slashed."

"Sexual assault?"

"Too much water damage to know for sure."

"And lemme guess—boyfriend had an alibi?"

"Airtight," he confirmed. "Then November nineteenth that same year, another woman went missing, this time from a dog park. Same county. Her remains were discovered in a ravine six months later."

"Not a lot to work with by that point."

"You'd be surprised. A forensic anthropologist examined what was recovered. Marks on the bone indicated another throat cutting."

"So now the boyfriend's off the hook and you're look-ing for a serial killer."

"*I* wasn't looking for anything yet. They didn't call me in until that next fall. Another missing woman, an-other body dumped in a remote area. Dara Langford. Twenty-three. She'd just graduated from college and found a job in Redding." He visualized Dara's smiling young face on all the fliers he'd seen tacked to lampposts and stoplights throughout the area. "She was living with her parents at the time. They reported her missing when she didn't come home from a jog on October thirtieth."

Allison tipped her head to the side. "So it's the dates that match up, not just the MO?"

"Looks that way. That same year, we had another dis-appearance on November nineteenth. Sheryl Fanning, thirty-five-year-old mother of two. And another woman the following fall, Jillian Webb."

"October thirtieth?"

"Yes."

Her brow furrowed. "What do the dates mean?"

"Good question. I wish I knew."

"Maybe some kind of Halloween connection? Day of the Dead, that sort of thing?"

"We looked into that. Came up with zip. Which isn't to say it isn't a factor; we just don't know how it fits." Mark gazed down at his beer and swallowed his frustra-tion. He'd worked hundreds of cases, but this one stuck. For years he'd studied it, and still he hadn't put all the pieces together.

He glanced up. She was watching him closely, as she had been all evening. He doubted she missed much, which meant she'd sensed this was personal.

"So five women." Her eyes had turned somber.

"That we know of."

"Were all of them found?"

"Sheryl Fanning—the mother of two toddlers—was never recovered. Some search dogs found her running shoe near the path, but that was it. They combed the area repeatedly, so we're thinking she might have been taken someplace else."

Allison gazed away, looking pensive. "Stephanie Snow went missing October thirtieth."

She didn't recite the rest. Many of the details—too many of them—had appeared in the local paper. Mark had read the articles online after catching a news snippet on CNN. Most murders didn't get a mention in the national media unless there was something sensational about them. Stephanie Snow had been a swimming star at the University of Texas. She was a hometown hero.

The media hadn't connected Stephanie to the killings in California yet. Maybe they never would. Maybe nobody would, and Mark was spinning his wheels here.

But he didn't believe that. From the way Lieutenant Reynolds had reacted in their meeting today, he could tell there were some holes in the case against Stephanie's ex-boyfriend.

And besides that, Mark had a hunch. This murder *felt* connected, and his hunches about cases often turned out to be right—mainly because they weren't hunches, but predictions based on dozens of different factors, all viewed together through the lens of experience.

"So," Allison said. "Three years in a row you get these close-together murders in Northern California, and the dates match up."

"Also, the MO. The crimes are remarkably similar."

"How?"

"You haven't seen the case file?"

"It's not my case."

"Maybe it should be."

She looked uncomfortable now, and he could tell he was touching on something that was going to make her life complicated.

But she didn't mind complicated, or she wouldn't be here, wearing a snug-fitting black shirt and drinking a beer with him.

"So, then what?" she asked.

"Then nothing. He's been inactive, as far as we know, for a decade. Now this."

Allison leaned forward on her elbows. "You're the expert, not me. But I didn't think serial killers worked like that. That they just stopped."

"They don't, usually. After about five years without anything similar popping up in ViCAP—that's the database we use to track violent crimes—"

"I know what it is," she cut in, defensive. He often had that effect on local investigators.

"After five years with no hits, we began to think he might be dead or in prison. By ten years, we were sure of it."

"But now he's at it again."

"Maybe. Depends who you want to believe—me or your lieutenant."

She eyed him silently, and could see the gravity of the situation sinking in. November 19 was two weeks away.

"I'd much rather believe Reynolds," she said. "I just don't think I do."

• • •

Allison drove him back to the motel without talking. Her mind was tied up with Stephanie Snow and the smiling graduation photo she'd seen in the paper the other day. Allison hadn't looked at the crime-scene pictures. Hadn't wanted to. She'd been content to let more experienced investigators handle this one—until today.

Until she'd met Mark Wolfe.

She pulled into the pitted parking lot and slid into an empty spot beside his burgundy sedan. The rental car, the suit, the laptop. He was a fellow law enforcement officer, but in terms of lifestyle, they were worlds apart.

"You should put some ice on that welt," he told her.

His eyes were almost black in the dimness, and the lights of the motel made the angles of his face stand out. A day's worth of stubble darkened his jaw, and she thought he looked tired. He didn't look old, though, as he'd hinted back at the bar. He looked experienced. Confident. Smart. It was a combination she found attractive, even though the confidence bordered on arrogance.

He reached for the door handle. "Don't beat yourself up about today."

She scoffed.

"You did fine."

"It's embarrassing. I walked right in on it, didn't even realize it was happening." She looked at him. "What was your tip-off?"

"Saw the car running out front."

She'd heard the rest. He'd parked in back and quietly slipped in the door Sal had left unlocked after his smoke break.

"Bet you realized it before you think," he said.

"What, you mean when he pointed the gun at me? Snaps for me."

"You knew it before that. Think, Allison."

It was the first time he'd used her name. She turned away and gazed out the window at the parking lot. She visualized the scene again.

"I guess, yeah," she said, "I knew something was up."

"Something felt off in the store."

"It was Sal. He had this look on his face. Tight." She glanced at him. "And then when he saw me, suddenly it was pure relief."

"You're a regular there. He knew you'd be armed."

"And then there was the guy . . . I don't know. Even from the back, I could tell he was a tweeker. His movements, his hygiene, everything."

"All those silent cues you pick up on without even noticing. Your mind pulls them together and sends you a warning."

Holdup. She remembered thinking it even before she saw the gun. Maybe she wasn't as oblivious as she thought.

She looked at Mark again and tried to read his expression. His tall, athletic build filled up her passenger seat. Her gaze settled on his long-fingered hands. No ring, but he hadn't wanted to talk about that. She could tell she made him uneasy, which was okay. She liked to keep men off balance.

He pushed open the door and got out. "Thanks for the beer."

"Thanks for saving my life." She said it as though it was nothing, but they both knew she was serious.

He leaned a forearm on the door and ducked down to peer inside the pickup. "Get your lieutenant to listen to you about Stephanie Snow."

"It's not my case."

He just looked at her. Something in his expression put the responsibility on her shoulders.

"It belongs to Jonah Macon," she said. "He's a good cop."

"Then, how come you're here and he's not?"

She couldn't answer that without being disloyal to her squad. Mark Wolfe was the outsider, and Jonah really did care. But he liked the suspect they'd already developed.

"Read the ME's report," he said. "Reynolds wouldn't let me see it, but maybe you'll have better luck." He looked at her gravely. "And do it soon. November nineteenth isn't far away."

He started to slam the door, but she leaned across the seat. "Wait." She looked up at him in the bluish light of the motel sign. It panicked her a bit for him to throw all this information at her and then leave. "What am I looking for?"

"You'll know it when you see it," he said. "Pay attention to the hair."

Allison kicked off her morning with a domestic and a purse snatching. By ten a.m. she had two men in custody and a caffeine headache, not to mention a boatload of reports to write.

She spotted Jonah in the bullpen.

"Glad I caught you," she said, cornering him at his desk, where he was logging off of his computer and collecting his car keys.

"You been talking to the fed." He stood and shrugged into his blazer.

"What, am I under surveillance now?"

"Sean saw you at the pool hall." He gave her a look that was part big brother, part local cop defending his turf. "Guess you got your second wind last night, huh?"

"Guess so." She sat on the side of his desk and peeked inside the white paper bag. "Such a cliché," she said, and helped herself to a glazed doughnut.

"He tell you his theory?" Jonah asked.

"No, his favorite sexual position."

His face hardened. "You want to be careful here, Doyle. Bender's already got a lawyer involved. If you start circulating some new case theory and he hears about it—"

"No one's circulating anything." She chomped into the doughnut. The icing melted on her tongue and made the roof of her mouth sticky. "I just want to see what we've got."

Jonah gazed down at her, and she was reminded of Mark Wolfe. Both men towered over her, but Jonah was bulky while Mark was just big. Maybe he'd played basketball at one time. He definitely had the build for it.

Jonah sighed and shook his head. He reached for a thick brown file in his in-box.

"Murder book's in Reynolds's office," he said, referring to the official receptacle of all info in a homicide case. "This has the highlights—copy of the autopsy, initial police report, first round of interviews. You want to see the book, you're going to have to go through Reynolds."

"Why all the secrecy?"

"Just being careful. Like I said, the ex-boyfriend's got a lawyer. A good one. We don't need any screw-ups."

Allison sucked the sugar off her fingertips before taking the file. It was heavier than it looked.

She glanced up at Jonah, who happened to be one of the best detectives she'd ever met. "What makes you so sure about the boyfriend?"

He waited a beat. "This hasn't been in the news yet—"

"And you think *I'm* going to leak it? Thanks."

He ignored the jab. "Stephanie Snow took out a restraining order on her ex the day before her disappearance. I interviewed the guy who served the papers, too, and Bender was pissed."

"Timing's pretty incriminating."

"Tell me about it. I've worked more than a few cases where the restraining order was found at the scene of the crime."

"Some men don't take rejection well."

"No shit."

"But I'd still like to see where we are."

"Have at it. You got anything to add, go talk to Reynolds. He's holding on tight to this one." Jonah looked at his watch. "I got a deposition in twenty. Put that back when you're done."

Jonah took off, and Allison carried the file into the same interview room where she'd viewed the convenience store video last night. As unpleasant as that had been, this was going to be worse by a factor of a thousand.

Her thoughts went to Mark Wolfe. Why was he so convinced this case was connected to the ones in

California? *You'll know it when you see it,* he'd said, and she hoped he was right. She took a deep breath and opened the file.

The police report was on top, stapled to a sketch of the crime scene. Everything was stamped COPY. She flipped through the paperwork. No crime-scene photos, which made her both relieved and annoyed. She'd have to look harder for details about the hair. Allison found the ME's report tucked beneath an interview with the dog walker who had found the body. The report had a coffee ring on the top page and was already smudged with fingerprints. Someone had spent time with this. Probably Jonah. And if Allison knew her colleague, he'd shown the report to Ric Santos for a second opinion. The two detectives weren't the oldest on the squad, but they were the best, and they always sought each other's input.

Allison had noticed because they so rarely sought hers. Not that she was bitter or anything—she hadn't given them a reason to. She hadn't proven herself. She had only one homicide case under her belt, and that was as a member of a task force. She was well aware that some people—particularly the older guys—thought she'd only been promoted to detective because she was a woman. It was possible they were right. But she'd worked her ass off, too. She'd put in a lot of long hours and she'd aced her detective's exam, and now she was determined to show she could handle the job as well as any man.

She thought again of Mark. When she'd first met him, he'd been cool and detached, but at the bar last night he'd loosened up. She pictured him across the table from her with his sleeves rolled up, his hand settled comfortably around his beer. He'd looked relaxed as she'd shared what little she knew about the case, but she got the impression that really, he wasn't relaxed at all.

Allison skimmed through the ME's findings. He described an arc-shaped cut from the victim's left ear to her right. Sharp force trauma was listed as the cause of death. Manner of death, homicide. Scratches on the inner thighs. Signs of sexual assault. A rape kit had been collected, but the results weren't included in the report. Probably not back from the lab yet, if the kit had even been sent. She'd check the status with Jonah. No mention of her hair.

Allison flipped to the next page and looked at the sketch. The ME, or maybe his assistant, had drawn little lines out from various wounds on the body and scrawled notes in the margins: *abrasion, lower left forearm. Missing, upper right incisor. Contusion, right temple.* Allison frowned. Bruises would mean her attack had been prolonged. Allison read one of the notes scrawled beside the head: *Cut.*

That was it.

She flipped through the remaining pages in the stack. She reached the end and found a Polaroid clipped to the final page. Not an official crime-scene photo, but something taken indoors, with Stephanie Snow lying atop a steel table, her sightless eyes staring up into space. A bright rectangular light—in the autopsy suite, presumably—was reflected in both of her irises.

Allison picked up the picture and examined it. A chill skittered down her spine as she studied the jagged angle of Stephanie's brunette locks. She'd been wearing a ponytail when she died.

The killer had cut off her hair.

• • •

The 7:50 to Washington Dulles was full, but the 9:15 wasn't and Mark was able to get a row to himself. Now he sat in 26C with his computer balanced on his lap and his knees crushed against the seat in front of him. The seat beside him was occupied by a stack of files containing photos and descriptions that would have caused even the most seasoned homicide detectives to look away. Not yet noon and Mark had been through them twice already. He'd studied the pictures coolly and objectively, looking beyond the brutalized bodies for clues he might have missed all those years ago when he'd first joined the investigation. He'd gained experience since then, and he hoped something important would jump out at him now, but nothing had, so he'd set the photos aside and turned to his computer.

Alone in his room last night, Mark had gone through the old files and transferred his key case notes to his current laptop. It had been something to do to keep his mind off his insomnia. And his wife, who wasn't his wife anymore. And a slender brunette who drove a pickup truck older than she was.

Mark scrolled through the document entitled UNSUB CA-39. He'd originally named the file DEATH RAVEN, but then thought better of it. It was the sort of moniker that would look good in a headline if some reporter should ever get wind of it. Better to keep it private.

The dread that had been building for days now settled heavily in his stomach as he reviewed the notes. He wished he was wrong, but he knew that he wasn't. And he wished he'd managed to convince a provincial Texas police lieutenant to take him seriously, but he knew that he hadn't.

Mark had failed to accomplish his objective yesterday, and now it would probably take the death of yet another innocent woman to get anyone to believe that the unidentified subject who had been the focus of so much attention ten years ago was back. The UNSUB was on the hunt again, which meant Mark was hunting, too.

"Bloody Mary?"

The flight attendant smiled down at him, and he glanced at his empty plastic cup.

"Just the mix," he said. "I'll take the whole can."

She handed over a can of spicy tomato juice and a fresh cup of ice. Another liquid lunch. High in vitamins, high in sodium. Kind of a win-lose, but he needed the fuel. After thirteen years living in airplanes and motel rooms, he'd learned to get his nutrients wherever he could find them.

Mark glanced at the woman in 25D. Blond, barely twenty, probably an undergrad. She had a chemistry textbook tucked into the seat pocket in front of her, but for most of the flight she'd been listening to her iPod. Now the little wires had disappeared, and the man next to her seemed to have spotted his opening.

"Run out of battery on you? Mine does that, too."

The woman responded, and Mark knew he was about to get a lesson in Predatory Tactics 101.

"Name's Jason."

Pause. "Isabella," she said.

"You from Washington?"

"Austin."

"Me, too. Nice town. Taking a little vacation, though. Just hope I can get a cab." His dark head moved closer. "It's gonna be hell getting a taxi on a Friday like this. Business travelers and all that."

Isabella's hands fidgeted with the iPod, as if she wanted to put it on again. But she was in the conversation now, and she probably didn't want to seem rude.

"You visiting family?" he asked.

"Friends."

"Me, too. 'Course, they aren't expecting me until tomorrow, so I'm cabbing it. Pretzels?"

"No, thank you."

"I don't blame you. Taste like cardboard. That's what we get for flying roach class, huh?"

She laughed politely.

"This your first time in Washington?"

"It is, actually." She tucked the iPod into the pocket with the book. "I was supposed to be on the eleven o'clock, but I was so early, and they had a seat on this one, so . . ." She sighed. "Then I found out my friend—she's at Georgetown?—she couldn't meet me because she has a midterm at one. I told her I'd take a taxi. You think I'll have to wait?"

"I know you will," he said with authority. Ice cubes rattled as he sipped his drink.

Jason had been on Mark's radar since the boarding area. New blue jeans. Old tattoos. Sinewy build. No luggage. Mark had taken one look at him and made him as an ex-con—a very recent one.

Isabella managed to stuff the earbuds into her ears for the rest of the flight, but Jason chatted her up on the way off the plane until she smiled and bid him good-bye.

Mark caught up with her in the baggage claim area, even though he made a point never to check bags when he traveled for business.

"Excuse me, Miss?"

She kept walking.

"Miss?"

She turned around, startled, and gave him a "who, me?" look.

"Do you have a moment, please?" He was careful not to stand too close to her, but she looked suspicious anyway, which he thought was ironic.

"That man you were talking to on the plane. Jason."

She took a slight step back. "What about him?"

"He's going to offer to share a cab with you. Don't accept."

Inside Mark's pocket, his phone vibrated.

"But . . . how . . . ?" She looked puzzled and definitely uncomfortable being approached by a strange man more than twice her age.

"Don't accept," he repeated. "You don't want to get mixed up with him."

She watched him skeptically, still uncertain what to think. Her gaze darted to a nearby security guard.

"Um, thanks." She slunk away.

Mark sighed. His phone continued to vibrate and he pulled it from his pocket. "Wolfe."

"Hey, it's me."

Allison Doyle. It had taken getting out of Texas for him to hear the Southern lilt in her voice. He heard something else in it, too—urgency.

"What's wrong?" he asked.

"Where are you?"

"Just landed at Dulles."

"*Damn* it."

"What happened?"

The baggage carousel groaned to life, and a throng of people eased forward. Isabella and the other Austin passengers vied for a spot near the front.

Jason walked up to her, smiling. They exchanged words. She shook her head. More words and she shook her head again. The man's smile vanished and he stalked away.

"Mark? Are you listening?"

He watched the man disappear through the automatic doors. Then he turned his full attention to Allison.

"I'm listening."

"Stephanie Snow. I saw the autopsy photos. He cut off her hair, right? That's what you were talking about."

"He does it to all of them."

"It jarred something loose in my mind, something from a year ago. A woman up in Wayne County, couple counties north of here. Jordan Wheatley."

Mark gritted his teeth. A *year* ago. Jesus, how many had he missed?

"She was kidnapped from a park there. Raped. Beaten. The whole thing. He cut off her hair and slashed her throat, ear to ear."

Mark's shoulders sagged. He felt tired suddenly. And he knew he couldn't be tired. Tired was a luxury he couldn't afford, not with that date looming on the calendar. He tried to think how he was going to juggle his heavy caseload and his meeting schedule and all the dozens of things he had to do besides provide long-distance assistance to nail an active UNSUB.

But she wasn't talking about long distance.

"Mark, we need you on the next plane. We need you here. I need your help with the interview."

"What interview?"

"Jordan Wheatley. I'm going out there tonight."

"You mean—"

"Mark, this woman survived."

CHAPTER 4

Mark Wolfe pulled into the station house parking lot in the same model car he'd had yesterday, only this Ford Taurus was dark blue instead of burgundy. Allison shoved her hands into the pockets of her barn jacket and hunched her shoulders against the cold as he claimed a space beside an idling patrol unit. She ignored the cop's curious glances at the tall guy in the suit, so obviously an out-of-towner. Didn't take much to start the rumor mill around here.

Mark got out and leaned an arm on the top of the door. He looked her up and down as she tromped over, clearly not impressed with her choice of attire for a witness interview.

"She canceled," he stated.

"Postponed. Something about her husband. She's available tomorrow morning, first thing."

He muttered a curse and checked his watch. Then he surveyed her appearance again, and his gaze lingered on her muddy duck boots. The cuffs of her jeans were muddy, too.

"You have anything else to wear?" she asked.

"No."

"Not even some jeans or, I don't know, khakis?"

He just looked at her, and she sighed. She trudged across the parking lot to her truck and opened the tool-box in back.

"What are you, a twelve?" She glanced over her shoulder, and he was frowning at her from beside her back bumper.

"Thirteen."

She rummaged through everything—tire jack, road flares, traffic cones—until she came across a pair of bat-tered work boots. She pulled them out and handed them over.

"Whose are these?"

"My ex-boyfriend's." She glanced at his feet. "They'll pinch some, but you'll live."

He leaned a palm against the truck as he rested his foot on his knee and unlaced the shiny black wing tips. "Where are we going?"

"Crime scene." She smiled as he stuffed his feet into Roland's boots, which looked pretty ridiculous with the suit pants. "Don't worry, no fashion police out there."

Mark pulled the keys from his pocket and headed back to his sedan. "I'll drive, you navigate," he said over his shoulder.

"How about I drive, since I know the way?"

He stashed his dress shoes in back and slid behind the wheel.

Annoyed, she slammed the toolbox shut and crossed the lot. She hesitated for a second before giving up and climbing in. It was deliciously warm inside, but she gave him a scowl.

"Your controlling side is showing."

He started the engine without comment. No cough. No sputter. He glided backward out of the space.

"Where to?" he asked.

"North."

He glanced at the digital compass before turning right onto Main Street.

"How was your flight?"

"The usual."

"You have time to go home first?"

"Went by the office instead. Picked up some work for the week."

So he planned to stay. She tried to hide her relief, but he was good at reading body language. And anyway, he was probably used to women wanting him around. It wasn't only his looks—which would have been fine on their own—but also the way he radiated a certain masculine self-assurance, as if he'd seen a lot and was prepared for anything. Allison knew better than to let all that alpha-male confidence have an effect on her, but it did.

"Third light up ahead here, you're going to hang a left."

She scanned the storefronts as they drove through downtown. Most businesses on Main Street shut down at six o'clock. Those near campus stayed open later— the bars, the restaurants, the convenience stores. He approached University Boulevard, and she glanced around. Not much pedestrian traffic for a Friday night, but that was probably because of the cold snap. The temperature had dropped this afternoon, and it was expected to sink into the twenties tonight.

She turned to look at him. "You're holding out on me. Don't think I don't get that."

He glanced at her, then back at the road.

"How'd you know about her hair? You didn't even see the ME's report."

"I talked to Reynolds," he said.

"I'm surprised he told you about it."

"He didn't. But he didn't deny it, either."

Allison looked out her window again. "What else? There has to be more. You got on a plane for this case, without even knowing the specifics. Something tipped you off."

Mark hung a left onto the road that led to the outskirts of town. He looked at her as if debating whether to trust her, and she felt a spurt of irritation. Why was he being so secretive? He was the one who'd come down here and stirred up all this business about a serial killer when everyone in her department had been perfectly content with the suspect they already had.

"There are other elements in play here," he said vaguely. "Things that haven't been in the media. We need to keep it that way."

It was the second time that day a fellow investigator had implied that she might leak something to the press, and she was starting to get ticked off.

"It's an online connection," he elaborated, probably picking up on her annoyance. "That's why I flew down here. It's part of his pattern."

"You mean he's stalking these women online?"

"And communicating online."

"With who?"

"Us. Law enforcement. It's part of this game he's got going."

"What do you mean by 'communicating'?"

"Before each murder, he posts these taunts on various Web sites. He's got certain phrases, lines of poetry he uses over and over."

"If he's online, shouldn't we be able to track him?"

"We should, yes."

"How can you be sure it's him?"

"Because of the first one. He posted a photograph."

"Crime-scene photos sometimes get leaked. Are you sure—"

"She was still alive when the picture was taken."

Allison's blinked at him. *Alive?* That was just . . . she didn't know. She didn't have words for what that was.

Mark pulled up to a stoplight. He reached behind her and took a thick manila file from the backseat, then rested it in her lap.

"Here." He glanced up at the light to make sure it was still red as he flipped open the folder. After shuffling through a few pages, he tapped his finger on what looked like an e-mail. "Read this."

Allison checked the date. It was from ten years ago, almost to the day. The sender was listed as E. Poe and the recipient was a K. Langford at some company Allison had never heard of.

"Where'd this come from?"

"Our UNSUB. Dara Langford's father got this in his in-box at work the week after his daughter's body was recovered."

Allison read the words aloud: " 'In the startled ear of

night / How they scream out their affright / Too much horrified to speak / They can only shriek, shriek.'"

A chill snaked down Allison's spine. She pictured a grieving father reading a message like that.

"I assume you tried to trace this?"

"We've had some of our best people on it," Mark said as Allison thumbed through the other papers in the file—police reports, interview notes, an autopsy report. "He's been good at covering his tracks, unfortunately. His communications have been completely untraceable. Is this the turn?"

"Veer right up at the fork."

Allison stowed the file at her feet as they approached the sign for Stony Creek Park, which until this morning had been closed to the public. The CSIs had finished days ago, but the chief had wanted to deter curious teens and reporters from nosing around. Not that that had stopped them. Allison had been here this afternoon and seen the tire treads of what she guessed were news vans.

Mark turned onto a dirt road that led to a trailhead. The trail was flat, making it a favorite for joggers and dog walkers. It made a three-mile loop through the woods, skirting the property where Allison's apartment was located. He pulled up beside a wooden sign and looked at her.

"I'm assuming you're on this case now?"

She opened her door. "That depends on tomorrow." If he could be vague, so could she.

She climbed out of the car and stood there for a moment in the near-darkness. Mark left the headlights on, and she heard the persistent ding of a warning bell before he closed the door.

"Place closes at sundown," she said, surveying the empty lot. "Sometimes we get teenagers who come out here to park, although the murder's probably scared them off for a while."

"Or made them curious."

Allison dug into her pocket and pulled out a mini flashlight, which she pointed at the path. The footprints in the mud were new, and they didn't look like athletic shoes. Reporters, maybe? Allison switched the light to her left hand, freeing her right hand, just in case. Last night's humiliation was still fresh in her mind.

She trudged into the woods with Mark close behind her. The air smelled of damp leaves and earth. As they moved into the trees, they lost the light of the parking lot and everything darkened.

Her flashlight beam landed on a familiar tree stump. She stepped off the trail.

"Through here," she said, ducking under a branch.

"You've been out here already?"

"Earlier this afternoon, with one of the detectives—Jonah Macon. You met him yesterday."

"Briefly," he said. "How many entrances to this greenbelt?"

"Vehicle entrances? Only one. But it's not fenced or anything, so the possibilities are pretty limitless for someone on foot." Allison followed her flashlight over the carpet of dead leaves. "We have reason to believe she was actually killed here, not just dumped. A lot of blood had seeped into the ground around the remains."

The remains. It sounded so cold, when actually she

was talking about a vibrant young woman who'd had her whole life ahead of her.

Mark's footsteps crunched behind her. He had no trouble keeping up, despite the poor visibility and the awkward clothes.

Her flashlight beam sliced through the darkness. It landed on a little orange flag attached to a stake in the ground.

"Here." She stopped beside it.

"Scene's been released?"

"It's hard to keep people out, so yeah. Think we got everything, though. I talked to one of our CSIs. They spent a lot of time here."

Mark crouched beside the freshly turned earth, where crime-scene investigators had removed soil and debris. It had been carted off to the state crime lab with the other evidence, in the hopes that some of the blood might belong to the perpetrator and not just the victim. Of course, given the backlog at the lab, it was unlikely they'd see those test results anytime soon.

Mark stood up and glanced around. There wasn't much to look at, and she suddenly felt silly for bringing him all the way out here to view a patch of dirt.

"Anyway," she said, "thought you'd want to see it."

He made a 360-degree survey of the surrounding blackness.

"He chose this place," she said, "so I would think it reveals something about him. I mean, I'm no profiler, but that seems pretty obvious."

"You're right. Turn off that light, would you?"

She did. Darkness enveloped them. She stood silently beside him and wondered what thoughts were going through that mind of his. Everything surrounding them was quiet except for a faint gurgle of water.

"That's Sage Creek," she whispered. She wasn't sure why she felt compelled to whisper. Maybe because this place felt hallowed in some way. A woman's life had ended here.

An owl hooted in the distance. Allison shivered.

"I can't imagine her fear," she said quietly. "Being kidnapped and dragged out here, probably knowing what he had in mind, or at least an idea of it."

"Fear is a good thing."

She glanced in the direction of his voice, but it was too dark to see him.

"If more people listened to their fear, we'd have far fewer crime victims."

"You're not blaming the victim, are you?" She couldn't keep the disdain out of her tone. "For all we know, he pulled a gun on her."

"I'm not blaming anyone but the person who killed her. I think—"

"Shh." Allison touched his arm. "You hear that?"

Snick.

She whirled around. Footsteps in the distance. She switched on the flashlight and took off in that direction, plowing through vines and branches toward the trail.

Leaves rustling. Muffled words. A grunt. Allison rushed toward the sounds. Her toe snagged on something, but she caught herself on a tree. Footsteps crunched. Bushes snapped. Her flashlight beam bounced over the path as she pursued the noises, which were getting farther and farther away.

Something lashed her cheek.

"Ouch!" She staggered backward and bumped into a hard body.

"Easy."

Mark's hand curled around her arm. She tried to pull away, but his grip tightened.

"Let go! They're getting away!"

"They're already gone."

Squeaking metal. Slamming doors. An engine roared to life and she heard the squeal of tires on asphalt.

Mark's hand dropped away. She stood there, clutching her cheek and brimming with frustration as the noise faded into the night.

"Chances are it was just kids, right? I mean, what are the odds it was *him* returning to the crime scene?"

Mark glanced at Allison in his passenger seat. She was still hyped up from the chase.

"Happens more than you might think," he said. "Serial killers frequently return to the scene to relive the moment, re-experience the thrill. But in this case, I'd say you're right—it wasn't him."

Allison flipped down the vanity mirror and craned her neck to see her cut. It was still bleeding. She'd found some hand sanitizer and started dabbing it on her face with a woolen glove.

"I'm guessing it was bored teens. Although it would be nice to know." She sent him a glare. "I can't believe you stopped me from going after them."

"A tree stopped you from going after them. Want me to pull into a pharmacy?"

"No." She wiped the blood off her face. "I just wish I could be sure."

"Trust me, it wasn't him. That was at least two people back there. Our UNSUB is a loner."

"You're certain?"

"Yes."

Silence settled over the car as he neared downtown again. He needed to take her back to the station where she'd left her truck. He needed to check into his motel, too, but he didn't really want to.

"You hungry?"

He glanced at her. "Shouldn't you take care of that injury?"

"I'd rather eat," she said. "Actually, I've been starving for hours. What about you?"

Mark considered it. The calzone he'd eaten while waiting for his flight seemed ages ago, but he didn't like the thought of sharing dinner with her two nights in a row.

"There's a Sonic right up here. Great chili dogs." She flipped the mirror shut and looked at him. "They have wraps, too—in case you're on a health kick."

He sighed. Work or food? But it wasn't really that simple. This was a small town. People would see them together and get the wrong idea. She might get the wrong idea.

"You know you're hungry."

He glanced at her. She was right. And to his surprise, he'd discovered he liked her company—which was unusual because there were so few people he liked to be around anymore.

Screw it. It was only a hamburger. He spotted the sign and pulled into the parking lot.

"One chili dog, all the way, side of tater tots."

He shot her a look.

"What? They're good."

He ordered her food and added a cheeseburger and fries for himself.

"Don't tell me they're really going to bring it out on roller skates," he said.

"Yep."

"Very retro."

She smiled. "We like things quaint."

He left the window open, and the faint sound of a marching band could be heard from a football stadium across town. Something about the percussion noises mingled with the brisk November air was so very *heartland*, and it made him glad to know there were still places like this scattered across America.

"Friday-night lights," she said, leaning her head back against the seat. "Only game in town."

He watched her for a moment. She'd stopped the bleeding, but he still didn't like the look of that cut marring her smooth cheek.

She glanced over and caught him staring.

"You grow up around here?" he asked.

"South Side High, home of the Wranglers. You're listening to them now."

"So you have family in town?"

"My sister. South Side homecoming queen, by the way." Her voice was laced with pride and maybe a hint of sarcasm.

"What about you?"

"Me? No. You have to be popular for that. And wear a dress."

He smiled. "Your parents live here, too, then?"

She gazed out the window. "My mom's still in the house where we grew up."

Okay. Evasive.

She turned to look at him. "Where're you from?"

"West Virginia." He could say it now without a trace of shame—that's what two degrees and a federal badge had done for him.

"And now you live near Quantico?"

"Alexandria."

"Never been there."

"It's like everywhere else. Used to be a town, now it's a suburb. Anyway, I don't spend much time there. I'm on the road a lot."

"Bet that's hard on a marriage."

He looked at her. "It was," he said, answering her unspoken question.

Something in her eyes told him the next question was going to be even more personal, and he didn't feel like talking about his ex-wife or his one-bedroom apartment, still crammed with moving boxes two years after his divorce. A freshly minted psychologist would probably say he was in denial, but Mark knew the reason was far less interesting: He was a workaholic and hadn't had time to unpack.

"Tell me about Jordan Wheatley," he said.

"What about her?"

"What do you know about her case, besides what you said on the phone?"

"Jordan Wheatley," she said crisply. "Thirty-three, Caucasian, college graduate. She lives up in Wayne County with her husband."

"Kids?"

"No."

"Job?"

"She works at GreenWinds, I think. They're an energy company here. Also, she's a marathoner. She was training for Boston when she was attacked near a jogging trail."

A woman glided up on skates and attached a tray to Mark's door. The scent of fried potatoes wafted into the car, and he heard his stomach growl. The waitress dispensed the orders with a wink, and Mark watched her roll away.

He handed Allison her food, and she was smiling slyly.

"What?"

"Nothing," she said.

"Jogging trail's in Red Oak Canyon, correct?"

The smile faded. "It's a state park about thirty miles north of here."

"And does the sheriff up there know we're interviewing her tomorrow?"

"Not exactly."

"What about your lieutenant?"

Her silence answered the question.

"So you're *not* on this case."

She picked at her tater tots.

"Allison?"

"Jordan Wheatley's a sexual assault, far as everyone here is concerned." She looked up at him. "Sheriff's deputy I talked to said they've exhausted their leads on it. Unless I can prove there's a connection between her and Stephanie Snow, her case is on ice. And if there *is* a connection—like the one you're describing—then we're talking about a serial killer. No one wants me opening up that can of worms."

"He said that?"

"That's what he meant. He didn't even want me talking to Jordan Wheatley, even though I can talk to whoever the hell I want. I only called him and told him out of professional courtesy."

"And to get a look at her case file, I hope."

"That, too." She sucked on her straw.

"And?"

"He wouldn't give me anything without talking to the sheriff first, so I said, 'Fine, talk to him.' Which he did. The sheriff said I'm outside my jurisdiction."

Mark shook his head. He was surprised and he wasn't. Small town didn't always mean small minded, but it usually meant territorial. And resentful of outside interference. They had their work cut out for them tomorrow.

Still, if Allison had her facts straight, it meant he had something he'd never had before in this case: a witness who'd seen the killer up close and lived to tell about it. Mark was keenly interested to hear what she had to say.

He was also keenly interested in getting someone on the local police force in his corner. Offering FBI assistance in a serial murder case was futile if the police department in charge didn't even believe they were looking for a serial killer.

And November 19 was looming.

"Ah, hell," Allison said.

Mark followed her gaze and saw a very tall, very skinny guy walking down the street toward them. He was stark naked.

Allison was already getting out of the car, and Mark grabbed her arm.

"Whoa. He might be dangerous."

She shook him off. "He's not. Can I borrow your jacket?"

Mark looked at her.

"Mine's not long enough."

He unclipped his seat belt and took off his suit jacket. "Be careful. He's probably mentally unstable."

She took the jacket and climbed out. Muttering a curse, Mark followed her. She sauntered up to the man without a trace of trepidation, which Mark didn't like.

On the other hand, the guy clearly wasn't armed.

"Evening," she said, stepping into his path. The man scowled at Allison, then at Mark. "Your daughter know you're out here, Mr. Pitkin?"

He mumbled something. A horn blasted behind them as an SUV loaded with teens rolled by, kids whooping and hanging out the windows. Mark eased around, positioning himself between Allison and the man.

"Pretty cold to be out here without your clothes." She held out the jacket. "Let's put this on, okay?"

He stuck his chin out defiantly, but didn't say anything.

"Okay?" Allison held the jacket up by the shoulders. The guy scowled again and slipped his arms in.

"How 'bout we give you a ride home now, Mr. Pitkin. Does Marcy know you're out here?"

The man looked at his feet and said something.

"What's that?" Allison put her hand to her ear.

"She made tacos again." His voice was gravelly. "I hate spicy food." He frowned at the Sonic they'd just come from.

"I don't blame you." Allison took his elbow and guided him toward the car. "I bet she'll fix you a sandwich, though, if you ask her nice."

Mark opened the back door for him. "Watch your head."

He got inside without a fuss, and Allison mouthed the word "sorry" at Mark as he shut the door.

Mark went around and slid behind the wheel. "Where to?"

Allison gave directions as she passed her food sack into the backseat.

"You take your medicine today, Mr. Pitkin?"

He said something around a mouthful of food. Mark glanced in the rearview mirror and watched him devouring the tater tots.

A few minutes later he pulled up to a one-story brick house where a woman stood in the front yard, talking on a cell phone. She paused for a moment, then rushed to the car and yanked open the door.

"Dad! You can't *do* that! I've been calling everywhere." She cast an anxious look at Allison. "I'm *so* sorry. Where was he?"

"Main Street."

Mark went around and helped the man out while Allison spoke to his daughter.

"Oh! Sorry about your suit. Should I . . . ?" The woman cast a glance over her shoulder. Several neighbors were watching from their front porch.

"I'll get it later," Allison said. "Make sure he takes his meds now, all right?"

The woman shuffled her father inside as Mark and Allison looked on.

"He do that a lot?" Mark asked.

"Oh, you know. Maybe once a year. Usually he's in his tighty-whities." She shuddered. "The joys of small-town policing, huh?"

Mark glanced at her as he got behind the wheel and thought she looked embarrassed. He pulled away from the house and drove down the tree-lined street.

"It's nice to see people taking care of each other," he said. "You don't get that much in big cities."

She sighed. "I don't envy Marcy what she's going through. Anyway, sorry about your coat. I'll get it back."

"No hurry. I've got another one just like it."

"You buy them in bulk?"

"Makes for easy packing," he said, turning onto Main Street. He glanced at her and she was smiling.

"What?"

"Nothing. Hey, you mind doing a quick drive-by? It's probably a waste of time, but I wouldn't mind having another look."

Mark didn't need more explanation. He'd been thinking about that crime scene, too. He wended his way through town and headed back toward the park entrance. When they neared the sign, he cut the headlights and rolled down the window. Cool air filled the sedan as they eased past, silently scouring the area for any more visitors. Mark peered into the woods. Wind whipped through the dark leaves and he heard the owl again. But there were no car noises or any other signs of trespassers.

They drove back to the police station in silence. The parking lot was nearly empty, and Mark pulled into a space beside her pickup.

She pushed open the door. "I'll pick you up at seven-thirty sharp tomorrow. The appointment's at eight."

He'd intended to drive, but he decided to choose his battles. "Seven-thirty, then."

She reached into the backseat and grabbed the muddy boots he'd borrowed.

"And about the interview—I'll take the lead," he told her.

She looked instantly suspicious.

"I've got a lot more experience, Allison, and that's not a knock against you—it's just a fact. You want in on this case, you need to stay in the background."

Her eyes simmered, and he could tell she didn't like it, but whatever her objections, she didn't voice them. Maybe she knew how to choose her battles, too.

"You got it, Special Agent." She slid out of the car and started to shut the door.

"Wait." He studied her face again. It had two dings now: one from the meth addict and one from earlier tonight. "Want me to follow you home?"

She looked amused, and he hoped she didn't take it as a come-on.

"Make sure I get in okay?"

"Something like that."

She shook her head at him. "I'm the law around here, Wolfe. If I'm not safe, who is?"

CHAPTER 5

Jordan Wheatley lived in a small A-frame cabin on the banks of Dry Creek. True to its name, the creek had not a drop of water in it when Allison's pickup bumped over the low-water bridge and rumbled up the dirt road leading to the house. Railroad ties marked off a parking area beside a large pecan tree, and Allison swung in beside a dark green hatchback. Her Chevy shuddered and coughed when she cut the engine, and she avoided Mark's gaze as she climbed out.

"Right on time," she said.

Mark stood beside the car, studying it. Leaves had collected at the base of the windshield. The tires were low. She wondered if he was drawing the same conclusion she was.

He glanced up at her. "Remember, I take the lead."

She gave a noncommittal look as the front door swung open and a German shepherd bounded out.

"Maximus, stay!"

The dog halted, his body quivering with restrained energy.

A tall woman stood in the doorway. She held a

cigarette in her hand and wore a baggy gray sweat suit. A thick pink scar on her neck stretched from one side to the other like a necklace.

Allison stepped forward. "Hi. I'm Allison Doyle."

"Who's he?" She nodded at Mark, who had crouched down to pet the dog.

"Morning, Mrs. Wheatley." Mark stood up and walked over to the weathered porch steps, hands in his pockets, very low-key. The dog followed him. "I'm working with Detective Doyle on one of her cases, and she asked me to come along today." He held out a hand. "Special Agent Mark Wolfe, FBI."

She gave him a long, cool look. "Come on in," she said at last, and held open the door.

Mark went inside. Allison followed, attempting to ease the tension with a smile.

"Thank you for meeting with us, Mrs. Wheatley."

"It's Jordan."

Her house shoes snapped against the wood floor as she led them inside. Allison noticed her hair—the brunette pixie cut was matted on one side, as if she'd just gotten out of bed.

"Y'all want coffee?"

"I'd love some, thanks," Mark said.

"Detective?"

"No, thank you."

Jordan showed them to a large, open room that smelled like cigarettes and . . . soil, Allison thought. She glanced around the open floor plan. Casual furniture, throw rugs, a TV. Upstairs was a loft that looked out over the main room. Through the wooden railing Allison saw a king-size bed with a green comforter bunched

at the foot. If there was a second bedroom, she couldn't
see it, which confirmed her information that the Wheat-
leys had no children.

Jordan was on the kitchen side of the room now,
pouring two cups of coffee.

"You take sugar?"

"Black."

Jordan slid the mugs into the microwave, and Allison
studied the home more carefully. She spotted the source
of the soil smell—a wooden table beside the window
where someone was potting herbs. Allison wandered
over to it, aware of Maximus's attentive gaze tracking
her around the room.

The house backed up to a sloping hillside. Through
the windows Allison saw six neat lines of trees—pear,
lemon, some young pecans.

"Nice orchard." Allison turned around. Jordan was
leaning against the kitchen counter, puffing on her cigarette and watching her.

"It's Ethan's." She flicked her ash into the sink. "He's
a landscape architect. Raises plants, too, to supplement
things. He's on a delivery right now."

The oven dinged, and she retrieved the mugs, deftly
handling them and her cigarette as she made her way to
the sitting area. She set the coffee on the table and sank
onto the couch.

Mark took his cue and lowered himself into the armchair near his mug, leaving Allison with the futon. Maximus brushed past her and plopped down at Jordan's feet.

"So." She took a deep breath. "You want to hear about
my rape."

Allison was surprised by the bluntness. Jordan gave

her a challenging look as she sucked on the cigarette. She dropped the butt into a Coke can and blew out a stream of smoke.

"That's what I'm supposed to call it, according to my shrink. No euphemisms, no avoidance."

Mark eased forward in his chair. "You're been seeing a counselor?"

"Twelve months now. Once a week, every week. Got the empty bank account to prove it."

"Do you find it helpful?"

She shrugged. "I don't know. If it's supposed to make me forget about it, then I'd say no, it's not too helpful. Haven't swallowed a bottle of Ambien, though, so she must be doing something right."

Allison cleared her throat. "They never made an arrest in your case, is that correct?"

"You tell me. You're the investigators."

Okay, clumsy opening.

"According to Deputy Sheriff Brooks," she tried again, "the suspect sketch and the vehicle description you provided haven't yielded any leads."

"Don't forget the rape kit. I provided that, too, for all the good it did."

Allison shifted in her seat. This woman radiated hostility, and she wasn't sure quite how to handle her. She glanced at Mark for help, but he was focused on Jordan.

"You're angry with the local investigators," he stated.

"Wouldn't you be? I had a goddamn pelvic exam right after getting my neck sewn up. I sat with a police artist for two hours the very next day. I talked to detectives, even though my throat felt like it was on fire the whole time. I told them about his car, his clothes, everything.

And have they arrested anybody? No. My case has been dead for months. How would you feel?"

"I'd be furious," Mark said.

She stared at him for a long moment. Then she took a deep breath. "Thank you." She reached down to pet her dog between the ears and seemed to be collecting herself.

"So, the FBI's involved now. You think he's done this somewhere else." She said it as a statement, not a question, and her tone was somber.

"We believe that, yes."

"And the other woman . . ." She looked from Mark to Allison. The cautious hope in her eyes made Allison's chest squeeze.

"We know of six other women who suffered attacks similar to yours," Mark said. "They didn't survive."

Jordan looked stricken. *"Six?"*

He nodded.

"Oh my God." She closed her eyes.

Silence fell over them. No one moved. The distant chirp of the birds outside the windows sounded out of place, like giggling at a funeral.

Jordan shook her head. "I knew there were others. Somehow I knew that, but . . ." She stared at her lap. "Something about the way he did it, the way he talked to me. I knew he'd done it before. And he's done it again, too, hasn't he? That woman in San Marcos." She glanced up, and Allison saw the fear in her expression. "Do you think he lives around here?"

"We're working on a profile of him, to help investigators," Mark said. "Part of that will be determining where he lives."

"When they didn't get anywhere with the sketch and

the vehicle, they told me he was probably a transient."

"Unfortunately, we don't know where he is, we only know where he's been." Mark paused. "Hopefully, you can help us get a more complete picture of him."

She gazed down at her lap. For a while, she didn't talk, and when she looked up again her eyes were moist but clear.

"You're a profiler."

"Some people call it that."

"Then before I help anyone, I want something from *you*." Her voice was uneven. "I want to understand how he did this to me. I want to understand how it happened. I never thought I was a victim."

"You're a survivor," Mark said. "Not a victim."

"Then how did I get like this? Look at me!" She pounded a fist on her thigh. "I've gained thirty pounds. I'm scared to leave my house. I can barely look at my husband. My whole life is destroyed. Why did this happen to me? What did I do *wrong*?"

Mark leaned forward on his elbows. "Let's get one thing straight, Jordan. You didn't invite this attack, no matter what you did."

She watched him intently, and Allison could tell she was clinging to every word.

"He's very skilled. We think he has a sophisticated method of luring women into his trap, which is how you can help us. We need to know more about his MO so we can find him before he does it again."

Her brow furrowed. "I don't know what you want me to say that I haven't already said to police. You're the expert on human behavior."

"No, Jordan, you're the expert." He paused until she

looked up at him. "You sensed the danger that day, probably from the moment you saw him."

She didn't reply.

"You know when you're in the presence of danger. It's your most sharply honed survival skill. Think back."

She gazed away, at the windows.

"What were your instincts telling you when he first approached you?"

She took a deep breath and nodded, as if she knew what he was getting at. "It just felt . . . off, I guess. From the beginning." She looked at Mark. "He said he was having car trouble and he needed help, and he kept smiling. It seems like nothing, but looking back, I see that I didn't trust it. Something about his smile."

Mark watched her, but didn't say anything overtly encouraging. It was all in his face, in the utter focus he was giving to her.

"And then he acted like it was assumed I should help him. Like, 'Hey, we're stranded here together. What are the odds we'll get a tow truck?' "

Mark nodded. "Forced teaming."

"What?"

"It's one of the most sophisticated methods of manipulation: Create a shared purpose where one doesn't exist."

Her gaze sharpened. "That's just how it was. And then when I hesitated, he said something like, 'I bet you don't have time to play Good Samaritan,' and suddenly I'm agreeing to help him, trying to prove him wrong about me." She blew out a breath. "I mean, how stupid was that? Why did I care what some total stranger thought of me?"

"He's an expert manipulator."

Another deep breath. Jordan stroked Maximus between the ears. The dog seemed to be providing her some sort of comfort so she could keep talking.

"And then there were little things, too. They seemed minor at the time, but they just, I don't know, seemed off. He kept mentioning his wife. And then he started talking about his mechanic. I remember thinking it was odd."

"Interesting."

Allison looked at Mark. "You think he's married?"

"It's possible." His gaze went to Jordan. "It's also possible he was saying that to put you at ease. And the detail about the mechanic . . . that's part of his effort to deceive you. When people are being truthful, they don't feel the need to throw in extra details to support what they're saying. But if they're deceiving you, they think they need that to make themselves more believable. Those extra details are a sign of deception, and you picked up on it."

Allison watched Mark, fascinated. She used that signal all the time in suspect interviews, but she'd never pinpointed what it was.

"I've been over it and over it," Jordan said. "There were so many little warnings I let myself ignore."

Mark watched her, and Allison caught an intensity in his gaze that she hadn't seen before. This woman was a treasure trove of information about someone he'd been hunting for more than a decade.

"Just . . . he looked so *normal*, you know? He had a minivan. He wore glasses and a Rice University sweatshirt. God, that's my alma mater. I mean, I was wary at first, but I kept telling myself I was being paranoid." She stopped talking and stared at her lap. Tension hung in the air, and Allison knew they were coming to the tough part. "Then he attacked me. I turned my back and he was on me. I screamed and kicked, and he kept saying, 'Shut up and I won't hurt you.'" She looked Mark in the eye. "But I knew that was a lie. I *knew* it." Her voice was fierce now. "He said it over and over again, when he threw me into the van and then when he was raping me. I wouldn't stop struggling, because I knew in my soul that he fully intended to kill me."

She stopped talking, and her words seemed to hover in the quiet room.

"The van," Allison said gently. "Do you remember anything else about that, anything the police didn't ask about?"

"Like what?"

"Anything inside it, for example."

She shook her head.

"What about smells?" she pressed. "Maybe food? Or tobacco? Or some sort of cologne?"

Jordan looked away. "Paint."

"There was paint in the van?" Mark asked.

"It wasn't that strong. And maybe it wasn't even paint, but some kind of chemical. I don't know. That part is fuzzy, really. I mainly remember fear."

She looked from Allison to Mark. "It was so *complete.* I knew he wanted me dead. So I pretended, hoping maybe he'd stop. And then he slit my throat and dumped me out." Her hand drifted up to her neck. "He was in a hurry by that point, I guess because I'd put up such a fight, maybe he thought someone would hear us or find us. He just shoved me out and peeled away, and the last thing I remember was staring up at those trees and thinking of Ethan."

Her voice broke on the last word and she turned it into a cough. Allison watched her fighting the emotions and had to blink back tears.

Jordan took a deep breath. "Next thing I know, I'm in the hospital, some emergency room. I wake up, and it's all these doctors and sheriff's deputies, and everyone's telling me I'm lucky to be alive." She looked at Mark, then Allison. "People tell me that a lot, you know—that I'm lucky. It's a shitty thing to say."

The ride back into town was long and cold, and it wasn't just because Allison's heater was on the fritz. She couldn't bring herself to talk. Mark was probably used to hearing stories like that, but Allison wasn't, and she felt hollow inside. She remembered a similar feeling last summer, when she'd worked her first murder case. She'd learned that people were capable of unspeakable cruelty, and she wondered if she'd ever get used to knowing that. And if she did, what would that say about her?

"You all right?"

She glanced at Mark. "Why wouldn't I be?"

"You seemed a little uncomfortable back there."

She tamped down her annoyance. She'd hoped he hadn't noticed, but he seemed to notice everything.

"Honestly? I found it hard to be around her. I bet a lot of people do. That's one of the things that sucks about what happened." She shook her head. "If you want to know the truth . . ." She trailed off, unsure if she should talk to him about this. She didn't really know him.

"If I want to know the truth . . . ?" He was looking at her expectantly, and she settled her gaze back on the road.

"The truth is, she's my worst nightmare. I mean, here's this strong, determined woman. She's tall. She's in excellent shape—or at least she was. She was a freaking marathoner. And now she seems so . . . lost, I guess." She gripped the steering wheel, upset for reasons she couldn't articulate. Or didn't want to.

"You identify with her."

"How could I not?" She glanced over, and he was watching her with concern. She focused on the road, hoping he'd let it go. She didn't feel like talking about it anymore—it felt too emotional.

"There's a rape kit," Mark said now, and she was grateful for the change of subject.

"Yeah, I asked about that."

"And?"

"Sheriff's deputy said it didn't go anywhere."

"What does that mean exactly?"

Allison stopped at a juncture and turned onto the highway that would take them back to town. "I assume it means they tested the DNA and didn't get any hits."

"Never assume."

She looked at him. "What, you think he was being literal?"

He reached over and turned up the heater, as if that would help anything. Cold air blasted out, and he switched it off.

"I think every crime lab in the country is backed up," he said. "Your state lab's probably worse than Quantico. You want to know what they ask when an agent sends in a DNA sample for analysis?"

"What?"

" 'When's the trial?' "

Allison's throat tightened with frustration. She jerked her phone out of her pocket and dialed the Wayne County Sheriff's Office. Deputy Brooks was off for the day, but she'd chatted with their dispatcher before, and she managed to finagle his home number.

"The Jordan Wheatley case," she said by way of greeting. "What happened to her rape kit?"

The deputy paused, as if digesting this. "It's at the lab."

"Still? It's been a *year*."

"Hey, talk to Austin. I don't run the state crime lab."

"Well, have you ever thought of picking up the phone? What have you guys been doing up there?"

Beside her, Mark shook his head at her apparent lack of judgment. She supposed she was expected to play nice with these people, even though their laziness might have cost a woman her life.

"We're not exactly front of their line." Brooks sounded pissed now. "You know how many cases they get? And we don't even have a suspect yet. You're talking about a blind DNA test."

"What about a private lab?" she asked. "The Delphi Center's one of the best in the world, and they're practically in your backyard. I can't believe you didn't—"

"Look, *Detective*. Don't call me on a Saturday at my *home* and start criticizing the way we conduct an investigation. We don't have the luxury of hiring private labs whenever we feel like it. We have rules around here. Budgets. If we had a suspect to compare it to, that'd be one thing. But we don't. And we don't throw taxpayer money around on blind DNA tests every time someone gets assaulted."

"She almost *died*." Allison couldn't believe she was hearing this.

"I know, all right? I interviewed her in that hospital. But the fact is, the sketch she gave us went nowhere. The vehicle description went nowhere. We don't have a suspect, and until we do, that's it. We're waiting on state. You don't like it, talk to the sheriff."

Allison clenched the wheel. She felt Mark watching her, probably disapproving of the way she was handling this.

"How'd it go with her, anyway? She doing any better?"

His voice sounded concerned now, and some of Allison's anger subsided.

"She was okay. Still having a hard time, I think." She glanced at Mark, who was gazing out his window but obviously listening. "We may have a new lead, though. I'll keep you posted."

"I heard y'all brought a fed in on your homicide," he said. "You really think it's connected?"

"Yes, I do."

"Shit." A heavy sigh on the other end of the phone. "He wore a condom, you know. Chances are, that rape kit isn't going to give us much."

Allison bit back a curse. Jordan hadn't mentioned the condom. But then, she'd skimmed over the most brutal part of her attack with only a few words. Had she been sparing Allison's feelings? Mark's? Or maybe it was just too difficult to talk about.

"I'll give Austin a call," Brooks said. "See if I can rattle a few cages."

Like you should have done ten months ago.

"Thank you," she said instead, then tossed her phone in the cup holder with maybe a bit too much force.

Mark looked at her.

"Her kit's sitting in Austin, untested. He pleads backlogs and budgets."

Mark didn't seem surprised.

"Anyway, her attacker wore a condom, so it could still be a dead end."

"I doubt it."

She glanced at him.

"They can get DNA off a single skin cell. Jordan fought hard, from the sound of it. That rape kit should include her clothes, her nail clippings. They should be able to get a profile."

Allison shook her head. "I keep thinking of all the time wasted."

"You're going to have to make nice with that deputy. I want a look at their suspect sketch. Hell, I want a look at their entire case file."

Allison's phone buzzed from the cup holder, and she checked the screen. Not Brooks. His apology would have to wait.

"Hey, Kelsey, what's up?"

Allison listened for a moment, and her stomach filled with dread. It was becoming a familiar feeling.

She hung up with her friend. Then she checked her

mirrors and pulled a U-turn in the middle of the highway.

Mark glanced at her. "Change of plan?"

"That was a friend of mine, Kelsey Quinn. I called her yesterday with some questions about the case."

"Kelsey Quinn. Where have I heard that name before?"

"She's a forensic anthropologist," Allison said grimly. "We're going to go look at some bones."

CHAPTER 6

The Delphi Center looked like a Greek temple that had been inexplicably transported to the heart of the Texas Hill Country. Mark remembered the fanfare when the place opened—first, because it was a cutting-edge forensic research facility, and second, because they'd managed to hire away some of the Bureau's top scientists. Now, only five years later, the lab boasted the largest body farm in the country—which they proudly referred to as the body "ranch"—as well as a stellar reputation in law enforcement circles.

Allison said Dr. Quinn would be meeting them in the lobby, but Mark hadn't expected her to blow in from outdoors. She strode up to them wearing an olive green ski vest and faded jeans with mud on the knees. He took one look at her auburn ponytail and recalled where he'd met her before.

"Special Agent Wolfe. Good to see you again." She turned to Allison. "We met once at the FBI Academy. I was giving a talk to a room full of police chiefs."

"Postmortem interval," Mark supplied.

"I'll take your word for it. It was a busy week." She turned to the weekend security guard. "We all checked in, Ralph?"

He nodded silently from his place by the door, and Mark and Allison followed the young anthropologist into a narrow hallway. They passed a knot of people clustered in a doorway. Detectives, probably. Every one of them was packing and Mark had seen their unmarked vehicles in the parking lot.

"Deliveries," the anthropologist said, following his gaze. "We get a lot on weekends. Cops bringing in blood and ballistic evidence. Always a few rape kits."

"The staff works weekends, Doctor?"

"Call me Kelsey. And yeah, evidence clerks do." She paused beside a door and flattened her palm against a panel to open it. "Plus, there's that group that seems to be here no matter what day it is."

"Which includes you," Allison said pointedly.

"Hey, look who's talking." She nudged Allison with her elbow and glanced at Mark. "I don't always work Saturdays, but we're on a research dig."

"I noticed the vultures."

"That's not us, thank God." She shuddered. "I hate those nasty birds. Today's recovery is fully skeletonized."

Mark eyed her with amusement. The last time he'd seen the woman, she'd been giving an enthusiastic lecture on maggots, and yet a few birds gave her the shivers.

Or maybe it was the temperature. The corridor they were in sloped down dramatically, and it was colder than the one they'd come from. Mark felt like he'd stepped into a meat locker.

She stopped before a door with a small black flag depicting a skull and crossbones pinned up beside it. Again, she pressed her palm against a panel to gain access.

"Osteology," she announced. "Otherwise known as our Bones Unit. You ever seen one before?"

Mark scanned the office, which looked like any other room full of cubicles. He glanced up. She'd been talking to him. "No, I haven't."

"Well, we're not *quite* as well-staffed as the Smithsonian. It's just me and a handful of grad students." She tossed her jacket over a chair and grabbed a lab coat from a hook on the wall. "But wait till you see our lab."

They followed her through the desks to yet another door, and again she did the palm-print thing. Mark had to admit he was impressed with the security here. The guard downstairs had wanted to see two forms of ID in exchange for their visitors' badges, and those were only valid for two hours.

"Here we are." She stepped into what looked like an autopsy suite, complete with stainless steel tables. Sinks and hoses lined the far wall. He noted the fume hood and the hanging scales, as well as a stove with a giant metal pot that brought back memories of his grandparents' farm. He didn't want to think about what it was used for.

"I got the call this morning." Kelsey went to the sink and washed up as though scrubbing in for surgery. Then she donned some latex gloves and handed pairs to Allison and Mark.

"Who found the bones?" Mark asked.

"Hunters. Actually, the find occurred last winter. But until now, we haven't had an ID. Through here." She led them into an adjacent room, only this one was narrow and lined with drawers, hundreds of them, from the floor up to Mark's shoulder. Kelsey strode about halfway down the row and pulled one open. Mark watched Allison's body stiffen as she peered down at the drawer.

"Is this . . . all?" she asked Kelsey.

"These remains were scavenged, unfortunately. They conducted a full-day search, but it was pretty hopeless and we were lucky to get the skull and femur. The recovery site is right beside a river in Evans County, so I'm guessing many of the bones were swept away in that flood two summers ago."

Mark tensed. Two years then, at least. How many victims had he missed while he'd been distracted with other cases? People sometimes asked him why he took on such an impossible caseload. This was the reason. For every case he helped close, there were countless more where someone was out there destroying people's lives with impunity. Too many crimes and not enough crime fighters. There would never be enough.

"The hunters found the femur first and called the sheriff," Kelsey said, "and he in turn called me to see if it was human."

Mark looked at her. "You went out there yourself?"

"Not at first. You wouldn't believe how many of those calls I get, especially with a long bone like this. Often it's just a cow or a deer. Or in the case of a smaller bone, sometimes people think they've found a baby on their property, when in fact it's an adult raccoon. We have a reference collection for comparison—animals native to Texas. But in this case, I knew it was human as soon as I saw the photo."

"How can you tell from a picture?" Allison asked.

"Trained eye," she said. "I could see right off this was a human femur, left side. And I confirmed that through microscopic examination."

"*Left* side?" Allison sounded doubtful.

"The shape tells you." She ran her gloved hand over the ball-shaped end of the bone. "This end fits into the pelvis. Then the shaft angles slightly inward to the knee." Kelsey smiled faintly. "In grad school one of my professors used to fill a big brown grocery sack with human bones. We had to blindfold ourselves and identify every single one by touch."

"How old are these remains?" Mark asked.

"It's not an exact science. Based on the bleaching, the drying, the way they were discovered, I put the PMI— postmortem interval—at two to five years."

"Why five?" Allison asked.

"That's where the skull comes in." She put the femur down and picked up the skull. "This is called the cranium, to be precise, because it's missing the mandible."

"Not a lot to work with," Allison said.

"Actually, for such a limited recovery, this is almost a best-case scenario. Ideally, you want a skull and pelvis to determine the Big Four: race, sex, age, and stature. I can do that almost as easily with a skull and long bone."

"So, what can you tell us?"

Kelsey nodded. "Caucasian female, fairly petite— about five-one." Sadness flickered over her face. "I'd say early twenties, based on the cranial sutures and also the tooth development."

"Any idea how she died?" Allison asked.

"That's trickier. No visible trauma. A few scratch

marks, but I examined them under a microscope, and they look to be from scavengers, as opposed to, say, a knife or a saw."

"What about the missing teeth?" Mark pointed to an upper molar.

"Good catch. Her teeth were intact when we got her, but our forensic odontologist removed one to examine the filling. It's a synthetic material that came into use about five years ago—hence, the timeline I gave you. She most likely didn't die before then. The other tooth, I sent to Mia."

"Mia?" Mark glanced up.

"Mia Voss. She's one of our DNA tracers. She got a profile from the molar, had it entered into a database of missing persons. It contains samples from families that are missing a loved one." Kelsey turned to Allison. "After we talked yesterday, I made a few calls searching for any recent IDs of young females in this area. This one *just* came through. Her name's Rachel Pascal, twenty-six. She disappeared from the parking lot of her workplace up in Austin."

"She wasn't jogging?"

"Not according to the detective I spoke with. He said she was leaving work."

"But if we can't tell how she died," Allison said, "how do we know she's connected?"

"The date," Mark said. He looked at Kelsey for con-firmation.

"I'm afraid so. And it also corroborates my time-of-death estimate. Rachel Pascal was last seen three years ago, the night before Halloween."

• • •

Allison was tapped out, both physically and emotionally. The bleak mood she'd been in after leaving the interview with Jordan had gotten worse when she'd seen those two lonely bones. So much loss. So much suffering. For years, she'd wanted to be a homicide detective, and now that she was, she wondered if it was really for her. How could you deal with so much death and violence and not become hardened to it? Not lose some of your humanity? She couldn't imagine what it must be like for Mark, day after day, wading through a steady stream of the very worst society had to offer.

"Looks like you need a drink."

Allison snapped out of her funk and looked at the woman beside her. Mia had sensed her melancholy on the phone and insisted on dragging her out for margaritas.

"Still working on this one." Allison picked up her fish-bowl-size glass and took a halfhearted sip. Avoiding Mia's gaze, she glanced around the bar. Tonight El Patio was noisy, crowded, and much too festive for Allison's mood.

Mia gave her a nudge. "What's with you tonight?"

"I don't know. Work."

When she didn't elaborate, Mia shook her head. As a cop's fiancée, she knew how tight-lipped detectives could be about their cases. But Mia didn't pry, which was one of the reasons Allison liked hanging out with her.

"What's with *you*?" Allison asked. "I've hardly seen you in weeks."

"The lab's been inundated."

The chair beside Allison slid out and Kelsey plopped down in it. "Hi." Her cheeks were flushed from cold as she unwound a purple scarf from her neck. "What'd I miss?"

"Nothing. We'll get you a margarita."

"Man, it's cold out there. Think I want a beer instead. And speaking of man . . ." She turned to Allison. "What'd you do with Wolfe?"

Mia's eyebrows arched. "What'd *I* miss? Who's Wolfe?"

"Nobody."

"Ha." Kelsey rolled her eyes and turned to Mia. "He happens to be a very hot, very unattached, very intriguing FBI agent who's in town right now working on Allison's murder case."

"It's not my case," she pointed out, but Mia was distracted.

"You didn't mention this guy, and we've been here nearly an hour?"

Allison sighed. "Nothing to mention." She turned to Kelsey. "And how do you know he's unattached?"

"See? I knew you were interested." Kelsey sounded pleased with herself. "And I asked around. I've got some friends in the San Antonio field office. Remember my ex, Blake? He says Mark Wolfe's got quite a reputation at the Bureau. Fact, he's practically a legend, although I'm not sure you want to know what he's legendary for."

"Womanizing?" Mia guessed.

"He's got the unenviable distinction of having worked more serial murder cases than any other profiler they've got over there," Kelsey said. "We're talking hundreds of cases."

"Hundreds?" Mia looked at Allison. "How old is he?"

"Old," Kelsey put in, and Allison bristled. Too late,

she noticed Kelsey watching her reaction. "But not *old* old. More like experienced." She turned to Mia. "A little gray around the temples. Nice eyes. And he's got this intensity about him. Am I right, A?"

She looked away and tried not to let Kelsey get under her skin. "Maybe a little."

"I knew I wasn't seeing things." Kelsey smiled. "I think it's mutual, by the way. The way he was looking at you at the lab—"

"Wait, when were you at the lab?" Mia asked. "Is this the Stephanie Snow case? I didn't even know you were on that."

"I'm not." Allison gritted her teeth. She'd spent her afternoon at the station house, trying to talk Reynolds into putting her on the case. No dice. And he was still hung up on Joshua Bender, their original suspect.

"Who *is* on the case officially?" Kelsey asked.

"Jonah and Ric," Mia said. "Although that's all I know about it. Ric doesn't usually discuss his cases with me."

"Allison Doyle?"

She glanced up to see a man glowering down at her. He had a stocky build, ruddy cheeks, and bloodshot eyes that beamed aggression at her.

"What'd you do to my wife?" he demanded.

Allison blinked up at him. She smelled alcohol on his breath as he leaned over their table.

"Uh, ex*cuse* you," Mia said.

"Sir, I don't know who you are, but—"

"Ethan Wheatley. Now answer me, damn it!" He pounded his fist on the table. *"What'd you do to my wife?"*

Conversations hushed. People turned to stare. Chairs

scraped back, and all three men at the neighboring table rose to their feet.

Crap. Allison stood up, too. "Sir, you're causing a disturbance. I'm going to have to ask you to step outside."

An off-duty firefighter appeared at Allison's side, along with an off-duty patrol officer. This guy had picked the wrong place to start something—it was a cop hangout, which was probably how he'd found her.

"It's either outside or at the police station, Mr. Wheatley. Your pick."

He scowled and stalked toward the door, and the crowd cleared a path.

"You're not really going to go out there, are you?" Mia looked horrified.

"I know what this is about. I just need to calm him down." She grabbed her jacket and moved for the exit, and the patrol officer caught her arm.

"Want me to arrest him?"

"For what, being a dickhead?" Allison shook his arm off. "I'll handle it."

She followed Wheatley out of the bar. The firefighter stayed behind her, but she ignored him.

Outside, she met with a wall of cold air. She spotted Wheatley sitting on the curb beside the parking lot. His big shoulders were hunched forward.

Allison walked over and saw that he was weeping. Far from the giant bully he'd been moments ago, he now looked soggy and pathetic. She stood there for a minute, not sure of what to say.

"How is Jordan?" she finally asked.

He shook his head and looked away. He rubbed his hand under his nose and seemed embarrassed.

Allison sat down on the curb beside him.

"She's upset, I take it?"

"She was in bed when I got home. Hasn't moved all day—all she's done is cry."

Allison felt a stab of guilt. "Our interview this morning— I guess it dredged up some things."

He nodded and looked at his boots. They were sturdy work boots caked with mud, and she remembered Jordan saying he'd had a delivery this morning. She'd probably postponed the interview so her husband wouldn't be there, and then didn't even tell him about it. Both Allison and Mark had left their business cards on the kitchen table.

"She gets like this." His shoulders hunched more. "I never know what to do. And then she won't talk to me. Didn't tell me you were coming, or I would have put my foot down." He turned and looked at her with his blood-shot eyes. "She can't handle when people swoop in like that and want to ask questions. It was happening every week for a while, and then . . ." He shook his head.

And then the case went cold and there was nothing left to ask.

"We think we might have a lead in her case," Allison said. "We think it might be connected to some others."

He sighed heavily and closed his eyes. A pickup truck tore out of the parking lot, and Allison watched its tail-lights fade down the street.

"He took her away, you know that? She's there still, but not really."

Allison looked at him. He sounded so defeated, as if the last twelve months had worn him down. He swayed slightly, and she smelled the booze again.

"Let me give you a ride home."

He went still.

"Mr. Wheatley? Jordan needs you right now, whether she says so or not."

"I'm fine." He heaved himself to his feet, and Allison stood, too.

He set his jaw and looked fiercely off at the parking lot. "I'm sorry for coming on like that. This isn't your fault. I just—"

"I'll drive you home."

"No, I got it."

"I insist." She pulled out her keys and glanced over her shoulder. The off-duty firefighter was still standing beside the door, watching protectively. "I'm going to drive Mr. Wheatley home," she called over to him.

"Really, I'm good. I got my truck here."

"Yeah, you know what? So do I. And I really don't feel like hauling you in for a DUI and filling out a bunch of paperwork, so save us both the trouble, okay?"

She walked toward her truck. He followed. When they were belted in safely, she got the engine started and steered out of the crowded lot.

He closed his eyes and rested his head on the window, and she desperately hoped he wasn't going to puke. After a few minutes on the highway, she decided he was asleep.

Allison focused on the narrow country road and the sleet coating her windshield. She flipped on the wipers and listened to the steady *swish-swish* of the blades.

"I hope you catch him this time."

She glanced over, startled.

"Don't bother arresting him. Call me up, I'll come slit his throat for you."

"I'm not sure you want to be saying that to a police officer."

He sighed heavily.

Allison pushed on through the night thinking about loss and pain and how even people who closed themselves off couldn't get away from it.

When she crossed the low-water bridge for the second time that day, Ethan Wheatley was fast asleep.

Allison lived in a generic beige apartment building that reminded Mark of his own. He wondered if she spent much time there or if she liked to spend her Saturday nights drinking and socializing, like most people her age. The silent door to 116 offered no clues, so he knocked.

Nothing.

But then the peephole went dark for a moment and the door swung back.

"Hi," she said, in a tone that meant, *What the hell are you doing here?* She wore a black tank top—no bra—and blue pajama bottoms with SpongeBobs all over them. Mark immediately regretted coming over.

She shivered. "Damn, it's *cold*. Come inside—you're letting all my heat out."

"Sorry to bother you at home."

He stepped into her warm apartment and quickly realized that while the outside looked much like his place, the similarities stopped there. Mark's apartment was depressing and anonymous, while hers was cozy and inviting. Her blue slip-covered sofa looked old yet comfortable. Her bookshelves were crammed with paperbacks and picture frames. Mark's gaze fell on a leafy green plant in the corner of the living room, and he tried to imagine being home enough to keep something like that alive.

He turned to look at her. "Sorry to interrupt."

"You said that already." She smiled slightly and crossed her arms. When he didn't say anything, she huffed out a breath. "Okay, be mysterious about it." She padded into the kitchen. "How about a drink while I try to guess how you found me? I've got beer or bourbon."

"I'll take a beer."

He followed her into a kitchen, trying not to stare at her bare feet. He distracted himself with her surroundings. Several unread newspapers lay on the counter. Dishes filled the sink. She opened her fridge, and he glimpsed an assortment of beer, yogurt, and carryout boxes.

"Where's your cat?" he asked.

"I don't have one."

"You were buying kitten chow the night of the holdup."

"Oh, *that* cat." She looked at him over her shoulder. "Budweiser okay?"

"Sure."

She used the hem of her T-shirt to twist off the top and then handed it to him. "He's just a stray that hangs around my patio. I call him Kitty-Kitty, but everyone in the building has a different name for him."

Mark sipped the beer and watched her. This woman had a soft side that she tried to downplay. He'd be willing to bet that one of these days she'd scoop up this cat that wasn't hers and take him to the vet for shots.

She was watching him with suspicion. "So, what'd you do, run me through the system?"

"Simple Internet search."

"But I'm unlisted."

"Very few people are really unlisted," he said. "Try it sometime. You'd be amazed."

She walked into the living room and sank down on the couch. To his relief and disappointment, she pulled a zippered sweatshirt on over her thin top.

"Okay, so you're not prying, you just happened to look me up on the Internet so you could crash my Saturday evening. What's up?"

Mark sat down beside her and rested his drink on an issue of *Runner's World*. "I've been working on the profile."

"I was wondering when you'd get around to that. You planning to share it with me?"

"Are you on the case yet?"

"Not officially, but I'm getting closer."

Mark watched her. She had that determined look that seemed to be her default expression whenever the subject of her job came up. She was trying to prove herself, and this case was a test.

"I've been working on this profile for a long time," he said. "Our interview today helped clarify a number of things."

"Glad it helped someone," she said bitterly.

"What's that mean?"

"Forget it. What did it clarify?"

He watched her for a moment and decided to let it go. "The UNSUB's sweatshirt. Rice University. Jordan Wheatley said that's her alma mater."

"Yeah?" Allison's gaze narrowed. "You think he was a student there?"

"I think he knew *she* was a student there."

She leaned forward to put her beer on the coffee table. "You think he stalked her?"

"I know he stalked her. He stalks all of them. I hadn't realized the extent of it until today."

She looked incredulous. "You're not talking about him spotting her on some jogging trail and learning her routine. You're talking about him researching *her*, specifically. Stalking her using personal information."

"Exactly. You heard what she said. Seeing that sweatshirt helped put her at ease, made her let her guard down. It's just the sort of tactic he'd use."

"But . . . maybe it's a coincidence. Maybe he actually went to school there."

"I don't think so. And I don't believe in coincidences—not in this case. Every move this guy makes is deliberate."

She stared at him, obviously uncomfortable with the notion that someone could be that calculating. She was naive. But then, she hadn't seen the things he had.

"It's not that hard, Allison. Think of all the social media sites where people post information about their backgrounds, their interests. All he needed was a name, and he had all kinds of information at his fingertips— information any skilled predator can use to gain an advantage."

She sat back against the sofa and blew out a sigh. "Wow."

"I found you—not only your home address, but your previous addresses, some of your hobbies, your date of graduation—all in a matter of minutes just by surfing the Net."

"But I'm not on social media. I hardly even have time to read my e-mail."

"It doesn't matter."

"You just said—"

"You were on the track team in college. Your name's still on their Web site because you hold the record in the sixteen-hundred." Which showed how recently she'd been an undergrad. "And utility companies have your old addresses. A simple name search yields all that. And the Habitat for Humanity project you did, back when you were a senior? That's out there, too. You're quoted in a newspaper article. Also, I can tell you're a cop because there's another write-up from when you spoke at a retirement home. 'Mail Scams and How to Protect Yourself,' I believe."

Allison drew back, surprised.

"This UNSUB uses the computer to select his victims. Then he goes out and targets them in real life. It's becoming more and more common."

"Okay, but . . . what's the common thread? How does he pick them off the Web?"

"I'm still working on that," he said. "I'd like more on Jordan Wheatley's background. And Stephanie Snow's. I spent half the day putting together victimology reports, but there are some missing pieces." He paused. "How's that case file coming from Wayne County?"

Her expression clouded. "I'm doing my best. Unfortunately, that's kind of limited right now, because I'm not officially on the case, and everyone knows it." She stood up and started pacing back and forth in front of the TV, her brow furrowed with frustration.

"You really think he's that sophisticated?" she asked.

"I was thinking about the exercise connection. I figured he was some jogger who'd noticed these women out on the trails."

"It goes beyond that. There's something about these specific women and these specific dates. Another thing I'd like to get a look at is Stephanie's computer. She might have been in contact with someone online."

"I heard they didn't find a computer at her house. She uses the one at work, apparently. And maybe her phone—our guys took that into evidence already."

"It seems odd for her not to have a computer at home. What's the status of her apartment?"

"It's probably been released by now," Allison said. "I could find out for you."

"I should see it. It might offer some clues, maybe even some insights into how the killer picked her."

Allison stopped and faced him, hands on hips. "Okay, I want to hear this profile. You're obviously the expert. Tell me who this guy is."

He held her gaze.

"Are you afraid you're wrong?"

"I'm not."

"Then, let's hear it."

Mark took a sip of his beer. He rested it on the table.

"We're looking for a white male, between thirty and forty-five."

She scoffed. "*I* could have told you that."

"College dropout," he continued. "High IQ, probably one-fifty or above. Works a menial job, probably owns a van or at least drives one. He lives outside a metropolitan area. Not married, but I wouldn't be surprised if he was in a relationship, possibly living with someone."

She looked skeptical. "And do you think she knows her boyfriend slashes up women in his free time?"

"It's possible," Mark said. "I think she at least has a hunch. She probably knows something's off about all the time he spends away from home. Stalking takes time. Maybe she's noticed the mileage on the van, or items of clothing that disappear, or scratches on his arms or face. But she could be in denial about what it all means.

"I believe his parents are dead. That he has at least one sibling, maybe two, and he had a domineering mother who physically abused him."

"Yeah, blame the mom. Next you're going to say he kills these women because they remind him of her. That's no excuse."

"I didn't say it was," Mark said. "I've sat in prisons and listened to every rationalization you can think of for why people do things, but the real reason is, they get off on causing pain. They have the impulse to hurt someone and they don't bother to control it—that simple. It's like the man who beats his wife because she mouthed off to him or burned the toast or forgot to put his favorite pair of jeans in the dryer. It's all bullshit."

"So you don't buy into the abused-kid defense?"

"There are a lot of abused kids out there, Allison. Not all of them grow up to be murderers."

She looked at him for a long moment, probably realizing he was speaking from experience. She had good instincts about people.

"What about his physical appearance?" she asked.

"We have that from Jordan, but it's possible he's smaller than she described. Victims have a tendency to exaggerate size as a result of their terror. Also, she described a goatee and glasses, but those are easily changeable features, along with hair color and eye color."

"Why would he care about disguising himself if he planned to kill her?"

"Witnesses," he said. "In California we found several eyewitnesses who thought they might have seen the UNSUB around the time the victim disappeared from the trails. They couldn't describe much about him physically, but said he drove a dark-colored SUV."

"Pretty weak."

"You're right, but that was all we had."

Allison watched him, and he could tell she was interested, but not necessarily convinced he knew what he was talking about. Mark was used to that reaction. He'd learned not to let it bother him, but at this moment it did. He wanted her trust. Not just that, he wanted her respect.

Hell, he wanted to impress her. And the fact that he wanted to bothered him more than everything else because he couldn't afford to be distracted right now, and somewhere along the way she'd become a distraction.

She stood there in her pajamas, arms crossed, probably mentally poking holes in everything he'd said.

"Another detail Jordan mentioned was the paint," he told her. "That's new, and we should use it. Reynolds needs to check out every paint contractor within a hundred miles of here."

Allison rolled her eyes. "I'm sure he'll get right on that. As soon as he finishes beating Josh Bender's lawyer over the head with all the evidence we have against him." She gave a frustrated sigh. "I'm fighting an uphill battle, you know. My lieutenant's a moron. He's stubborn, too, and as far as he's concerned, I don't even exist on this squad."

"How'd you get on it, then?"

She looked away. "Long story."

Mark wanted to hear it. Someday. But what he needed to do right now was get out of her apartment and get back to work.

She was giving him a look now that he couldn't read.

"You know, there's something you never told me about this case."

There were plenty of things he'd never told her. He hadn't wanted to burden her with every grisly detail. Was he being protective or sexist? Maybe both.

"What do you mean?" he asked.

"You've flown down here twice. First time, completely of your own accord. Correct me if I'm wrong, but doesn't the FBI have plenty to keep you guys busy without looking for investigations to butt into?"

"The UNSUB crossed state lines to avoid police. It's a federal case."

"Okay." She waited. "What else? I can tell you've been losing sleep over this thing and I'd like to know why. You've seen hundreds of cases."

He put his beer down. She could sniff out a lie, so he might as well just tell her.

"When they called me in ten years ago, it was my first case as a lead agent. I got more involved with the families than I should have. Sheryl Fanning's family in particular—that was harder than I'd expected. When you're the lead, everyone's looking to you for answers."

Mark stared at his hands. He remembered Sheryl's husband, her parents. Their grief had been enormous, and he'd felt powerless.

"They didn't even have anything to bury," he said. "I felt like I needed to give them some kind of encouragement, so I made them a promise. I said the investigation wouldn't end, that I wouldn't give up, until we got an arrest."

It was a foolish promise—he knew that now—but he'd made it. And now ten years later, he still hadn't delivered. So, yeah, this case was personal. Mark no longer made promises to people, but that long-ago one stuck with him.

"Every November nineteenth I get a call from her husband." He looked up at her. "You know he still looks for her? Couple times a year he borrows a dog team from the local fire and rescue, goes tromping through parks and wilderness areas searching for her bones."

Allison gazed down at him and those hazel eyes looked sad. Damn, why was he telling her all this?

He stood up. "Thanks for the drink."

"You're leaving?"

"I've got work to do."

"Now?" She glanced at her watch. "But it's—"

"It's November seventh, Allison. We're running out of time."

CHAPTER 7

Allison crossed the bullpen and yanked off her jacket.

"Reynolds is an idiot," she said, tossing her keys on her desk.

"Nice way to talk about your boss."

She glanced at Jonah, who was two cubicles away, doing what she should have been doing with her Sunday afternoon—catching up on paperwork.

Jonah leaned back in his chair and frowned at her. "What happened to your face?"

"Ran into a tree."

He smiled. "And Reynolds is the idiot."

She ignored him as she sank into her seat. "We now know of three women within an hour's drive of here who have been attacked on October thirtieth. Not to mention a clear link between those crimes and others out in California. But are we looking for a serial killer? Heck, no, we've got the boyfriend."

Something flickered across Jonah's face, and Allison narrowed her gaze at him. She sprang to her feet.

"You're doing it, too, damn it!" She was beside his cube in two strides. "What are you not telling me?"

"It's not your case, Doyle."

"It should be. *I'm* the one who found the Jordan Wheatley link. And Rachel Pascal."

"Who had an accident, for all we know. A skull and a leg bone? You can't even prove she was murdered."

"Aha! You've checked out her case."

Jonah looked annoyed. "Of course I've checked it out. I'm a detective. That's what I do."

"You know I'm onto something. And you're holding out on me." *Just like Wolfe did,* she thought, and her anger bubbled up all over again. "What does Reynolds know about Bender? Why is he so stuck on that, when we've even got the FBI down here saying we should be looking for a serial killer?"

Jonah sighed with resignation. He glanced around the room, which was practically empty except for a patrol officer on the phone.

"Bender won't give us an alibi," Jonah said. "And in this case, that's a red flag."

Allison thought about that for a moment. He was right—that was odd. "Because this is recent, you mean."

"Exactly. If I came up and asked you what you were doing, say, the evening of January ninth last year, you'd have no idea, right? In fact, if you *did* tell me right away where you were that night, I'd probably bump you to the top of my suspect list. But for something that happened a few days ago?"

Allison dragged a chair over from a neighboring cube and sat down. "So, what's he saying?"

"Practically nothing. It's one reason Reynolds is so set on him. He's acting guilty."

"Okay. Well, what do we *know* about what he was doing the night she disappeared?"

"There you go with the 'we' again." Jonah looked irritated as he reached across his desk and picked up a fat black binder. This would be the actual murder book, complete with all the info Reynolds didn't want reporters or anyone outside the inner circle to see.

"I intend to get on this case, Jonah. Eventually, there's going to be a task force."

He held up a hand. "I've heard your theory, all right? And I've even listened. You and the fed have some good points, far as I'm concerned. But I'm telling you, Bender looks bad in this. He won't give us the slightest detail we can corroborate about where he was the night Stephanie died, and it's not helping his case any."

Jonah opened the binder and flipped to a report. It looked to be several pages of typed interview notes.

"Here's what he told us in the original interview, before he got a lawyer—that he was at work from eight a.m. to five-fifty, with the exception of his lunch break. We've confirmed that with his employer."

"The car dealership, right?"

"Yeah, he sells Toyotas. After that, he says he went home and watched TV. End of story. Didn't leave his apartment until work the next day."

"That right there is an alibi."

Jonah gave her a baleful look. "First off, the guy's lying through his teeth. I took his statement. Second, he was served with a restraining order the night before, and his reaction to *that* was to call up Stephanie, probably to ream her out. We have records of fourteen phone calls placed to her cell phone, from Bender, the day before her murder. No idea what he said to her, but I doubt it was friendly."

"The restraining order includes phone contact."

"Yeah, which goes to show how much respect he had for it. Then the day of her murder, he disappears at noon—three people at his work confirm this—comes back two hours later. Was he making plans? Buying a murder weapon? Buying a sandwich? We don't know. Five hours later, Stephanie gets home from work, changes, and goes jogging. She pulls over for gas on the way—we've got that on tape from the gas station. Parks her car at her favorite park. She passes a woman walking her dog as she sets out on the trail. That woman was the last person to see her alive, that we know about. Eleven hours later, a female jogger strays off the path with her Weimaraner and sees Stephanie's partially clothed body lying in the woods. And where was Bender while all this was happening? Home watching TV, according to his original statement. He didn't make a phone call. Didn't send a text. Didn't log onto his computer. Didn't have a friend over. Nothing. Just home alone, watching the tube."

"What about DNA? She was sexually assaulted."

"The ME sent swabs to the lab, but you know how that goes. By the time we hear back, this case'll probably be stone cold. Meantime, only solid suspect we've got is Bender."

Jonah culled through the file and pulled out another paper, this one with several incidents listed on it. The descriptions took up almost a full page. "He's got a temper. Stephanie's neighbors in her apartment complex called us out twice because they were fighting, and it sounded like Bender was hitting her. She herself reported him once for splitting open her lip. After she dumped him, she called twice to report him stalking her before finally getting the restraining order. Two days after he gets served with papers, Stephanie turns up dead."

Allison stared down at the report.

"Come on, Allison."

"Okay, you're right, it looks like Bender. The guy's a dirtbag. He beats women. But the thing is, he didn't kill her."

Unless he killed the other ones, too.

The thought startled her. She pulled the file toward her and studied the interview notes. Bender's date of birth was listed at the top, beneath his name.

"Twenty-eight years old," Allison muttered. That didn't fit Mark's profile. And he would have been seventeen when the first victim was killed in California. But still . . .

"Where'd he go to high school?" Allison asked.

"North Side High. Starting quarterback." Jonah leaned back in his chair again and crossed his arms. "Took his team to state his senior year, as a matter of fact."

"That explains his ego. And probably his penchant for knocking people around."

"Not every athlete's a wife beater, Allison."

"I know that, I'm just—"

"I get it. You're trying to build a profile." He gave her a hard look, and she knew he was thinking about her sudden friendship with Mark.

She looked away. Mark was right. These cases were connected. If there was anything Allison had taken from her interview with Jordan Wheatley, it was that the man who attacked her had a ruthless MO. He was skilled, smart, and shockingly cold in his execution. Mark believed he'd killed five women in California, at least two in Texas, and that he would go right on doing it unless someone tracked him down and put a stop to it. Allison believed it, too. And *her* law enforcement agency was in a position to do something. They had the freshest case, the warmest trail.

And yet they were completely off track.

"Why won't he provide a solid alibi?" Allison looked at Jonah.

"How the hell do I know? Maybe his lawyer told him to keep his mouth shut."

"But even during the initial interview. He claims he went home and watched TV, and you say he was lying."

"I know he was—I just can't prove it."

"I bet I can." She felt the adrenaline rush as her idea took shape.

"You want to *provide* our prime suspect with an alibi." Jonah smiled ruefully and shook his head.

"I want to eliminate him. It's the only way to convince Reynolds. Now, listen." She leaned forward. "Why would he lie about where he was? I mean, *why*, for Christ's sake? This is a death penalty state."

She saw him understand where she was going with this.

"Because the truth would make him look guilty," Jonah said.

"That's right. And what do we know about Bender? What do we have on record? That he's abusive. That he's violent. That he's followed the victim out on dates and harassed her. He probably *was* stalking her the night she got killed, Jonah. Even if he wasn't the one who killed her."

Jonah pursed his lips, considering the idea.

"Where's Stephanie's apartment?" she asked.

"'Bout three blocks off campus. It's that new complex over by the movie theater."

Allison pictured the redbrick building with the pool and the landscaping. She'd bet her next paycheck it had security cameras.

She stood up and went to get her jacket. "Come on, let's go."

"Where are we going?"

"To see where Bender was the night Stephanie disappeared."

Mark entered Randy's Pool Hall and saw the typical array of football fans and bored husbands he'd expected on a Sunday night. What he hadn't expected was Allison. She was seated at the bar with a drink in front of her, deep in conversation with the bartender.

So much for his plan. He'd come in to ask a few subtle questions of the wait staff. Now he ditched the idea and approached Allison. Once again, she was in jeans and a tight-fitting shirt, her dark hair loose around her shoulders. She glanced up.

"Hey." She looked pleasantly surprised to see him. "What are you doing here?"

"Looking for a drink." He ordered a beer and nodded at her almost empty glass. "What is that, bourbon? You want another one?"

She smiled at the bartender. "Another Coke, please.

Make it a double." She slid the neighboring stool toward him with her foot. "Sit down."

Mark did, although he didn't like having his back to the door. He swiveled sideways to face her.

"Catching the game?"

She scrunched up her nose. "I don't watch football. Actually, I'm waiting for someone."

Of course she was. Mark glanced at the entrance. He should probably give up his stool, but he didn't.

"So," she said, "what'd you do in the cave all day?"

He lifted an eyebrow at her.

"I passed the motel a couple times, saw your car."

"Work, mostly. Did a couple errands."

"That explains the jeans." She leaned back and looked him up and down critically. "I see you found our outlet mall. This mean you plan to stay awhile?"

"That depends." The bartender delivered his beer, and he took a sip. "Did you have the day off?"

"Not really. Spent the afternoon disproving Joshua Bender's alibi."

"*Dis*proving?"

"Turns out he spent the entire night of Stephanie's disappearance parked in front of her apartment building, waiting for her to come home."

"He admitted this?"

"Surveillance cam." She stirred her drink with one of those little red straws. "Anyway, contradicts what he told us, which was that he was home by himself. Also eliminates him as a suspect. Reynolds is rethinking his theory now, thanks to me." A smile spread across her face. "Score one for the rookie detective."

Her eyes sparkled, and Mark's heart gave a kick. She

held his gaze for a moment, and the triumphant smile turned into something warmer, more intimate.

He looked away.

"Think your friend's here," he said.

She turned to look at the door, where a brawny man had just stepped in from the cold. He wore jeans and cowboy boots, but the way he carried himself was pure cop. His gaze went from Allison to Mark and instantly turned suspicious.

Allison swiveled on her stool as he approached. Six-two, two-twenty, buzz cut. Mark wondered if he owned a pair of size-twelve work boots that he'd left with his ex-girlfriend.

"Cal, thanks for coming." Her tone was brisk. "This is Special Agent Mark Wolfe with the FBI. Mark, meet Deputy Sheriff Calvin Brooks."

They shook hands and spent a moment sizing each other up. The deputy turned to Allison.

"Talked to Austin this afternoon. Not sure I got anywhere." He looked at Mark. "Maybe you got some other strings you could pull on that rape kit." He reached into his camo-print jacket and pulled out an envelope. "Here's the highlights. All copies, but it's a start. You didn't get this from me."

"Understood."

"I'll work on Denton."

"Thanks, I owe you." Allison dropped the envelope into the purse at her feet. "Can I buy you a beer? You drove all the way down here."

"I'll take a rain check. Keep me posted on the case."

"Will do."

Mark watched him leave, then glanced down at the envelope.

"The Jordan Wheatley file. How'd you manage that?"

"I took your advice and made nice with the deputy." She rattled the ice cubes in her glass. "Plus, I did a favor for Ethan."

"Ethan?"

"Jordan's husband. Turns out he's got some friends up in Wayne County. Word gets around."

He looked at her, intrigued. "What was the favor?"

"Are you always this nosy?"

"Yes."

"Helped him avoid a drunk-driving charge. Our paths crossed last night, and he was kind of on a tear."

"And who's Denton?"

"The sheriff. He and Reynolds have some kind of pissing contest going back to God knows when." She turned to face him and tilted her head to the side. "Hey, I've been thinking about your profile."

Mark sipped his beer and waited.

"Was that the full thing, or did I get the nutshell version?"

"You got a lot of it. Why?"

"Then you know he's left-handed, right?"

Mark gave her a sharp look. "Where'd you get that?"

"From the autopsy report. The ME noted abrasions on Stephanie's back, indicated he was on top of her during the struggle. She had bruises on the right side of her face, and he knocked out a tooth, too—upper right side." Allison made her left hand into a fist and mimicked a swing at Mark's jaw. "See? He's a lefty."

Mark just looked at her.

"Also, the throat cutting," she said. "Someone left-handed would probably slash right to left, because it's a more natural motion. Cut penetrated deepest on the *left* side of Stephanie's neck, which seems to support that."

Mark shook his head. Clearly, he'd underestimated her. It probably happened a lot.

"Well?"

"Nice logic—sounds like he's left-handed."

"But you already knew that, huh?"

"I didn't."

"Come on." She narrowed her gaze at him.

"It's a new detail. An important one, too. Roughly eighty percent of people are right-handed."

"You're telling me *I* told you something you didn't know?" She smiled. "Well, okay then. That's three things I did right today." She signaled the bartender. "Think I'll quit while I'm ahead."

The bartender dropped off the check, and Mark picked it up.

"Hey, you bought last time."

He ignored her and put some bills down, leaving a generous tip in case he decided to come back to interview the staff.

Allison shrugged into her leather jacket and led him out of the bar. When they were on the sidewalk, she glanced over her shoulder at the traffic on the interstate.

"It's supposed to be icy tonight." She turned to face him, and her breath was a puff of steam in front of her face. Her cheeks were pink. Her mouth, too. She caught him looking at it, and there it was again—that pull he'd been trying to resist since he first met her.

He stepped closer and touched her cheek. She went still and gazed up at him as he traced her jaw with his finger.

"How's the bruise?" he asked.

"Better."

She looked up at him and he knew what she was thinking, because he was thinking the same thing. For a moment he let himself picture her in the dimness of his motel room. He pictured himself peeling that leather jacket off her and tossing it down on the bed. He pictured her eyes going dark with desire.

The door slapped open and several men filed out of the bar, trading good-natured insults as they headed for their trucks.

Mark's attention settled on his rental car parked in the nearest row. It was always the same—rental cars, airplanes. Motel rooms, police stations. Torn-up families. Neglected relationships.

Mark let his hand drop. He stepped back and a cold gust filled the space between them.

"Good work today," he said. "See you at eight tomorrow."

Confusion flitted over her face. He was giving her mixed signals, and he needed to stop.

"What happens at eight?" she asked.

"Reynolds set up a meeting. Wants me to present the profile."

"So he's on board." It was her cop voice now.

"From the sound of it, yeah. He's pulling together a task force."

"You could have told me."

"I figured you knew."

"I didn't. Which means I'm not on it. Damn it, I've had it with that man." She stomped her foot. "What do I have to do—"

"Allison, calm down, you're on it."

Her gaze turned suspicious. "What did you do?"

"Nothing."

"Bullshit. Tell me what you did."

"You did it yourself." He pulled out his keys and started for his rental car. "You've got a long day ahead of you. A long week. Get some sleep, and we'll tackle it again tomorrow."

Jordan stared at the rafters as the wind rattled the windows and the cabin creaked. Beside her, Ethan snored. She turned to look at him. The only time she ever looked anymore was when he was asleep and she could do it in private. In sleep, he seemed so young. Boyish. And she felt a pang of regret for all the pain she'd put him through this past year.

She turned her gaze back to the ceiling and forgave herself. It was the only thing she could do. She regretted what she'd done to him, but what had been done to her was worse, and she couldn't take on everyone's hurt—it was more than she could stand.

At the end of the bed, Maximus lifted his head. His ears perked, and Jordan sat up on her elbows.

What is it, boy?

He turned to the window, a low growl in his throat, and hopped off the bed.

Jordan glanced at Ethan. She heard Max's paws on the wood as he trotted downstairs.

Easing out of bed, she followed her dog. She crept

down to the living room, where everything was washed in moonlight. Max approached the door, and she watched from the shadow of the staircase as he gazed outside. He turned to look at her.

What is it?

He scratched at the door. It was his signal, and she walked over to let him out. She shut the door quickly against the icy air and locked it as he bounded down the porch steps and sniffed around the yard. They had no fence, but Maximus was well trained. He'd come to her that way—not as a puppy, but a fully grown guard dog. He'd been a present from Ethan, and at first she hadn't wanted him, but now she felt profoundly grateful. She'd fallen head over heels for the dog, and she preferred his company to people. Ethan knew it, too, and it probably hurt his feelings, but that didn't make it any less true.

Max sniffed at the edge of the orchard. He paused beside a tree. His muscles tensed, and Jordan felt a chill of fear.

Is he out there, boy? What is it?

She eased deeper into the shadows and gazed through the glass. Her heart pounded. Her palms began to sweat.

You know when you're in the presence of danger. The special agent's words came back to her, but they didn't help. The problem was, she *didn't* know. Her instincts were muddled. She didn't trust herself—not anymore.

But she trusted Maximus. He stood rigid beside the orchard, tail up, ears pointed skyward. Jordan's fear became a brick inside her stomach.

One one-thousand, two one-thousand, three one-thousand . . . If she got to ten, she'd call 911.

Suddenly, Max relaxed. He crossed the yard again

and climbed the stairs to the back door, where he sat and gazed up at her expectantly.

Jordan blew out a sigh. She let him in, and he licked her knees and rubbed his cool, thick fur against her calves.

She scanned the woods one last time as she bolted the door. Another night. Another nobody. Max was halfway up the stairs already, and she followed him back to bed.

CHAPTER 8

———— ❧ ————

Allison's knocks on Mark's motel room door went unanswered early the next morning. She stood in the parking lot beside his frost-coated Taurus and scanned the frontage road for possibilities.

To the north was a Denny's. To the south, an IHOP. But somehow she couldn't picture him hunched over a greasy plate of eggs. She glanced at his motel again, and this time her gaze landed on a set of railroad tracks stretching east into the sun, and a figure in the distance. He was running. The unexpected sight of his tall, broad-shouldered form pounding along the train tracks made her breath catch.

Intensity. Mark Wolfe had it in spades. Kelsey had put a name to it, but Allison had sensed it from the very beginning. It was in the way he moved, the way he spoke, the way he made an argument. It was in his laser-sharp focus when he talked to a victim. It was in the way he looked at her sometimes—as if he could see straight into her mind and read her private thoughts.

She wondered what it would be like to have all that intensity directed at her in bed.

He reached the parking lot and stopped beside his car. His Georgetown T-shirt was soaked with sweat, and his chest heaved up and down as he looked her over.

"Morning."

He nodded.

"How far'd you go?"

He jerked his head east. "Out to the bridge."

"That's got to be eight miles."

"Six." He watched her, still breathing hard. His legs were long and powerful, and the sight of them made her stomach flutter.

Behind him, the muffled ring of a phone. He glanced over his shoulder at the door.

"That'll be Reynolds," she said.

He raised an eyebrow and took a keycard from the pocket of his running shorts. She followed him into the room but remained near the door as he crossed to the nightstand and reached for the phone.

"Wolfe." He glanced up at her. "Okay."

Allison turned and checked out his room as he took the call from her lieutenant. Draped over the desk chair was a plastic dry-cleaning bag. He'd taken his shirts in, apparently. On the desk was a closed laptop computer and a tall stack of files. She stepped over and read the labels. Case numbers. Lots of different ones. All the folders were fat with papers, and it occurred to her just how much work he was juggling in order to be here. This case seemed to have him by the throat, and she wondered if it really was all because of some promise he'd made ten years ago.

She glanced up to find him watching her reproachfully.

Okay, so she was nosy. Came with the job. She surveyed the rest of his living quarters. The wastebasket contained a Coke can and a Subway wrapper, evidence of a solitary dinner at his desk. A black garment bag sat in the corner, patiently awaiting the next journey. On the dresser lay a worn black billfold and a rental-car key. The wallet was the most personal item in the room, and all at once she felt terribly lonely for him. What sort of life was this that he'd built for himself?

Mark hung up the phone. "Meeting's been moved," he said.

"Eleven o'clock."

He grabbed a towel from the rack beside the sink and rubbed the sweat from the back of his neck. "He didn't explain why."

"He does that sometimes. Power trip."

He crossed the room and stood in front of her, hooking the towel around his neck, and she noticed the stubble all along his jaw. He watched her, still waiting to hear what she was doing here.

She cleared her throat. "So, we've got a good three hours until the meeting. I'm on my way to Austin."

His eyebrows tipped up.

"I'm authorized to pick up the rape kits for Jordan Wheatley and Stephanie Snow. We're hoping to get faster turnaround at the Delphi Center."

"You're officially on the task force."

"Yep."

"Congratulations." He gave her one of those long, penetrating looks. "What do you need me for?"

She shoved her hands in the pockets of her blazer. "Just thought you might want to come, that's all. Case there's any red tape."

The side of his mouth curved up. "You're using me for my FBI badge."

"Is that a problem?"

"No."

She glanced at her watch again. "Look, you want to come or not? I need to get going if I'm going to be back for that meeting."

"I need a shower. Give me ten minutes."

"Five," she said firmly. "I'll wait in the car."

Four hours later, Mark Wolfe looked every inch the federal agent as he stood in front of a room full of skeptical small-town cops and presented his profile. He didn't shed the jacket, or loosen the tie, or even lay off the Quantico-speak as he went through his points, and damned if Allison didn't admire him for it.

She knew how it felt to be the odd man out in this particular arena, and she didn't envy the task Mark had in front of him. Even with Jonah on board and Reynolds reluctantly cooperating, he had a long way to go to persuade the newly formed task force to accept his case theory. After an hour of discussion, the cops around the table still seemed unconvinced that a serial killer who'd eluded investigators for more than a decade had traveled all the way from California to terrorize their community. The whole thing seemed unreal, like something out of a movie, and Allison could see from the body language around her that they didn't fully believe it.

Surely Mark, skilled profiler that he was, could see it, too. And yet he continued to stand up there and make his case in that confident voice Allison had come to respect.

"What do you mean by 'low-risk victim'?" asked a

detective at the other end of the table. A fellow member of the Crimes Against Persons squad, Sean Byrne had spent the entire meeting with his chair tipped back and his arms folded over his chest.

"Low-risk victim, high-risk crime," Mark said. "In other words, each of these women had a low-risk lifestyle. They're not prostitutes or drug addicts—people who routinely put themselves in vulnerable situations. We're talking about students, moms, corporate executives—women who are not only connected to their communities, but who habitually take measures to protect themselves. Dara Langford had self-defense training. Sheryl Fanning kept a tube of Mace on her key chain and made a point never to jog after dark. The fact that these women were targeted anyway makes the crimes high-risk for the perpetrator."

"So, why were they targeted?" Sean asked. "You still haven't told us why he picked them all."

"*If* he picked them all," Reynolds said. "All due respect, I still don't see as we can say these murders are all connected. Maybe it's a copycat. Someone coming here all the way from California? I think it's a stretch."

"People move around," Mark countered. "Ted Bundy crisscrossed the country committing murders in at least five states, even escaping from jail twice before ending up in Florida."

Mark surveyed the faces around the room, meeting Allison's gaze only briefly. She'd been careful not to say much this morning because she didn't want to stir up trouble with her boss, who clearly had put this task force together for appearance's sake.

Mark shuffled through a stack of files and drew out a

photograph. "Okay, don't take my word for it. You tell me what you see."

He passed the eight-by-ten to Reynolds, then selected another picture from another file. And another. And another. Soon photographs from four separate case files were making their way around the table.

"Each case, someone abducts a woman from a nature trail or park, beats and sexually assaults her, slits her throat, chops her hair off, and then dumps her body in the woods."

"What does the hair mean?" Ric Santos asked.

Allison glanced across the table at her friend's fiancé. He wasn't much of a talker, and she didn't know how he felt about the investigation yet.

"The hair is very telling," Mark said. "Combined with the brutal sexual assault, it reveals what his crime is really about. It's his way of showing his contempt for women. Degrading them. We're talking about someone with a lot of pent-up hatred, a need to humiliate his victims and feel power over them. As I said, it most likely goes back to some childhood trauma, a very volatile relationship with an abusive mother."

Reynolds snorted. "So now you're making excuses for him?"

"No," Mark said. "I'm tracing the roots of a behavior."

"Guy's sick," Sean said scornfully, and tossed one of the photographs away. It was a picture of Stephanie Snow, whose murder was particularly disturbing to everyone in the room because it had happened on their home turf.

"Careful how you use that word," Mark warned. "Especially in front of the media. This UNSUB shows clear signs of being a psychopath, but that doesn't mean he's not mentally competent, that he can't tell right from wrong. He can. He does. And he chooses to do it anyway. Some attorney down the road may try to use an insanity defense for him. We shouldn't lend credibility to that by talking about how he's 'sick in the head' or 'mentally ill' or whatever."

Allison leaned forward on her elbows and cleared her throat. "When we interviewed Jordan Wheatley, she said her attacker referred to his wife several times. You do or don't think he's married?"

Mark nodded. "Married is unlikely, I'd say. All indications are that he has a disdain for conventional society, along with its institutions."

"Where'd you get that?" Jonah asked.

"It goes back to the Internet posts I mentioned from when he started this, and the latest one that coincided with Stephanie's death. He indicates a deep dislike for societal institutions, and I would bet that extends to marriage. But it *is* possible he's in a relationship with a woman, maybe even lives with her."

"He hates women, but he lives with one?" Sean asked.

"I didn't say he was nice to her. Most likely he's abusive and controlling. I worked a serial case once where the perpetrator had a girlfriend for ten years, but he treated her like an animal. Wouldn't allow her to bathe or leave the house. Made her sleep on the floor beside his bed."

Allison gritted her teeth. Where did these assholes come from?

"Cutting off the victim's hair is a key element of the attack," Mark continued. "It's important to him emotionally. You could say it's his signature."

"How's that different from MO?" Sean asked.

"Signature stays the same. Modus operandi can change over time, evolving as the killer gets more skilled. For example, switching vehicles or finding new ways to approach a victim."

"Why was Jordan left in the park where she was jogging, and the others were taken to a secondary dump site?" Jonah asked.

"You're right, that's unique," Mark said. "I think he probably intended to take her somewhere, but she put up such a struggle, he couldn't control her. So he got in a hurry and changed his plan. He dumped her out in the same parking lot where he first approached her, and she was discovered a few minutes later by some hikers, which is why she survived."

Quiet settled over the room at the reminder of Jordan Wheatley. No one wanted to think about the aftermath of her attack. In some ways, it was easier to think of the victim dying rather than surviving because she wasn't still suffering now, today, as everyone sat around a conference table with their coffee cups, reviewing what had been done to her and conjecturing about her attacker's emotional problems. Having met Jordan face-to-face, Allison now understood the anger that seemed to seep from her pores.

How could this man still be out there after what he'd done? What had anyone been doing about her case for the past year?

"Another point," Mark said. "He probably follows his crimes in the media. He's interested in knowing what we know and feeling superior because he's evaded police for so long. He's probably got news clippings somewhere, pictures of his victims. Maybe he follows the story online.

"We also know he takes souvenirs. Several of the victims were missing jewelry. Dara was wearing a gold bracelet when she disappeared that was never found. And Stephanie"—he shuffled through a file and produced a photograph—"was wearing this opal-and-diamond pendant on a chain around her neck."

Mark held up the photo that showed Stephanie in her graduation cap and gown. She had soft green eyes, a beautiful smile, and a cascade of glossy dark hair that flowed over her shoulders.

"What about the hair?" Jonah asked. "That a souvenir, too?"

"He leaves it at the crime scene. It's the act of cutting it off that satisfies some need he has. Although we wouldn't know if all he takes is a few strands."

"That poetry he puts out with his Internet messages," Ric said. "Who'd you say that was again?"

"Edgar Allan Poe."

"Yeah, what does all that mean, exactly? The poems?"

"I don't know," Mark said frankly. "Could be it has some psychological importance to him. Could be—and this is my personal opinion—it's all just a gimmick. Means nothing. He uses obscure references because it makes him feel smart. Don't forget, we're talking about someone with a very inflated ego who likes attention. Maybe he thought the poetry would get him a cool nickname in the media like the Zodiac Killer or the BTK Killer. We've tried not to emphasize the poetry to keep that from happening."

"But do the poems tell us anything?" Ric asked.

"In one case, it helped them recover a body."

All eyes swung toward Allison. She'd spent the ride up to Austin perusing Mark's case files and questioning him about the details that were new to her.

"Jillian Webb," she said. "Someone posted a few snippets of poetry on the Web site of the local paper covering her disappearance. The poem was about a lake with 'waters lone and dead.' Detectives heard about it and started searching a reservoir near the park where she disappeared. Cadaver dogs found her body that same day."

"Unfortunately, that was the last time he gave us anything useful," Mark said. "The other verses we've come across have been more obscure."

Allison studied the faces around the room. She saw skepticism. Because Mark was a fed? An outsider? Because they thought profiling was a bunch of psychobabble? Every last one of these men was action-oriented.

"So, if your theory holds," Reynolds said, "you're telling us we should brace ourselves for another murder on November nineteenth."

Something sparked in Mark's eyes. "That's exactly the wrong way to look at it. I'm here—we're all here—to prevent that from happening."

"Agreed," Allison said. "So what do we *do*?"

"If it were a serial bank robber, we'd harden the targets," Jonah said, and people nodded in agreement. "We'd put up extra security everywhere and then leave one vulnerable target, let him walk into a trap."

"Not a bad idea," Mark said. "And it's a technique we've used before. But in this case it doesn't work because these aren't crimes of opportunity. He doesn't go to a park and wait for a vulnerable woman to come along.

He selects *these* women. And if we knew how or why, we'd have a better idea where to find him."

"Okay, what else?" Allison said. "I plan to deliver the rape kits to Delphi this afternoon, see if we can get a rush on them. What about the paint?"

"What paint?" Reynolds wanted to know.

"In our interview with Jordan, Detective Doyle asked about smells." Mark acknowledged Allison with a nod. "Jordan recalled a strong chemical smell in the van, possibly paint. That's a new lead."

"I'm on it," Jonah said. "I'll check out paint outfits in the tri-county area. Maybe we can find someone with a criminal background."

"I'll help," Ric said. "That's a lot of people. We should check deck and fence companies, too. Those wood stains they use smell like paint."

"I'll keep pushing on the Internet angle," Mark said. "And the victim profiles need work. Allison, you've got the Jordan Wheatley file, so you can help with that."

Everyone's gaze settled on Sean, who hadn't volunteered for anything.

"I'll work on the vehicle angle," he said. "Wayne County says the green minivan was a dead end, but maybe they missed something."

And with Sean's offer to help, the tables were officially turned. Allison wasn't sure how it had happened, but every cop in the room was at least pretending to be on board.

"Okay, that's it, people." Reynolds re-asserted his authority over his squad as chairs scraped back and notebooks flipped shut. "We got work to do. And remember, no one talks to the press besides me or the chief. That's an order."

"One more thing," Mark said. "You've got ten thousand women enrolled at the university here. Someone needs to coordinate with campus security and make sure these students know what to watch out for."

"I'll do it," Allison said.

"You think he's been on campus?" Reynolds looked alarmed.

"I don't know," Mark said. "But it's a target-rich environment and I'm sure he's taken notice."

Mark walked out of the police station and stood on the steps to get some air. He hated meetings. He preferred to walk a crime scene or interview a witness or search an apartment. Sitting around a conference table always felt like a waste of time, especially when he knew he was right.

He glanced up at the dull gray sky and remembered a similar day nearly a decade ago. It had been cold and cloudy then, too, as he'd stood beside a creek bed watching a young woman be zipped into a body bag. Even with a task force working round the clock, they'd still been too late. Mark didn't intend to be too late again.

He pulled out his phone and scrolled through his messages, but instead of seeing the words he saw faces. Dara Langford. Sheryl Fanning. Stephanie Snow. That coldness started to creep in again. He felt it sometimes when the cases began to bleed together and he'd spent too many hours sifting through crime-scene photos and occupying the minds of soulless people.

In college, Mark had read a quote by Nietzsche that

he'd never forgotten: *Whoever fights monsters should see to it that in the process he does not become a monster. And when you look long into an abyss, the abyss also looks into you.*

When he'd first read the words, Mark had glommed onto the idea of fighting, of lashing back at his father and all those things he'd been powerless to take on when he was a kid. All his life he'd wanted to be a fighter instead of a weakling, and so he'd joined the FBI. But the longer Mark did this job, the more it seemed that he wasn't fighting monsters so much as he was fighting that abyss.

He thought of Allison in the meeting just now, studying those crime-scene pictures. He remembered her at the Bones Unit. She'd had an intense distaste for what she was seeing—outrage, even. Allison was still in the fighting stage. She had that unchecked passion, that thirst for justice. Being around her reminded him how he'd felt when he'd first started this job, and part of him wanted that back.

Another part of him knew he couldn't have it. Time marched on. What he had now was experience.

A pickup chugged up to the curb and Mark watched as the window slid down. Allison leaned across the front seat and peered out at him.

"We're going the same direction," she said. "Want a lift?"

"How do you know where I'm going?"

"Delphi Center. Home of the best cyber-crimes lab in the country." She smiled slyly, and he knew she liked making digs at the Bureau. Perversely, he liked it, too.

He looked out over the parking lot full of police cars. He looked at the woman offering him a ride. Either she was oblivious to local politics, or she didn't care.

"I need to be back by three to take a conference call," he said.

"Fine."

"No detours for tater tots."

"Fine."

He got in the truck, which was warm for a change. He stowed his briefcase stuffed with files in the back of the cab.

She shot him a peevish look as she pulled away from the curb. "But if I pass out from hunger, I'm blaming you."

CHAPTER 9

❧

"What's your in with the DNA lab here?"

They hiked up the wide marble stairs and passed through a pair of Greek columns.

"What makes you think I have an in?" Allison asked.

Mark shifted the packages he was carrying and opened the door for her, demonstrating those old-fashioned manners again.

"Expediting evidence is no easy task," he said. "And you volunteered."

"Maybe I like a challenge."

He looked at her patiently.

"Okay, yes, I have an in," she said. "A friend of mine is a DNA tracer here."

"The one Kelsey was talking about Saturday. Mia Voss."

"Not bad, Wolfe. Now I see why you're a cop."

They approached the reception desk and presented IDs in exchange for visitors' badges.

"Actually, it should be *Ric's* in," Allison said. "He's engaged to the woman. But until about an hour ago, I'm not sure he thought much of your case theory." She clipped the badge to the lapel of her blazer and headed for the evidence room. "By the way, nice going earlier. You did well back there."

Allison glanced up at him, but he didn't acknowledge the compliment. Then again, Mark knew he was good. He didn't need her to stroke his ego.

"Mia's very passionate about what she does," she told him. "And she's got a thing about untested rape kits. When I explained the situation, it wasn't hard to get her to put us at the front of her line."

"At Quantico, even 'front of the line' doesn't necessarily mean soon. What's her time frame?"

"With her, soon means soon. We could have something within a week. Like I said, she's very dedicated. She even offered to do the tests for free."

"What's the catch?"

"They get grants here," Allison said. "Private funding to help clear the backlog of biological evidence. You know how this place was founded?"

"Wealthy oil heiress left them her estate, right?"

"Massive endowment. This woman's daughter had been raped and murdered by a convicted sex offender."

Allison plunked her packages on the counter and greeted the evidence clerk, whom she'd met on several occasions. The woman handed over a familiar form for Allison to fill out while she checked in the evidence, which consisted of several cardboard boxes and over-sized envelopes. The clerk entered some notes in her computer, printed out bar codes, then tagged everything and gave Allison a receipt.

"Very efficient," Mark said as they retraced their steps to the lobby.

"You know, their elevators are on that biometric security thing. I think we need an escort to get up to Cyber Crimes."

"My contact said he'd meet me in the lobby," he said. "Finish telling me about the founder."

Allison was pleased he was interested. Some of her close friends worked here, and she had a deep respect for the lab's mission.

"Before this ex-con attacked the founder's daughter, he'd assaulted something like six women while he was out on parole," Allison said. "His DNA was in the system, and he should have been locked up again, but the rape kits were collecting dust in various evidence rooms. I remember the media uproar when it came out how he'd slipped through the cracks."

"Happens all too often."

"Well, the victim's mother agreed with you, which is why we have the lab."

They reached the lobby, where a twenty-something man in jeans and a T-shirt was talking on an iPhone. He took one look at Mark and stepped forward, stuffing the phone in his pocket.

"Special Agent Wolfe." He thrust out a hand. "I'm Ben Lawson, Assistant Director of Cyber Crimes."

Allison compared the two men as everyone traded introductions. Ben was tall like Mark, but the similarities ended there. With his shaggy goatee and faded *Pub Scouts of America* T-shirt, Ben looked more like an aimless college kid than an investigator. And yet he was one of the best cyber sleuths in the country.

Ben led them to the elevator and did the palm-press thing before jabbing the button for the sixth floor.

"You guys got the penthouse," Allison said as they got on.

"Us and DNA—we lucked out. Bones is stuck in the basement. Man, I hate it down there." He made a face. "Like the catacombs or something. Here we go."

The doors dinged open and they followed him down a glass corridor. On one side, a row of windows looked out at the Texas Hill Country. On the other side, glass walls revealed a room filled with computers, monitors, and all sorts of electronic equipment.

"How many people you have working here?" Mark asked.

"Twenty-three," Ben said proudly. "We're growing. There's been a surge recently in identity theft and crimes against children."

He held the door open for his visitors and led them to a cubicle where no fewer than five computer screens formed a semicircle atop the spacious desk.

"All of these are yours?" Allison asked, thinking of her putty-colored CPU back at the station house.

"We share workstations here in the lab. I've got my own in my office, but this has better software, so . . ." He dragged a chair over from a neighboring cube. "Here, sit down."

Mark rested an elbow on the wall of the cubicle and looked at Ben. "You read my e-mail, so you know what we're looking for."

"Death Raven." Ben rolled his eyes. "What a handle."

"He calls himself Death Raven?" Allison asked Mark.

"It's one of his aliases."

"I looked him up already," Ben said. "That name isn't

really original. It's all over the Net, so it'll take some time to sort out what's him and what isn't."

"I realize that."

"And aside from the one link you sent me"—Ben swiveled in his chair and opened an e-mail on one of his computer screens—"which was posted on October twenty-ninth, you don't have anything dating from the last decade."

"That's correct."

Ben grinned. "So I'm looking for digital footprints from eleven years ago. In Internet years that's, like, an eternity."

"I know."

Ben looked at Allison. "Good thing I like a challenge. Let me guess," he said to Mark. "You've got someone at Quantico working this, too, right?"

"You have an issue with that?"

"Not at all. Just want to know who my opponent is."

"Your opponent isn't the FBI," Mark said, and Allison heard the edge in his voice. "It's this UNSUB. He's murdered at least seven women in two states, and he's planning his next strike now."

Ben's grin vanished. "Seven?"

"Maybe more."

"Damn, I had no idea."

"We're reasonably certain he's finding his victims online," Mark said, "and using information about them to develop ploys to lure them in."

"Who's 'we'? You mean the Bureau?"

"As well as the local task force that's been set up to work the case."

Ben leaned back and gave Mark an appraising look.

"Okay, now I'm getting it. That means you're a profiler, aren't you? Part of that new FBI cyber team."

Allison shot Mark a look. "Cyber team?"

"I read about you guys," Ben said with admiration. "Online profiling."

Mark nodded. "I'm spearheading the project."

"We've been doing some of that here, too, trying to create software that can track down child predators on the Net. You guys have come up with some cool techniques."

"Uh, someone want to fill me in?" Allison felt a twinge of irritation. How come she was just now learning about this special project?

"It's a new focus within BAU," Mark said. "We're developing ways to profile criminals based on their online activities."

"Such as . . . snooping through their e-mails?" she ventured.

"Way beyond that. More and more, criminals are online in connection with their crimes. They post videos, blogs, leave comments on Web sites. They send threatening mail or pictures, tying to intimidate their victims beforehand, or they brag about their crimes afterward."

"It's an exciting area," Ben said. "Wish we were doing more of it."

Allison looked at Mark and saw the glint in his eyes.

"No offense to the geeks in the room," she said, "but what's so exciting about it?"

"The Internet is everything now," Ben said. "You can use it to buy a car, sell a child, start a revolution."

"And it's a whole new type of profiling," Mark added.

"People behave differently on the Internet than they do in real life. We get a unique glimpse into what makes them tick."

"It's the anonymity," Ben said. "Or perceived anonymity. People think they can do anything in cyberspace, no consequences."

"That's part of it," Mark said. "People hide behind their Internet persona. They let their guard down and reveal things about themselves they wouldn't reveal in face-to-face contact. For investigators, it's a potential jackpot of information. But you have to know where to look."

Mark pulled a folded piece of paper from the inside pocket of his suit. "These are the dates and URLs of the Internet activity we believe is his. Only one of these is recent. I need you to see if there's anything else from the intervening years."

"What are his other aliases?" Allison asked, peering over Ben's shoulder.

"Only one that we know of: E. Poe. It's a reference to Edgar Allan Poe, who wrote 'The Raven.'"

"The original dark poet," Ben said. "Did you see the verse he posted to that newspaper site after his second kill? 'My love, she sleeps . . . Soft may the worms about her creep.' This guy likes the macabre."

"Maybe," Mark said, "but I also think he's being practical here. Poe's been dead since 1849."

"Aha. Public domain." Ben leaned back in his chair. "That's very clever."

"Wait, back up," Allison said.

"His work is in the public domain." Ben looked at her. "That means it's everywhere. People post his stuff on poetry sites or anyplace they want. Imagine running an Internet search for someone who liked to post comments accompanied by Bible verses. You'd get a zillion hits and have to wade through all of them to find the ones you were looking for. He's hiding his messages in plain sight, which is like a big F-you to investigators." He looked at Mark. "Am I right?"

"That about sums it up." Mark glanced at his watch. "Now, what I need is a name and a location. Current. And anything else you can dig up. Phone number, birth date, Social Security number—"

"Hey, no problem. Why don't I just whip out my superpowers and beam him on over here for an interview?"

Mark looked deadly serious. "The Bureau's cyber-crimes unit has logged more than three hundred hours on this case to date. That's not counting all the time I've spent on it. This guy's good, but he's not perfect. And he's out there somewhere, which means he can be found. No one at Quantico's managed to do it yet, so I'm looking for someone with fresh ideas on how to outsmart him."

"Fresh ideas." Ben took a deep breath and nodded. "That case, I'm your man."

Allison kept a heavy foot on the gas pedal to make it back in time for Mark's conference call, but the icy roads were slowing her down.

"Think he'll come through?" Allison asked.

"He seems motivated."

"You were baiting him with all that Quantico stuff. He's competitive about the Bureau."

"Whatever works."

The pickup skidded through the next turn, and Mark sent her a look.

"Sorry."

"I can be a few minutes late," he told her. "I'm the one leading the call."

She looked at him in the seat beside her. He seemed tense. Ten minutes ago, he'd downed three aspirin without even a sip of water.

"You juggling a lot of cases?" she asked.

"Always."

"How many?"

"Couldn't tell you. I stopped counting a long time ago."

"Someone's been counting. I hear your workload is legendary."

He gazed out the window. "Record number of cases." He glanced at her. "That stat's misleading, though. Everyone else I started with has left for private practice or to write books."

The books, she'd heard about. She'd even read a couple when she was a brand-new detective, even though at the time she'd been busy working car thefts, not chasing down murderers.

"You think you'll ever do that?"

He glanced at her. "Which one?"

"The writing. I bet you've got some interesting stories."

"If we all sat around writing books, who'd be left to work the cases?"

"Good point. But it's not your job to work *all* the cases."

He didn't look at her, and she realized maybe he thought it was.

"What kind of private practice?" she asked, shifting the topic.

"Consulting, mostly. Private security stuff. Forensic psychology. And there's always my law degree."

"You ever consider leaving to do that?"

"Not really."

He looked out the window. From the way he clammed up, she figured this was another taboo subject, right along with his marriage. Didn't matter. Allison could probably guess the story. Many of the cops she knew were either divorced or headed there because of the hours, the stress, the drinking. She even knew a few guys on the job who swore they'd never get married simply because the divorce numbers were so high. But Allison didn't buy into that thinking. Numbers were just numbers. If she let statistics intimidate her, she wouldn't have a detective's shield right now.

"I hope you won't take this the wrong way, but I need to give you some advice."

Allison glanced at him, immediately defensive. But then she took a deep breath and steeled herself. She was on a task force with a world-renowned FBI profiler, and he could probably teach her a thing or two if she'd let him.

"I'm all ears," she said.

"You should team up with Macon on this."

She looked at him, surprised. "Jonah?"

"He seems sharp. He's got some tough cases under his belt. His work on the school shooting last year was solid."

"You checked out his background?"

"He'd be a good mentor for you as you get your feet wet."

Allison trained her attention on the road and tried not to feel slighted. Was this really about work, or was he trying to find a tactful way to put distance between them?

"Are you trying to tell me something, Wolfe? Because if you are, I'd rather you come out and say it."

He turned to look at her, and she felt anger welling up.

"I've been doing this a long time, Allison. Let me tell you how it works. I come into town. They're putting together a task force. Some people listen to what I have to say. Some people don't. Often, we make an arrest. Occasionally, we don't. But there's one thing that always happens. Without fail." He paused. "There's always a bump in the road, a setback. And when that happens, guess who the bad guy is?"

She rolled her eyes.

"Your chief, your lieutenant, your detective friends— every one of them will happily feed me to the sharks if the case goes sideways or if another victim turns up. And you know what? I don't blame them. Always easier to make a scapegoat out of the outsider. They're the ones who have to live in this town long after I'm gone."

"You think *you're* the outsider here?"

"I am."

"Try being one of only two female homicide detectives in the entire county, one of only four women in my whole department." She didn't usually talk about this because she didn't want to be seen as a whiner.

She glanced at Mark, and he was watching now with

one of those unreadable looks that drove her crazy. Maybe he *did* think she was a whiner.

"That's a fair point," he said, surprising her. "We're both outsiders. But it just reinforces what I'm saying. You should team up with Macon, not me, or you're going to get burned. Something goes wrong on this case—and it will—I'll be the one taking the fall."

She scowled. "Are you trying to make me feel sorry for you?"

"I'm giving you a warning. You've got a promising career ahead of you. Don't blow it right out of the gate by making enemies with the people you need to help you."

"I'm making enemies by working with you? That's ridiculous."

The truck lurched forward. Allison clenched the wheel and glanced at the dashboard as it abruptly slowed, then lurched, then slowed again and sputtered to a crawl.

She slapped the steering wheel. "Damn it!"

She eased onto the shoulder and coasted to a halt, then glanced at Mark. He didn't look surprised at all—just resigned.

"I'm not out of gas," she said. "That gauge is broken."

He unbuckled his belt and pushed open the door.

She cursed as she jumped out after him.

"Pop the hood," he said.

She ducked back inside and pulled the lever. Steam spewed out from the front, and she felt her cheeks flush with embarrassment.

The hood squeaked as Mark lifted it. He plunked his hands on his hips and gazed at the filthy engine. In a suit and tie, with his badge and his Glock on display, he looked like the quintessential federal agent—which was not what she particularly needed right now.

She needed a damn tow truck.

"This happen before?" He looked at her.

"Not in a while."

He went back to the passenger door, which was still standing open.

Allison ducked under the hood and waved the steam away. Her automotive knowledge was less than extensive, but she wasn't a complete idiot.

"I'm not out of gas," she reiterated. "The gauge is busted. I filled up last night."

He reappeared at her side, minus the jacket now. He'd shed the tie and rolled up his sleeves, and she watched with interest as he reached across the engine. He examined a black hose and a gray one. He crouched down and peered beneath the truck. Then he stood up and frowned.

"Oil," he said.

"No way. I get the oil changed every three thousand miles. I'm religious about it."

He looked at her and the corner of his mouth ticked up. "Religious, huh?"

He leaned in again and fiddled with some more hoses.

"This engine's a 350," he said. "You've probably got a fuel-pump seal failure. That's right beneath your crankcase. Drains the oil out of the engine. Pretty common on these old pickups." He straightened and looked at her. "Got any backup?"

She stared at him. In the space of two minutes, he'd gone from being a staid federal agent to a sexy car guy.

His eyebrows arched impatiently.

"I'll check."

She yanked her keys from the ignition, then unlocked the built-in toolbox behind the cab.

He leaned against the truck. "Where'd you get this thing, anyway?"

"My grandfather." She moved a wooden caddy filled with rusted hammers and screwdrivers. She shoved miscellaneous items aside: a pair of fishing waders, a tire iron, the work boots Mark had borrowed the other night, a flannel shirt stiff with dirt. Allison's grandfather was a pack rat, and she hadn't gotten around to cleaning anything out yet.

She glanced up, and Mark was watching her with interest. "What?"

"Not a bad deal. My granddad left me a barbecue pit."

"He's still alive." She tossed some more tools aside. "He's in a nursing home. Alzheimer's. Before it got bad, he asked me to look after his truck for him."

She culled through the remaining junk and found what she was looking for—a quart of motor oil. A second quart lay on its side, and some of the oil had leaked out.

"I'm guessing these have been in there a while." She handed the containers to Mark. "Watch your shirt. That gunk won't come out."

He shot her a look as he bent back under the hood.

"This'll probably get us back into town," he said. "But you need to get the fuel pump and seal replaced or you'll blow the engine."

She watched him work and felt a warm pull of attraction. His forearms were tan and muscular, his fingers deft.

"Where'd you learn about cars?" she asked.

He didn't respond, and she thought he'd tuned her out. She looked away from him as another pickup roared by.

"My dad was a mechanic," he said, pouring the oil. "Started working for him when I was eight."

Allison looked him up and down, trying to mesh this new information with what she'd assumed. She'd definitely pictured a more white-collar background.

"Georgetown University seems like a stretch for a mechanic's family. How'd you afford it?"

He smiled and shook his head. "That's tactful."

"Just an observation."

"I went to college on my jump shot."

"Basketball?"

He raised an eyebrow, and she felt stupid.

"So, if your dad's a mechanic . . . does that mean you're a car buff?"

"Nope."

"What do you drive at home?"

"A Ford."

She laughed. "Is it blue?"

"Black." He glanced up and gave her a wry smile. "I couldn't care less about cars. Just need to get where I'm going."

Allison shook her head and looked out at the horizon. The barren hills rose up around them and the grass was yellow from cold. A gust kicked up, whipping straight through the thin blazer she wore to conceal her holster. She wanted to get her jacket, but she didn't want to be a wimp when Mark was standing there in his shirtsleeves.

He screwed the cap back on the fill hole. "That should do it."

She handed him the old flannel shirt to wipe his fingers.

"Get back in and give it a try."

She climbed behind the wheel, and after a few failed attempts, got the engine going. He slammed down the hood. Then he tossed the shirt and the empty oil containers in back and slid inside the cab.

"Sorry about this," she said. "You're definitely going to miss your meeting."

He didn't comment.

"Thanks for the help. I owe you one."

"Get your truck to the shop." He glanced at her. "And next time, I drive."

CHAPTER 10

~~~

Mark stood outside Stephanie Snow's apartment building in the chilly dusk and watched as Jonah used a pocket-knife to cut through the official crime-scene seal on the door.

"This place gets released tomorrow morning," Jonah said, turning the knob with a gloved hand. He held the door open for Mark and reached inside to flip on a light switch.

Mark stepped over the threshold and tried to take a mental step into the victim's life. He scanned the room for a moment, wanting to get a feel for it. A few minutes in a person's home could be more revealing than hours of interviews with friends and loved ones.

"Her parents been by yet?" Mark asked.

"Only her aunt last week. She needed some clothes for the funeral home. Think the mom sent her over because she didn't want to come in here."

"I don't blame her."

The apartment was cold, dim. Everything was tidy but had an off feel—the result of countless law enforcement officers tromping around and poking through things, without putting a single item back precisely where they'd found it.

Mark glanced around, looking for the source of the Superglue smell. He noted the purple smudges on the doorknob.

"Styrofoam cup method?" he asked, referring to the technique sometimes used to develop prints with cyanoacrylate. The cup trapped the Superglue vapors so detectives didn't have to remove the doorknobs.

"Did all the knobs in the unit," Jonah said. "There were only seven."

"Anything interesting come back?"

"Stephanie's prints, the ex-boyfriend, and a few others. No hits with AFIS on the unknowns, though."

Mark stepped deeper into the living room. The one-bedroom unit was small but new. It had been new to Stephanie, too. She'd moved in this past summer right after graduation. According to her parents, she hadn't managed to find a paying job yet, so she'd taken an unpaid internship at an engineering firm in town to build her résumé. Jonah had said the parents were very involved in Stephanie's life, and Mark guessed they were subsidizing her living expenses, too.

He surveyed the furniture—a modern blue sofa beside a green, seventies-era lamp. A flat-panel TV and a slumping tweed armchair. It was a mishmash of old and new that Mark had seen in many first apartments, and it spoke of trips to IKEA and forays into parents' attics.

"We been over it all twice," Jonah said from across the room. "Ric found a stack of letters tucked into the box springs. Something we missed on the first pass."

"Letters?" Mark stepped into the kitchen. "Hardly anyone writes letters anymore."

"Addressed to Stephanie in Germany. She spent a semester there, spring of her junior year."

"Who sent them?"

"Some guy back here. Ex-boyfriend. We checked him out already. He's in law school up in Dallas."

Mark shot Jonah a questioning look.

"Alibi checks out," he said.

Mark donned a pair of latex gloves and opened the refrigerator. Diet sodas, salad dressing, a bag of slimy brown lettuce. The freezer was chock full of Lean Cuisines.

He opened a few cabinets and drawers and saw the expected assortment of basic kitchen supplies. The drawer closest to the breakfast nook contained a stack of bills bundled together with a rubber band. Mark thumbed through them: cable, electric, cellular phone service.

He glanced up at Jonah. "No landline?"

"Just the mobile. We ran the account already. Nothing unusual."

He flipped through the bills again. Only four months' worth—not even enough to warrant a filing system.

Mark sighed. Twenty-three years old. Young enough to be his own daughter, if he'd ever had one.

Just four years younger than Allison Doyle.

"No computer, either," Jonah said.

"That's unusual."

"She used the one at work, evidently. And used her phone for e-mail."

Mark headed into the bedroom and flipped on a light

switch. Most of the space was taken up by a queen-size bed with a floral bedspread and coordinating pillows. The bedding was rumpled. On the far wall stood an oak bureau with all the drawers slightly open. The mirror above it hung askew. The smooth surfaces in the room showed traces of fingerprint powder, and Mark looked at smudges regretfully. It was one of the many things that would be painful for Stephanie's parents to see when they mustered the strength to come in here and pack up their daughter's things.

Mark walked into the bathroom. A pair of black high heels lay on the floor beside the vanity cabinet. A wicker laundry hamper sat beside the door, and a black skirt and ivory blouse had been draped over the lid. Her work clothes, presumably.

Mark tried to visualize her last minutes in her apartment. She'd come home from her unpaid job, probably tired and restless. She'd changed into running gear. A plastic cup beside the sink contained an assortment of elastic bands, and he pictured her standing in front of the mirror and pulling her hair into a ponytail before heading out for a run. She'd stopped to collect her iPod, too, which had been found in the woods near the jogging trail.

Mark disliked iPods. He didn't understand why so many otherwise intelligent women made a habit of disabling one of their key warning systems every time they went out to exercise. How many homicides had he worked where the victim never even heard her attacker coming?

The iPod bugged him for another reason. Where had she downloaded her music?

Mark stepped back into the bedroom. Jonah stood in the doorway, patiently waiting for him to finish second-guessing his team's work.

"Her computer at her job," Mark said. "You know if she kept music on it?"

"No idea. Why?"

Mark's phone buzzed inside his pocket. He checked the number. Allison.

"Wolfe," he said briskly.

"Hey, it's me. I'm celebrating my rare night off by making something for dinner that doesn't come from a freezer. You like spaghetti?"

He didn't say anything. Clearly, she hadn't listened to a word he'd said earlier.

"Hello?"

"I'm thinking."

"It's spaghetti, Wolfe. Not a marriage proposal. I've got some ideas about the case."

He glanced at Jonah on the other side of the room. He was going through the nightstand drawers now.

Mark sighed. "What time?"

"How about eight? I'm just getting home from the store."

"That works."

He ended the call and shoved his phone in his pocket, almost sure he was making a mistake. But it would be a working dinner. She'd be wearing something besides pajamas.

He hoped.

Mark's gaze homed in on the stack of books and magazines on the nightstand. He crossed the room and moved the stack aside to reveal a slender black tablet.

"Bingo," he said, opening the case. He looked at Jonah. "An iPad."

"Shit, how'd we miss that?"

Mark tapped the screen. It was out of battery, but that could be remedied quickly enough.

"I'll take it in," Jonah said.

"I need some time with it. I want to see what she's been doing online."

"Let me run it by our CSI first," Jonah said. "This is the kind of thing she might carry around with her. Could be someone's prints on it besides hers."

Mark was still thinking about the overlooked iPad when he arrived at Allison's half an hour later. Missed evidence was a bad sign, and it didn't do much for his confidence in the local investigators.

Allison's parking lot was crowded, and one of her neighbors was having a party. She opened the door looking ticked off.

"You'll have to ignore the noise," she said. "My neighbor's a rabid Cowboys fan."

Mark stepped inside, and the aroma from the kitchen made his mouth water.

"You started already."

"Just the garlic and onions." She walked into the kitchen and he forced himself not to stare at her hips in those jeans. She wore a black T-shirt and had thick woolen socks on her feet. There was nothing at all sexy about the outfit—except that he'd developed a weakness for this girl, and it had nothing to do with clothes.

He was attracted to her, and it was starting to get in the way. It had gone from being a fleeting annoyance to an ongoing distraction. He found himself thinking about her when she wasn't around—and when she *was* around, which was worse. She'd be looking at him, talking about the case, and he'd be standing there thinking about her mouth or her hands or, hell, her *hair*, and wondering what it would look like fanned across his pillow instead of up in one of those no-nonsense ponytails she wore to work each day.

"Mark?" She turned and gave him a quizzical look.

"What?"

"I asked how it went at Stephanie's."

"Fine. How'd you know I was there?"

"Sean told me."

Of course. News traveled fast in small-town police departments—yet another reason he needed to be careful here. Some patrol officer had probably already noticed the rented blue Taurus parked in front of this apartment.

Allison pulled a beer from her fridge—same brand as last time—and twisted off the top for him.

"Thanks." He leaned back against the counter and watched her. She took a swig of her own half-finished beer and turned to the stove.

"So, what'd you think?" She stirred something in a big soup pot and looked up at him.

"The apartment may not generate any real leads. Our UNSUB was most likely a stranger to her. He learned about her online. It's unlikely he visited her home."

"But you wanted to see it anyway."

"I like to be thorough."

She lifted an eyebrow at that as she transferred some browned meat from a skillet to the pot.

"Want to help?" she asked.

"Sure."

She handed him a manual can opener and plunked a few cans beside him: stewed tomatoes, tomato paste, black olives.

Mark hadn't cooked in a long time, and he realized he missed it. He missed a lot of things—cooking, sleep, sex—but lately his life had become one long workday, punctuated by some long-distance runs to keep him sane.

He glanced at Allison in her sock feet. She seemed more relaxed than he'd ever seen her.

"You're making this from scratch?"

"I can't eat it from a jar," she said. "My maternal grandmother's Italian."

"Ah . . . that explains it."

"What?"

He opened up the cans. "Your coloring. And your attitude."

"Thank you, I think."

"It's definitely good. The attitude. You'll need it in this profession."

"Well, my grandmother had quite a lot of backbone, if that's what you mean." She added the contents of each can to the pot and stirred. "But if I really wanted to take after her, I'd be married with about five kids by now. And I wouldn't use tomatoes from a can. Blasphemy."

She glanced up at him. "You have any kids?"

Mark had been wondering when she'd get around to that. Women always asked. They had a strong interest in what sort of emotional baggage a man carried around, unlike most men Mark knew, who didn't give a damn. There were agents he'd worked with for ten years who'd never asked him a single personal question, even during his divorce, which had been public knowledge at the time. Trisha was a defense attorney in D.C., and their circles tended to overlap.

Marked sipped his beer. She was still waiting for an answer, and his silence had raised a red flag.

"No kids."

"You sure?" She smiled. "You had to think about it there."

"My line of work doesn't tend to produce good fathers."

"What's that supposed to mean?"

And here was the minefield of too-personal issues he'd wanted to avoid.

"I spend my days studying the very worst men are capable of." He waited for her to meet his gaze. "It's ugly stuff. I don't believe in happy endings anymore, Allison. I've seen too much shit."

She turned to face him, tipping her head to the side. "Kind of a sad way to live, don't you think?"

"No."

She reached an arm around him, and he stiffened. She pulled a half-finished bottle of red wine from the counter behind him and uncorked it.

"*I* think it is." She poured a bit of wine into the sauce and stirred. "Have you always been like this?"

"What, cynical?" He folded his arms over his chest. He didn't like to talk about himself so much, and he wasn't sure how he'd allowed it to happen, especially with her.

"I mean, did your job make you cynical about people, or did you grow up that way and, hence, go into law enforcement?"

"What do you mean?"

"I mean, the FBI Academy . . . not the kind of thing you just stumble into. Pretty elite group. And they don't get paid much, compared to some of the other things you could probably do with a Georgetown law degree."

She turned and looked at him with that frank expression he'd come to expect from her.

"I'm guessing most people are drawn to the Bureau because they have at least *some* level of faith in humanity," she said. "It's about helping people, right? Working for justice. If you're a *complete* pessimist, what would be the point?"

He watched her talk, uneasy with what he thought she was getting at.

"Maybe you're not as cynical as you think," she said.

"I could find a few people who'd tell you otherwise."

"You mean your ex-wife?" She gave him a knowing look. "I take what people's exes say with a grain of salt."

Mark reached for his beer. "Why do I feel like I'm being psychoanalyzed all of a sudden?"

"Me?" She widened her eyes with mock innocence. "Psychoanalyze *you*? Never. I only have a few measly psychology courses to my credit."

She took some herbs from her pantry and sprinkled them into the pot.

"My dad was from a family of cops, but he became a firefighter." She looked at him and smiled. "I know— almost the same thing, right?"

"Almost."

"He worked here in town, eventually became an arson investigator. Growing up, he used to tell me he was a fire detective."

"And he died . . . ?"

"When I was twelve."

Christ, no wonder she had a cop complex. He'd sensed it from the beginning. But she had a daddy complex, too, which was much worse. Some selfish middle-aged ass-hole was going to come along and take advantage of her someday. But it wasn't going to be him.

"I probably would have been one, too, if I thought I could handle the physical aspects."

"Women do it." He picked up the new topic and ran with it.

"Yeah, but not a lot of women who look like me." She waved a hand at herself. "I'm not exactly built for it. And those hoses are damn heavy. But I always knew I wanted to help people in some sort of law enforcement capac-ity. So I got my degree in criminology and landed at the police academy."

"The physical requirements there weren't challeng-ing?"

"Ha. They were hell. First day, I could barely do a chin-up. But I got my butt in gear, managed to improve. Size isn't everything." She turned to stand in front of him, hands on her hips. "Fact, I've learned to use it to my advantage."

"Like you did in that holdup?"

She looked stung, and he immediately wished he hadn't said it. The holdup would be a sore subject for her. The worst label any cop could get was to be called unsafe.

"I meant that I learned not to make threats I can't back up," she said. "I don't go shooting my mouth off, telling some two-hundred-pound drunk I'm going to kick his ass if he doesn't cooperate. I'm not afraid to call for backup when I need it. And I've learned it's a lot easier to talk somebody to jail than to drag him there."

"Good for you. Talking is preferable to force. Most of the time." Mark could recall a few moments when force was the only option, and he hadn't hesitated to use it.

Hesitation could get you killed. He hoped she knew that.

She took a swig of her beer and eyed him sullenly.

"Didn't mean to pick on you about the holdup," he said.

"No, you're right. It was poor judgment." She sighed. "Live and learn, right?"

She crouched in front of a cabinet and took out another big pot. She filled it with water and shook in some salt.

"Linguini okay?"

"Great."

"Good, 'cause that's what I've got." She took a package down from the cabinet and put a finger to her mouth. "Shh. Packaged noodles. Don't tell Gram."

Mark watched her move around her kitchen as the sauce simmered. Some of the tension he carried around seemed to drain out of him. She had music playing in the other room—something soft and bluesy. Her kitchen smelled amazing. Mark hadn't had much of a home life in years, and he felt a pang of regret over what he'd lost. He didn't miss Trisha, really. And he knew for a fact that she was better off without him—only two years since their divorce, and already she had a new husband and a baby on the way. What he missed was companionship. Sometimes he came home from a long day or a business trip and he walked into his empty, silent apartment, and he couldn't help wondering how things might have been different if he'd paid more attention to the people in his life and not just his work.

Allison picked up her beer and looked at him. "Uh-oh."

"What?"

"You're looking serious again."

He cleared his throat. "You said you had some ideas about the case."

She poured a few drops of olive oil in the water, then added the noodles.

"Right, so I've been going over the victim profiles you copied for the task force. All eight cases. Had them spread out on my rug in there—they covered the whole thing."

"Anything jump out?"

"Yeah, something did." She set the timer on her oven and then leaned back against the counter, crossing her feet at the ankles. "Although it's going to sound weird now that I'm actually saying it. I'm not a profiler."

"You profile people every day."

"Uh, no, that would be you."

"A profile is basically just a guess about who someone is and what they're likely to do," he said. "You do it all the time. Every time you maneuver through rush-hour traffic, you make a thousand tiny predictions about the people around you. Your brain picks up cues from all different sources and makes judgment calls about whether to tap the brakes or change lanes or speed up."

"That's not really profiling."

"Sure it is. And you're a cop, too, which gives you a

whole other layer of experience to draw on. When you worked patrol, you profiled people every time you made a traffic stop. You looked at all sorts of factors—their car, their driving ability, the time of day, the day of the week—to determine whether the person behind the wheel might present a danger to you."

"All cops do that."

"That's my point. They're good profilers, whether they realize it or not. Waitresses, too. And teachers. All those groups make better-than-average predictions about human behavior because they've honed their instincts for it. I wish more people would listen to their instincts."

She stared at him, and he realized he was getting carried away again.

He rubbed the back of his neck. "Sorry. This is a hot-button issue for me."

"Clearly." She put her hand on her hip. "You said something about this when we were out at the crime scene. So go ahead, enlighten me."

He paused. She was mocking him now, but still he wanted to talk about it.

"People—the most highly intelligent creatures on the planet—so often ignore their instincts. I don't know how many times I've sat down to interview a crime victim, and the first words out of her mouth are about how she got this weird feeling about the guy, but she told herself she was being paranoid. Do you think an animal in the wild gets a signal of danger and stops to wonder whether it's being paranoid? Hell, no. It acts on its most important instinct: to protect itself."

"I never thought of it that way." She looked at him for a long moment, and he saw respect in her eyes.

Shit, he needed to shut up now. He hadn't come here to lecture her. He wasn't sure why he'd come, but it hadn't been to get on some soapbox in her kitchen.

"Tell me what you noticed about the case files," he said. "I'm interested in your take."

"Well, it struck me that all the victims are so different."

"Okay."

"I mean, really different. In almost every way. We've got a mom. Several professionals. A few wage earners. Their jobs are all over the map. Their ages, too. Their physical appearance, religions, hobbies. But there is this one thing . . . I notice the career women were working for pretty unpopular companies."

Mark went back through the files mentally. "Okay."

"Dara Langford was the one who made me notice it. I found a news article, about a month before her death, in which she was quoted at a press conference. She was a PR flack for some timber company. And Jordan Wheatley was in the PR office at her firm, too. I think she mainly worked behind the scenes, but still."

"Jordan Wheatley worked for GreenWinds. She quit right after her attack."

"I know."

"Aren't they an alternative-energy company? How is that unpopular?"

"All right, *controversial* is probably a better word. At least in some political circles. And both women dealt with the media, the public. And then there's Jillian Webb. She volunteered at a women's shelter and was quoted in a newspaper article about one of their fund-raisers."

"Okay." He looked at her, holding the idea up against the other victim information he had filed in his head. "I like that line of thought, but I'm not sure how far it goes. Sheryl was a stay-at-home mom, Stephanie Snow was at an engineering firm. The first victim worked in retail."

"Yeah, but what about before that? Has anyone checked her previous job? And what did Sheryl Fanning do before she had kids? Anyone check that?"

He nodded. "We should."

"And the engineering company Stephanie worked for has been in the news lately over some dam they're building. I've got a message in to talk to her supervisor about what all she did there. Her father told me her job was pretty varied because she was an intern, but her college transcript listed a minor in communications. I wonder if maybe they had her writing press releases or something where she might have been interfacing with the public."

Mark watched her, impressed. It was a thin connection, but a connection nonetheless. And it had taken someone new on the case to see it, someone able to connect dots between a victim from the past and the present. Maybe she was onto something.

"You do that blank expression thing very well, by the way," she said. "It's impossible to read your reaction half the time."

"I think we should check into it."

A cell phone chimed, and Allison crossed the room to get it. She kept her back to him as she took the call.

"Okay, I'm on my way in." She hung up and turned off the stove. "We've got a problem at the park."

"I thought you were off tonight."

She reached for her keys. "I'm on for this."

CHAPTER 11

~~~~~

Allison strode into the bullpen and found Jonah leaning against the doorway of what had come to be called the war room. She heard Ric's and Sean's voices inside. She walked up and joined the group, ignoring the looks of interest when they saw that she was accompanied by Mark.

"Where is she?" Allison asked.

Jonah glanced from her to Mark and back to her again. "Interview Two," he said. "I talked to her already, but see what you get."

She was familiar with the assignment. She frequently got called in to talk to female witnesses. Women tended to be more forthcoming when interviewed by Allison than, say, a man the size of a refrigerator.

She left Mark to fend for himself and headed for Interview Two, which sounded very official but was simply a ten-by-ten room equipped with a table and chairs. That was it. No phone, no computer, no windows, no sharp objects.

The woman beside the table looked young and unhappy to be there. She wore a trendy black tracksuit with

Nike sneakers and had a pink fleece scarf around her neck. Allison immediately noticed her long blond pony-tail and that her green eyes were swollen from crying.

"Lauren Reichs?" She reached across the table and of-fered a handshake, forcing the woman to put down her cell phone. "Detective Allison Doyle. Nice to meet you."

"Nice to meet you, too. Do you know if I can go now?"

"Something the matter?"

"I've been here an hour. I've got a paper due tomor-row, and I'm *so* behind."

Allison slid into a chair. "You're a student?"

"Yes." She blew out a breath. "No offense, but I al-ready told them this already. I told them everything. I don't get what's going on. Why is this such a big deal?"

Allison glanced up as the camera in the corner of the room shifted. Someone—probably Jonah—had acti-vated the closed-circuit TV and was now watching the interview from another room.

"I understand." Allison smiled. "There are a few last details we'd like to clear up before you leave."

"Am I in trouble or something? Because my dad's a lawyer."

"You're not in trouble," Allison said. "We're just try-ing to understand what you saw tonight."

"This is about that girl, isn't it?" Her eyes filled with tears. "You think it was him, don't you? That guy who killed her?"

"Let's just go over what you saw, all right, Lauren? Could be it was nothing important."

"I knew I should have gone to Fairfield instead." She shook her head. "My roommate *told* me I was stupid to go to Stony Creek after what happened. But, I mean, I had my dog with me. Sadie's very protective. I figured I was fine."

"Where is Sadie now?"

"Downstairs. They wouldn't let me bring her up here." A tear spilled out and Lauren brushed it away. "She's probably terrified. She gets nervous around strangers."

"Excuse me one minute, okay?" Allison stood up and opened the door to the interview room. She spotted Mark across the bullpen, already headed for the stairs. He waved, and she knew he'd read her mind.

She returned to the table and smiled. "So, you're a senior here at the university?"

"I graduate in May."

"And what's your major?"

She took a deep breath and seemed to be bracing herself for a litany of questions. "Art history."

"Cool. I took some art in college. You know what you want to do when you graduate?"

She gave a watery chuckle. "No idea. But I know I'm *not* moving in with my parents. I'll wait tables if I have to."

"Do you have a job now?"

"Not since the summer. I'm trying to keep my grades up."

"And what did you do in the summer?"

"I worked at the bookstore. You know, on campus? It was part of my work-study."

The door opened and a yellow Labrador darted into the room, going straight for Lauren.

"Oh!" She gathered the dog against her legs. "Thank you!" She smiled gratefully at Mark as he handed over the leash.

"No problem. You two need anything?"

Lauren didn't even hear him—she was too busy fussing over her dog.

"We're good now, thanks." Allison shot him a look, and he slipped out.

"So, about this evening," Allison said. "You were coming *back* from your jog when you saw the van? Or just setting out?"

"Coming back. Sadie, *sit.*" Lauren pointed at the floor beside her chair, and Sadie put her rump down, tail thumping. Lauren looked at Allison. "I only did two miles today. Usually, I do four, but like I said, I have a paper due, so . . ."

"I understand. And where exactly was the van parked?"

"On the far end of the lot. It faced out, like he'd backed into the space. It was white. I pointed out a picture from one of those car books here, but I couldn't be sure. It was either a Dodge or a Ford." Another apologetic look. "I didn't get the license number or anything—they already asked me."

"It's okay." Allison smiled reassuringly. "And the driver. Did you get a good look at him?"

"It was dark. I don't usually go after dark, but I had Sadie, so I figured no big deal, right? Anyway, it was still light out when I started. Sunset. But when I finished, it was dark, so I didn't really see him."

"Didn't see him at all?"

"Just, you know, the side of his face. There was a light in the parking lot, but it wasn't all that bright."

"And you only saw one side? A profile?"

"I was across the lot, off to the right. He had a beard, though. I'm pretty sure I saw that."

Allison nodded. "And he stayed in the van the whole time?" She already had this detail from the phone conversation she'd had with Jonah on the way over, but she needed to confirm.

"That's right."

"Did he gesture at you or try to communicate in any way?"

"No. He just . . . I don't know." She paused. "This is going to sound weird, but . . . he just looked at me."

Allison leaned closer. "Looked at you?"

"Yeah. I told the officer. Mr. Macon."

"How did you feel when he looked at you?"

"That was the creepy part. That's why I called 911. He just *watched* me, you know?" She gave Allison an imploring look, as if hoping she'd understand.

"Did it feel sexual?"

"*Yes*. I mean, this is totally gross, but I got the feeling he was . . . you know . . . jerking off or something there in the van. *While* he watched me. Don't ask me why I think that, but I do." She shuddered. "Trust me, it was disgusting. I jumped in my car and hauled butt out of there."

By the time they rehashed everything and left the station house, it was nearly eleven. The pasta sitting in Allison's kitchen was well past its prime, and there wasn't even talk of trying to salvage dinner. She convinced Mark to grab a drink with her instead.

It took some strong-arming. He had a definite reluctance to being seen in public with her, and she wasn't sure what that was about. When they walked through the door to El Patio, she got a better idea.

"Yo, Doyle." Sean waved her over. "Come have a brew with us."

Several guys she knew had staked out a big table near the patio doors. She glanced at Mark. His carefully blank expression told her what he thought of hanging out with cops tonight.

"You go over." He sounded resigned. "You want a beer?"

"Bourbon and Coke."

He headed for the bar, and Allison joined Sean, Ric, and a detective she'd never liked much named Vincent.

"So, what's your take on the girl?" Sean wasted no time asking as Allison sat down.

"I think we shouldn't let her out of our sight."

"You really think she's a target?" Sean leaned back in his chair, looking skeptical.

"I don't know," Allison said. "But until I do, I plan to keep an eye on her. And she promised not to go jogging alone."

"I don't think she'll be jogging anywhere, alone or not," Sean said. "She seemed pretty freaked out."

Mark appeared with the drinks, and Allison glanced up, surprised. She looked over her shoulder and noted it was Connie at the bar tonight, which would explain the speedy service. She never missed a chance to flirt with a new man.

"Thanks," Allison said.

Mark walked around the table and took the chair across from her, leaving the one beside her empty.

"What's the profiler say?" Sean crossed his arms and gave Mark a challenging look. "You think it's our guy?"

Mark scanned the faces around the table. "I think a lot of men observe women at parks. Some of them drive vans."

"Knew it." Sean nodded at Ric. "Different pervert. World's full of them."

Allison looked at Mark. "Don't you think it's a *little* coincidental that he's hanging out at the same park where we just had a murder? Maybe he's returning to the crime scene."

"Except he's in a *white* van," Ric pointed out.

"It's been a year since Jordan Wheatley was attacked," Allison countered. "People change vehicles."

"Hey, no shit." Sean pointed his beer bottle at her. "And you want to know what I did today? Ran down green vans in the tri-county area. We're talking hundreds of records. Add in white ones, and you get into thousands. As leads go, this sucks."

"You want me to take over the vehicle search?" she asked, and the question seemed to ruffle his feathers.

"Hey, I didn't say I wouldn't do it. But I think it's going to a take a crapload of man-hours. And according to him"—he jutted his chin at Mark—"we've got another attack coming."

"Fine," she said. "I'll run the vehicles."

"I *said* it's no problem."

"No, let me. I believe in it. You don't. Take on something you can get behind."

"Yeah, like Lauren Reichs," Vince quipped. "I could definitely get behind some of that."

Allison rolled her eyes. Typical Vince. She glanced at Mark, who was once again wearing his poker face.

Allison looked at Sean and started to get an idea. He

was young, single, and had a protective streak a mile wide.

"You know what? That's not a bad idea, Vince," she said. "Sean, why don't you give Lauren a call, see if she needs company when she goes jogging?"

"Yeah, right," Sean said.

"I'm serious. It would allow us to keep tabs on her and put an extra set of eyes on that park at the same time."

Sean sneered. "Yeah, you guys work the case while I dick around with some sorority chick. You trying to get me arrested? Jesus. Her dad's a freaking lawyer. How many times did she mention that?"

"I didn't say you should *sleep* with her. Just, you know, keep an eye on her."

"Come on. Didn't you hear Wolfe?" Sean nodded at Mark. "It was probably just your garden-variety jerkoff. End of story. He's not our UNSUB."

"That isn't what I said," Mark corrected. "We should keep tabs on this woman, at least until we see where this lead goes."

"You think we should tail her?" Ric asked.

"Wouldn't hurt."

"Great." Sean shook his head. "As if I don't have enough to do." He swigged his beer, then set the bottle on the table and looked at Allison. "Fine, but you just bought yourself the vehicle search."

"No problem. I'll handle it." She'd add it to her list. So far, she had a hand in nearly everything, including the all-important DNA evidence. She glanced at Ric. "Hey, speaking of assignments, how's that DNA coming? A hit on that would be a godsend right now."

"I'll check with Mia." He stood up and tossed some bills on the table.

"What, you leaving?" Sean asked. "That was your first beer."

Ric smiled slyly. "Sorry, bro. Some of us have a woman to get home to."

Vince checked his watch and stood up. "I'm out, too. See you guys tomorrow."

They took off, leaving Allison, Sean, and Mark, all sitting in an awkward triangle.

Sean swigged the rest of his beer and plunked it on the table. "Guess that's it for me, then." He stood up and nodded at Mark, then Allison. "Later, you two."

They watched him leave. Then Mark's gaze settled on Allison. She couldn't read it. She glanced at the smaller table to their left and wished they were sitting there, but she had the feeling if she suggested moving, he'd make an excuse to call it a night.

"So, what do you think?" She put her elbow on the table and rested her chin on her fist. "You're the expert. You think it was him tonight?"

"Yes."

"Then what was with the 'world's full of perverts in vans' spiel?"

"The world *is* full of perverts in vans. I think the one from tonight also happens to be our UNSUB."

"In that case, I'm seriously concerned about Lauren Reichs. Maybe she's his next target."

He nodded. "It's possible."

"Aren't you worried?"

"I think you guys need to keep a close watch on her."

"You think she's in danger?"

He studied his beer and seemed to weigh his answer. "Even if she is his target, I don't think she's in any real danger until November nineteenth. That date's very important to him. He hasn't strayed from the pattern yet."

"That we know of. And anyway, that's a pretty big gamble to take with a woman's life." She narrowed her gaze at him. "And you know what I'm noticing? You're not nearly worried enough about this. What aren't you telling me?"

He didn't say anything.

"Oh my God. You've already got someone on her, don't you? Otherwise, you wouldn't even be here."

He took a sip of beer, set the bottle on the table. "I made a few calls."

"I knew it!" She slapped the table. "What'd you do? Conjure up a few MIBs from the San Antonio office?"

"I put someone on surveillance."

He said it so coolly that she was reminded how much clout he must have at the Bureau. Part of her was annoyed that he'd orchestrated something like that without going through Reynolds, but maybe it was for the better. Her lieutenant might have objected purely to prove he was in charge of the investigation. If Lauren really was in danger, her safety mattered more than some petty rivalry.

"So . . . what about Sean?" she asked.

"What about him? He'll probably do a half-assed job tailing her while we have an agent in place doing it right."

"Doesn't sound like you're too impressed with our Detective Byrne."

He just watched her, his face unreadable. What else was new? This man was an expert at keeping his feelings masked. And for some reason, she was beginning to relish the challenge of getting a reaction from him.

"Reynolds gets wind of what you're doing, he'll be ticked," she said. "He's very territorial. I'm surprised he even wants you here."

Mark leaned forward on his elbows and looked at her. "I bet he doesn't. But here I am."

She looked into his dark brown eyes and saw flecks of gold she'd never noticed before. The bar bustled around them. She heard the clink of bottles, the hum of conversation, the faint din of football highlights playing on the TV behind the bar. Suddenly she was acutely aware of the big empty table around them and the man in front of her. His dark gaze made her insides tighten. She glanced down at his fingers, curled around the beer bottle.

Allison's pulse pounded in her ears as she gave in to the urge. She eased forward. "Wolfe?"

He arched his brows. God, he had no idea what she was going to say.

"Come home with me."

It was a whisper, but he heard it because something sparked in his eyes. He held her gaze, and she felt a warm buzz of anticipation as she waited for him to say yes.

He wanted to. She could see it. His gaze dropped to her mouth and she felt a flutter of excitement.

He leaned back in his chair, breaking the spell.

"I can't."

She eased back. "*Can't.* You mean you can't because you've got some kind of problem or—"

"You know damn well what I mean." He gave her

a sharp look, and she felt a little shot of triumph. She'd touched a nerve.

"Come on." He slid back his chair and stood up. "I'll run you home."

She looked up at him and almost laughed because it sounded like something you'd say to a babysitter. But then the urge to laugh vanished as he stared down at her, utterly serious.

A sour ball formed in her stomach. *This* was what rejection felt like. She hadn't been here in a while, but it was just how she remembered it. She stood up and took her time slipping into her leather jacket. He guided her out of the bar and reached around to open the door for her.

The cold whipped against her cheeks as they walked to his rental car. She opened the door for herself before he could reach for it.

They rode across town in silence, and she pretended to be interested in the view outside.

This was fine. Better, really. She didn't have time to get involved with him. She hardly had time to sleep these days, much less plunge into a sexual relationship that was sure to be consuming.

She darted a glance at him in the driver's seat. *Consuming*. That was exactly how he'd be. If she ever got him to let his guard down, he'd consume her by fire.

He pulled into her lot and expertly slid into a narrow space right in front of her apartment. He reached for his door handle, and she grabbed his knee.

"Don't walk me up."

He looked at her across the car, and she saw guilt in

his eyes, which was a million times worse than an attraction he wouldn't act on.

"Allison—"

She held a hand up, but he ignored it.

"—I'm sixteen years older than you are."

"I get it."

He laughed. "No, you *don't* get it or you wouldn't have brought this up."

Maybe it was the laugh that did it, but she was suddenly angry. She turned in her seat to face him.

"Okay. Why don't you explain what I don't *get,* since I'm not in possession of your infinite knowledge?"

He looked her directly in the eye—and she liked him even more because he didn't shy away from her temper.

"I have a federal badge. I wield influence in all kinds of law enforcement circles, including your task force. You're a rookie detective."

"So?"

"So, a sexual relationship between us would be totally inappropriate."

"Inappropriate."

"Yes."

"That's why you don't want to sleep with me."

He hesitated. It was only an instant, but it was enough.

"No."

She tipped her head to the side. "What is it, then?"

"You're not my type."

She gazed at him across the car, and she knew—with certainty—that he was lying his ass off.

She should just let it go. She should climb out of the car and let him leave things the way he wanted. Instead, she eased closer and rested her hand on his thigh. Every muscle in his body tensed as she leaned close enough to smell the last traces of aftershave lingering on his collar.

"You know something?" She looked up at him, but he didn't answer. "I can tell when you're lying."

She combed her fingers into his thick hair and felt his hand clamp hard around her wrist as she pressed a kiss just beneath his ear where his pulse thrummed. She waited for him to push her away, but instead he held her there with his iron grip. She could hear his heart pounding—or maybe it was hers. His skin tasted salty, male, and she found his mouth and slid her tongue over the firm line of his lips. She felt his resistance, felt his hand clamped painfully around her wrist. And then suddenly he shifted, and it was *his* mouth seeking hers, *his* tongue tangling with hers, tasting her. Excitement flooded her and with a low moan, she sank into the kiss.

And he pulled back. His eyes blazed down at her—a mix of desire and conflict and . . . guilt.

Slowly he brought her hand down to her lap, and she knew that although she'd proven something, she still hadn't changed his mind.

"I can't do this," he said. "I don't mean to hurt your feelings, Allison."

Her chest squeezed. Talk about a sour end to an evening. And she still had to work with him now, which was going to suck, because what she really wanted to do was smack some sense into him.

She shook her head and pushed the door open, letting a chilly gust of air into the car.

"Good night, Wolfe." She glanced at him over her shoulder as she got out. "Hope you sleep well."

CHAPTER 12

Allison stretched her arms over her head and eyed the brightening sky. Roland was late, but she was lucky he'd agreed to come at all. She jogged in place to get warm as she watched a pair of headlights turn into the lot. His familiar SUV slid up alongside the unmarked patrol unit she'd borrowed from work.

"Nice ride," he said, joining her at the trailhead. Dressed in shorts and a long-sleeved T-shirt, he looked almost naked compared to her. In deference to the morning's frosty weather, Allison had on two thick layers and a fleece headband that covered her ears.

She rubbed her hands together. "You're not planning to whine at me, are you?"

He gave her a "get real" look. "I never whine. How many miles?"

"Six."

He shook his head. "Always a slave driver. That's what I miss about you." He started down the trail.

"Don't you even want to stretch first?"

"Stretching's for wusses."

She caught up to him and they fell into a brisk pace.

If things had gone differently, she'd be waking up in Mark's motel room right now. Instead, she was running her butt off and he was on a plane back to Quantico.

I need to go handle something.

He'd left the message on her voice mail at precisely 5:45, as she'd been groggily groping for her phone.

Was he running away?

No. She hadn't known him long, but he wasn't the type to run away. If he was getting on a plane this morning, it was because someone needed him somewhere. He'd already proven, on more than one occasion, how important this case was to him.

And yet he hadn't said when he'd come back. Or if.

Not that it mattered. Allison was determined to work the hell out of this case, with or without him. Her department would make an arrest, with or without him. Without him was probably better, anyway, because Allison's emotions wouldn't get tangled up.

"So let's hear it," Roland said as they passed the half-mile marker.

"What?"

"You need a favor."

"What makes you say that?"

He sent her a sidelong glance. "One a.m. would have been a booty call. Six a.m. is work. What do you need?"

This was what she missed about Roland. No bullshit. And also, having a jogging partner—that had been cool. Really, Roland had some excellent boyfriend qualities. On the downside, his aversion to monogamy was a deal breaker.

"A? Come on, out with it."

She pulled her thoughts together as she took the next

curve. Like many other scientists at the Delphi Center, Roland was constantly getting hit up for favors. Sometimes he said yes, sometimes he didn't. But the best approach with him was simply to ask.

"I need some evidence examined."

He didn't respond.

"I doubt my lieutenant will approve a formal request, and he definitely won't approve a rush fee even though I need it quickly."

"What's 'quickly'?"

"Oh, you know. Yesterday would be good." She was trying to make light of the favor, but he didn't seem to be in the mood. Maybe in the back of his mind he'd been hoping this *was* a booty call.

"Sounds important."

"It is." She glanced at him. "You've read about Stephanie Snow?"

"Who hasn't? She died right in this park."

"They've put together a task force to investigate, and I'm on it."

He pounded alongside her, looking pensive. "Thought the boyfriend did it."

"He's a suspect, but we're looking at some other angles, too."

"Such as?"

"Such as maybe it's connected to a sexual assault case from last October. Mia's running the rape kit for us."

He grunted, and she could tell he wanted to hear more. Roland liked to have as much info as he could get when he took on a case. He said it helped him know where to look.

"We think the UNSUB uses a van," Allison said,

sounding a little winded. She hadn't run in a while. "The rape victim was in it during her attack, said she thought she smelled some sort of chemical, maybe paint. Two of our detectives spent a full day working that lead, and they got nowhere."

"A day's not much time."

"In this case it is. We have reason to believe this killer is going to strike again. Soon. We really need to know what substance he has in his van, see if it points us anywhere."

They veered around a couple walking a golden retriever. Allison waited for Roland's response.

"What's your fed think?"

"Who?"

He gave her a slight smile. "The hotshot FBI guy you've got heading up your task force."

Allison didn't think Reynolds would care much for that comment, but she let it go.

"He thinks the paint is a good lead."

"But they can't analyze it at Quantico?"

"Why can't you guys do it?" she asked, getting frustrated now. "The evidence is with Mia already. How much trouble would it be to walk down there and—"

"Relax, I'll do it."

"You will?"

He nudged her elbow. "Just giving you a hard time about the fed. I hear you're hot for him."

"Where'd you hear that?"

"Word gets around." He grinned at her. "Although I have to say I'm surprised. Wouldn't have pegged you for an older-guy kinda girl."

She ignored his baiting.

"I seem to recall you've got a *lot* of energy. He can't keep up with you, just give me a call—"

She threw an elbow, but he dodged it, grinning.

"Hey, no need to get feisty. Just thought I'd offer."

As he did in place after place, year after year, Mark entered the home of a victim and tried to imagine what killed her. Hannah Eckert had been found at a rest stop this morning off Interstate 95 near Richmond. As with Rita Romero just a few days before, the cause of death was a single gunshot wound to the forehead.

But Mark believed Hannah Eckert's true cause of death lay on the coffee table in her filthy apartment. He picked his way through a sea of trash and looked at the homemade crack pipe.

"She have drugs on board at the time of the shooting?" Mark asked the young FBI agent standing behind him.

"No tox screen yet."

Mark's gaze scanned the room. The three-hundred-square-foot efficiency was one of twenty units in a ramshackle building that faced a busy stretch of Interstate 70, right outside Baltimore. The paper-thin walls did little to keep out the traffic noise, and Mark wondered how anyone managed to sleep here.

"How long have they been living here?"

"Three months," the young agent informed him. Donovan was his name. He'd been on the job for about five minutes. "The building rents by the week. Manager said they're two weeks behind and he was getting ready to evict them."

Mark surveyed the kitchen area, which was littered with trash. A sour-milk smell permeated the room and he attributed it to the sink filled with dirty dishes. He stepped over and pulled open the door of the rust-spotted refrigerator. The shelves were empty except for a carton of milk. Mark checked the date. Three weeks expired. He pulled open a drawer and found a half-finished package of hot dogs.

Mark studied the living room again. The sofa had a blanket and pillow bunched at the end and looked as though it doubled as a bed. In the far corner of the room, two plastic patio chairs—the kind sold at Walmart for a few bucks each—sat side by side with a Dora the Explorer blanket draped over the top. This would be Kaylie's space, and Mark stepped over to take a closer look. He crouched down and peered into the child's fort. Inside was a sofa cushion with a striped beach towel spread out on top of it. Tucked into the makeshift bed was a stuffed blue dolphin. Beside the cushion, a row of small plastic ponies was lined up neatly against the wall.

Mark stood up. His gaze landed on a pair of pink sequined flip-flops parked beside the fort. A knot of anger formed in his chest as he thought about a six-year-old's efforts to create order amid the chaos swirling around her. Kaylie Eckert had had the odds stacked against her from the very beginning, and those odds only worsened with every hour she remained missing. Same for Rita Romero's daughter.

"Hannah Eckert's cell phone. Who's checking the records?" Mark turned to Donovan, who was watching his every move, as if he might pick up some kind of superpowers just by being in the same room.

"Sir?"

"Her phone. It wasn't in the car, correct?"

"No, sir. We're not even sure she had a phone. And there's no landline—"

"She had one," Mark said. "Rita Romero had one, too. Both phones were stolen from the victims at the time of the shootings."

"Yes, sir."

"We need records, ASAP, from whatever companies provided the cell-phone service."

"Maybe they were using throwaway phones."

Mark glanced at the door, where a homicide detective stood waiting impatiently. Mark could tell by his tone that he wasn't thrilled about the FBI's involvement in this investigation, but the Bureau had been brought in almost immediately because of the missing children.

"They weren't," Mark said. "Neither woman has a computer, which means the phones were equipped with e-mail, Internet access, probably cameras, too. You get those phone records, you're going to find one number that called both women the day of the murders."

"To set up the meetings," Donovan said. "At the rest stops, you mean."

"That's right," Mark said. "You find the person who owns that phone number, and you find the two missing girls."

If they're still alive. Mark didn't say it because it was understood.

The agent hurried from the room as the phone buzzed inside Mark's pocket. The detective in the doorway was still eyeing him skeptically, and Mark turned his back on him.

"Wolfe."

"It's Allison Doyle."

She sounded perfectly polite, which grated on his nerves. He hadn't spoken with her in five days.

"What's going on?" he asked.

"I just got a message from Mia Voss, the DNA specialist at the Delphi Center."

"And?"

"She finished the profiles and ran them through the database."

"She got a hit?"

"She got something. But she said it's complicated and she'll explain tomorrow. Said she needed to confirm a few things first. I'm meeting her at the lab at eight a.m."

Mark checked his watch. That was fourteen hours away. He bit back a curse.

"I'm in the middle of a situation," he said. "I probably can't make it."

"I'm aware of that, but you said you wanted to be kept informed."

"Thank you."

A tense silence stretched out between them as Mark stood in the center of the squalid apartment and thought of all the reasons he couldn't go to Texas right now.

But he wanted to. Badly. Which was exactly why he should stay the hell away.

"Let me know what you hear, would you?"

"Of course," Allison said, and hung up.

As she walked down the glass corridor to the DNA lab, Allison noticed the ominous gray thunderhead rolling in over the hills.

"Don't envy Kelsey today," Mia said. "She was supposed to have a dig this morning."

"Grad students?"

"CSI training. You know she's running two sessions a month now? That's a lot of revenue into the lab. They're going to have to build a statue in her honor."

They passed the DNA section, and Allison could see half a dozen lab-coated men standing at worktables and peering into microscopes.

Mia glanced at Allison again. "Hey, you notice anything weird with her lately?"

"Kelsey? No, why?"

"She's been acting . . . I don't know. Off."

Mia ushered her into her office, which was really a glorified workroom equipped with gadgets and microscopes that probably cost more than Allison made in a year.

"'Off' as in distracted?" Allison asked.

"That." Mia dropped her purse in a chair and slipped into her lab coat. "And maybe depressed."

Allison frowned, thinking about it. She hadn't noticed anything weird with Kelsey, but really, how much attention had she been giving her friends lately? She'd spent the past few weeks battling an impossible workload, a boneheaded boss, and now an inconvenient attack of lust.

She'd hardly given Kelsey a thought.

"Maybe there's trouble in paradise," Allison suggested. "Didn't she fly out to see Gage a few weeks ago?"

"Last month. And yeah, I know. Where has the time gone? It's been so busy lately." Mia crossed over to her slate-topped work counter and booted up the notebook computer sitting there. Allison pulled up a stool beside her.

"I just wanted to see if you knew anything," Mia said. "I'm starting to get worried."

"Sorry. I've been buried at work."

"Yeah, me, too. The good news is, I've made some serious progress." The phone on the wall rang, and Mia reached for it. "DNA." Her gaze went to Allison. "Okay, good. Send him up."

Allison's nerves fluttered.

"That was the front desk. Mark Wolfe is on his way up. I thought you said he was at Quantico?"

"He was. He had some other cases come up, so I figured he was done here."

Mia watched her, and Allison felt her words being analyzed.

"What?"

"Kelsey's not the only one acting weird," Mia said. "What's up with you two?"

"Nothing."

Mia's eyebrows arched.

"What? You think I'd be dumb enough to start something up with some fed who lives on the East Coast?" She tried to make it sound absurd, but it really wasn't. That was exactly what she'd been trying to do.

Mia just looked at her. Her gaze moved over Allison's shoulder, and for a second she thought Mark was standing there. She turned but saw nothing.

"Anyway, go ahead. He can catch up." Allison nodded at the laptop. "You have the results on your computer?"

Mia returned her attention to the screen. "These are my notes. I have a form I use while I work. Keeps me organized." She tapped a few keys. "I had a pretty amazing stroke of luck with this sample. Actually, I shouldn't say *luck*. Not when you consider the high rate of recidivism when it comes to violent offenders—"

"Dr. Voss?"

Allison turned around, and now he *was* standing there, filling up the doorway. He wore a gray trench coat over his suit today, and the shoulders were damp from rain. His hair was damp, too, and mussed slightly, as if he'd combed his hands through it when he'd come in from outside. He looked ridiculously attractive, and Allison felt the sting of his rejection all over again.

He cut a brief glance in her direction as he stepped into the room.

"Mark Wolfe." He shook hands with Mia while Allison looked on. He didn't spout his title, she noticed. And he had that confident, commanding air about him that made him seem in charge in any setting—whether he'd been there before or not.

"Please, pull up a stool," Mia said, returning to her computer.

Mark followed her across the room, but instead of taking a seat, he stood beside the worktable.

"What'd I miss?" He shrugged out of his coat.

"Nothing yet. Mia was just opening the file."

Allison didn't look at him. He smelled like rain and aftershave, and she realized he must have gotten in late last night and stayed at the motel. And he hadn't called her, of course, because maybe he didn't want her showing up at his door like a little welcome wagon.

She felt his gaze on her and glanced up. "What?"

"Doing some jogging?"

She glanced down at her running clothes and sneakers. "So?"

"In Stony Creek Park?"

From his disapproving look she could see he already knew the answer to that question, so she ignored him and turned to Mia.

"So, you were saying? About the DNA?"

Mia was pretending to be immersed in her computer file. "Okay, so I ran the samples from both rape kits—Stephanie Snow and Jordan Wheatley. The vaginal swabs revealed traces of lubricant, but no semen. It appears the attacker wore a condom in both cases."

"That's what we expected," Mark said. "What about nail clippings?"

"That was my next step. Jordan Wheatley's clippings yielded skin cells belonging to someone besides her—presumably her assailant."

Allison listened anxiously. They were so close to a break, she could practically taste it, and yet she could tell there was some sort of catch.

"With Stephanie, nothing under the fingernails. I did, however, get touch DNA from the waistband of her pants. Using the tape-lift method, I recovered material from the elastic. Analysis revealed skin cells from someone besides her, most likely left by her attacker as he pulled off her clothes." Mia paused. "Same genetic profile as what I got from Jordan's nail clippings."

Allison held her breath. She felt Mark tense beside her.

"We ran it through CODIS," Mia said, referring to the nationwide DNA database maintained by the FBI, "and it came back negative. No perfect match. I did, however, manage to find a partial."

"Familial DNA," Mark said.

"That's right. Whoever contributed the sample isn't in the system, but has a relative who is."

"A relative?" Allison was surprised. "You can tell that?"

"It's a very close profile," Mia said. "I would expect it to be a brother, or possibly a son, of the offender we have on file."

"Who's the offender?" Mark asked.

"David Moss."

"Moss?"

"Like the plant."

Mark shook his head. "Never heard the name. Don't think we ever interviewed a 'Moss' in connection with any of the crimes. I'll double-check. Where'd you get this?"

"You mean his DNA profile?"

"Yes. I didn't think the FBI condoned sharing partial matches across state lines."

"The rules are in flux," Mia said. "Anyway, this one's in California. They're paving the way out there with this investigative technique, so I figured they'd be open to my inquiry about a partial match, which they were." She looked at Allison. "The state of California has the third-largest DNA database in the world, and since your case has a California connection, I thought I'd at least try. I'm glad I did, too, because we got this lead. But fair warning: It could result in some controversy for you guys."

"We'll be careful," Mark said.

"Wait, why the controversy?" Allison turned to look at him. "Why shouldn't states share DNA profiles? Think of all the crimes we could probably solve."

"Full matches are one thing," Mia said. "Partial matches are a whole different ball game."

"The Bureau's worried about backlash," Mark said. "Specifically, civil rights groups and privacy activists."

Allison scoffed. "In my book, you pretty much forfeit your right to privacy when you commit a felony."

"Yeah, but what about your cousin?" Mia asked. "Does he get to forfeit your privacy for you?"

Allison looked at her, shocked. "Listen to you. I thought you were all about using DNA to solve cold cases."

"I am. I'm just playing devil's advocate," Mia said. "A lot of people don't agree with DNA technology being used for this. Sins of the father being visited on the son and all that. Plus, there's the Big Brother aspect. Some people don't like the idea that some relative commits a crime, and now the whole family is under some sort of perpetual genetic surveillance."

Mark nodded at the computer screen. "Tell me about California."

"Well, they've solved some high-profile cases this way." Mia looked at Allison. "You may have heard of the Grim Sleeper case in L.A.? Investigators found a partial match with a felon already in the system and linked his DNA to a string of killings. Police zeroed in on a new suspect—the incarcerated man's father—and confirmed the DNA through a slice of discarded pizza. They ended up charging the father with ten counts of murder."

"Wow," Allison said.

"There's a new saying in law enforcement circles," Mark said. "'If your brother's doing time, don't commit the crime.'"

"What about *our* case?" Allison asked, getting impatient.

"Like I said, it's only a partial, but it's still very useful. Are you familiar with how we do DNA profiles?"

"More or less."

"When we compare DNA, we don't actually analyze the entire chromosome. That would take ages. Instead, we look at thirteen designated genetic markers where the DNA is highly variable among people, and we compare those." Mia paused to make sure they were following. "In this case, the samples matched at eleven of the thirteen." She turned and nodded at the report pulled up on her screen. "I was here late last night double-checking my work with a peer's findings, just to be sure. I feel confident saying the UNSUB you're looking for is closely related to David Moss, who was once in the California prison system."

"Was," Mark said. "But he's not anymore."

"That's right." She consulted a notepad on the counter. "I contacted the law enforcement agency listed with the record, and they had him in for aggravated sexual assault. He served six years in San Quentin, was released four years ago." She took a deep breath. "And you're not going to believe where he is now."

Allison's heart lurched, and she knew what Mia was going to say.

"Texas," Mark said for her.

"That's right. And not only that, I have an address." She ripped a sheet off her notepad and handed it to Mark. "He's in prison in Huntsville doing life for murder."

"David Moss, twenty-nine. Sentenced to life, no parole, for the murder of Patricia Stewart, a twenty-year-old waitress in Arlington, Texas." Mark wrote the victim's name on the dry-erase board beside the mug shot of the man who shared almost the same genetic fingerprint as their elusive UNSUB. "Okay, what else do we know?"

He scanned the faces in the room, which included everyone they'd been able to drag in thus far: Allison, Sean, and Jonah. Ric was tied up with a domestic complaint and Reynolds was missing in action. Mark figured he was hiding in his office, where he wouldn't have to be overshadowed.

"Born in Redding, California," Allison said, reading from the file that had been faxed over by Arlington PD. Mark had skimmed the fax when it came in, but hadn't had time to study it. For the last half hour he'd been on the phone with an agent in the San Antonio field office who was running down every available detail on David Moss.

Allison glanced up. "So our UNSUB's from Shasta County, like we thought."

"Why'd we think that again?" Sean asked.

"The first murder occurred there," she told him. "Serial killers often strike first in the place they're most comfortable." She looked at Mark. "Isn't that how you came up with that piece of the profile?"

"Also, the location of the attacks and the recovery sites shows a strong familiarity with the area." Mark wrote the name "David" on the board and circled it. "Let's get back to his family. Particularly the males."

Allison looked down at some papers. "Okay, parents: Paul Michael Moss and Sheryl Randolf Moss. Both parents deceased, like you said."

"When did the dad die?" Sean asked.

"I looked up Paul . . ." Her voice trailed off. "It was 1984, so he's not our man."

Mark had already drawn an "X" over Paul's name and was waiting for Allison to continue.

"Okay, one brother. Damien Michael Moss."

"Shit, his name's really Damien?" Sean asked.

"Really is. Born December 6, 1976, also in Redding, California."

Mark turned his back on her and continued jotting facts on the white board. Damien Moss fell right within the profile age range.

"No sisters listed here," Allison said. "So, looks like a family of four, with the father dying when the kids were young."

"Let's hear about Damien," Mark said, although he already knew she'd hit a snag. The San Antonio agent who was helping him had been running into walls, too.

Allison slid the papers aside and flipped open a notepad. "Here's what I got, just in the last two hours. Damien was issued a California driver's license at the age of sixteen. It was never renewed. California DMV has zilch on this guy besides his original driver's license. Texas doesn't even have that much. I've got nothing here at all for a Damien Michael Moss. Or Damien Moss. We've got three Michael Mosses, but they're totally the wrong age."

"What about tax records?" Sean asked.

"Nothing in Texas. He must not own property here."

"How about California?" Sean persisted. "They pay state income tax out there, right?"

"You better believe it," Jonah said.

"No tax records in either state on this guy," Allison said. "No criminal record. No voter registration. I've got nothing. It's like he doesn't exist. I thought you said he went to college?"

Mark turned around. She was looking at him, and he saw the frustration on her face. Everyone was feeling it. They had a potential ID now, but it was getting them nowhere. No record of a Damien Michael Moss living anywhere in Texas or California. They'd found several in other states, but the ages didn't fit at all. Even so, Mark had his contact running down the IDs. The Bureau had access to much better databases than a small-town cop shop.

"I still believe he went to college, but I think he dropped out," Mark said.

"Then how come there's not a record of him in the California university system?" Allison asked.

"Maybe he went private," Sean suggested. "Wolfe said he's some kind of whiz kid, maybe he was at Stanford."

"We're checking on it," Mark said.

"Who's 'we'?" Jonah wanted to know.

"I've got a couple agents out of San Antonio giving us a hand."

No one objected, which was good. They were getting down to the wire here. November 19 was only three days away, and this UNSUB's name was useless if they couldn't get a location before he made his next kill.

"This is unbelievable," Allison said. "I called phone companies, electric, gas, water, you name it. I called freaking ISP providers. *Nobody* has a record of Damien Moss."

"Why don't you let Wolfe call?" Sean said. "Probably

have better luck dropping the word 'FBI' into the conversation."

"I already dropped it."

Mark shot her a look. "You impersonated a federal agent? You know that's a felony?"

"Ask me if I give a damn."

"Nice going, A." Sean winked at her. "Way to take the bull by the horns."

"Anyway, I didn't say I was FBI, I said I was calling on *behalf* of the FBI. That's different."

Jonah laughed. "No, it's not."

"Telemarketers do it all the time," she said. "Anyway, what the hell are we arguing about? We need a location on this guy. Soon." She looked at Mark. "What did your people get?"

"They're working on it, same as you. They're also looking for any other close male relatives."

Mark's phone vibrated in his pocket. He pulled it out and read the text message coming in from the agent in San Antonio.

"His age doesn't work for a son," Allison said. "Even if David Moss got someone pregnant by the age of thirteen—which is highly unlikely—that kid would only be sixteen now, and these murders have been happening for more than a decade."

"I talked to Mia," Jonah said. "She thinks the brother's our best bet. Something about the DNA. She said it's likely these two share the same mother, although there's a small chance it could be a cousin on the mother's side."

"Great," Sean said. "Now we're not even looking for guys named 'Moss.' We're looking for 'Randolfs' and who the hell knows what else."

"I think we should follow Mia's advice and focus our attention on Damien," Allison said. "Somebody somewhere has a record of the guy."

"Just not in Texas or California," Jonah said.

"I received a text from someone who was checking on prison visitation records for me," Mark said. "David Moss had no visitors in lockup either in California or Texas, with the exception of his defense attorneys."

"Shit," Sean said, tossing his pencil on the table. "The leads just keep pouring in."

The door opened and Ben Lawson poked his head inside. "Got here soon as I could." He stepped into the room and grabbed a chair next to Allison.

Jonah shot her a look that said, *Who the hell is this guy?*

"Ben, meet some other members of our task force, Jonah Macon and Sean Byrne."

Ben nodded distractedly as he pulled a notebook computer from his backpack and powered up.

"Ben's with the Delphi Center," Allison added. "He's been running down some Internet leads for us." She turned to Ben. "I hope you've got something, because we're coming up with zip on Damien Moss. It's like he's totally off the grid."

"That's because he is." Ben's computer chirped to life and he tapped at it for a few seconds as everyone watched impatiently. He glanced up.

"He is—just as you said—totally off the grid. That applies to California, Texas, nationwide. The last actual record I have of him is from twelve years ago"—*tap, tap, tap*—"when he received a citation for illegal lodging in Golden Gate Park. He wasn't carrying any ID at the time, but they ran his prints through the system and came back with a name." Ben leaned back in his chair and looked around the room. "Since then, nothing."

"So, you're saying he's what, a vagrant?" Allison looked at Mark. "What about a vehicle? A job? A residence?"

"It is possible he has all those things, and yet he doesn't register them with any state," Mark said. "I said before, he's got a deep-rooted dislike for institutions."

Sean snorted. "Yeah, and I've got a deep-rooted dislike for the IRS. Doesn't stop them from collecting my taxes. Who does this guy think he is?"

"That's exactly the point," Mark said. "He thinks he's better than all of us. He doesn't need to register his car, or pay taxes, or have a license to drive. He can, and does, do whatever he wants. The complication is, he has to be careful so that he's not caught and forced to interact with the system." Mark looked at Ben. "I want to hear what you found. I'm guessing he only interacts with the system on *his* terms, is that right?"

"That's one way to look at it." Ben tapped a few keys. "First off, you all should know it is possible to do a lot using fake identities. He could have a phone, and a house, and an e-mail account, like the rest of us do, only he doesn't use his real identity. Maybe he's living with someone, the house is in her name. Or maybe he has a phone, but not a cell-phone contract. And any first-grader can set up an e-mail account. All you have to do is get access to a machine and fill in a few blanks." Ben slid his laptop into the middle of the table so everyone could see it.

"What's this?" Allison asked.

"His e-mail account."

"What?" Allison gaped at him. Mark edged closer for a better look.

"I hacked into his Hotmail account," Ben said as everyone stared at the screen.

"You've got to be kidding me," Jonah muttered, looking at the list of messages in the in-box.

"How do you know it's him?" Allison asked.

"This account ties back to the blog comments Wolfe provided." Ben nodded at Mark. "All of those tied back to this user."

"Great," Sean said. "We can read his mail. Now how do we find him?"

Ben's brow furrowed. "That part's trickier. This account's free, so no payment records. The profile it's set up with is totally bogus. And it's old, too. He hasn't sent a message from here in almost a year."

Mark skimmed the list of messages. All appeared to be generic spam, and none of them looked to have been opened.

"I assume you've gone through these looking for any record of him doing business with someone?" Mark looked at Ben.

"It's all junk mail. Nothing personal whatsoever. He hasn't sent *out* anything personal, either. About once a year, he sends a blank message to another e-mail account, also used by this alias, just to keep things active. At least that's why I'm guessing he does it. Who knows? Maybe he's just bored."

"But why have the account if he doesn't use it?" Sean asked.

"That's" where it gets interesting. A lot of Web sites

require an e-mail address in order for you to post comments. They don't post the e-mail address necessarily, but they use it to 'verify' identity, which is really a joke, but it makes people feel more secure." Ben glanced at Mark. "It took some hacking, but I ultimately traced the posted comments on those sites you gave me back to this e-mail address. The user name he entered for it is E. Poe."

"What about Internet service providers?" Mark asked. "If he sent anything at all, it had to have gone through a server."

"I traced the comments he posted the day before Stephanie Snow's murder. They all went through the server at the university."

"You mean here in town?" Allison asked.

"That's right. There's free Wi-Fi all over campus, so he could have sat down on a park bench or whatever and used a phone or a laptop to visit the Web sites. I was hoping he used a home system, but no such luck. I can tell you he was in the area, but we already knew that because of the murder. I can't tell you where he lives."

The room fell silent. Jonah rubbed the bridge of his nose. Allison looked at Mark helplessly.

"We have a name," she said. "We even have an e-mail address. And still we're getting nowhere!"

"We're not nowhere," Mark said. "We're much better off than we were yesterday—or even an hour ago."

"Where are we on motive?" Sean asked. "Maybe that would help narrow the search."

Mark glanced at Allison. "I've made some progress on that front." He looked around the room at the other detectives. "Allison noticed that several of the victims had been working in some sort of PR capacity, which made them interface with the public. I did some checking, and turns out, *all* of these women's names were in the media—either through a press release or a personal blog or a news article in which they were quoted."

"So you're saying he has a beef with women in the public eye?" Jonah asked.

"Could be—and this fits with his profile—he doesn't like outspoken women or women in positions of power," Mark said. "He feels the need to degrade them, put them in their place. As a motive, it fits. Problem is, we're at a point where motive doesn't help us that much. We need to find him, not analyze him, and we're running out of time."

Mark turned to look at Sean. "You've been keeping tabs on Lauren Reichs. Any news there?"

He sighed. "We've been jogging every evening this week. No sign of any vans, green or white. And no sign of any other scumbags hanging around." Sean folded his arms over his chest. "I've been checking into her background, too, for anything similar with the other two victims down here. Didn't find anything."

"We need to check out her online activities. She might have crossed paths with Moss somewhere." Mark looked at Ben. "Could you look into it?"

"It would help if I had her e-mail address and social media account info."

"I'll get it for you," Sean said.

Mark turned to Jonah. "What did you get on those paint contractors?"

"Nothing interesting," Jonah said as someone's phone

chimed. "But now that I have a potential name, I'll circle back, see if anything hits."

Allison checked the number on her phone and stood up. "I need to take this. Put me down for vehicles. I've got a lead on something." She answered her call and slipped out of the room.

Mark looked at the remnants of his task force—even though it wasn't his. Reynolds was in charge. But when Mark encountered a leadership vacuum, he had a habit of filling it. It didn't always make him popular with the locals, but solving cases was his top priority, and nothing got in the way of that, ever. It was something that set him apart from most investigators, even those at the Bureau, which was notorious for demanding that its people make personal sacrifices for the job.

In Mark's case, the sacrifices were somewhat easier because he didn't *have* a personal life. Not anymore.

"So, that's it?" Sean asked.

"That's it."

Chairs scraped back as everyone stood to leave.

"If anyone gets a break, call it in ASAP," Mark said. "We've only got three days left, so the clock's ticking."

Allison spotted him outside the station house. "Mark, wait up."

He turned to face her. He had his trench coat on again, and she glanced up at the sky. It was threatening rain.

His expression looked equally threatening.

"Thanks for stepping up in there. No idea where Reynolds is."

He nodded.

"We've got a lot new to work with now," she said, "thanks to our trip to Delphi."

He just looked at her, definitely not inviting further conversation. He flicked a glance over her shoulder, and she heard a group of cops exiting the building. He was worried about appearances again.

"Listen, I was thinking," she continued. "We should interview David Moss out in Huntsville, see what shakes loose."

He didn't look surprised by the idea. "We have no reason to believe he's had any contact with his brother in the last twelve years."

"But we can't prove he *hasn't*, right?"

He didn't answer. It started to drizzle, and Allison glanced up at the sky. Mark did, too.

"The other leads we discussed are more promising," Mark said.

"His brother's doing life. He's probably bored out of his mind and willing to talk. *That's* promising. What harm could it do to interview him?"

His eyebrows shot up. "What *harm*?"

"Yes."

"How about wasting what little time we have left? This isn't a research project, Allison—it's a manhunt. You need to be here, working the leads."

Mark's phone buzzed and he jerked it from his pocket.

"Wolfe." His brow furrowed and he turned away slightly. "Yeah . . . yeah. I told you—Craigslist, Kijiji, Zac's Page. Hit every goddamn one of them. Ryan can help you interpret what the ads mean." Pause. "She was pimping out her kid, Donovan. She's not going to come right out and say—" He flicked a glance at Allison, and turned away again. "Yeah . . . No . . . No, that's *not* him. We're looking for a loner. He took them for personal use."

Allison's blood chilled as she stood there, eavesdropping. *Personal use?* Good God, what kind of case was that? She tried to imagine it as he finished up the call.

He stuffed the phone in his pocket and turned around, clearly not happy to see her still standing there.

He looked tired, she realized. Despite the smooth shave and the tie, the lines in his face were more pronounced than they'd been a few days ago and he seemed as though he carried the weight of the criminal world on his shoulders. She wanted to reach out and touch him, but the look in his eyes told her to stay away.

"I don't know how you do it," she said quietly. "I think I'd go crazy."

His jaw tightened. He glanced at his watch. "I need to call my office, so . . ."

"I want to talk to David Moss. You're a federal agent. One simple phone call and you could probably set it up—"

"Not happening." He took his phone out again and started down the stairs toward the parking lot, completely dissing her.

"Get to work, Allison," he said over his shoulder. "You've got more than enough to do here."

CHAPTER 13

It was a three-hour drive to Huntsville, and Mark spent the last ninety minutes on his phone, listening to a rookie agent out of San Antonio read the transcript from the sentencing phase of David Moss's trial. The defense attorney's account of Moss's childhood provided a wealth of information Mark had only guessed at before. It also read like a primer on how to raise a psychopath.

Paul Moss died when Damien was four and David was only one. He was killed in an accident at a timber mill in Northern California, leaving Sheryl on her own with the boys. The timber company paid the family some sort of death benefit, even though Paul's accident was attributed to drinking on the job, and apparently Sheryl used this money to keep her family afloat. When the funds ran out, though, they ended up with Sheryl's grandmother, who passed away soon after. Sheryl inherited her grandmother's house, but also a hefty set of responsibilities she was ill-equipped to handle.

And that, evidently, was when the trouble started. Beginning when David was just five, Child Protective Services went out to the house three times after neighbors reported noisy confrontations between the mother and children. Sheryl told social workers that her boys were "wild" and "uncontrollable," and oddly enough, the younger one seemed to be the bigger problem. Around that time, David started setting fire to outbuildings on the property. His mother's response to this behavior— as noted in reports—was to give him "time-outs" in an unfinished basement. And although the mother claimed these punishments only lasted a few minutes, one social worker noted a strong odor of urine and feces down in the basement and suggested the possibility that one or both of the children might be spending a lot of time there. The social worker made note of a chain and a set of handcuffs attached to a basement pipe and recorded the puzzling conclusion that this had something to do with the family dog.

Two years later, a clerk at the nearby grocery store called CPS when Sheryl Moss brought both of her boys into the store with matching black eyes. She claimed they'd beaten each other up, but the clerk was suspicious and CPS was sent to follow up. The caseworker reported an unclean house and two cases of head lice, but she documented no overt signs of abuse.

She didn't go into the basement.

At trial, Moss's defense attorney made a lot of noise about these incidents, claiming they proved a pattern of abuse by a single parent who was by turns violent and neglectful. And instead of being removed from the home, the children were left in the care of an abusive woman who spent years on the cusp of a mental breakdown.

Why did the state let her keep her kids?

Who knew? Mark had seen worse offenses go unaddressed by overworked, underpaid bureaucrats. It was no excuse, but it was reality. At any rate, the Mosses were apparently left to their own devices until three years later when the fire department was summoned to handle a fire on the neighbor's property, where this time *Damien* Moss, then thirteen, admitted to locking a puppy in a storage shed before setting the structure ablaze. On this occasion, a sheriff's deputy made it out to the Moss house, but CPS was never notified.

The sheriff's office, Child Protective Services, the school system—all bore the blame, according to Moss's lawyer, for letting a troubled young boy slip through the system.

"That's some sob story," Mark said, then realized he sounded unbelievably jaded, even for him.

"Yeah, too bad the jury didn't think so," said the agent who had been reading him the transcript. "They spent only an hour deliberating and came back with life, no parole."

"I'm thinking they didn't like the shovel," Mark said.

"Probably not."

David Moss had been convicted of picking up a waitress in a bar, taking her home to her house after her shift ended, and beating her to death with a shovel that had been sitting on her back porch. Had she gotten bad vibes from the previously charming stranger and decided not to invite him inside? Had they had an argument in the car? The events leading up to the murder remained murky, according to the transcript. But what wasn't in doubt was the existence of David Moss's fingerprints all over the shovel as well as the garbage bag used to dispose of the victim's body in a nearby Dumpster. Another damning bit of evidence was a smear of her blood on the gearshift in David's car.

"Or it could have been these photos," the agent said. "Not something anyone on that jury's likely to forget. They're just . . . shit, you don't want to know what a two-hundred-pound guy can do with a shovel. You really wouldn't believe it."

Unfortunately, Mark was quite familiar with what an angry man with a shovel could do to a defenseless woman. But he didn't mention any of that because he was busy formulating questions that might pertain to the current case.

Fire setting—a component of the homicidal triad that included torturing animals and bed wetting—was a definite part of both brothers' repertoire. Also, their father had worked at a timber company. Dara Langford had been a PR rep for a timber company. Did Damien Moss blame the company where his father died for causing the event that left him in the care of a violent mother? And was there any significance to the fact that the boys' mother had the same name as of one of Death Raven's victims?

The questions were piling up faster than Mark could answer them. At the moment, they were only useful insofar as they provided insight into David Moss's life, which would help Mark relate to him during the interview. Mark's brother, Liam, was a former Marine, and he'd passed along one of his favorite military sayings: Prior planning prevents piss-poor performance. Mark took the advice to heart.

"Anything else in there?" he asked as his phone beeped a low-battery warning.

"Sure, plenty. But as far as relevant to this Damien you're looking for? I'm not seeing anything. The public defender left me a voice mail after lunch. Said he never met anyone in Moss's family. Said as far as he knew, everyone was dead but the brother, and they were estranged."

"Thanks for the help." Mark spotted the Huntsville exit and cut over to the right lane. "Call me if anything new comes in."

Mark clicked off and plugged his phone into the charger. The screen told him he'd missed a call from Allison, but he had no intention of returning it. At least not right now. He didn't want to muck up the excellent job he'd done of pissing her off on the steps of the station house. He needed her mad at him. He could handle her anger. He could even handle the shocked indignation he'd seen on her face when he'd essentially patted her on the head and told her to go play cop in her backyard. She'd probably decided he was a condescending prick, and he didn't blame her.

What he couldn't handle were those smoldering eyes that looked up at him and promised heaven.

Come home with me.

He could still hear her voice, low and sultry, as she'd gazed at him back at the bar. Her eyes had promised not just sex, but *sex*. Ecstasy. The kind of soul-searing heat that might actually succeed in distracting him from the soul-numbing drudgery that had become his life.

What her eyes *didn't* promise was an easy out. She was too young, too vulnerable, too idealistic—although she'd flat-out deny the last two. And there was no getting into it with her and getting out without someone—namely Allison—winding up hurt.

Another hurt, bitter woman was not something Mark needed in his life right now.

He exited the highway and passed a big green sign: WELCOME TO HUNTSVILLE, HOME OF SAM HOUSTON. Mark thought it was an interesting motto for a town that was much better known for being home to the busiest execution chamber in the nation, not to mention six prisons. He drove through several intersections and took the familiar highway that would lead north of town to the Ellis Unit.

It had been years since he'd been to the Ellis Unit, which for decades had housed Texas's infamous death row. After seven condemned inmates attempted an escape, the row was moved to the newer, more secure Polunsky Unit a short drive away.

Mark remembered Ellis from that previous visit, when he'd interviewed a convicted murderer who had managed to kill three wives before detectives caught on to him. Prison had taken a toll on the man, and he'd looked defeated during their two-hour meeting. He'd described the prison as "hell on earth" and said the worst part about it wasn't the violence or the food or the boredom—it was the noise.

Mark had heard the complaint before. Noise carried inside the concrete walls, and the incessant shouts and taunts and clanging doors drove many men over the edge.

Mark had been interviewing prisoners for years now, but this meeting was liable to be especially challenging.

First, he needed to establish a rapport. Information flowed much better when the subject felt at ease. Mark's habit was to make a production of asking the guards to remove the handcuffs, which immediately established a small degree of trust. Next, Mark would offer something—a smoke, a stick of gum, a business card, whatever. Didn't matter. Again, it was about building trust so the convict would talk freely. Finally, the questions would begin. He'd start with the easy ones first—basic biographical info and maybe the undisputed facts of the case—to establish a baseline. Once he had a grasp of the prisoner's default expressions, he'd go for the hard stuff—MO, motive, elements of the crimes that remained in dispute.

Mark had discovered that most convicts—especially lifers or those condemned to death—had only one thing left, and that was an abundance of time. They didn't generally mind being interviewed, but for the meeting to provide any value, Mark had to get at the truth. Many career criminals were skilled manipulators and some relished the idea of spending a few hours jerking around a fed. So Mark had learned early on to separate the truth from the lies.

Mark's colleagues often said he was a "gifted" interviewer because he had a talent for seeing the invisible. But what he saw wasn't invisible—it simply took a trained eye. Mark picked up on every little stress signal—from a small change of expression to a slight shift in voice or pitch. He picked up on extra bits of information that were added to a story just before the lie came. He picked up on body language, and all the subtle cues that signaled a person's stress level was mounting.

Mark was an expert at reading both verbal and non-verbal cues because he'd been doing it all his life. Children from violent households made great lie detectors because their ability to read people and situations wasn't just a hobby—it was a survival skill.

The problem with David Moss was that he could very well be the most difficult sort of interview subject: a psychopath.

Psychopaths were brilliant liars. Stress while lying was caused by worry and feelings of remorse, but true psychopaths had no conscience and hence, no stress. They lied easily and without breaking a sweat. Even while deceiving people, their demeanor tended to be glib, shallow, sometimes even charming. If David Moss fell into this category, Mark would adjust his strategy. He'd do the very thing he despised doing, but had been forced to do on countless occasions to get a convict to open up and reveal details about his life.

He'd feed his ego.

And although Mark hated pumping up the ego of a sadistic killer, he believed the ends often justified the means. He'd learned to hide his contempt while he talked to people. Some of the brag sessions Mark had listened to over the years had yielded information that led to re-opened cold cases and recovered bodies and closure for families who had waited years for news about a loved one.

Mark tapped the sedan's brakes as the highway curved through a dense thicket of trees. The road looked familiar here. Through the swishing wiper blades, he soon spotted the redbrick sign for the Ellis Unit. He entered the prison grounds and pulled into the visitors' lot near the building. It was relatively empty, as today wasn't a normal visiting day, but Mark had put in a call to the warden to arrange a special interview due to the exigent circumstances of the case. He left his phone in the charger—he wasn't allowed to take it in the interview room anyway—and jogged through the downpour to the building's front entrance.

In the lobby, he brushed the rain from his sleeves and combed his fingers through his hair as a potbellied guard shoved a binder across the counter.

"Name, badge number, agency," the guard intoned.

Mark passed the man his ID and jotted his information on the first line at the top of the page. He slipped his Glock from its holster and placed it on the counter, then added his spare magazine, his handcuffs, his key chain, and his wallet to the pile of contraband.

"Any cell phones, pagers, laptops, knives, cash, tobacco, lighters, matches—"

"Just my smokes." Mark smiled and patted his breast pocket.

The guard pursed his lips, then nodded. The man had a pack of his own in the pocket of his uniform.

"Proceed through the double doors, left at the first hallway, first guard station is on your right," he said. "Captain there will show you into the attorneys' room. We got y'all set up in there. Prisoner's already on his way down."

"Already?" Mark checked his watch. He was half an hour early, and the guard hadn't even made a call.

"The detective's back there waiting."

A cold feeling settled in Mark's stomach. He glanced

at the log. He flipped to the previous page and zeroed in on the name at the bottom of the list.

Mark felt his temper rising as he pocketed his badge. He plowed through the double doors and strode back to the first guard station. The man buzzed him through and Mark entered a secure corridor where a single door stood ajar.

Inside the room, Allison sat in a chair, staring down at her notebook and clutching a pencil. She looked like a college kid about to take a final exam.

Mark swallowed a string of curses and stepped through the doorway.

"What are you doing here?"

Her gaze snapped up. She narrowed her eyes at him. "I *knew* it. You lied to me."

"What are you doing here?" he repeated, and his voice sounded amazingly calm, given that his stress level had just shot through the ceiling.

"What does it look like? I'm interviewing Damien Moss's brother."

"You came here by yourself?"

She glanced over her shoulder at the empty room. "Looks like. Why?"

Mark gritted his teeth. He looked her over. She had on those slim-fitting black pants and the gray blazer he'd noticed at this morning's meeting. She wore one of those stretchy white shirts underneath, which clearly outlined the shape of her breasts. She had on heeled black *boots*, for Christ's sake. If someone ordered a stripper dressed as a detective, she'd show up looking exactly like Allison did at this very moment.

Mark felt like his head was going to explode.

She leaned back in the chair and crossed her arms. "What exactly is your problem?"

"I don't have a problem."

"Reynolds sent me here. He knows the warden and helped me get the interview set up."

Reynolds, of course. Mark could have throttled the guy. He took a deep breath and changed tactics.

"You know, you're right," he said, pulling the door closed for privacy. "This is a good idea. I'm glad we're pursuing it. But we're up against a time limit here, so why don't I go ahead and—"

"I was here first."

He laughed, but there was no humor in it. "*That's* what you're going with? Finders keepers?"

Her expression hardened. "Don't patronize me, Wolfe. I'm here to do my job. This could help us locate Damien."

"You're right. But *I* will conduct the interview."

She shrugged. "Fine, we'll both do it."

"Allison." He felt his control slipping. He was getting dangerously close to losing it. He clenched his teeth and struggled for calm. "Let's at least agree that I have *years* more experience conducting this sort of interview. Can we agree to that, please?"

She stood up, looking affronted now. "What is it you have against me doing my job?"

"Nothing at all. And your job is in San Marcos."

She fisted her hand on her hip and stepped closer, and God help him, he could smell her shampoo.

"Our best lead is right here," she said. "It's entirely possible he could point us straight to our suspect. We could *arrest* said suspect before he has a chance to murder any more women."

"Do you even know who we're dealing with?"

"Yeah, and he's a dirtbag. So what? I deal with dirtbags all day long."

"Not like this."

She rolled her eyes. "He could help us get an arrest, Wolfe. Which just happens to be my chief objective right now. So, sit in if you like, but I plan to talk to him."

"No."

Her jaw dropped. *"What?"*

"No. You're not talking to him. End of discussion." Goddamn it, how had he lost control of this?

"You can't tell me what I can and can't do! Who the hell do you think you are?"

His argument had lost all logic, so he simply pulled rank. "I'm a federal agent. I have a bigger badge than you. Live with it."

He heard clanging at the other end of the hall and shot a desperate glance at the door.

"I will *not* live with it! I came here to do my job, and I plan to do it."

She stepped around him to reach for the doorknob, and he caught her arm.

She shook him off. "Jesus, Wolfe, *what* is your problem?"

"I don't want to watch him look at you!" he boomed, and she jerked back. "I don't want him seeing you! Thinking about you! I don't want him goddamn *smelling* you, all right? He's a piece of shit and you don't belong in the same room with him!"

She stared up at him, looking intimidated by him

for the first time since he'd met her. And she *should* be intimidated. She should run away at top speed. All that calm, cool composure he wore like armor had vanished, and she was seeing the real Mark Wolfe, a man on the edge.

She looked at the floor, and he could tell she was shaken. But she was backing down, which meant his completely losing his shit in front of her hadn't been for nothing. He didn't care what she thought of him—he just wanted her out of here.

She looked up. "I'm sorry you don't believe in my ability to do my job."

What?

"Allison, that's not it."

"That's exactly it. But I assure you I *am* capable of conducting this interview."

A rap on the door. Mark looked over his shoulder as a guard poked his head in. "Inmate's here. We ready?"

Mark looked at her, but she was ignoring him now. She squared her shoulders. "We're ready. Send him in."

CHAPTER 14

David Moss stepped into the room, and Allison instantly noticed his eyes. His irises were a brilliant shade of blue and he had thick, dark lashes that any woman would envy. But the flash of envy turned to unease as his attention homed in on her like a guided missile.

"Special Agent Mark Wolfe, FBI." Mark stepped between them and offered a chair. He didn't offer a handshake, though, as the prisoner wore cuffs attached to a loose leather belt around his waist. "Have a seat."

Moss's shackles clinked as he shuffled across the room. He had short hair—almost a crew cut—and wore white pajama-looking pants with a white cotton T-shirt. On his feet were gray rubber shower shoes.

She lifted her gaze and found him staring at her again as he sat down.

"And who are you?" he asked her.

"This is A.J. Doyle, one of my colleagues."

She shot Mark a look. He'd positioned two more chairs on the other side of the table and indicated for her to take the one nearest the exit. An armed guard was posted on the other side of the door and the button to summon him was on the table within easy reach.

Allison took a seat and studied Moss again, keeping her expression neutral. The man had a tall, powerful build and was surprisingly good-looking. If she saw him in a bar, she'd definitely look twice.

Allison thought of the waitress who'd gone home with him. She wondered if those same blue eyes had been the last thing Patricia Stewart had seen as she lay dying from a crushed skull. A shiver of fear moved down Allison's spine. She kept her face blank, but the corner of Moss's mouth curled up, and she knew he'd read her thoughts.

"No visitors in a while."

He turned his attention to Mark. "No, sir."

"Not even your attorney's been to see you in the last two years."

"Nope. Just you guys." He looked at Allison. "'Scuse me, ma'am." He nodded at her. "Just you *two*. My last appeal tanked, so. You know how it goes."

He sounded relaxed. Nonchalant. Completely unlike what she would have expected from a man who'd been condemned to spend his life behind bars. He was only twenty-nine. She figured he had at least that many more years ahead of him inside these walls.

"That would be the appeal you had in front of Judge Roth." Mark said it as a statement, not a question, and Allison realized he'd done more homework than she had.

"That's the one." His voice was tinged with sarcasm now. "Guess the D.A. fucking the judge in my case doesn't get me a new trial." He cut a glance at Allison. "If you'll 'scuse my language." Then back to Mark. "So that's pretty much it for me."

A door slammed down the hallway, and Allison glanced at the window. The guard hadn't moved.

"So." Moss's gaze was on her again. "What brings *you* here? I'm guessing the FBI didn't send you out to talk about my appeal."

"We're seeking information about your brother," Allison said.

His attention shifted to Mark and then to Allison again. A smirk spread across his face.

"My brother."

"When was the last time you saw him?" Mark asked.

He glanced up at the ceiling. "Ah, let's see." He looked at Mark. "It's definitely been a while. Mind if I bum a smoke?"

Allison looked over, startled, as Mark reached into his jacket and pulled out a pack of Marlboro Reds. He tapped one out and passed it across the table.

"Bet they took your lighter, didn't they?"

Mark nodded.

Moss smiled as he tucked the cigarette into his pants. "Ah, that's okay. I'll save it for later." He leaned back and gave Allison a smug look. "You were saying? About Damien?"

"*You* were saying you hadn't seen him in a while," she said. "You remember when it was, exactly?"

"Well, maybe not *exactly*."

Another gaze at the ceiling, and Allison waited, watching him think. She had no doubt this "aw, shucks" routine was designed to be charming, like the "ma'am" and the "sir" bit. She glanced at Mark, but he was wearing his most inscrutable FBI face now, and he hardly resembled the man who'd been shouting at her a few minutes ago. If not for the slight tension in his jaw that told her he was grinding his teeth to nubs, she'd think she'd imagined it.

I don't want to watch him look at you!

Well, the man was looking at her now, and she knew that behind the bland facade, Mark was absolutely hating it.

"Musta been twelve? Thirteen years ago?" Moss glanced at Mark.

"Do you know where he's living now?" Mark asked.

"That I don't."

"Where would you guess?"

"I wouldn't." He looked at Allison and his gaze dropped to her breasts.

"He ever visit you in San Quentin?"

"Nope."

"Did he come to your trial?"

"Nope." Moss smiled. "We're not what you'd call a close family."

"You two came to Texas about the same time," Mark said. "I assume you were together?"

Moss looked surprised by this, and Allison probably did, too. It hadn't occurred to her that the brothers might have moved down here together.

"Nope." Moss shifted in his chair and his smirk disappeared. "Like I said, haven't seen him. What's this about, anyway?"

"We'd like to question Damien about some crimes in central Texas," Allison said, and Moss's expression didn't change.

"What sort of crimes?"

"Homicides," Mark stated.

"Homicides, plural?"

"That's right."

Moss made a *tsking* sound and shook his head. Allison wanted to reach across the table and slap him, but she focused on keeping a blank face.

"Well, now, *that* sounds like some serious shit. Why would I want to help you hook up my brother for murder?"

And here was the sticking point. There really *wasn't* much reason for Moss to help them. Barring a new trial—which looked very much impossible after his failed appeal—he wasn't going anywhere.

"You know, I'm curious," Mark said. "Why Texas?"

Moss watched him. He pulled the cigarette from his pants, along with a book of matches. Despite a limited range of motion, he somehow managed to lean forward and get the end lit. Then he sat back in the chair and blew a stream of smoke at the ceiling.

"Now, *that* I can tell you. Damien loves it here, ever since we were kids."

"You came down here as kids," Allison clarified as he took another drag. She itched to pick up her notepad, but she didn't want to stifle the conversation now.

"You been out to Waynesboro?" He squinted at her through the haze of smoke. "Good bird hunting. Dove, quail, you name it. Damien's good with a shotgun."

"Who taught you to hunt?" Allison asked, thinking of the time line. Moss's father had died when he was practically an infant.

"That would be Uncle Brad. Married to Theresa, my mom's sister."

"And her last name is . . . ?"

"Gillis," he said.

Allison wanted to rush outside and call Ric. She wanted him to look up every Gillis in Wayne County. They could narrow their vehicle search to the county as well.

The blue eyes turned to her. "She's dead, though, if that's what you're thinking."

"What about Brad?" Mark asked.

"Him, too." Moss shook his head. He took another pull on the cigarette, then leaned back and looked at Allison. "So, A.J. How long you been at the Bureau?"

"I'm with the San Marcos police."

"San Marcos."

"Where one of the victims lived."

He nodded. "Not a real common field for a woman." He flicked an ash on the concrete. "Being a cop, that is. You like it?"

"I do."

"I've met some lady cops. Dykes, every last one of 'em." He gave her a slow, appraising look that chilled her skin. "But you're not a dyke, so it must run in the family. I bet your dad was a cop."

She could feel Mark's gaze boring into her. He didn't like this conversation, but if he tried to put a stop to it, Moss would gain the upper hand. She hadn't realized the complexity of the dynamic she'd created by insisting on this three-way interview.

"He was a firefighter."

Moss's eyes widened, as if he was impressed. "A *fire-fighter*. Now, those guys are cool. Always liked those guys." He gave Mark a knowing look, and she realized

Moss was telling him he knew that *they* knew about his criminal history.

"When was the last time you heard from your brother, David?" Mark's voice sounded tight now.

"Hold on, now. I want to hear about A.J." He dropped the cigarette butt on the floor and let it smolder. "So, I bet you were a daddy's girl, huh? Why aren't you carrying a hose?"

She forced herself not to look at Mark for guidance. This had been her idea.

"Maybe flames aren't your thing?" Moss pressed. "You said your pop's dead. What'd he do, run into a burning building?"

Allison felt the blood drain from her face. Her chest squeezed. She forced her lips to move and heard words coming from her mouth.

"My father's retired."

"Retired?"

"Yes."

"Now, that's too bad." He shook his head. "We need those firefighters."

"When exactly was it you moved down to Texas?" Mark asked.

Moss's insolent gaze didn't stray from Allison. "Five years ago."

"Tell me how you got your job with the roofing company."

Now he looked at Mark. "They needed a roofer."

"And you had some experience?"

He shrugged. "Not rocket science. Did some construction here and there along the way."

"Damien do any?"

"Here and there."

"Any house painting?"

"I doubt it." He focused back on Allison again. "Damien never liked all that manual labor. He was into the computer." He cut a look at Mark. "You know he took some SAT test when he was sixteen? Perfect score."

"Where did he attend college?" Allison asked, and she waited for him to say Rice University, where Jordan Wheatley had gone.

"Wish I could remember."

"You don't remember where your brother went to college?" The second the words were out, she regretted them. Of course he knew. And now he knew they *didn't* know, and he could be smug about that, too.

"David." Mark waited for Moss to look at him. "We're looking for your brother. It would be good if you helped us. Sooner rather than later."

"What, you're worried he'll strike again soon as the sun goes down?" He smiled at Allison. "Sorry. Wish I could help you out."

He turned to Mark and the smile vanished. "It'd take more than a free smoke to make me rat out my own brother." He turned to Allison. "Lemme let you in on a secret: You're never going to catch Damien because he's too smart."

"Is he smarter than you?" Mark asked, maybe trying to stir up some resentment.

"I don't know, Special Agent. You tell me. I'm in here. He's not." He tipped his head, as if considering it. "Yep, sounds like he's smarter than me."

Moss's gaze settled on Allison. "I can tell *you're* smart."

He jerked his head at Mark. "He's pretty smart. But Damien's in a whole different league." Moss stood up, and Mark instantly got to his feet.

Moss smiled. "You won't find Damien if he doesn't want to be found." He pressed the button to summon the guard. "Think I'm done here." He nodded at Allison. "Nice talking to you guys."

Allison stood up. It seemed like the thing to do. She glanced at the window, but the square of glass was empty. No guard.

Everything after that happened fast.

Mark grabbed her arm and shoved her just as the prisoner lunged. Moss grabbed the front of her jacket with both hands, flung her onto the tabletop, and smashed an elbow against her throat.

"One move, I'll break her neck!"

Allison struggled to breathe. His elbow was jammed against her windpipe.

"Back the fuck off, or I'll snap it like a twig!"

"Let her go, David." Mark's voice was steady, calm. "You don't want to do this."

Allison gasped for air. She tried to kick her legs, but he pinned her to the table with his hard body. She tried to reach for his eye sockets, but her shoulders were pinned. The face above her was red and contorted, the blue eyes wild. The edge of her vision started to blur.

"David, look at me," Mark commanded.

Amazingly, he obeyed.

"You hurt her, they'll throw you in the hole. You don't want that."

"Don't tell me what I want!"

"Let her go." Mark's voice sounded farther and farther

away. Her throat burned. "You hurt a cop, they'll make your life hell, David. Let her go."

The door burst open with a *boom*. Moss's body jolted. Mark hauled him off of her and heaved him against the wall.

"Stun him again!" someone barked.

Mark's face loomed over her. Allison tried to sit up, but her limbs tingled. She couldn't move, couldn't speak.

"Medic!" Mark shouted at the guards who'd filled the room. "We need a *medic*!"

"No," she rasped. "I'm . . . okay."

Across the room, Moss was sprawled on the floor. Everyone was yelling. A pair of guards grabbed the convict by the ankles and shoulders and hauled him away.

CHAPTER 15

———

Mark was down to his last shred of patience by the time he reached San Marcos. He'd spent three hours on a narrow country highway driving through darkness and torrential rain, and with every wreck and disabled car he passed, he got angrier at Allison. Finally, after his fourth attempt to reach her, she picked up the phone.

"Where are you?" he demanded. "I thought you were going to wait for me."

"Sorry, I just . . . I had to get out of there. Every time I turned around, someone was making me fill out another report."

He'd left her in the prison infirmary while he met with the warden. It never occurred to him she'd finish up and take off without so much as a conversation.

"Where are you now?" He tried to keep frustration out of his voice, but it came through anyway.

"I just dropped by the station. Ric and Jonah were there, and I handed off these leads so they can get going. We'll regroup in the morning."

She was still working the case, then. Mark gritted his teeth. He'd allowed himself to entertain the possibility that maybe—just maybe—today's disaster had had one positive outcome, and she'd decided to bow out. But of course he'd been wrong. He *wanted* her to drop the case, so why would she do that? Why would she do a single damn thing he wanted her to when it was so much easier to do the exact opposite?

"Don't go anywhere," he said. "I'm coming over."

"What, here?"

"Are you home yet?"

"I'm pulling in right now."

He whipped into her apartment complex just in time to see the taillights go dark on her battered pickup. The unmarked police cruiser she'd taken to Huntsville—the one he hadn't recognized in the prison parking lot— must be back at the police station.

She turned to look at him through the back window as he slid into a space. It was still pouring. She made a dash to her apartment and waited for him under the overhang as he jogged across the lot. They stood at her door, soaked to the skin, and he gazed down at her and realized it was the first time they'd been alone since the argument in the interview room.

"I'm glad you're here," she said over the rain. "I need to ask you something." She unlocked the door and shoved it open. "God, it's *wet* out there."

He followed her inside and closed the door on the storm. Her apartment was dark and cold. She dropped her purse and keys on the hall table and made a beeline for the thermostat.

"Jonah's digging up whatever we can on these Gillis people out of Waynesboro," she informed him as she switched on the heater. "Ric is going to run a vehicle check for Wayne County, see what comes up."

"I think you should drop the case." There. He'd said it. But by the look she gave him, he could tell the idea was going nowhere.

"Why would I do that?" She peeled off her sodden blazer and tossed it toward the armchair—which she missed—as she headed for the kitchen. She unbuckled her holster with movements that were brisk and clumsy. Clearly, she was still amped up.

Mark picked up her jacket from the floor and draped it over one of her bar stools. She put her weapon and holster on the counter and grabbed a dish towel.

"Allison, maybe you need some time off. From this case."

She dried her face and squeezed the towel around her ponytail. The only light in the room came from the dim bulb of the fixture above the stove, but even in the meager light he could see she looked rattled.

"Time off," she repeated.

"Yes."

She shook her head and muttered something he couldn't hear as she turned to her refrigerator. She took out a can of Coke, popped open the top, and proceeded to pour half of it down the sink.

"What I need is a favor," she said, looking him squarely in the eye for the first time in hours. Her face was pale, taut. Everything about her seemed agitated. She still hadn't had the adrenaline crash that he felt certain was coming very soon, and it pained him to see her this way.

In that moment, he would have done anything for her. But he somehow knew that he wasn't going to like whatever this favor was.

"I already talked to the warden about it," she said, "so now it's up to you."

He waited for her to finish, but instead she opened a cabinet and took down a bottle of Jack Daniel's. She poured a few glugs into her Coke.

"Drink?" she offered.

"No."

She took a sip and headed back into the living room with the can, pulling the band loose from her ponytail as she went.

"I need you not to mention this incident to Reynolds," she said over her shoulder.

"'Incident'?" He followed her. "Did you really just say 'incident'? You were *assaulted,* Allison."

"I'm aware of that." She set her drink on the table in the foyer and stopped to unzip her boots and kick them off.

Mark tried to tamp down his temper. "You were *assaulted* on an assignment your idiot lieutenant sent you on alone. He should be out of a job."

"Wolfe, listen." She stepped closer and her eyes pleaded with him. "I need your help. This could unravel my career."

"It wasn't your fault!"

"I know that and you know that, but you also must realize how this looks. It's the second time in just a few weeks that I've let a situation get out of control." She walked down the hall to the bathroom and flipped on the light. "I can't take another hit like this. I'll be ostracized.

How can anyone trust me to have their back if I can't even watch my own?" She stripped off her shirt and stood in front of the mirror.

Mark halted in the doorway, stunned by the giant purple bruise on her shoulder.

"Jesus *Christ*." He stepped up behind her. She lifted her chin and examined her neck in the mirror. There was another dark bruise on the underside of her jaw, and Mark's gut clenched with fury.

"It doesn't hurt anymore." Her gaze met his in the mirror. Then she dodged around him and walked into her bedroom.

In only her bra and slacks. Mark tried to blink away the image of all that smooth, bare skin because, god*damn* it, she'd been attacked today and—

His gaze fell on the shirt she'd tossed on the counter. The seam at the shoulder was ripped, and he got an instant visual of Moss throwing her down on that table.

He grabbed the shirt and stormed into the bedroom. "Did he cut you? Did he fucking *cut* you?"

One scratch and she could have some deadly diseases.

She was standing there, still half undressed, but she was holding a bathrobe now.

"He didn't cut me." She took a deep breath. "I'm just banged up."

Mark tried not to look at her. He looked at the shirt bunched up in his fist and felt the blinding fury all over again.

"Will you help me?"

He glanced up at her, not understanding. The only thing he grasped at the moment was rage.

"This is my career, Wolfe."

Mark looked at her with disbelief. She wanted him to *help* her downplay her assault—an assault he'd *let* happen right in front of him because he'd feared for her life. Moss had had his elbow on her larynx, and Mark had had no doubt that he could have crushed her neck with one blow.

And now she wanted him to let that go.

"You know, I really, *really* need a hot shower," she said. "Just think about it, all right? I'll be out in a minute."

Mark turned his back on her and returned to the kitchen, where he threw the torn shirt into the trash. He lifted the bag out and carried it to the Dumpster across the parking lot. It was still pouring, but he didn't care. Maybe the rain would jar him out of this funk he'd been in for the past four hours. He couldn't remember the last time he'd been so affected by something. He was furious with himself, with Moss, with Reynolds.

He was furious with Allison, too, and somehow that made the rest of it worse. He had no right to be upset with her.

He replaced the bag in her kitchen trash can and stood at the counter, listening to the pipes run. He pictured her in that plain white bra with those bruises marring her skin and he felt an overwhelming urge to just . . . just . . .

Goddamn it, *how* could he be thinking about this? It was wrong. In every way. What he really needed to do was leave, right now, but instead he found himself standing in the middle of her kitchen, imagining her naked in the very next room.

He grabbed the bottle on the counter and poured a shot of bourbon into one of her juice glasses. He slugged it back. It burned all the way down but did nothing to ease his tension.

He heard the pipes shut off. A few minutes later, the bathroom door opened. Then he heard the faint scrape of drawers opening and closing back in her bedroom.

He should go now, while he still could. Before she walked back in here all wet and beautiful—

Too late.

"So, what's the verdict?" She was in the bathrobe now—a white terry-cloth thing that practically swallowed her. He thought about the drawers opening and closing and wondered what else she'd put on.

If he had a decent bone in his body, he'd leave.

"I need to ask you something," he said instead. It was possibly the worst time for him to ask this question, but he needed to know. It had been eating at him for hours.

She stepped closer and gazed up at him. All that wet, dark hair was combed back from her face, and he could really see her eyes. There was curiosity in them, and something else, too, something he wasn't sure he wanted to put a name to.

"What happened to your father when you were twelve?" he asked.

Her expression clouded. She looked down. When she looked up again, her eyes were somber.

"He died on the job."

Mark's heart sank. But he'd known the answer. He'd known it from the look on her face when Moss had taunted her. For about the thousandth time that day, Mark honestly wanted to kill the man.

"You know, it's weird." She looked down at her bare

feet. "That—what he said about my dad—feels like more of a violation than when he was choking me." She looked up, as if searching his face for some kind of understanding.

"I'm sorry," he said. Two inadequate words that didn't help anything.

"It's not your fault."

Mark scoffed and looked away.

"Mark." She reached up and turned his face to hers. She stood dangerously close and he forced himself to look at her eyes. "It was my choice to be there. It was his choice to hurt me."

Her fingers were cool against his skin and she smelled just as fresh and young and beautiful as she actually was. He had to get out of here. But he had this compulsive need to make things right first. As if he could.

"Allison." A bitter lump rose up in his throat. "I want to erase what happened, but I don't know how."

Her hand dropped from his cheek, and he instantly missed it.

"I do." She took his fingers. Slowly, she turned his palm up and kissed it. The touch of her lips electrified him. She pressed his fingers gently against her throat, right beneath her bruise.

He gave up trying not to look at her—at the curve of her neck, at the deep V where her robe came together. She slid his hand over all that soft skin and underneath the fabric and cupped his palm around her breast.

Mark needed to leave. He knew that. But when she smiled up at him, he couldn't bring himself to move. Except his thumb, which was stroking circles around her nipple now. She tipped her head back and sighed.

And it was that soft, tiny sound that finally sealed his fate.

Allison felt the exact instant when he surrendered, and the sweet thrill of it was something she knew she'd carry with her the rest of her life. He pulled her against him and crushed his mouth against hers. His kiss was hot, hungry, and the fierceness sent a shot of lust straight to her core. He tasted like heat and sex and the whiskey she'd offered him, and she grew dizzy just from tangling her tongue with his. There was no finesse here—just raw, desperate need that confirmed everything she'd always suspected about him.

He pulled back and gazed down at her, and the intensity in his eyes made her legs weak. She stroked her hands up behind his neck to pull him down for another kiss.

"You taste good," she murmured, rubbing against him, and the texture of his damp suit and the coolness of his tie against her skin sent a shiver through her. Her fingers combed his hair. She opened her eyes and smiled up at him, so relieved that he was finally touching her. This closed-off, powerful, impossibly unattainable man wanted *her*. And he was done resisting. She'd been fantasizing about him, but the reality of him was so much better. She had him *here,* in her kitchen, damp and mussed from rain and with a day's worth of beard darkening his jaw.

She backed out of his arms and he stopped, breathless just like she was. Smiling, she planted her palms on the counter and hitched herself up so she'd be closer to his height. His gaze heated as she hooked a leg around him and pulled him to her.

"I've been dying to do this," she said, reaching for his tie. She kissed him and tugged at the knot. After a few fumbled tries with him watching her intently, she managed to get it loose. She jerked it from his collar with a *snap* and draped it over her thigh. Next, his shirt. His big hands slid down from her breasts and circled her waist possessively as she worked the buttons. She pulled the shirttail from his pants. He was still wearing his holster. She made a low growl of frustration, and he took it off.

She leaned back to watch. Her robe was open now, and she loved the way his gaze locked on her body as he got rid of his shirt and assorted weaponry. When at last she had him naked from the waist up, she ran a hand over his chest and wrapped her legs around him.

Her breasts brushed against his skin. He had well-muscled shoulders and flat abs, and although she'd known he kept in shape, she'd been prepared to overlook some extra pounds because of his age. He didn't have any, though. He looked good in a suit, but he looked even better like this, and she felt lucky to be one of the few people who probably ever got to see him this way.

She kissed him deeply, wanting to swallow him as his hands stroked up the backs of her thighs and he dragged her hips to the very edge of the counter. He glanced around desperately. His gaze landed on her breakfast table and she saw him consider it briefly, then change his mind.

"Here," she whispered, pushing him away and hopping down from the counter. She took him by the hand and led him to her bedroom, where she'd left only the closet light on. She turned to look at him.

Uh-oh. Second thoughts. She could see it in his eyes. He was overthinking this again, and she wanted him to stop.

She tugged him toward the bed and got on her knees on it.

"I don't want to hurt you." His voice was low and rough, and she responded by hooking a finger into his pants and pulling him to her.

"You won't," she whispered. She shrugged out of her robe just to erase any lingering doubts he might have that they were doing this and they were doing it *tonight*. Her skimpy black panties seemed to have the desired effect, and he quickly got rid of the rest of his clothes. She saw his gaze dart to the nightstand where she'd left a condom. His eyes locked on hers.

Okay, busted. Yes, she'd planned to lure him back here. But that wasn't much of a secret, now, was it? She'd wanted him from the very first night, and those dark glances he'd been giving her had told her he wanted her, too, despite his brush-offs. And the brush-offs were over, evidently, as he came to her again and pulled her into his arms. He kissed her roughly, deeply. He planted his knee between hers and eased her down onto the bed.

Her throat closed. She made a panicky sound, and he jerked back.

"Sorry, just—" She got to her knees again. "Sorry."

He stood up, and she knew that was it. She'd spooked him. But instead of backing off, he cupped his hand around her face and gazed down at her, and the total concern in his eyes had her heart melting. He felt responsible for what had happened. He had this protectiveness about him that both touched her and drove her crazy, because how crazy was it for him to feel responsible for everyone everywhere and all the bad things that happened?

She brought his hand to her mouth and kissed his knuckles. "Let me be on top," she whispered.

His eyes heated at the words. She pushed him back onto the bed and loved the raw desire she saw on his face as she straddled his thighs.

All at once she felt exhilarated. Energized. Whatever she'd lost earlier today, she was determined to get it back, right now, this moment, and with *this* man. Mark Wolfe was the most powerful, commanding man she'd ever known, and it was a huge rush to have him utterly at her mercy.

She stroked her fingers over those strong shoulders that were always so burdened with responsibility. She stroked his chest, his arms. He watched her intently and his fingers gripped her thighs as she ran her hands over his body. Then she bent over him and felt a jolt of desire as he pulled her forward and his mouth fastened on her breast. His hands moved over her hips, pulling off her last bit of clothing.

She rubbed and writhed against him, and suddenly he surged up and rolled her onto her back. He pressed his weight against her, and she was elated all over again because it felt good instead of terrifying, and she wrapped her legs around him and pulled him closer.

He kissed her mouth, her neck, her breasts. His hand slid between her legs and stroked her until she was panting and moaning and mindless. He watched her face and knew exactly where to touch her, how to touch her, how to make her forget everything in the world except *him*. And right when she thought she was going to fly apart, he pulled away from her and sat back on his knees.

She made a whimper of protest, but then she opened her eyes and he was putting on the condom. He bent over her and kissed her mouth again as his legs parted her thighs. He pushed himself inside her, and all she could think of was *yes*.

She squeezed her legs around him and fisted her fingers in his hair as he drove into her again and again. She finally had it, right there in her arms—that fierce intensity she'd sensed from him since the very beginning. That relentless, driving power that defined who he was and everything he did was directed at *her* now. He was losing control with *her*, at last, and knowing she'd done this to him made her feel giddy, greedy, empowered. And then the heat of it was all too much and her control shattered. He made a raw, guttural sound and with a forceful thrust, his shattered, too.

She lay there panting, staring up at the ceiling, as the weight of his hips pinned her to the bed. Every inch of her body was in shock. She drew a deep breath and let it out with a sigh.

Something felt different. She could breathe. She glanced around and realized he was propped on his elbows, trying to keep from crushing her as she wallowed in bliss.

Carefully, he shifted her thigh and pulled their bodies apart. He rolled over onto his back and lay there, chest heaving, gazing up at the ceiling of her bedroom. Before she could think of anything to say, he got up and walked into the bathroom. When he came back, he stretched out beside her on the bed. They lay in the dark without words—only the dull pitter-patter of rain against the windowsill.

She studied his profile in the dimness. He had strong, manly features and a chin that was maybe a little too big. She decided it was her favorite feature.

He turned to look at her. "What?"

"I'm just admiring." She propped up on an elbow and smiled down at him.

"Are you okay?"

"Very okay," she said, making the comment about sex even though she knew that wasn't what he'd meant. She didn't want him to worry about her.

He looked at the ceiling again. Something came over his face, and she sensed it was reality, crashing in on him.

She flattened her hand on his chest and felt his heart thudding against her palm.

"Stay," she said.

He looked at her, and his expression told her he'd been thinking the exact opposite.

Without giving him time to respond, she nestled her head against his side and pretended the decision was made.

Regrets already. Something pinched inside her. She'd at least hoped she'd have him until morning. But this had been her idea, not his. She'd pressured him into it, using every tactic she could think of. And now that the lust was satisfied, he was thinking clearly enough to see exactly what had happened. He was probably lying there realizing that she was manipulative and calculating. Or wondering how soon he could tactfully leave.

Allison closed her eyes. The bubble of euphoria she'd created gradually started to deflate. Here it came—the crash after the adrenaline-soaked day. She'd been expecting it, but still it hit her out of nowhere. She suddenly felt more exhausted than she'd ever been in her life. Every muscle seemed immobilized. The whole day sank down on her all at once, and she felt too weak to even lift an eyelid.

"Hey." He squeezed her shoulder. "Are you all right?"

"Fine," she murmured, and drifted off to sleep.

CHAPTER 16

Mark awoke with a hangover that had nothing to do with alcohol and everything to do with the woman sleeping soundly beside him.

The gray light of dawn slanted through the blinds. The rain had stopped. He glanced at the fan of hair across his arm and felt a sharp pang of guilt.

Mark squeezed his eyes shut. He'd refused her. He'd flown across the country to get away from her. And still he'd managed to end up naked in her bed—a situation he'd never intended to let happen.

Except, of course, in his fantasies. In his fantasies, Allison was naked and smiling and pulling him into bed with her. In his fantasies, her bed was a place where he could forget the chaos and the loneliness and the gut-churning stress that had become his life, a place where he could pound himself into her and get rid of this clawing *need* that had somehow taken hold of him.

But it was no longer a fantasy, because that was exactly what he'd done. And because it was reality instead of a dream, there were consequences.

One of these, apparently, was that all that need he'd hoped to get rid of hadn't gone anywhere.

What the fuck had he been thinking? He couldn't blame it on alcohol. Or even fatigue, really. He'd been tired his whole career, and he'd somehow managed to keep his baser impulses in check until last night.

The smooth, slender thigh resting on his leg shifted, and he looked down at her.

God, she was young. And warm. And so beautiful he didn't want to touch her for fear she'd . . . he didn't know. Vanish, maybe. Along with the faint feeling of contentment he'd been sensing for the past six hours. Mark stared at the ceiling. When was the last time he'd felt this way? When was the last time he'd gone an entire night without getting up to pace or open his laptop or sift through case files? It had been years—since before his troubles with Trisha.

She shifted again, and it was more purposeful now. He needed to get up before this grew awkward. He needed to leave.

Only his body hadn't quite received the "time to go" message his brain was sending.

"Are you always this tense in the morning?"

She propped up on an elbow and looked at him, and he realized she was fully awake. And she was smiling. The slight curve at the corner of her mouth reinforced what her leg was saying—she was feeling playful.

Instead of answering her question, he looked at the clock on the nightstand. "I need to call in."

She laughed. "It's five-fifty."

"Six-fifty in Virginia."

Her brow furrowed. "People actually work at—"

"Yes."

He gently eased her leg off him and got up. He hazarded a glance in her direction as he zipped his pants.

Her eyes were cool, assessing, and she looked tough enough to handle what he had to say.

"How's the shoulder?"

She watched him warily. "Fine."

He didn't believe her, but she was obviously waiting for him to talk about last night. He sat down on the edge of the bed.

"Allison." He picked up her hand. "This can't happen again."

Her eyebrows arched and she pulled her hand away. "Are you seeing someone?"

He hesitated. It would have been a good excuse, but he hadn't laid any groundwork and she'd see right through it.

"No."

"Then what's the problem? And if you say our age difference again, I may have to slap you."

"I live in another state, for one thing."

"And?"

"And you deserve more than just—" He searched for the right word. Came up empty.

"A cheap one-night stand?" She kicked the covers off and threw her legs over the opposite side of the bed. She reached over to her nightstand and snatched up the black lace panties that had mesmerized him last night. He watched her step into them and plunk a hand on her hip defiantly, and he was mesmerized all over again.

"You deserve someone who can be here for you," he said. *Someone who won't screw up your life.*

She laughed dryly. "What I deserve is someone who's man enough to be honest." She jerked a drawer open and grabbed a bra. It was black lace, too, and she wrestled it on. "This isn't about me and what I deserve. It's about you."

He stood up, annoyed with himself for letting this get messy when he should have simply left last night.

Actually, what he should have done was never come over here in the first place.

She advanced on him now, eyes flashing, all skin and lace and temper. And he knew exactly why he'd come, and he also knew that given the chance to do it over again, he'd be just as incapable of staying away.

"You know the really sad thing, Wolfe?"

He had no idea, but he knew better than to guess.

"The sad thing is, you underestimate me. And I thought you were smarter than that." She grabbed a T-shirt off the floor and headed for the bathroom. She stopped in the doorway and turned to look at him.

"Sex isn't the only thing you need, Wolfe. I've never met anyone in such dire need of a friend."

Kelsey took her usual morning dose of caffeine down to her office, and was surprised to see Ben Lawson slouched beside the door. She plastered a smile on her face and braced herself for a conversation she didn't really want to have.

"What brings you down here, Ben? Thought you hated our little bone basement."

"Just thought I'd drop by."

Kelsey let herself into her office, but bypassed her desk and went straight into the lab, where there weren't any chairs to encourage lingering. Ben followed.

"You're in early," he said as she traded her jacket and scarf for a white lab coat. "Again."

She glanced at him, noting the emphasis he'd placed on the last word.

"I've got a lot to do today. I'm running a training session Saturday that I haven't had time to plan yet." She took a swig of her latte, hoping it would somehow manage to wake her up. Meanwhile, Ben glanced around. His gaze paused on the shelves of animal skeletons, and she waited for him to get to the point.

"You doing all right?" He leaned back against the counter and watched her closely. He was in his typical jeans and microbrew T-shirt, but his look at the moment was very parental.

"Fine."

"Because you've seemed kind of . . . distracted. Since you got back from vacation."

Unbelievable. Kelsey's friends hadn't even noticed, and here was Ben Lawson giving her the third degree.

"Well, you know, we've been swamped," she said. "Training workshops. Couple of cold cases. I've hardly had time to sleep."

"Guess that's why you look tired, huh?"

"Is there something you needed?" she asked tersely. "Because I really have a lot to do."

"The Stephanie Snow case," he said. "I hear you're working on it."

Kelsey pursed her lips. He must have heard about Mark and Allison's visit.

"I'm giving them a hand with a cold case that might be connected," she said.

"Rachel Pascal."

"How'd you know?"

"They brought me in on it, too. They're trying to trace the killer through his Web activity."

"Have you found anything?"

"Not a lot," he said. "I'm running down some Web IDs at the moment, but ran into some walls."

"Never known that to stop you before."

"Yeah, well, that's true. Usually when I run into an obstacle, I just hack on through." He smiled. "Kind of like your boyfriend, only using computer code instead of C-4." His smile faded. "Unfortunately, looks like this case is a little more complicated."

Kelsey ignored the mention of Gage, an obvious fishing expedition. Ben and Gage weren't friends—they'd never even met. Kelsey's boyfriend was a Navy SEAL who had been out of the country fighting terrorists for the better part of their relationship.

"And what exactly is it you need?" She glanced at the clock, hoping he'd get the hint.

"GPS coordinates from Rachel Pascal's recovery site."

She watched him, trying to figure what on earth he might do with that information. Who could guess? What Ben lacked in tact he made up for in raw intelligence. The man was rumored to be a genius—possibly the smartest person working at the Delphi Center, which was brimming with brainiacs.

"I figured you'd have them," Ben said, clearly taking

her silence for reluctance. "You use a Garmin every time you do a recovery, right?"

"I've got them." She crossed the lab to the laptop computer she'd left sitting on the counter yesterday. She booted it up and located the file. She hadn't even had a chance to update it yet with the woman's identity. But the date and location of the recovery were listed clearly at the top of her report.

"What do you need with these?" She glanced over her shoulder at Ben, who was fiddling with the midsize mammal bones displayed on one of her shelves.

"Oh, you know. Tossing some ideas around."

"Well, I've got two locations—a cranium and a femur. Both recovered along the Blanco River in northern Evans County. I'll give you the coordinates, but you're going to have to do better than 'tossing some ideas around.' What exactly are you up to?"

He put the skull down and leaned a palm against the counter. "I've been working on this software program. It's called Mind Sweep."

"Catchy name. What does it do?"

He hesitated, and she could tell he was the one uncomfortable in the conversation now.

"You ever heard of geographic profiling?"

"Hmm . . . Don't think so. What is it, like catching criminals based on their victims' locations?"

"That's it in a nutshell. Think of it as one of those old-fashioned wall maps with the stick pins, only it's all computerized. Investigators enter geographic data about connected crimes into a software program. The goal is to find an offender's base of operations—which usually means his home, his workplace, maybe his girlfriend's house."

"They've got software that does this?"

"Depends who you ask." He shrugged. "Basically, what's out there now is complete crap. I've been working on something better. Still getting the kinks out. Haven't got a patent yet or anything."

"I had no idea we had anything like that in development here."

"Most people don't. But this project's been going on for years. It's a natural offshoot of what we do here at the lab."

"How's that?" she asked, and he got that look on his face. Ben became impatient having to explain things to the mere mortals around him.

"Well, the mathematics behind it is complicated. The software is based on various algorithms. The first computer programs were used to prioritize tips and suspects, run address-based searches of criminal records, do neighborhood canvasses—that kind of thing. But the programs had some major faults, including not being based on enough data to link crimes together in a reliable way. The Delphi Center's changing all that. With all the work we're doing here to build out the national DNA database, we're adding thousands and thousands of data points into the system in the form of genetic profiles. You follow?"

Kelsey nodded.

"For example, used to be some detectives in a city might get together and say, 'We think we have a serial rapist operating on the east side of town. We think he's raped five women, and we're guessing he lives or works in the area.' That's so basic, it's essentially common sense. Now with DNA, we can definitively link that same offender to a whole host of crime scenes across different jurisdictions."

"Sounds impressive."

Now he almost looked bashful. "Yeah. I mean, *I* think so, anyway." He glanced up at her. "It's kind of under wraps till the patent comes through. I know I can trust you not to talk about it."

"Sure, no problem. Here are two new 'data points' for your collection." Kelsey took a sticky note and started copying the GPS coordinates as the phone rang at her desk. "I need to get that." She handed him the paper. "Jot those down. And I can send you the full report if you want."

She rushed into the other room and snatched up the phone.

"Osteology."

"I'm calling for Dr. Quinn."

"Speaking."

Silence on the other end. Some people didn't expect a woman, and Kelsey had learned not to let it bother her.

"This is Sheriff Chuck Denton in Wayne County."

"What can I do for you?"

"I've got some deer hunters out here, just stumbled across a bone you need to come see. You're the expert, but looks to me like we got ourselves a leg."

"Actually, what I'll need you to do, Sheriff, is take a photograph of it so I can rule out a nonhuman bone, such as a deer or a cow. Be sure to use a ruler for scale. Or if you don't have one handy, just put a dollar bill in the picture. E-mail me the photo at—"

"Ma'am? Think we can rule out animals in this case."

"You'd be surprised, Sheriff. Oftentimes—"

"All due respect, ma'am, I've dressed my share of deer over the years, and that's not what I'm looking at."

The certainty in his voice filled Kelsey with dread. Wayne County was adjacent to Evans County, where Rachel Pascal had been found.

"Now, I can send the picture if you want," he said, "but I'm telling you right now—this bone I'm looking at is from a person."

A sharp rap at the door startled Allison and made her drop the photo in her hand. She got up to answer the knock, blaming half a pot of coffee and a set of grisly Polaroids for her jumpiness this morning.

She peered through the peephole, hoping to see Mark standing there looking needy and apologetic. But of course, that wasn't what she saw.

She opened the door. "Hi."

Mia stared at her for a moment before stepping inside.

"Come on in," Allison said crossly.

"Why aren't you at work?"

She laughed. "What are you, my truant officer?"

"Ric said you missed the task force meeting."

Allison went into the kitchen.

"Coffee?"

"No," Mia said. She stood at the bar now, about a foot away from the square of counter space Allison had occupied just last night.

Allison topped off her mug of coffee and took it into the living room, where she wouldn't be distracted by memories or crime-scene photos.

"I'm working from home this morning," she said, sinking into a chair.

Mia perched on the sofa arm. She was in her typical cold-weather work attire of a cable-knit sweater and jeans, minus the lab coat.

"Ric's worried about you. He said you were all wired at the station house last night."

Allison put down her mug. "Did you come here from the lab just to check in on me?"

"He also mentioned you had a bruise on your neck that you didn't want to talk about."

Allison sighed.

Mia walked over and stood in front of her. Grudgingly, Allison lifted her chin. Even with a lot of concealer, it was still visible.

"Allison! What happened?"

"Nothing."

"Did Mark Wolfe have something to do with that?"

"God, no." Allison frowned. "Why would you say that?"

"How am I supposed to know what to say?" Mia sank into the nearest chair. "Ever since he came into your life, you've been acting strange. And now you're not at work during a murder case? I've never even known you to take a sick day."

"I'm not sick. I'm just working from home. I'm not getting along with my lieutenant now, and it's easier to avoid him." Or rather, avoid a conversation about her prison interview until she figured out exactly what Mark and the warden had told him. She was pretty sure she knew what the warden would say—nothing. He didn't want the bad publicity any more than she did. But Mark was a wild card. He'd been very upset last night.

Among other things.

"Well?" Mia was still looking at her expectantly.

"Well, what?"

She rolled her eyes. "Are you going to tell me what happened?"

"I had a little scuffle."

"With David Moss," Mia stated.

Allison didn't respond.

"The convicted *rapist* and *murderer*."

"I'd really appreciate it if you'd drop it, Mia. I don't need any more crap from the guys at work."

Mia looked down and folded her hands in her lap. She knew how it was working in a male-dominated field. But she was also a concerned friend, and Allison didn't need her running to her fiancé and feeding him stories that would reinforce anyone's ideas about Allison being incompetent. It was bad enough Mark probably thought less of her after everything that had happened.

"Look, Allison." Mia met her gaze. "I really don't want to meddle in your life—"

"Then don't."

"Okay." She paused. "I understand. I'll downplay it with Ric. But are you sure—just between you and me— are you sure you're really all right?"

"Fine."

"And Mark? Is he fine, too?"

"I don't know. He was fine this morning when he left here."

It was a risk, putting it out there like that. But Allison hoped confiding in her friend at least a little would keep her from worrying too much. And anyway, Mia was good at reading her. She knew there was something going on in Allison's love life.

Love life. Yeah, right. As if a one-night hookup constituted a love life. It was ridiculous. But considering the hookup had been with Mark, it somehow wasn't. He was a serious person—possibly the most serious person Allison had ever known. And she doubted he took anything lightly, including sex. Maybe the intensity of it was what had freaked him out. It sure as hell was freaking *her* out. She'd been thinking about it all day.

And she'd been thinking about him, too. Not just the sex, but the man—the one who'd fixed her truck and helped her make spaghetti and lifted a two-hundred-pound assailant off her and heaved him against the wall as if he weighed nothing. When she'd first met Mark in that convenience store, he'd seemed larger than life, like a superhero, and she'd expected him to shrink to normal size as she got to know him. But if anything, the opposite had happened. The more she knew him, the bigger impression he made. And glimpsing his humanity—such as when he interviewed Jordan or when he lost his temper yesterday—only made her like him more.

Allison bit her lip, disgusted with herself. She knew better than to do this. If she wasn't careful here, she was going to get her heart pulverized. A relationship with Mark Wolfe was not an option. He'd made that abundantly clear.

And crap, now Mia was staring at her, more concerned than ever.

"Are you sure you're okay?" she asked. "I mean, really. That bruise looks awful."

"I'm fine." Allison stood up and looked at her watch. "But I'm actually leaving soon to follow up on some things."

Mia took the hint and stood to go. "You're still working on the Stephanie Snow case?"

"Absolutely." Allison walked her to the door. "I've got an appointment up in Waynesboro in an hour."

Mia looked at her over her shoulder. "Are you meeting Kelsey?"

"Meeting her where?"

"In Waynesboro. Your appointment."

"Why is Kelsey in Waynesboro?"

"I just got off the phone with her," Mia said. "She's been up there all morning digging up bones."

CHAPTER 17

———◦◦◦———

Kelsey hunched over the grave site in the biting cold, using a small bamboo spatula to free a bone from the earth.

"You try the plastic trowel?"

She glanced up into the face of her assistant. As her most experienced graduate student, Aaron made a habit of not only helping out on her digs, but offering advice when he disagreed with her methods. Kelsey didn't care much for criticism, but she'd learned to listen to him because he had good ideas.

She swapped the bamboo tool for the plastic one. When unearthing a possible homicide victim, it was critical to use non-metal tools that wouldn't leave marks on the bone that could later be misinterpreted as coming from a murder weapon.

"How's the sifting going?" she asked.

"Wet."

Which meant that instead of simply sifting the debris through their screens—which would have been time-consuming enough—they had to run water over each batch to rinse away mud. If they had had access to a hose, that would have been one thing, but out here in the sticks, the water supply consisted of five-gallon buckets that had been transported by pickup truck from a nearby creek. Grad students with frozen fingers poured pitchers over each and every screen in the hopes of finding bits of bone or pieces of evidence.

Kelsey glanced over at the huddle of students.

"There any coffee left?" she asked.

"That was gone hours ago."

Kelsey would have to drum up some more, even if it meant taking a break from digging to go inside the trailer and brew a pot herself. Her team had been at it for hours in the miserable chill, and she was worried about morale. Low morale led to distraction and distraction led to missed evidence. Missed evidence was unacceptable when an entire murder trial might hinge on a lump of chewing gum or a scrap of clothing.

Kelsey bent back over her work. She'd get to the coffee later, as soon as she finished this ulna. She was almost to the hand, where she hoped to find something that would help with an ID, such as a class ring or a wedding band. Engraved jewelry was a forensic anthropologist's buried treasure.

A chorus of barks went up from the base camp, where the cadaver dogs were resting. She glanced over her shoulder and saw an unmarked police unit bumping over the field. Allison was in the passenger seat and it looked like Jonah Macon behind the wheel.

"SMPD," she told Aaron.

Kelsey got to her feet, wincing as she straightened her abused knees for the first time in hours. Even the volleyball knee pads she always wore did little to combat the soreness. Human patellas weren't designed to bear weight for hours at a time.

A sheriff's deputy met the two detectives at the car, and Kelsey watched them flash a pair of badges.

Aaron looked at her. "Not good news, I'm guessing?"

"No."

There was only one reason for these two to show up at a burial site nearly fifty miles outside their jurisdiction.

The deputy nodded in Kelsey's direction and they tromped over. Kelsey glanced at Aaron, who as a grad student wasn't supposed to be privy to all the investigative details. "You mind getting another pot of coffee going?" she asked him.

Aaron gave her a sour look and headed off to the RV. Kelsey stepped over the yellow twine that cordoned off the grave site.

"What do we have?" Jonah got straight to the point.

"Some hunters were cutting across that clearing and came across a femur." Kelsey pulled out her mittens. Her fingers felt like icicles, and the woolen gloves she wore for digging had the tips snipped off for better dexterity. "About eight-thirty this morning, I confirmed it was human. The sheriff got the cadaver dogs out here and zeroed in on this grave."

"Hunters again." Allison glanced at Jonah. "You think there's any significance to that? It's the second victim found near a deer lease."

"Practically this whole county is a deer lease," Jonah said.

"I wouldn't read too much into that," Kelsey said. "It's not uncommon for hunters to find bones this time of year. They often travel with dogs and tromp around in areas that don't otherwise get a lot of traffic."

"Who owns this land?" Allison asked.

"Some rancher. He's got a couple thousand acres transected by a highway, from what I understand."

"Full skeleton?" Jonah asked.

"Looks like."

"Recent?"

"In my world, that's a relative term. The rotted bits of clothing we're finding are probably from the past few years." She looked at Allison. "Women's clothing," she said, anticipating her friend's question.

"How'd the femur get way over there?" Jonah asked.

"The grave's about two feet deep. A heavy rain could have removed some of the topsoil, then scavengers got to it. There are teeth marks on the bone. The canine team also recovered a few foot bones."

Jonah stepped closer and examined the excavation area. "Isn't that pretty shallow?"

"You're the detectives, but I'm guessing someone was in a rush."

Another chorus of barks as a second sedan pulled up—a blue Taurus. Special Agent Wolfe climbed out and flashed his creds at the deputy.

Allison cut a glance at Jonah. "You call him?"

"Nope."

Everyone watched as the agent trekked across the muddy field. He wore a trench coat and a stern expression, and he couldn't have looked more out of place on a Texas prairie. Kelsey sighed. She didn't like a lot of cops at her recovery scenes. They weren't qualified to dig, so all they really added were more pairs of feet possibly trampling evidence.

"Who called you?" Allison asked when he reached them.

"Ben Lawson." Mark nodded at Kelsey. "Another female?"

"Looks like. Is the *entire* task force planning to come? I think we're fresh out of doughnuts."

Mark ignored Kelsey's sarcasm. "How long to get her out of there?"

"Five, maybe six more hours," Kelsey said. "Anyway, how do you know this is connected to your case?"

"We have reason to believe our killer has ties to Waynesboro, that he may be living there," Mark said. "In fact, Ben tells me this is right in his sweet spot."

"What the hell does Ben know about it?" Allison asked.

"He's creating a geoprofile," Mark replied without looking at her. He glanced at Jonah instead. "It's a computer-based map showing where the killer is likely to live or work."

"But I thought your other victims were merely dumped, not buried," Kelsey said.

"It's an important change in MO," Mark said. "He spent a lot of time hiding this victim, which leads me to think he knows this one. There could be some personal connection that would point us to him. How soon can we get an ID?"

"Well, first I need to get the remains unearthed, and this weather is not exactly ideal. Then I'll get a bone sample to Mia for comparison with samples of known missing persons—of which there are none currently on record in this county, according to the sheriff."

"None at all?" Jonah asked.

"No females. Looks like you guys have some work ahead of you."

"How much longer on the digging part?" Mark asked, and Kelsey was starting to get annoyed. Typical fed, he showed up with his fancy badge and suit and expected everything done yesterday.

"Well, it'd be a lot quicker if I had a backhoe. Thing is, heavy machinery tends to destroy evidence. We use this instead." She held up a bamboo tool the size of a teaspoon.

Three faces frowned at her.

"The excavation process is slow and tedious," Kelsey said. "But it has to be done right or critical items get missed. You'd be surprised how many people take a smoke break after they dig a grave, then toss the butt inside right before the body. Or sometimes they toss in condom wrappers that they opened with their teeth while they were holding down a struggling victim. Those things tend to be sources of DNA, which we try to hang on to whenever we can."

Kelsey knew she sounded bitchy, but she was cold, sore, and hungry, and she had about eight hours' worth of work to cram into a five-hour window of daylight.

"Our guy's too smart for that," Allison said. "He wouldn't leave condom wrappers."

"Really? Because most of the trials I've testified at involve guys who *think* they're smart, but actually they're careless and in a hurry."

"You already have the femur," Mark said. "What if you take a break from your digging to get a bone sample to the DNA lab?"

Kelsey looked at him. Everyone's gaze settled on her, and she felt the combined tension of three tightly wound detectives. She was used to dealing with tightly wound detectives, but there was something particularly tense about these three.

"We have less than forty-eight hours left to locate this perpetrator before he makes his next kill," Mark said. "I think he personally knew this victim, or he wouldn't have bothered to bury her. If we get her identity, it will likely point us to a location."

Kelsey nodded, feeling guilty now for giving them a hard time. "I can get you the Big Four by this evening— race, sex, age, stature. The rest is up to Mia. If I get her a bone sample within the hour—"

A whistle went up near the RV camp. Kelsey glanced over and saw Aaron waving at her.

"Excuse me." She hurried across the grass, knowing from his body language that he'd discovered something important.

Aaron stood beside the screen setup, where grad students had been rinsing debris for the past two hours. He looked excited, but the students huddled around him with their water pitchers appeared baffled.

"Check it out." He pointed at the screen.

Kelsey immediately spotted what had caught his attention. She crouched down and picked up a small silver object from amid the leaves and twigs.

"What is it?"

She turned around to see Allison peering over her shoulder. Mark and Jonah were right behind her.

"A prosthetic patella."

Blank looks.

She turned the object over and pointed to the tiny, barely visible serial number that had been stamped on it by the manufacturer. It would link to a database, which would link to a specific doctor and a specific procedure.

"She had a knee replacement." Kelsey held up the piece of titanium. "Run down this serial number and you'll find the name of the victim."

They gathered in the war room, where yet another young woman's picture had been added to their wall of photographs. Meredith Devins, thirty-eight, of San Antonio, who had been reported missing by her husband last fall.

She'd gone missing one day after Jordan Wheatley's attack.

Following Kelsey's suggestions, Allison and Jonah had spent yesterday afternoon tracking down the artificial knee, which had led them to the victim's identity. Their luck hadn't held out, though, and all the other leads the task force had been following yesterday had netted them nothing.

And meanwhile, the clock was ticking.

"Gotta say, I think Wolfe's right about this one." Sean stood beside the victim wall and surveyed the pictures. "She's different from all the rest. Older, short hair. She wasn't out jogging at the time of her abduction."

"Maybe he needed a substitute when Jordan Wheatley didn't turn out like he wanted," Ric said. "He could have seen on the news that a jogger was attacked in that nature park and survived. Maybe he just grabbed the next woman he saw, no planning."

Allison wasn't sure she bought into the theory. But

if it was true, then it made sense that the killer actually knew this victim and explained why he'd gone to some effort to hide the body, unlike before. The woman had worked as a librarian on the outskirts of San Antonio. Had Damien Moss visited this library and known the woman personally? Had he been in there frequently using their computers?

Mark had gone to the library yesterday and flashed the suspect sketch around. One staffer said he looked "familiar" but that they got hundreds of people a week in and out of their doors. And the place was open to the public, no library card required unless someone wanted to check out material.

"We should stake out her workplace," Jonah said from the other end of the conference table. He was poring over a stack of e-mails that had been printed out from Stephanie Snow's account, hoping to figure out how she'd crossed paths with her killer.

"Think Wolfe's already there," Sean said.

Allison shifted in her seat. She hadn't seen Mark all morning. Or last night, for that matter. She'd foolishly allowed herself to hope he might come over at the end of their grueling workday, but of course he hadn't. Her doorbell and her phone had remained silent and she'd gone to bed alone.

She glanced around the table now and realized everyone was looking at her.

"What?"

"You know where he is?" Sean asked pointedly.

"No. Do you?"

He gave her a baleful look and turned back to the

board. "Okay, what about hunting licenses? That lead pan out?"

"What hunting licenses?" Allison asked.

"David Moss told you his brother likes to hunt," Jonah said. "I figure maybe he applied for a license with Parks and Wildlife."

"That doesn't mesh with the profile," she pointed out. "Wolfe specifically said he doesn't like to interface with government institutions, he doesn't like to get anybody's permission to do his thing."

"Yeah, well, the game warden doesn't give a damn what he likes," Jonah said. "Those guys are more powerful than God. They can go onto anyone's property without a search warrant and demand ID from any hunter they see. And they dole out hefty fines. If Damien Moss hunted around here, he probably wouldn't want to risk drawing attention to himself by hunting without a license."

It was a thought. Allison still wasn't sure it had potential, but they were getting desperate now. Time was running out for getting a location on this guy and bringing him in.

The phone in the conference room rang, and Ric grabbed it. "Santos." He looked at Allison. "Yeah, we're in a meeting right now. I'll put you on speaker."

Ric shoved the phone to the middle of the table. "It's Roland over at Delphi. He said he was running some trace evidence for you."

"Hey, I got those results back." Roland's voice came over the phone line.

Jonah looked at Allison. "What'd we send to Roland?"

"Jordan Wheatley's clothing. It was collected with her rape kit."

"So, Allison told me the victim reported smelling paint in the van where she was attacked," Roland informed them. "I looked at her clothes under the stereomicroscope, and she was right, that's exactly what I found: paint residue. Lots of colored spheres, no bigger than the head of a pin."

"What kind of paint?" Sean asked. "We talking house paint?"

"That's the thing that caught my attention. Even at a glance, I could tell it's not house paint. Not unless he's painting Walt Disney's house. This is a rainbow of colors. Stuff you wouldn't see on a house. And not only that, the spherical shape is typical of aerosol paint, which forms spheres when it floats in the air and then adheres to surfaces."

"The kind of paint used for graffiti?" Sean asked.

"Higher quality than that. This stuff's more expensive."

"Help me out here," Allison said. "You're saying he paints things *inside* the van?"

"No, but maybe he grabbed a drop cloth from wherever he does paint, put it on the floor of the vehicle. Maybe if he was trying to keep blood off the floor? Or for easy cleanup?"

"Damn, that's cold," Sean said.

"So, anyway, these polymers I saw are commonly found in decorative paints. Think signs, metal furniture, that sort of thing."

"Car paint?" Ric asked.

"Not cars," Roland said. "That's a whole different kind of paint."

"So our guy maybe works in some kind of paint shop," Allison summarized. "Or knows someone who does, and that's where he got the drop cloth. It's a decent lead." She was already firing up her laptop to search for sign-painting businesses anywhere between here and San Antonio. Their target area now included four counties.

"That's not all," Roland said. "It wasn't just paint I found on her clothes, but very fine dust. Looked at it under a microscope, turns out it's glass. And this isn't just any glass; it's a special kind of safety glass. The stuff they use in fancy shower doors, things like that."

"Shower doors?" Ric straightened in his chair and reached across the table for a thick manila folder. "Shit, hold on." He started flipping through the file.

Allison leaned closer. "What's that?"

"List of green or white vans in all four counties we're looking at." Ric flipped through the pages. "I struck out with the name 'Moss' but I've got a 'Thompson' here who has a green van registered to his business. *Shit*, look at this: Thompson Shower and Bath Solutions, 646 Mesquite Creek Road." Ric looked at Allison. "That's in Waynesboro."

Jonah whistled. "Best lead we've had all day."

"Hey, Roland, I owe you one." Allison got to her feet and grabbed her coat. "Let's go."

Mark was operating on almost no sleep and didn't have time for coffee. And yet he entered Home Depot at precisely ten a.m. and went straight to the lumber aisle, as he'd been instructed. It smelled like sawdust, and he couldn't resist running his hand over the pile of smooth two-by-fours stacked waist-high about midway down the aisle.

"Agent Wolfe."

He turned around and saw Jordan walking toward him with Maximus at her side. She wore jeans and a canvas barn jacket. Mark noted the green scarf wrapped around her neck and wondered if she wore it to keep out the cold or to hide her scar.

Maximus strained against his leash and wagged his tail as they reached him. Mark petted the dog's head as Jordan held out an oversized cup from Starbucks.

"Black," she said. "This is the biggest they had. Figured you'd need it."

"Thank you." He took the cup and rested it on the pile of lumber. "This is a first for me. Don't think I've ever been invited to breakfast at Home Depot."

"Yeah, well, most places don't like dogs." She rubbed Maximus between the ears. "I've thought about getting one of those harnesses and people would think he's a service dog. Because he sort of is."

Mark looked at her and tried to conceal his pity. When he'd first seen her car covered with dust and leaves, he'd figured she was practically a shut-in. She seemed to be confirming that.

"But . . . ?" he prompted.

She arched her brows at him as she took a sip of her coffee.

"You were thinking of getting a harness, but . . . ?"

She set her cup down beside his. "I don't know. It's

like saying I have a disability." She shook her head. "In some ways I guess I do, but I'm not ready to give in to that."

Mark was glad to hear it. This woman's life had been decimated, but she was still fighting. He wondered how much courage it had taken her just to come out here today, even with a protective German shepherd at her side.

She stared down at their coffee cups, and Mark waited for her to tell him what she needed.

"Look, I can imagine how busy you must be today." She glanced up at him. "I know what tomorrow is."

He waited.

"Still no arrest?"

"No."

She nodded. "I figured I would have seen it on the news." She cleared her throat. "I was watching this morning. I saw the coverage about that woman from San Antonio. Meredith Devins." She looked at him somberly, and Mark knew what she was going to ask him even before she said it. "I need you to tell me—do you think he killed her because he didn't kill me?"

Mark gazed down at her. He couldn't bring himself to lie to her, but he didn't want to burden her with what he believed to be the truth, either.

She looked down and closed her eyes. "That's what I thought."

"We don't know for sure why he killed her. We only know that she was abducted the day after you were."

"It's okay. I just—" She shook her head as her eyes welled with tears. "I just needed to know. I feel responsible. I realize that doesn't make sense, but still it's how I feel."

"Jordan." Mark waited for her to look at him. "You can't do that to yourself. You can't take that on."

For a few moments, she simply looked away and seemed to be trying to compose herself. Then she met his gaze. "Sometimes it amazes me," she said. "How one person can be so destructive. Can ruin so many lives. Ever since it happened, I've had this huge inadequacy thing. I can't stop thinking about it."

"How do you mean?"

"It's this feeling of . . . not being worthy. That maybe my life was spared for some kind of reason, only I have no idea what it is. Some days I can barely get out of bed, and I don't know why God would choose *me* over someone else, someone who's a much better person than I am."

God didn't choose you—Damien Moss did. Mark wanted to tell her that, but he didn't want to quibble with her religious beliefs.

"It's like he pried this door open into my life, and I can't get away from him," she went on. "There are times I'm outside, in my garden, and I feel like he's watching me. And I feel like that in my bed in the middle of the night, like I'll open my eyes and see him standing in the doorway." She shook her head. "One time I even thought I saw him in the window, standing out on our deck, and I *totally* flipped out."

Mark went on alert. "You saw him at your home?"

She looked at him with watery eyes. "No, I just *thought* I did, but of course it was nothing. See, it's like I'm going crazy. I'm so scared all the time, and I can't tell anyone because they'll think I'm unstable or something. And then I get so *angry*." She clenched her hand into a fist. "And it's like he's destroying my life all over again, every day I give in to it. Every day I let myself be too afraid to even do anything. I used to be so blissfully ignorant, so *stupid*. And now I wish I had that back."

Mark frowned down at her. Much of what she was describing could result from post-traumatic stress disorder. But what if there was more to it? What if Damien Moss was, in fact, still stalking her?

She produced a tissue from the pocket of her jacket and dabbed the end of her nose. She looked up at him. "Do you have kids?"

The question caught him off guard. "No."

"I used to want children more than anything. Back before . . . what happened, we'd been trying for a year." She looked away. "Now I don't know. I'm not sure I have the heart for it. Too many what-ifs." She looked at him. "Do you know what I mean?"

Her gaze was so direct—it was as though she could read his mind. *Too many what-ifs.* In a few simple words, she'd just articulated the reason he'd never caved in to Trisha's relentless pressure, even though it had cost him his marriage.

"I know what you mean," he said.

She looked away again. She took a deep breath. "I think my husband's planning to leave me."

Mark didn't say anything.

"I'm not sure I blame him."

He watched her, uncomfortable now, and not only because she was dumping her marital problems on him.

"Jordan . . ." He waited for her to meet his gaze. "Your instincts, they're always a response to something. They always have your best interests at heart. Don't discount that, no matter who tells you you're paranoid."

She smiled slightly. "So, you think he *is* leaving?"

"I'm talking about your safety. If you ever get that feeling—if you ever truly feel threatened—you shouldn't ignore it."

The stark look on her face made him feel guilty. He'd probably set her recovery back by months. But she needed to understand this.

"You think he's coming back?"

"I think we're going to find him before he hurts anyone else." They'd never been *so* close, and Mark was more determined than ever. "But I'm also a big believer in caution. You should take commonsense safety measures. Keep your doors locked when you're at home. Keep Maximus with you. Be wary of strangers. All the basic stuff you already do now."

She nodded, looking somewhat numb.

"You don't need to go around in a panic all the time, because that's not helpful, just exhausting. But if there *is* something to worry about, your brain gives you signals. You don't have anything to be afraid of until you *actually* feel fear." He stopped to make sure she was listening. "Does that make sense?"

"The only thing I should fear is . . . fear itself?"

"That's exactly it," he told her. "And if your instincts start yelling at you, sit up and listen."

CHAPTER 18

Mark was still thinking about Jordan an hour later when he should have been giving his full attention to the demonstration going on in front of him at the Delphi Center.

"And that's been the primary problem with these software programs in the past," Ben Lawson was saying. "Garbage in, garbage out. But in this case, the opposite is true. Quality data in, and you get quality results."

The Pub Scout—who today was sporting a faded Fat Tire Ale T-shirt—sat before his bank of computers, demonstrating one of the most impressive law enforcement software programs Mark had ever seen. Ben had somehow managed to combine practically every lead available in the Death Raven case, feed it into a program he'd developed, and come up with a map showing the killer's most likely places of work or residence.

Ben glanced back at Mark with a peculiar look on his face. It was pride mixed with . . . hope, Mark realized. This boy genius, who could run circles around the most gifted cyber-crime analysts on Mark's FBI team, was seeking his approval. As was happening more and more these days, Mark found himself playing the role of mentor to a cadre of investigators who seemed to be getting younger every day.

Or maybe it wasn't that the investigators were getting younger, but that Mark was getting older—not just in age, but in outlook.

"So?" Ben looked up at him expectantly. "What do you think?"

Christ, now he was supposed to give him a grade?

"I've never seen anything like it," Mark said truthfully.

"That's because there *isn't* anything like it," Ben said, full of youthful hubris now. Mark had lost that years ago, after hundreds of heart-wrenching cases had taken their toll. He no longer thought he was Superman. But that didn't stop him from getting up to do his job every day and seeking justice for the victims in each and every one of his cases.

"It's impressive," Mark said, leaning closer to get a look at the map. "What do the three orange triangles mean?"

"Those are my best leads, given our current data." He pointed to the color-coded map, in which cool-colored zones marked areas where the suspect wasn't likely to work or reside, and warm-colored zones marked areas considered high probability.

"The entire town of Waynesboro is a red zone," Ben explained, "but there are three locations *within* that area that became 'flagged' after I entered all the vehicle data."

Mark reached over to the mouse and clicked on one of the triangles, and a text box popped up showing an address.

"According to the state database, someone at all three of those addresses owns a green Chrysler minivan," Ben said.

"I want all three," Mark said, scribbling down the first one.

"These first two are residences and the vehicles are actually under women's names, but who knows if there's a man living in the house? Third address is a business: Thompson Shower and Bath Solutions."

"Sounds like remodeling," Mark said, feeling a faint buzz of excitement.

"They make and install custom bath enclosures," Ben said. "I called over there this morning—you know, just a casual inquiry. They also do bathroom renovations."

"Including paint?"

"I didn't get that far. But you said your guy might be working construction, so I figure it's a pretty good lead."

Mark finished jotting the three addresses and tore off the sheet of paper. "You figured right."

Allison sped down the highway, feeling the buzz of anticipation that came with a fresh lead.

"How will we know which house?" she asked Jonah, who was sitting beside her in the passenger seat.

"I'm hoping for a truck out front. Or maybe a sign in the yard."

Allison's phone chimed and she checked the number.

"Hey, where are you?" she asked. "I've been trying to reach you all morning."

"I've got a lead on something," Mark said. "There's a remodeling company in Waynesboro. I'm headed there now—"

"Thompson Shower and Bath. We were just there."

Silence.

"Mark?"

"Who's 'we'?" he wanted to know.

"Jonah and I. We interviewed the owner."

"And what exactly was your plan?"

"Um, maybe get some questions answered? What was yours?"

Mark didn't reply, so she kept going. "The owner said he hired a Damien Moss last fall to do some tile work. And get this, Thompson—the owner—says Damien asked to borrow his van a few times to haul some furniture when he moved. The owner has a *green* Chrysler minivan registered to his business."

More silence, and she could practically feel Mark's disapproval coming through the phone.

"He no longer works for Thompson," she said, "but the foreman there thinks he's doing some work for one of the local builders. We're on our way over there."

"You have a warrant in hand?"

"No."

"It ever occur to you to get one before you go off beating the bushes, sending our prime suspect back into hiding for a decade or so?"

"Listen, Wolfe—"

"You need to let the Bureau handle this. I've got an undercover team already en route."

"En route where?" She couldn't believe what she was hearing.

"They're headed to Thompson's," Mark said, "posing as building inspectors so they can get a look around, see if he's on the premises."

"Well, he's not. He's at a job site, which is where *we're* headed, so tell your guys to take off."

"Damien Moss has crossed state lines, as well as county lines, to evade police. This is a federal case. And I don't appreciate your going off half-cocked without checking with me."

"How am I supposed to check with you when you ignore my calls? You're avoiding me, which is so damn unprofessional, it makes me want to scream and—" She glanced over and noticed Jonah was watching her. This was just what she *hadn't* wanted to happen.

"I haven't been avoiding you," Mark said. "I've been working, like everyone else on this task force."

"Whatever." She didn't want to argue the point right now. She felt too emotional about it. "Anyway, we're not going to spook him, all right? We aren't even going to approach him. Not yet. We just need to get him in our sights."

"Pull over."

"What?"

"You heard me. Pull over."

"You can't just bark orders at me. I don't work for you."

"Allison." His voice was tight, as if he was down to the end of his patience. "He knows me, and he probably knows *you*, if he's been following the case. You can't go waltzing up to some construction site asking for him. Let our agents do it. They're in coveralls and they're driving a van. They can be plumbers, electricians, carpet layers. They can be anybody."

She didn't respond.

"Tell me where you are, and I'll meet you," he said.

She sighed, mainly because he was right. His plan was better. Ric and Sean were still back at Thompson's checking out the minivan. And the last thing she wanted to do was send the suspect into hiding.

"We're almost to the neighborhood," she said. "Walnut Glen. It's on the south side of town. West of the interstate."

Grudgingly, she checked her mirror and cut over to the right lane as Jonah frowned at her. She turned into a gas station.

"I'm waiting at the Exxon," she told Mark, then clicked off.

She was too steamed to deal with Jonah right now, so she pulled up to a pump and started getting gas. But the veteran detective wouldn't be put off. He got out and leaned against the truck bed as she watched the numbers scroll on the pump.

"Change of plan?" he asked.

"He wants his agents on this."

"*His* agents?"

Allison shook her head. "I don't know. He's got a team together, it sounds like."

"So you just handed over our case."

She looked at him. "We don't have jurisdiction here, Jonah, and we both know it."

"I don't need jurisdiction to go for a drive. And I don't need some fed telling me how to run an investigation."

"And if we spot Moss, then what?"

"Then we have a bead on him, finally. We shadow him until the warrant comes through."

The gas pump clicked off. She hadn't needed much fuel anyway. She jerked the nozzle free.

"So now we have some help. What's the harm?" God, was she really defending Mark now?

Jonah shook his head. "Drinking the Kool-Aid."

"What's that supposed to mean?"

He nodded at the car turning into the lot. "Here he is."

Mark pulled his car up alongside them and got out. He was in another dark suit today—no trench coat—and Allison was immediately struck by how good he looked. For the first time, it occurred to her that maybe he had ulterior motives for letting something intimate develop between them. Look how easily she'd relinquished control when it was time for an arrest. But it wasn't because she didn't care—it was because she knew how vitally important this case was to him and she trusted him to do what was best here. She *trusted* him.

And wasn't that convenient? Maybe she *was* drinking the Kool-Aid.

"Where's the neighborhood?" Mark asked, scanning the surrounding area.

Jonah nodded south. "Right over there. We got word he's on a job with Tall Tex Tile Company."

Mark pulled out his phone and turned around. He had a low, brief conversation with someone and hung up.

"We still don't have a warrant," Mark said.

"We could get one," Allison pointed out, "if we wait for him to discard something that would prove the DNA link—a cigarette butt, a soda can, maybe even a slice of pizza, like that case in Los Angeles."

"No time for that," Mark said.

"Then we get him under surveillance," she said, and Mark glared at her.

"I don't want him under surveillance," he said. "I want him in custody."

"He's not going to do anything with us watching—"

"Unless we lose him," Mark countered.

"I'm not planning to lose him. Are you?"

He gave her a heated look and turned to Jonah. "You were in this vehicle when you pulled up to Thompson's?"

"Yeah. Ric and Sean are still back there, looking at that van."

"And what were they driving?"

"An unmarked unit," Allison said.

"Perfect," Mark said. "So, we can assume everyone at that business knows some cops stopped by looking for Damien Moss. Let's just hope he doesn't have any buddies calling him with a tip-off right now."

Allison's temper flared. "What did you want us to do, Wolfe? Ignore the lead? We're talking *hours* left until his next attack. I'm not about to just sit on my hands here!"

"Allison, you don't need to prove to me how tough you are. I already know."

"This isn't about you. I have a commitment to my job, my community. Can't you understand that?"

Jonah eased between them like a referee. "This isn't helping anything." He looked at Mark. "What's the ETA on that team of yours?"

"Probably three minutes. And I've got another agent in a second vehicle as backup."

"Fine," Jonah said. "Let's both of us go find an inconspicuous place to camp out near the entrance to the neighborhood in case something goes sideways."

Mark returned to his car. Allison stalked around the

front of her truck and fired up the engine. She pulled away before Jonah had even closed the door.

"You need to lose the emotion," he told her. "It's not helping today."

Allison swallowed the bitter lump. He was right. But she couldn't get past the idea that maybe, just *maybe*, Mark was trying to sideline the locals so the FBI could take credit for the big arrest.

She neared the neighborhood marked by a redbrick sign: WALNUT GLEN. Over the scrub brush surrounding the neighborhood's perimeter, Allison saw dozens of homes in various stages of completion.

"How are they going to find him in there?" she wondered aloud. "Every house is a job site."

"They're feds. Figure they'll use their X-ray vision."

Allison shot him a look. He didn't like being elbowed aside by a federal agent any more than she did.

Of course, without Mark, they'd probably still be trying to build a case against Stephanie Snow's ex.

Allison spied the only logical place to park inconspicuously: the dark shadow of an oak tree on the street that intersected the subdivision's entrance road. A taco vendor had set up under a similar patch of shade nearby and was busy selling snacks to laborers.

Allison took out her cell and called Mark. "Okay, we're at the entrance to the neighborhood near a taco truck. Where are you?"

"North side. There's a dirt road being used by heavy machinery. I'll keep an eye on it. The team's on its way in."

At that moment a white van came into view. It looked generic in every way.

"Acme Services?" she asked Mark.

"That's us."

The sign was magnetic, she guessed. They probably kept it in back with some other generic signs. She figured they also had a bunch of surveillance equipment in back—stuff that budget-strapped departments like hers and Jonah's could only dream about.

Allison's phone beeped. She checked the screen.

"I've got a call coming in from Ric. Let me let you go." She hung up on him and clicked over. "What's up?"

"We nailed it." Ric's voice was tinged with excitement.

"What, the van?"

"We got dried blood in the crevices of the door track. It's right here, staring at us. We gotta get this to the lab."

Jonah sent her a questioning look.

"Blood in the van," she explained as her heart sped up. "Wolfe's going to want it," she told Ric.

"He's gonna have to duke it out with Sheriff Denton. He's already got this thing loaded on a flatbed and headed for the Delphi Center. You find Moss yet?"

"Still working on it."

"He's our man, Doyle. Sheriff's getting the arrest warrant right now. Whatever you do, don't lose sight of him."

"I won't." She clicked off and turned to Jonah. "Sheriff's involved. Van's on its way to Delphi."

"Now we just need to bag up our perp."

"Easier said than done."

Allison stared through the windshield, growing antsier by the second. Blood in the van. They had their crime scene. They had their UNSUB. Suddenly their whole case was coming together after days and days of maddening dead ends.

Allison drummed her fingers on the steering wheel. Tension gathered in her neck and shoulders as the minutes crawled by. She scanned the workers waiting in line for tacos, noting the height and build of each one. She had binoculars in her toolbox, but she didn't want to draw attention to their setup by climbing out to get them.

"Third guy from the end," Jonah said. "What do you think?"

Allison considered him. "Not tall enough."

"Why not? Wolfe said maybe Jordan Wheatley exaggerated his size because she was afraid."

Allison shook her head. "Not that much. Jordan's tall herself. He's barely five-five."

Her phone chimed and she snatched it out of the cup holder.

"We think we spotted the house," Mark said, and the "we" grated on Allison's nerves. "There's a Tall Tex Tile truck out front. Place is swarming with workers, most of them on scaffolding doing exterior paint. The tile guys are probably inside, working on bathrooms or kitchens."

"And what's the plan?"

"Our agents are posing as building inspectors. They're going to go in on some pretext about permits and have a look around. They've seen the suspect sketch as well as Damien's driver's license picture from California."

"He was a teenager then."

"It's still something."

"Where's this house?"

"There's a street that loops around the whole neighborhood, spits out at the entrance street. This house is five lots in, facing north."

Allison squinted through the windshield and counted rooftops. "Two-story? Big oak tree in back?"

"I don't know. I'm not looking at it. Just a sec, I'm getting something from the team." Mark's voice faded and she heard static in the background. He was on the radio with someone, and Allison would like to be listening in on the frequency, but her pickup didn't have a police radio.

"Okay, we got a guy in the front yard, cutting tile. He's wearing eye shields, so they're not sure, but it could be him."

"Description." Allison looked at Jonah.

"White male, six-one, one-fifty, black T-shirt, blue jeans, red bandana hanging out of his pocket."

Allison watched the back of the house. There was no fence yet, but her view of the first floor was mostly obscured by scrub brush. A man in a gray hoodie stepped through the trees and headed across the field. He had his hands in his pockets and walked with his head down, shoulders hunched forward. He cast a glance behind him, and Allison looked at Jonah.

"We've got another possibility," she told Mark. "White male, about six feet, one-seventy, gray hooded sweatshirt. Proceeding away from the house toward the entrance of the subdivision."

"He's on foot?"

"Yes."

More static as Mark conferred with his team.

"The guy cutting tile still looks good," he said over the phone. "Our agent's trying to get a name right now."

The man in the hoodie neared a blue Porta-Potty at the end of the street. He walked past it.

"Let's see if he's hungry," Jonah muttered.

Allison watched, her heart rate climbing with every step the man took away from the neighborhood. He did nothing obvious—no more backward glances or furtive looks around. But still, there was something in his posture, something very purposeful about the way he was walking away from that house. The man neared the taco line. He passed it.

Allison started the engine. The guy continued down the street, which was nothing but an empty cul-de-sac. Beyond the last lot was a utility easement and then a long row of fences marking another neighborhood.

"Pull out," Jonah said, and Allison was already shifting into gear.

"Wolfe, this guy's heading away from the neighborhood, no transportation in sight. He's walking down a dead-end road."

No reply. More static and voices as Mark talked with the undercover team.

Allison eased away from the curb. She rolled forward slowly, thinking about directions and access roads and natural barriers in and around the subdivision.

"The guilty runneth when no one pursueth," Jonah mumbled.

"What?"

He glanced at her. "Something my dad used to say."

Jonah's father had been a cop. Allison figured he had a kernel of wisdom or two. She focused again on the suspect. Maybe he was simply going home. Going to relieve himself. Going for a walk. He flicked a glance over his shoulder.

And broke into a run.

CHAPTER 19

———— ❧ ————

Tires squealed as Allison gunned the gas.

"Wolfe! We've got a runner!"

"Get me up on him!" Jonah shouted.

She sped past the line of startled laborers and raced toward the cul-de-sac, but the man reached the trees before she even ran out of asphalt. Allison lurched over the curb and bumped across the field.

"Let me out! You go around!" Jonah flung open his door. The instant she slowed the truck, he leaped out and bolted for the woods, where the suspect had vanished into the brush.

For a split second, she thought of racing after them. Instead, she jammed the gearshift into Park, reached over and yanked the door shut, then threw the truck in reverse and shot backward across the field. She bounced over the curb again and made a squealing J-turn before thrusting it into Drive. A crowd of gawking workers filled the street now, and she blasted her horn. She roared out of the neighborhood and skidded onto the highway.

"Allison?" Mark's voice sounded far away. Her phone was on the floor. She stooped down to grab it, struggling to keep from swerving as she took her eyes off the road to grope for the phone.

"*Allison?*"

"He fled to the next neighborhood! That's *west* of where you are."

"I'm on my way."

She repeated the physical description as she swerved around a cyclist. Damn, this was a residential area. *Not* good news. "Wolfe, you got that?"

"Got it."

"Call in your cavalry. I don't have a radio."

She stuffed the phone in her pocket and pulled a sharp right into the neighborhood. Good God, what time was it? Had school let out yet? They didn't need kids around.

She muttered a plea to Jonah, who, despite his size, was quick on his feet. Maybe he had him cuffed and Mirandized already. Wishful thinking.

Allison glanced around, desperately trying to get her bearings, and took the first right onto a through street.

A man darted across the road.

She stomped on the gas. He raced up a driveway, followed by Jonah.

Allison slammed on the brakes and swerved, barely missing him.

Jonah didn't even look. He kept running, then scaled a six-foot fence like it was nothing.

She hit the gas again and careened around the corner. A woman walking her dog leaped back onto the nearest lawn as Allison raced by.

There he was! He dashed across the street, spotted her, then changed directions, sprinted up the nearest sidewalk, and disappeared into a house.

God, don't let him grab a hostage. Allison swung into the driveway and jammed the truck into Park. She yanked out her gun and jumped out as a chorus of barks went up from the yard.

"Back here!" Jonah called.

Allison raced up the driveway just as a gray hood disappeared behind the back fence. She saw Jonah in hot pursuit, leaping onto the fence and heaving himself over it.

Allison glanced around frantically. Two doors down she spotted a utility easement that seemed to cut through the neighborhood. She ran for it and sprinted north across the open grass, hopefully gaining on Jonah and the suspect. She ran as fast as she could—arms pumping, Glock gripped tightly in her hand. Her heart pounded. Her thighs burned. She was even with them now—she could tell by the barks of alarm going up from all the local dogs. But then the houses ended and she reached the woods. She skirted behind the last row of homes. Up ahead, a commotion.

"Freeze!" Jonah shouted from a nearby yard.

It had a chain-link fence. Allison hopped it like a hurdle, using her left hand for support because her right was clutched around her gun.

Noise on the driveway now.

"Jonah!"

"He's next door! He doubled back!"

Allison raced for the gate. She tried to open it, but it stuck, and instead she clambered over the chain-link. More barking. A woman's yelp.

A flash of movement in her peripheral vision. He barreled into her, smashing her against a brick wall. She grabbed his sweatshirt. He twisted out of it and she fell back on her butt. She scrambled to her feet and rushed after him into a side yard. He ran past a line of garbage cans, heaving them at her as he went. Allison hurdled them—one, two, three. Her heart was about to explode as she darted around the garage and caught a blur of white as he leaped over another fence.

"Jonah! He's going for the woods!"

She stuffed her gun in her pants and jumped onto the wooden barrier, then hauled herself over. She landed on her side with an *oomf*. Ignoring the pain, she stumbled to her feet and ran for the line of trees.

A scream in the opposite direction caught her attention, and she drew up short. She spied an open gate and raced through it to find herself on yet another driveway.

Movement in the corner of her eye. She swung toward it just as a giant clay flower pot came hurtling at her. She caught it in the gut and fell backward. The pot shattered and she landed on her butt on the concrete, covered in soil. Her gun was buried somewhere, and she scratched desperately at the heap of dirt.

A terrified yelp from the driveway. Allison grabbed the nearest weapon—a long wooden pole leaning against the garage. She jumped up and raced around the corner, where a woman was flattened against the brick wall of the house, shrieking like a banshee as the man snatched the keys from her hand. He jerked open the door to her car.

Allison swung the garden hoe around like a hockey stick and swept his feet out from under him. He landed on his stomach and she jabbed him in the spine with the hoe. Would he think it was a gun?

"Freeze! You're under arrest!"

Allison dropped to her knees on his back and grabbed

the cuffs from her belt as a blue Taurus swung into the driveway and screeched to a halt. Mark jumped from the car, gun pointed.

"Don't move!" His hands were perfectly steady as he raced up the driveway. Allison tossed the hoe away and managed to get the perp's wrists cuffed.

Jonah burst around the corner of the house. He looked at Mark, then Allison.

"Ma'am, are you okay?" Allison glanced over her shoulder at the woman, who was now making some sort of keening animal noises. She turned her wide-eyed gaze to Allison and bobbed her head.

Sirens sounded in the distance. Allison sucked in a breath and let it out with a shaky sigh.

"You all right?" Mark cut a glance at her as he kept his weapon trained on the suspect.

She nodded sharply and started patting him down.

A sheriff's car skidded to a stop behind Mark's. Another cruiser pulled in. Deputy Brooks hopped out and rushed up the driveway.

"Sheriff's on his way. He wants to be the one to bring him in."

Allison glanced at Brooks. "Denton can kiss my ass."

Jonah helped her haul the prisoner to his feet. The man's T-shirt was ripped. Blood dripped onto it from a scrape on the side of his chin.

He turned and scowled at Allison, and she was staring into a pair of cobalt blue eyes she would have recognized anywhere.

"It's our smoking gun," Ric said from the end of the conference table.

"And we've nailed down the time line?" Mark asked.

Damien Moss had demanded a lawyer within minutes of his arrival at the Wayne County Sheriff's Office, which meant they were going to need a smoking gun because the chances of wringing a confession out of the man had just dropped dramatically.

Mark turned to the video monitor, where he'd been watching footage of Moss's non-interview with the sheriff. He'd gazed straight at the camera with those defiant blue eyes and asked for an attorney.

This guy was slick. Damien probably thought stonewalling investigators would help him avoid his brother's fate.

"Thompson's statement is crystal clear," Ric said. "He specifically remembers loaning Damien the van right before Halloween because his wife was nagging him about getting some folding tables out of there that she needed for a Halloween party."

"I thought the van was registered to his business?" This from Jonah, who was camped at the other end of the table with a can of Red Bull. It had been a grueling afternoon filled with statements and phone calls and paperwork, and no one had stopped even to eat.

"I talked to the owner," Ric said. "He's got two pickups he uses for glass and tile deliveries. The van's old and originally belonged to his wife. He had the seats in back removed and now he uses it for hauling stuff he doesn't want to get wet—drywall, carpet, that sort of thing."

"And Mia's already started on it?" Mark asked.

"She took some swabs of the blood we found. Says she should have something as early as Friday. Roland's already been over it looking for trace evidence he might match to Jordan Wheatley's clothes."

"Who's Roland?" Mark asked as his phone buzzed inside his pocket.

"Tracer over at Delphi," Jonah said. "Allison asked him to do us a favor and run the clothes. He found glass dust that linked back to Thompson's business, which was how we knew to look there in the first place."

Mark's phone buzzed again, and he checked the screen. Quantico. He stepped out of the room to take the call.

"Just saw your mug on CNN," Rob Doretti said by way of greeting.

"What's going on?" Mark asked him. No way had the Bureau's deputy director called to congratulate him on his TV appearance. Doretti had a deep dislike for the media spotlight and encouraged his agents to avoid it at all costs.

"Your buddy Ahmed's come up again," he said, referring to a homegrown jihadist Mark had interviewed several months ago. "We've matched his saliva to some letters sent last spring to the vice president. Director's going apeshit, wants to make sure he's not acting on behalf of Al Qaeda."

Ahmed sending letters. It was an interesting development, but Mark didn't have time for it at the moment. Of course, if the director was going "apeshit," he should at least pretend to care.

"I explained in my report, Ahmed's a lone operator." Mark stepped away from the door, although no one seemed to be eavesdropping. The San Marcos station house had been a hive of activity ever since word of this afternoon's arrest had hit the news. "I spent two full days with the man. He's been diagnosed with bipolar disorder and has delusions of grandeur. Any ties he has to Al Qaeda are wishful thinking on his part."

"Well, he's not completely incompetent," Doretti said. "He managed to construct a pipe bomb and plant it in a major shopping mall, didn't he? The director's worried that's just the tip of the iceberg."

Allison crossed the bullpen with a determined stride, headed straight for her lieutenant's office. She ducked her head in and said something, then went to her desk and picked up the phone.

"I'm not worried," Mark said. "We've had agents turning his life inside out for six months. No one's turned up a shred of evidence that connects him to Al Qaeda or any other terrorist group."

Mark watched Allison's back as she listened to her voice mail. She'd managed to get a shower, he noted. She wore fresh clothes and had her hair slicked back in a ponytail. Mark moved into an empty interview room where he wouldn't be tempted to stare at her in front of all her coworkers.

"Well, I'm glad you're convinced, but the director wants a meeting," Doretti was saying. "We need you here at nine tomorrow."

"I've still got to interview Damien Moss."

"Can't the locals handle it?"

"It's a tricky interview."

"You'll have to go back for it. Anyway, he lawyered up, didn't he? Thought I saw that on CNN."

"I still want a crack at him. Deep down, this guy's itching to brag. With the right kind of pressure, I think I can get a confession."

"Get it next week, then. Nine a.m. tomorrow, I need you outside the director's office with an updated report in hand."

Mark was cornered. When the director got an idea in his head, only carefully presented logic backed up by copious amounts of data could sway his opinion.

"I'll catch the last flight out." Mark clicked off and muttered a curse.

"Can I talk to you?"

He turned to see Allison standing in the doorway with her arms folded over her chest. He wondered how much she'd heard.

"I know you're busy," she said. "I just need a minute."

"Sure. I was just about to go get a drink."

She gave him a baleful look, but he ignored it and led her to the break room, where he figured the odds of her wanting to have a personal discussion were much lower.

He took out his wallet and bought a Coke he didn't want. Then he turned to face her, all too aware that this was the first time they'd had alone together since their half-naked argument Tuesday morning.

"What's on your mind?"

Despite his "stay away" body language, she stepped closer and leaned against the Formica counter. He had a flashback of her perched on her kitchen countertop, un-knotting his tie.

"I just wanted to say thank you," she said.

"For what?"

"For not telling Reynolds what happened at the

prison. It means a lot that you listened to me. You seemed very upset the other night." She watched him closely. "I wasn't sure you were listening."

Mark made a conscious effort not to shift on his feet. The other night he'd listened to everything—her sighs, her moans, her breathy voice telling him she wanted to be on top. The only thing he hadn't listened to was his conscience.

He'd messed up. And the evidence of his mistake was right here watching him with that hint of hope in her eyes. No matter how illogical it was, she thought they had a future together and she was here to argue her point.

And the twisted thing? He wanted to hear her. Some part of him wanted to hear her beg him for something he knew damn well would never work because he needed the stroke to his ego more than he needed not to hurt her.

"So, anyway, thank you. It means a lot."

"You're welcome."

She tipped her head to the side and looked up at him. "You know, there's something I've been wondering. When did you last take some time off?"

The question surprised him. "I took some vacation a few years ago."

"How much?"

"A couple days for some legal proceedings." At her quizzical look, he went on. "Trisha and I decided to go the mediation route so we could keep things private and not waste all the money on lawyers."

"You took a vacation to get *divorced*?" She moved closer and plunked a hand on her hip. "Mark." Her gaze raked over him, and his pulse automatically picked up.

"I know you take care of your physical health. But what about the rest of it?"

He stared at her.

"You're the expert in psychology. You shouldn't need *me* to tell you what chronic stress can do to you."

He felt like he was in the Twilight Zone. This wasn't at all what he'd thought she wanted to talk about. He was even less comfortable with this topic than he would have been with a relationship talk.

"I'm fine," Mark said. "And this is not something you need to worry about."

"You're right. You don't have anyone who needs to worry about you, and maybe that's part of the problem. But someone has to tell you this because you're obviously blind to what you're doing."

"And what am I doing?"

"Buying a one-way ticket to Burnoutville. What is this compulsion you have to be a martyr for the FBI? What good is it to the Bureau or your cases or *any*one if you have a meltdown and quit?"

He laughed. "I don't have meltdowns. And I don't quit."

"Are you sure? Because you seem very stressed out to me, and I think—no, I *know*—that if you keep on this path like some sort of robot, this career you've sacrificed so much for is going to suffer just as much as your personal life." She stepped even closer, and he could smell the shampoo she used, and he was flooded with memories of being in bed with her.

Mark glanced through the doorway at the crowded bullpen. How had this conversation gotten so derailed? He didn't want to talk about this here. Or anywhere.

He looked at Allison again and she seemed to be waiting for a response.

"I'm flying out tonight," he said abruptly. "I've got a meeting at nine tomorrow with the director."

"The director." Her eyebrows arched. "Of the *FBI*?"

Mark didn't answer. Instead, he watched her, looking for signs of disappointment because he'd crushed any hopes she might be harboring for a private good-bye. Or maybe he was the one harboring hopes. But this way was better. He felt relieved.

He also felt a stab of panic, and he wasn't sure why.

"So that's it?" she asked. "You're just going to take off in the middle of everything, leaving us high and dry?"

"It's not the middle. We've got our UNSUB in custody."

"Yeah, but the work is just beginning. We need to interview him. What if there are more victims?" Her cheeks were getting flushed with emotion. "There could be bodies we don't even know about. We need him to talk to us."

"I'll be back to help."

"When?" she asked. It was a simple question, but he didn't have an answer.

"We need you here now, Mark. These early days are critical. What if he digs in and decides never to talk? And what about Jordan?"

"What about her?"

She gaped at him. "Aren't you planning to circle back with her?"

Mark understood where this emotion was coming from. This wasn't about Jordan at all. This was about Allison not wanting to accept the fact that he had to leave. And damn it, he'd seen this coming.

"My God, we invited ourselves into that woman's home and made her relive the most traumatic event of her life so we could get a lead in this case," she said. "Don't you think we owe it to her to sit down with her again and tell her how it turned out? You're obligated to—"

"I'm not obligated to anyone," he snapped. "My obligation is to my job."

She pulled back, stung. For a moment she simply stared at him, absorbing the subtext of what he'd said.

"Thanks *so much* for clearing that up." She walked to the doorway and gave him a long look over her shoulder. "Good-bye, Mark. Don't be late for that flight."

CHAPTER 20

━━━ ❧ ━━━

Randy's was packed, especially for a Wednesday night. Weeks' worth of pent-up stress and frustration were being let loose as task force members traded jokes, slapped backs, and clinked bottles to celebrate a job well done.

Allison had managed to snag a stool at the bar, but she wasn't feeling very celebratory. Instead, she felt flat. Disappointed. And lonelier than she could ever remember feeling in her life, which was ironic because she was surrounded by some of her closest friends.

"Hey, Ace. What gives? Thought you'd be tying one on tonight." Sean sidled up next to her and rested an elbow on the bar.

"I am." Allison lifted her beer and gave his bottle a halfhearted tap.

"*Light* beer? What happened to Jack and Coke?" He glanced past Allison and winked at Kelsey. "She's going soft on us, Kels. We need to get this girl out more."

A warm hand settled on Allison's shoulder and she turned to see Roland standing behind her.

"I hear congrats are in order." He smiled. "Rumor is you guys made your collar."

"Allison made it," Sean said. "Moss never knew what hit him. Arrested by a ho."

Roland grinned. "I heard. And *that* is something I would have liked to see." He squeezed her shoulder. "Hey, where's your fed?"

Allison traded looks with Kelsey. She never should have come out tonight, but she'd had the misguided idea that a crowded bar would take her mind off Mark.

"Just girls tonight," Kelsey said.

"Man, he cut out on you again?" Roland pretended to be offended. "He worked the case and didn't even stick around for the party?"

"He had to get back to Quantico," Allison said. "Said to tell you thanks, though, for your help running that evidence for us." She clinked his bottle in a lame attempt to be festive.

"All in a day's work." Roland eyed her sharply as he tipped his beer back. Allison recognized the look. But he played it cool and shifted his focus to Kelsey.

"Haven't seen you here in a while, either. What have you been doing with yourself?"

"Working, mostly," Kelsey said.

"Well, it's good to see y'all out. You ladies work too hard." He nodded at Sean. "Make the rest of us look bad. Yo, Sean, how 'bout some pool? Allison and I versus you and Kelsey."

"I'm game."

Kelsey glanced at Allison and then smiled at Sean. "We just ordered another round," she lied. "You guys go ahead."

"Next game, then." Roland looked directly at Allison. "I'll be back."

She watched them head over to the pool tables, dimly aware of the attention they were attracting from other women.

Kelsey sighed wistfully. "That's one way to drown your sorrows."

Allison looked at her.

"He's hot."

"I'm aware."

"But?" Kelsey took a sip of her beer.

"But I know myself." She watched Roland chalk his cue. He really looked good. And he *was* good. But somehow the prospect of mindless sex—even with someone she considered a friend—just didn't appeal to her. She'd wake up feeling miserable. And guilty. The guilt part made absolutely no sense because she'd made no commitment to Mark and he'd made it abundantly clear he wasn't committed to her.

Her stomach knotted. What had she expected from a single night together? She shouldn't have expected anything, but she'd allowed herself to read too much into it. She'd thought there was something there.

Because there *was* something—it was just something uneven. From the moment she met him, Mark Wolfe had had an impact on her life. First, he'd saved it. Then he'd followed that up by helping her become a better investigator. He'd given her more confidence in her abilities. And then to top it off, he'd given her the most intense sexual experience of her life. She'd tried to give him something in return. She'd tried to take him away from the stress and death and ugliness that surrounded him and make him feel something special.

To her it *had* been special. To him it had been insignificant.

How had she allowed this to happen? How had she left herself open to a man when she knew—she *knew*—there was absolutely no future in it? Mark was married to his job. And even if she'd been willing to be his mistress, he lived fifteen hundred miles away. Even for a closet optimist such as herself, it was too daunting a prospect.

And that assumed he even wanted to try.

"You know yourself and . . . ?"

She looked at Kelsey. She was still focused on Roland. "And it wouldn't help."

Kelsey followed Allison's gaze across the bar. "Yeah, I know what you mean. Relationships suck." She gave Allison a meaningful look. "Especially long-distance ones."

"Oh, no." Allison's mood deflated even more. "Mia was right. What happened with you and Gage?"

Kelsey twisted her bottle on the bar. "I screwed up."

"You mean . . . ?"

"I didn't cheat on him or anything." She glanced up. "I just . . . I did something desperate. Something I never should have done. I ruined everything, and he broke up with me."

She stared down at her beer bottle as Allison watched. Once again, Allison felt guilty for being self-centered. She'd been so immersed in her own world lately, she hadn't done a thing for anybody else.

"This happened—" Damn, when had Kelsey flown out to California to visit him? "Four weekends ago?"

"Last month." Kelsey nodded. "I went to see him on his last leave."

Allison waited.

Finally, Kelsey looked up. "To be honest, this whole last year has been miserable."

"I had no idea." Allison said. "I thought you guys were in love."

"We were. We are. Were, I guess. *Shit.*" Kelsey swiped a tear from her cheek and took a deep breath as though to steel herself.

"What happened?"

"It's just . . . I've been going out of my mind with worry. You can't imagine what it's like." She shook her head. "When he's in combat, every time I turn on the news, or get on the Internet, or see a newspaper headline, my heart clenches. I have nightmares all the time. I can't sleep. I can't think. Every day I'm having visions of him getting shot or blown up or, God, *tortured.*"

"So . . . you broke it off?"

"No." Kelsey took a deep breath. "I gave him an ultimatum."

Allison gaped at her. "You gave an ultimatum . . . to a Navy SEAL?"

Kelsey smiled weakly. "Great plan, huh? I told him it was the job or me."

Allison tried not to cringe. She tried to imagine Mark's reaction if she suggested he choose between her and the FBI. It was unimaginable. She couldn't even picture it in her head.

"Turns out, not such a good tactic," Kelsey said. "We had this huge fight. He picked the SEALs."

"Ouch." Allison put her hand over Kelsey's and squeezed it. "I'm so sorry."

"I am, too. But I was desperate. We'd been having issues for a while. We'd both done some hurtful things." She shook her head, obviously not interested in elaborating. "Anyway, I made a last-ditch effort to save it and ended up killing it instead." She turned to look at Allison, and the tears were gone now. She looked stoic. "So take it from me. I know tonight's tough and everything, but I just came from the Land of Long-Distance Relationships and it sucks. I don't wish it on anyone."

"Allison, you're up, babe."

A hand settled on her shoulder and she turned to see Roland standing behind her with that look she knew well. The pad of his thumb felt warm against her neck.

"Who won?" she asked, stalling for time. She knew how this would turn out if she joined their game.

"Who do you think?" He smiled. "Come on, A. I'll even let you break."

Mark pulled into the parking lot of the bar and found a space in the same row as Allison's pickup. For a moment, he sat there, trying to figure out what he was doing here. It wasn't smart. It was selfish and showed incredibly poor judgment. But showing poor judgment was his new MO. So much for the psychology degree and the law degree and the decades' worth of experience dealing with impulsive, selfish people who hurt everyone in their path. Now it was his turn. Mark's new purpose in life was to take the one truly good person he'd met in years—someone who actually seemed to like him and respect him and, strangest of all, enjoy his company—and show her his true colors.

The parking lot was crowded. Music and laughter could be heard, even from outside. Mark braced himself for a crowd he had no interest in seeing as he pulled open the heavy wooden door.

He stepped out of the damp, chilly night and into the overheated room. It took him almost no time to spot Allison perched on a stool beside her friend the anthropologist. She was with some cop friends, too, but it wasn't the cops who captured Mark's attention. It was the tall, dark-haired gym rat who had his hand on Allison's neck and was whispering in her ear.

Mine, he thought.

The word surprised him. And yet it sat there, burning a hole in his brain, as Allison tossed her hair over her shoulder and smiled up at the guy.

Mark eased away from the door and out of the traffic pattern. He stayed on the periphery of the room as he took in the scene. It was a blue-collar crowd, as it had been before. Lots of cops and firefighters and guys who wore coveralls and Levi's to work. It was the kind of place where Mark's father would have been at home, and Mark stood out in his dark suit. He ignored the looks. He focused instead on Allison and the way she looked in her jeans and boots, with that cascade of dark hair.

When she'd first come on to him, he'd told her she wasn't his type, but that was a lie. She was young and aggressive and opinionated. She wasn't afraid to challenge him or tell him to go to hell. She was *exactly* his type, and it scared the shit out of him.

The man's hand curved around her shoulder, and Mark made his move.

"Well, hey." Kelsey nudged Allison. "Look who's here."

She glanced up and her smile vanished. "Hi." She blinked at him. "I thought you had a plane to catch."

"Change of plan."

Mark's gaze shifted to the man beside her, who was eyeing him with blatant resentment.

"Mark Wolfe," he said, reaching out a hand.

"Roland Delgado." They shook, and Mark managed not to flinch as the kid tried to break about twelve of his fingers.

So this was Roland, who'd run evidence for Allison as a favor. Mark glanced at his feet. He wore brown leather work boots—probably twelves—remarkably like the ones in the back of Allison's truck. He had one hand on Allison's shoulder now and the other around a beer.

Mark turned to Allison. "May I talk to you, please?"

She opened her mouth, but nothing came out.

"Alone."

She slid off the stool and smiled at her friends. "Excuse me."

Mark took her hand and led her to a hallway in back, where several women stood in line waiting to use a restroom. He squeezed past them and pulled her into an alcove stacked with kegs. It smelled like spilled beer, and Spanish radio drifted in from the kitchen.

Mark positioned his back to the wall so he could see people passing.

"What's going on?" she asked. "Did something happen?"

He looked down at her, and the concern on her face made him feel guilty. But not nearly as guilty as he was going to feel tomorrow morning.

"I'm not a martyr," he said.

She stared up at him, confused.

"I'm not a robot either." He raked his hand through his hair. "Yeah, I admit I've got some shit to deal with. Everyone does. But I'm not some . . . ticking time bomb. I'm not the guy who goes to work one day and shoots up the place."

Her eyes widened. "Are you seriously telling me this?"

"Yes."

"Mark . . . I *know* that." She looked around and seemed to realize they were standing in what was pretty much a beer closet. Her brow furrowed as she looked up at him. "Don't you have a meeting with the director of the FBI in, like, ten hours?"

"I moved it."

Her eyebrows arched. "Why?"

"I didn't want to leave on bad terms with you." In truth, he didn't want to leave at all. He was merely postponing the inevitable here, but for once he was being completely selfish and completely irresponsible and totally disregarding the long-term hurt he might cause to a woman he'd come to care about.

She gazed up at him, and the surprise seemed to be fading. There was something else in her eyes now, and it looked a lot like hope.

"Are you really going home with that guy?" Mark asked.

"Who? You mean Roland?"

"Boots back there. Your ex."

She didn't say anything. Mark felt a punch of jealousy so strong he could hardly breathe.

"Please don't." He slid his hands over her shoulders and gazed down at her, almost ready to beg.

She didn't respond, and for an agonizing moment he heard only the noise of the bar. Maybe she was going to show him up by doing the logical thing here—which would be to stop whatever this was right now by telling him to mind his own business.

Instead, she went up on tiptoes and kissed him—only it wasn't just a kiss. She pulled his head down to hers and licked her tongue into his mouth and pressed her body full against him. He slid his arms around her and kissed her like he'd been wanting to for days, like he'd been starving. Because he had been. Every time he'd looked at her, talked to her, been in the same room with her, he'd wanted to drag her against him and kiss the hell out of her—like he was doing right now. She rocked her hips, and he pulled her back with him against the wall as she licked her warm, sweet woman taste into his mouth.

Finally, he pulled away and she blinked up at him, dazed and breathless.

"Let *me* take you home."

"Umm." She kissed him again. Then she slid her hands around his neck and whispered, "Your motel's closer."

CHAPTER 21

By the time they made it into his room, Allison had managed to wrestle him out of his damp suit jacket. As the door swished shut on the rain outside, he was lifting the shirt over her head and freeing it from her arms.

She backed him up against the wall and pulled his head down for a kiss. His skin was damp. Hers was, too. It was chilly in the drafty motel room, but Mark was quickly warming her with his hands.

Allison's heart pounded, and it wasn't just because they'd practically sprinted from the car to the door. It was because she was here, with him, in his motel room when he should have been on an airplane. It felt so good to have him touch her and kiss her and let his guard down again, after struggling to pretend there was nothing between them. Allison *knew* she hadn't imagined it. She knew she hadn't dreamed up this need he seemed to have for her, when he probably could have had his pick of women back at Quantico or anywhere else. He was here with *her,* and she knew that tomorrow he'd be gone, but right now he was here, kissing her, making her body tremble with anticipation as they clung together in this dingy little room, dark except for the streetlights seeping through the flimsy curtains. His face was cast in shadows, but still she could see his desire. She could feel it. His powerful arms wrapped around her and his hands slid through her hair and over her shoulders. They slipped around her back and reached for her bra.

"Front."

He mumbled something against her mouth. She pulled away and looked up at him.

"It's in front."

His gaze landed on her black-lace demi bra, and he immediately dipped his head down and kissed her breast, right through the fabric. She moaned and arched against him as his hands closed around her waist. She combed her fingers into his hair and pulled him closer. His mouth felt so good. His hands, his skin, everything about him felt good. His warm fingertips dipped into the back of her jeans and sent a shiver of lust through her.

She pulled back and looked up at him. She gripped his biceps for balance as she unzipped her boots and kicked them aside. His eyes glinted down at her, and she unbuttoned her jeans and tugged the zipper down. He pulled them down her legs, and she stepped out of them and she leaned back against the wall, breathing heavily, just as he was.

He reached for the lamp, and suddenly she was standing in a halo of light.

"Hey!" She brought her arms up to cover herself.

"I want to see you." His voice was rough, but his hands were gentle as he took her wrists and lowered her arms to her sides. They were both soaked and winded and flushed, and she felt self-conscious being thrust into the spotlight, even a dim one from a forty-watt bulb.

But then she watched him watching her. Her skin heated as his gaze moved over her slowly, as if he wanted to memorize her body. She wasn't voluptuous by any stretch, but standing before him now in her lacy underwear, she felt more feminine and desirable than she had in her entire life. She'd never ignited this kind of need in someone, and the fact that she'd somehow done it with *this* man made her feel a surge of giddiness. She liked him. She respected him. And the fact that he'd come looking for her with that possessive glint in his eyes made her ridiculously happy. She should know better than to let that matter to her, but at this moment she wanted to enjoy the rush.

She grabbed his tie and pulled him to her for a kiss. His mouth was hot, fierce. His hands gripped her hips and he made a low, male sound in his throat as he pinned her against the wall. She loved the fact that she made him like this—raw and greedy—when the rest of the time he was so damn civilized.

She tugged at the knot of his tie, and together they got it loose. She pulled it from his collar and tossed it over the chair. Then she leaned against the wall and watched as he made quick work of removing his holster and belt, dumping everything on the dresser. He took a condom from his wallet and tossed it on the bed behind him.

Then he stepped closer and stood before her, watching her as he unbuttoned his cuffs. There was something so manly about the way he did it. He had thick wrists and strong hands. She eased closer and gazed up at him as she slid her palms over the crisp fabric of his shirt and started moving her hands down the buttons and opening them one by one.

"I like watching you do that," he said.

She lifted a brow. "I like doing it."

She peeled off his shirt. His undershirt stretched taut over his chest. She slid her hands under it and lifted it over his head, then dropped it on the floor. She traced the contours of his chest, running her fingers through the hair and admiring how masculine he looked in the lamplight. He had a thick scar on his collarbone she hadn't noticed last time.

"What?"

"Nice view."

He smiled slightly as he rested his palm against the wall behind her and leaned in to kiss her. It was hot, passionate, and she curled her fingers into his hair to bring him closer. Her body thrummed with the anticipation of what she knew was coming. He was very good at this, and he made her feel good at it, too, and she wanted to enjoy it for exactly what it was.

He pressed his weight against her, then cupped his hand around her thigh and pulled it up by his hip. He kissed her mouth, her neck, her breasts. His stubble scraped over her skin, and she arched against him, wanting more of that, too.

"Hold on to me," he said gruffly, and she gripped his shoulders as he lifted her other leg and pinned her against the wall.

She moaned with pleasure, but the sound was muffled against his mouth. He felt solid and strong, and the ridge pressing against her was setting her on fire. He flicked open her bra clasp now and cupped his palm around her breast.

"Mark," she gasped.

He hitched her higher against the wall and she gasped again.

This was going too fast, much too fast. Her heart was racing now. She felt the heat building inside her, and she knew it was going to be over soon, when she'd wanted to savor it.

"Mark, the bed."

He tightened his grip and carried her the few steps. The mattress squeaked as he rested his knee on it and eased her down. He quickly shucked the rest of his clothes as she untangled the bra from her arm and tossed it aside. He leaned on the bed again and hooked his fingers into the black lace at her hips and slid her panties down her legs.

His gaze moved over her body and then lifted to her face. "You're beautiful."

She went still at the compliment. He looked so serious. So sincere. He looked almost . . . sad, for some reason, as though he had regrets about being here with her.

"Hey," she whispered. "No guilt."

The muscle in his jaw tightened, and she knew she'd managed to read him.

"I know what this is," she said.

"What is this?"

"Temporary." She kissed him. "And it's okay."

He gazed down at her for a long moment. And then he kissed her. She wrapped her legs around him and pulled him in close, and moved against him to show him what she wanted. And then the sadness—if it had ever been there—was gone. The passion was back again, taking over everything and making the entire world about this room and this moment.

Allison soaked it in. Every touch. Every sound. Every look. He was leaving tomorrow, and she couldn't control that. But this moment was within her reach, and she knew what she wanted. She pushed his shoulders back and sat up.

"Here," she whispered, pushing him back against the bed. She loved the look on his face as she settled onto his lap and guided his hands up her body to cup her breasts. She closed her eyes and tipped her head back and let his hands stroke her. And like before, he knew. He read every sigh and every shiver and knew just where to touch her to make the heat build.

Then he took her wrists and pulled her up the bed, so he was leaning back against the headboard. She settled on his lap again and this time she opened herself up to him and pleasure speared through her. She flattened her palms against the wall and leaned forward, rolling her hips, making the pleasure mount as he touched her and licked her and kissed her into a frenzy. She'd thought she was in control this time, but she wasn't at all. He rocked inside of her, pushing her closer and closer to that sharp edge, making it impossible for her to turn back time. And then just when she thought it was about to end, he lifted her up and flipped her onto her back. He shifted her beneath him and plunged into her, and her world exploded into a million pinpoints of light. But instead of drifting back down to earth, the lights coalesced again as he drove himself into her over and over.

"Allison."

She opened her eyes and saw that his face was taut. The muscles in his neck strained as he hovered over her waiting for her to—

"*Yes,*" she gasped.

His muscles bunched under her hands. A sound tore from his throat as his body bucked and her world exploded all over again.

CHAPTER 22

⚬⚬⚬

Allison had slipped out at dawn. She was so stealthy about it that when Mark woke to the sound of the door closing, his gaze automatically went to the dresser to check for his wallet. It was still there, along with his gun. The one thing missing from the room had been her.

Mark should have predicted it. He should have known her comment back at the bar about his motel room being closer had nothing to do with how hot she was for him and everything to do with her pride. She couldn't let him make a habit of leaving first, so she'd wanted to be on *his* turf, so *she* could leave. He understood her motivations, but that didn't mean he wasn't pissed off.

Now, at the airport ticket counter, Mark took out his wallet and flipped it open. He handed his credit card to the smiling agent who was charging him a ridiculous amount of money to get on the 10:50 into Reagan National. Even with no delays, the flight would barely get him to Quantico in time for his rescheduled meeting—which besides costing Mark a fortune to attend had earned him an ass-chewing by the deputy director. Doretti didn't appreciate having his orders ignored.

"Will that be credit or debit?" the agent asked.

"Credit," Mark said, and she remained relentlessly cheerful as she swiped his card.

Mark stared down at his wallet and went back over the night in his head. He'd made love to Allison three times—the last one well after midnight when he'd nudged her awake and she'd eagerly pulled him on top of her. She'd wrapped those runner's legs around him and sent him to the moon.

A few hours later, she'd left without a word.

Mark should feel relieved. No strings attached, no hurt feelings, no dramatic scenes. It was the best-case scenario—he should be glad about it.

Instead, he was edgy. And frustrated. He'd spent the entire morning with the gnawing feeling that he was making a mistake here, a big one. Damned if he could pinpoint what it was exactly, but every instinct was telling him not to leave.

"And are you checking a bag with us today, sir?"

"No."

Mark's phone buzzed in his pocket, and he answered it without looking at the number. If it was Allison, he was going to let loose and tell her exactly what he thought of her sneaky little exit.

"Wolfe."

"Hey." Pause. "You sound pissed."

It was his brother. Mark bit back a curse as he stuffed his credit card back in his wallet.

"What's going on?" Mark asked. Liam rarely called him unless he needed something.

"You got a minute?" he asked. "I could use your help."

The agent was smiling again. "We only have a bulk-head seat left. Hope that's okay."

Mark held his phone to his ear with his shoulder as he collected his paperwork and stepped away from the counter. "What do you need?"

"I hear you're in Texas."

"Leaving Texas." Mark picked up his bag and looked around, reminding himself which airport he was in today.

"Damn, I was hoping you could do a quick favor for me while you're there."

"I'm getting on a plane. Why? What gives?" Mark cut through the mob of travelers and headed for the security gate.

"I've got a client in Austin. I wanted you to swing by and meet him for me, give me your take."

"What, you don't trust him?"

"I don't trust anybody."

It was a typical Liam thing to say. Typical Mark, too. They were a lot alike, and sometimes even their careers overlapped. Liam ran his own security consulting business and occasionally asked Mark for help, such as a quick profile on some nutjob who was stalking one of his clients. Or sometimes the nutjob was the client.

Mark bypassed the mile-long line and showed his badge to an official at the Authorized Personnel Only gate. The official held out a blue-gloved hand, and Mark gave him the leather folio containing his Bureau ID.

"Sorry, Liam. My flight boards in fifteen minutes."

"Any chance you could—"

"No."

Silence.

"Man, you are pissed. What's the problem? I bet it's that woman, isn't it?"

"What woman?"

"Whoever it is you're seeing down there." He heard laughter in his brother's voice, which ticked him off. "You think I didn't notice your reaction to Trisha getting knocked up?"

"What reaction?"

"Exactly."

The security official glanced from Mark's face to the picture, then took his boarding pass and scribbled something. Mark watched his gloved hand and noticed that he was a lefty, just like Liam.

The man handed back the boarding pass, and Mark stared down at it. Suddenly his blood ran cold.

"Mark? You there?"

The guard waved him through, but Mark's feet seemed cemented to the ground. Meanwhile, his thoughts were racing.

You know he's left-handed, right? He pictured Allison, back at the pool hall. He saw her feminine little fist coming at him in a fake punch.

"Mark?"

"Let me call you back."

Allison turned off the pitted road leading to Jordan's house onto the smooth asphalt of the highway. Not even noon, and already she felt wiped out. She could hardly think straight, hardly focus—and laser-sharp focus was typically her strength. She blamed her current condition on stress, an unusual number of bumps and bruises, and not nearly enough sleep.

Last night, for example, she'd barely had any.

Tears stung her eyes, and she angrily blinked them back. God, what was wrong with her? She didn't cry over men. It was a point of pride. And yet lately all her emotions were in turmoil. Somehow Mark Wolfe strode into her life and had managed to unlock all her most carefully guarded feelings. How had she let this happen, and in so short a time? She felt stupid and reckless and—worst of all—she felt weak.

A bitter lump clogged her throat, and she swallowed it down. She needed to get a grip. She had a job in front of her. The legendary profiler might have left the case, but there remained a lot of work to do, and Allison intended to do it. She planned to dot every *i* and cross every *t* and not give those anal-retentive prosecutors a single reason to bitch about anything.

She spied a dilapidated country gas station up ahead and decided to pull over. A jolt of caffeine would get her head back in the game. She parked her pickup in front and dialed Jonah's number as she entered the store.

"Where are you?" he demanded.

She grabbed a soft drink from the refrigerator. "On my way in. Why? Where are you?"

"I'm at the jail in Waynesboro. Is Wolfe with you? I thought he'd be here by now."

"He went back to Quantico."

Silence on the other end.

"Had a meeting with the director," she added, wondering why she felt compelled to make excuses for him.

"Listen, I was just at Jordan Wheatley's. She agreed to come in for a lineup."

"You're bringing her?"

"Her husband wanted to take her. He's cleaning up from a job right now. They should be there in the next half hour." Allison turned into the snack aisle and plucked a Snickers bar from the shelf as Jonah muttered a curse. "Why, what's wrong?"

"I can't believe Wolfe left. We need him to interview Moss today."

"I thought the sheriff wanted first crack at him."

"He does. That's the problem. Hundred bucks says he'll botch the interview and we'll never get anything. *Damn* it."

Allison paid for her snacks and turned around, nearly bumping into a woman behind her.

"Sorry," Allison said, but the woman didn't make eye contact. She stepped straight up to the register and paid for a carton of eggs.

With dimes and nickels.

Allison watched from the door as she counted out the coins while the clerk waited impatiently. The woman had that downtrodden look about her that Allison had seen many times before. She studied her face for bruises, but it was partly concealed by a mop of brown hair. A long-sleeved T-shirt covered her arms. Thirty-five degrees outside, and she didn't even have a jacket.

"Allison?"

"Yeah. Look, Mark's gone. We'll make do without him. Keep an eye out for Jordan, okay? I'm going to swing into town, pick up a vehicle from the motorpool. I'll be there by eleven."

"Make it quick, would you? This girl gets skittish on us, we're going to need you around."

"She won't get skittish. She really wants to do this." *It's an important part of her healing process.* But Allison didn't say that, because the guys on her squad wouldn't get it. Allison got it, which was why she'd paid Jordan a personal visit this morning to explain what had happened and ask her for her help.

Allison hung up with Jonah and held the door open for the coatless woman. She met Allison's gaze with a look of suspicion. She had watery blue eyes, pale skin, and chapped lips. She wore no makeup, but the sun glinted off a glittery pendant on a chain around her neck.

An opal, surrounded by diamonds. Allison got a quick flash of it as the woman stepped past her.

The door thumped shut and Allison stared after her. Where had she seen that necklace before?

Allison's heart lurched. The front page of the newspaper. Stephanie Snow. She'd been wearing a pendant just like that in her graduation picture.

We know he takes souvenirs. Several of the victims were missing jewelry.

The woman rounded the corner of the building as Allison stood frozen with shock. She couldn't let her leave. She needed to—

An engine grumbled to life. Allison followed the sound of it around the corner and saw the woman backing out of a parking space in a dusty white van.

Allison dropped into a crouch and ducked her head down, pretending to tie her shoe.

Too bad her boots didn't have laces. But it didn't matter—the driver didn't look her way as the van rumbled out of the parking lot. It turned right onto the two-lane highway and headed north. As soon as it was gone, Allison jumped to her feet and rushed for her truck.

Her pulse raced as she coaxed the engine to life. A diamond-and-opal pendant. A white van. Coincidence? It *could* be a coincidence. But taken with that look in her eyes . . . Allison wasn't sure why, but she felt almost certain the woman had some link to Damien Moss. Maybe she was his girlfriend. His wife. His accomplice. Allison had to find out.

She eased onto the highway as the now-distant van took a curve and disappeared. Allison followed, punching the gas to catch up. She looked herself over and made a quick plan. She was in civilian clothes. She had her pickup. With a bit of skill, she could keep a low profile as she tailed the woman to wherever she was going.

Allison took the first curve and saw that she'd closed the distance. Still, though, she wasn't close enough to read the license plate. And she couldn't *get* close enough without drawing attention to herself.

Another curve, and then the highway straightened out. Allison hung back, hoping not to attract the driver's notice in the rearview mirror.

Who was she? And if she knew Damien Moss, did she know he was in jail right now? Moss had used his one phone call to contact a lawyer, not a girlfriend. But maybe he simply hadn't wanted to draw attention to her. Or to his home, where police might attempt to execute a search warrant. The task force still had no current address on the man. The most recent address they had was from a job application at Thompson Bath Solutions. The information listed there had led them to a dumpy apartment in Waynesboro that was currently occupied by a family of five.

The van stopped at a juncture. No blinker, but the woman turned left onto another highway—this one leading *away* from Waynesboro and farther into the countryside.

Allison watched the van recede down the highway. She bit her lip. To follow or not to follow? She could call backup, but this wasn't her jurisdiction. This wasn't even her county. And anyway, she didn't need backup simply to explore a lead.

The real question was, *was* this a lead worth pursuing on a crazy-busy day when her colleagues needed her at a suspect lineup?

Trust your instincts.

Allison could almost hear Mark whispering in her ear. She took a deep breath. And followed the van.

Mark squeezed past the crowd of people pouring through the security gates. He found a place to stand and scrolled through his list of recently dialed numbers until he spotted the one he needed.

Shit. Let him be wrong about this. *Shit, shit, shit.*

"Wayne County Jail."

"Mark Wolfe, FBI. Get me the sheriff."

"Sheriff Denton's out right now—"

"Is Peabody on duty? Put me through to him."

"One moment."

Mark gripped his phone as he waited to be connected to the jail supervisor. God*damn* it, how had he missed this? And it was November 19.

"Peabody."

"Mark Wolfe, FBI. We talked yesterday. I need you to go see Damien Moss. Take him a form and make him sign off on his Miranda Rights."

A pause on the other end of the line. "We did that already."

"You had him sign a form?"

"No, we read his rights on camera. He said he understood. We got it on tape."

"I need you to put the form in front of him. Make him sign it. Come back and tell me which hand he uses."

Another pause.

"Do it now."

"All right, just . . . hang on a minute."

Mark stood in the concourse, waiting. A river of people ebbed and flowed around him as the minutes ticked by and a cold ball of dread formed in his gut. He didn't want to be right about this. He wanted more than anything to be wrong. But he knew that he wasn't.

Come on, come on, come on. He glanced at his watch. Eleven a.m. Just thirteen hours left. He might already have started.

"Agent Wolfe?"

"I'm here." Mark held his breath.

"I gave him the paper, gave him a pen."

"And?"

"He signed it with his right hand."

Jordan sat in the sheriff's office with butterflies in her stomach. She didn't want to be here. And yet she did. She didn't know what she felt, she only knew she'd had to ask Ethan to pull over twice on the way here so she could open the door and throw up.

"You okay?"

She glanced over at her husband, who was sitting beside her now outside the interview room.

"Fine," she said, and Ethan lifted an eyebrow at the lie. It was one of hundreds she'd told him over the last thirteen months. But instead of pushing the issue, he simply looked away. He was nervous, too. She could tell by the way he had his arms folded tightly over his chest. And he'd been grinding his teeth for the past ten minutes.

"Ma'am. You can come in now."

Jordan's stomach clenched. Ethan stood up.

"Alone, if you don't mind." The deputy gave Ethan a pointed look, and he started to object.

"It's fine." Jordan smiled and got to her feet, then turned her back on her husband and stepped into the room.

She'd expected a two-way mirror and was surprised to see plain cinder-block walls, just like the waiting area.

She turned a puzzled look on the deputy as he plunked a file on the table. Beside him were Moss's attorney and also the Wayne County D.A.

Jordan looked at the district attorney. "I'm sorry. Where's the window?"

He smiled. "This is a photo lineup."

"But I thought—"

"Problem with using real people is we gotta drum up five other guys the same basic description as the suspect. Some of the bigger sheriff's offices, that's no problem, but around here, we'd have to resort to throwing some of our deputies in the mix, and they look like what they are: cops. So, we'll be showing you a six-pack."

A six-pack. Six *pictures*. The relief was so intense, Jordan felt dizzy and had to sit down.

The deputy seated himself in the plastic chair across from her while the lawyers remained standing. Jordan took a deep breath. She felt three pairs of eyes on her as the deputy opened the folder, revealing a color copy: two rows of mug shots, three pictures per row. He turned the page to face her.

The room went silent. Jordan leaned over the page. She held her breath as she scanned the faces.

She looked up at the D.A. "He's not here."

CHAPTER 23

———⋙⋘———

Mark had been speeding down the highway for forty minutes before he finally managed to get a detective to pick up the phone.

"It's not him."

"We know." Jonah didn't sound surprised, just frustrated. "We heard from Waynesboro. The shit's hitting the fan up there. Jordan Wheatley failed to pick him out of a photo lineup, and I'm trying to figure out what the hell happened. I thought she saw the guy."

"She did." Mark spotted his exit and skated across three lanes of traffic. "Edgar Allen Moss, 10-30-70."

Silence.

"Damien's brother," Mark added.

"I thought his brother was in Huntsville?"

"Different brother, same gene pool."

"*Shit.* The D.A.'s going to go ballistic."

Jonah was right, but that was the least of their problems.

"I've been on the phone with the records office up in Sacramento County," he told Jonah. "Turns out there were three boys, not two. First kid was nine years older than his brothers. Which means—"

"He wasn't in the home when Child Protective Services went there."

Mark exited the highway and ran a stale yellow at the nearest intersection. November 19. Of all days for a screw-up of this magnitude . . .

"*Three* brothers?" Jonah was still in denial. Mark, on the other hand, had accepted the extreme shittiness of the situation and moved forward. "Shouldn't they have had this in a file someplace anyway?"

"California has some of the most overwhelmed social workers in the nation," Mark said. "We had to go back and find him through birth records after one of our agents turned up a Moss at Santa Clara University."

"So he did go to college."

"Made a perfect score on his SAT, too, like David told us. Everything he said about his brother was true, only he was talking about Edgar, not Damien, just to jerk us around. Anyway, I'm on my way up to Waynesboro, and we can go over this there. Is Allison with you?"

"No. Why?"

"I left her a message, but she hasn't called me."

"Think she's on her way in."

A police radio squawked on the other end of the phone.

"If you see her," Mark said over the noise, "tell her to call me, ASAP."

"What?" More noise.

"I said *have Doyle call me.*" The noise halted abruptly and his shouts reverberated inside the car.

"Jonah?"

"God*damn* it!"

"What is it?"

"Call just came in. We got another victim in Stony Creek Park."

A quarter-mile ahead, the van pulled off onto a gravel driveway. Allison passed the turn without slowing, but darted a glimpse to the side and saw the van rolling up to a ramshackle house. After the next clump of trees, she pulled over onto the shoulder.

She was now convinced this was no coincidence. The van, the jewelry, the location—it was too much to chalk up to chance. Allison needed to call Jonah, but she wanted that tag number first. It would tell her who owned the vehicle—including any criminal history or warrants— which would help the task force put together a game plan.

Allison eased the pickup into a clump of scrub brush, where it would be less conspicuous. She got out and un- locked the toolbox to retrieve the binoculars her grand- father had used for hunting. While she had the lid open, she also grabbed a baseball cap to keep her head warm and to conceal her face, in case someone should see her tromping around out here. She was pretty sure she could get a view of the plate from the edge of the property, but it paid to be cautious. She ducked under a barbed-wire fence—which meant she was officially trespassing—and kept her body low as she crept through the trees and crouched behind a juniper bush.

She lifted the binoculars. Clear view of the van. She called dispatch on her phone, while using her other hand to adjust the lenses.

"Hey, I need you to run a plate for me." The dispatcher would know who she was from caller ID. "It's a white Dodge van, probably mid-nineties. The tag is X-M-R . . . Six . . ." Allison adjusted the focus. "Hmm, just a sec." She heard the keyboard clacking in an office two counties away.

"Last digits?" The voice was terse.

Allison adjusted the lenses again. "Can't tell. There's mud on the plate. Can you hang on?"

"It's crazy here. I've got about six calls waiting."

"I'll call you back." Allison clicked off, not wanting to tie up the line when they were busy. She lowered the binoculars and surveyed the scene from a distance. One-story house. Chipping white paint, sagging front porch. Wind chimes in a rainbow of colors hung from the roof, and their jingle drifted over on the breeze. To the right of the house was a weathered wooden shed that leaned so severely, it looked as though it might blow over in the next storm. Allison saw only one vehicle on site—the van with the muddy plate. No movement in the yard. No yapping dogs.

She eyed the line of mesquite bushes stretching between her and the house. The brush had thinned out with the cold snap, but there was still enough cover to keep her out of view, provided she was careful. She switched her phone to vibrate and slipped it in the pocket of her jacket. She stayed low and walked closer to the house. She didn't have to actually approach the van—if she skirted around to the north, she'd be able to maintain her distance while getting a view of the front license plate. She stayed close to the trees, which got thicker as she neared the shed. She spotted another evergreen with enough bulk to give her cover and darted behind it. She lifted the binoculars.

This plate was clean. She called the dispatcher back and recited the digits.

Allison glanced around as she waited. The wind kicked up, and the chimes clinked louder, reminding her of a jack-in-the-box she'd had as a child.

She lowered the binoculars and eased her Glock from its holster. She wasn't sure why—just because.

"Ninety-two Dodge Caravan, white," the dispatcher said. "Registered to an Erika Phelps, eight-two-six Mulberry Court, Dallas, Texas."

"Wants and warrants?"

"Negative. Registration's expired, though."

Allison chewed her lip. She'd been hoping for an outstanding warrant that would give the task force a reason to raid the house.

"D.O.B.?" she asked.

"That's 12-14-85."

"There a caution code on her?"

"Negative."

"Okay, thanks."

She clicked off and slipped the phone into her pocket. Erika Phelps. Her age seemed to fit the driver, so Allison was going to assume the woman was Erika. She didn't have a criminal record—not in Texas, anyway.

But still, something was off. The pendant, the van, the expired tags. She stared at the wind chimes and wondered if they were homemade as she recalled what Roland had said about the trace evidence. *Not house paint. Not unless he's painting Walt Disney's house. This is a rainbow of colors.*

Allison felt a gut-deep certainty that Damien Moss was connected to this place and that she'd be back here within twenty-four hours with a search warrant and an army of investigators.

The hair on the back of her neck stood up. Allison whirled around, gun raised.

No one. Just grass and scrub brush. She turned and studied the house again. No movement. But her pulse was racing.

You know when you're in the presence of danger.

Allison eased out of her position and moved low and silently back toward her truck. She kept her senses alert, her grip tight around her Glock. She skirted some trees and spotted the back of her pickup jutting out from the mesquite bushes where she'd parked it. She ducked back under the barbed wire and reached for the door handle, and something hard jabbed the back of her neck.

"Drop the gun."

She registered a thousand details at once—the low, male voice, the cool muzzle pressed against her skin, the blurry reflection in the driver's-side window.

Don't give it up. If she surrendered her weapon, she was as good as dead—somehow she knew it.

"Now."

Allison's throat went dry. She tightened her grip on her gun. In the window she saw the other arm arch up.

A bright burst of pain and then the world went black.

Mark maneuvered through the tangle of emergency vehicles and parked beside a ditch. A yellow ambulance pulled onto the road and he watched it speed away, hoping the ear-piercing siren meant there was still a chance. He strode up to the huddle of cops in the parking lot. Jonah's face was grave.

"She's alive?"

"Barely." The detective looked past Mark into the street, probably worried about reporters. The media hadn't made the scene yet, but it was only a matter of minutes.

Mark scanned the gravel lot. He saw half a dozen uniforms, several task force members, and a handful of crime-scene techs, but no Allison. His gaze landed on a yellow Labrador sitting beside a police unit. A female CSI in coveralls was crouched beside the dog, trying to poke a cotton swab into its mouth.

Mark looked at Jonah. "Lauren Reichs?"

"Yeah."

"Is Allison here yet?"

"Haven't seen her."

"Yo, hotshot." Sean Byrne stepped in front of him, eyes blazing. The detective was a head shorter than Mark, but he looked ready to throttle him. "I thought we had our man, huh?" He shoved Mark in the chest. "You arrogant prick. Isn't that what you said? Said we had our guy?"

Mark glared down at him, and it took all his effort not to sock him in the jaw.

Ric clamped a hand on Sean's shoulder. "Hey, cool it."

"Fuck no, I won't cool it!" Sean shook off Ric's hand. "I shoulda been here. But I wasn't, was I, because fucking fed here said we had our collar!"

Mark looked at the other cops watching him. He looked at Sean. The detective was angry, but he had tears in his eyes. Mark knew the feeling.

"I was wrong," Mark said, and the words tasted bitter.

Everyone watched silently but without making eye contact. He could feel their resentment.

"Man, come on." Ric pulled Sean to the other side of the parking lot, and everyone resumed their work. Resentment or not, they still had jobs to do.

Mark looked at Jonah. "Tell me what we've got."

"Lauren Michelle Reichs, twenty-one, college student." He checked his notebook. "She showed up here about eleven this morning to go for a run with her dog."

"She gave a statement?"

"No. Witness saw her Honda Civic pull in. Forty-five minutes later, we got a 911 call from another jogger. Honda's driver's-side door was open, so looks like she was dragged away from her car and attacked in the woods. Apparently, her dog was going nuts. People heard the barking a mile away."

Mark looked at Sadie, whose coat was matted with blood. Even from where he stood, he could see her paws shaking. A uniform held her by the collar as she resisted the CSI's efforts to get the swab in her mouth.

"Perp Maced the dog, but it came at him anyway, by the looks of it. Probably the reason the vic's alive right now, although I hear she's slashed up pretty good."

Mark gritted his teeth and looked around again. "Okay, where's Allison? We need her in on this."

"She was up at Jordan's earlier." Jonah looked at his watch and frowned. "She should have been back by now, though."

Mark pulled out his phone and checked for messages. Nothing new. He dialed her number with a growing sense of unease. It wasn't like her to duck his calls. Even if she was upset with him for personal reasons, she'd still pick up. The investigation came first.

The call went to voice mail. "Call me, ASAP." Mark hung up and looked at Jonah. "When was the last time you heard from her?"

"About two hours ago. She was on her way in."

"Two *hours*?"

Jonah turned around. "Hey, Vince, you seen Allison anywhere?"

"Nope."

Mark turned to Ric. "Have you seen her?"

"Not today." Ric rejoined their huddle. "This is a fucking mess we got on our hands. Mia just called me. Damien Moss's DNA swab doesn't match what we got from the rape kit. Moss's lawyer's in front of the D.A. right now, trying to get his client released."

"We need to talk to him first," Jonah said. "He probably knows where his brother is. I'll head up there right now."

"I'll go, too," Vince chimed in.

"I'll finish up here," Ric said. "Give you guys a call with an update."

"Good plan," Jonah said. "I'll tell the lieutenant—"

"Wait. Just . . . *stop*." Mark held up his hand to cut him off. All three detectives looked at him impatiently.

"Where the fuck is Allison?"

Allison opened her eyes, but everything stayed dark. Pain crashed through her skull. She squeezed her eyes shut, but the throbbing wouldn't go away.

Above her, voices. Not just voices—arguing. She struggled to focus on the sounds, on anything that would take her mind off the relentless pounding in her head. She reached for the back of her head, but her hand wouldn't move. A metallic *clink* echoed around her.

Handcuffs. The word permeated the haze, and adrenaline overrode the pain. She touched her right wrist and confirmed that it was shackled to something.

She reached for her holster. Gone. She did a self pat-down and discovered she had no gun, no phone, no jacket. Even her belt was missing. Swallowing down panic, she groped around and tried to get her bearings. She was on a cool concrete floor. Her right hand was elevated above her head and cuffed to something hard and curved. It felt like pipe. The bracelet scraped against it, and fear shot through her.

The air smelled of chemicals—maybe paint—along with a foul odor she recognized as human waste. Her stomach churned and she wanted to retch, but instead she slumped back against the wall and forced herself to breathe. In and out. She couldn't panic. She couldn't lose it. She had to *think*.

Memories swam through her mind—crouching beside a tree, phoning in a tag number, returning to her truck. He'd come at her from behind and demanded that she drop her weapon. She hadn't cooperated, but instead of shooting her, he'd knocked her out and brought her here—which had to mean he wanted her alive, at least for now. It was the faintest glimmer of hope, but she forced herself to focus on it.

Damien Moss. He should have been in jail. Allison closed her eyes and visualized the man reflected in the truck window. Not Damien. She'd seen Damien, pursued him on foot, even cuffed and arrested him. The man reflected in that windowpane had been bigger and bulkier.

Something crashed overhead. Allison looked up. Noises above, a heavy thud as something hit the floor. A body?

"You stupid bitch! How could you lead a cop here?"

Glass breaking. A yelp. The sound was like a wounded animal, but Allison knew it was the woman—Erika. If that was even her name.

The male voice was talking again, lower now. Allison couldn't hear the words, but the tone was threatening, almost like a growl. Another thud. Another yelp. Allison blocked out the sounds, focused instead on the handcuffs. She had to break free. She ran her hands over the metal and was disappointed to discover that they weren't *her* cuffs. No, these were his. That knowledge, combined with the rank odors, told her she wasn't the first person to be locked up here. Maybe he kept Erika down here, too. Or other people, before he tortured them. They could have screamed out for help, but no one was around to hear.

Too much horrified to speak, they can only shriek, shriek.

The words came back to her, chilling her to the bone. She commanded herself not to think about it. She needed a plan.

She ran her left hand over the pipe and found the joint where it curved and turned into the wall. Was it possible to unscrew it? The metal felt thick and textured, probably from rust. She pulled on the pipe, but it didn't budge. She felt the joint, tried to make it move, but it held firm.

Allison glanced up at the ceiling. A chill swept through her. No more noises—just an eerie silence.

• • •

"Faster," Mark said as Jonah raced down the highway toward Waynesboro.

"You know, the lawyer's probably got him kicked loose by now." The detective glanced at the speedometer. They were doing eighty but he increased the speed. "We need a backup plan."

"I'm working on it," Mark said, pressing his phone to his ear. Ben Lawson answered on the first ring.

"I was about to call you," the computer tracer said. "I ran down Edgar Moss—DMV records, utilities, the works. Came up dry."

"He goes by Ed Moss, too. Did you try—"

"I tried all of it. What I'm working on now is the geo-profile. If you pull the van out of the equation, now that we know it was borrowed, we lose specific addresses, but I'm getting a big red hot zone in the rural area southwest of Waynesboro."

They were driving through that area right now—low hills and ranch land as far as the eye could see.

"We need something more specific," Mark told him as Jonah's phone buzzed beside him. Mark darted him a look, but he checked the caller ID and shook his head. Not Allison.

"Keep looking," Mark told Ben. "This guy's got to make a living somehow. There's a record of him some-where. You tried construction? Paint?"

"Checked everything with an online presence, but you know some of those outfits are just a guy and a truck."

"Find me the truck, then." Mark clicked off. He could see from Jonah's face that his call wasn't good news.

"What?"

"Dispatch had a call from Allison about an hour and a half ago," Jonah said. "She was running a vehicle plate."

"And?"

"Tag she requested comes up as a white Dodge van, registered to Erika Phelps."

A white van. Mark pounded his fist on the door. This was exactly what he'd feared. She was out there alone, following up on some lead.

"Registration's expired," Jonah continued. "Dallas address, which doesn't help us right now. No one's heard from Allison since that call."

"What about the GPS on her unit?"

"She's in the pickup."

Mark cursed again. He stared grimly ahead at the highway as the new information sank in. Ed Moss was at large after his latest attack, and Allison had been tailing a white van when she suddenly fell off the radar.

"Any chance she's mad at you?"

Mark looked at him.

"Maybe this isn't about work."

The suggestion set Mark's teeth on edge, but the man had a point.

"Let me have your phone."

Jonah passed it over, and Mark called her again, hoping desperately that this *was* personal—that she wasn't answering because she'd decided wanted nothing to do with him, not because she was in trouble. But the call went to voice mail.

"We need to talk to Damien," Mark said tightly, handing the phone back. Silence settled over the car, and he stared out the window. Somewhere out there was Allison.

"You know, she would've got on the task force anyway. She's a little pit bull when she wants something."

Mark looked at him. He remembered her showing up at his motel that first night, demanding to hear about Stephanie Snow. It wasn't even her case then. But would she have elbowed her way onto it if he hadn't pushed? He'd needed an ally, and he'd zeroed in on an eager young detective with a need to prove herself.

If anything happened to her now, it would be Mark's fault. He'd involved her in this. He'd put her at risk for the sake of the case.

Jonah's phone buzzed again. He talked for a few moments, and Mark could tell it was more bad news.

"Okay, hold on." Jonah muted the phone. "It's a buddy of mine at the jail giving me a heads-up. The meeting just let out and they're kicking Moss loose for lack of evidence."

"When?"

"They're doing his paperwork right now."

Mark looked at his watch. He looked ahead at the highway. Even with Jonah pushing ninety in the unmarked police unit, they were still ten minutes away.

"Want me to try and stall them?" Jonah asked.

Mark looked at the rushing landscape. He thought about Allison alone with Ed Moss.

"Get a list of Damien's personal effects when they booked him into jail," Mark said.

"He wasn't carrying ID."

"Have your buddy read the list out."

Jonah made the request. A tense silence filled the car. Mark thought of Allison warm in his bed last night.

He thought of that ambulance speeding away with Lauren Reichs inside, holding on by a thread.

"Yeah, I'm here." Jonah looked at Mark. "One leather belt. One pair athletic shoes. One plastic comb." He paused. "Sixteen dollars cash. One pack Camel cigarettes. One disposable lighter. One cell phone. What's that?" Another pause. "Okay, cell phone is the throwaway kind."

"What about car keys?" Mark asked.

"No car keys."

"Have your buddy toss the smokes," Mark said. "And tell him to call us as soon as Moss leaves."

CHAPTER 24

Mark leaned against a graffiti-covered wall of the gas station and waited. With each minute that ticked by, his brain invented more twisted scenarios. Not for the first time, he regretted knowing the mind-numbing depths to which people could sink. Mark's fists clenched at his sides and he thought about how it would feel to wrap his hands around Edgar Moss's neck.

Cars and pickups glided up to the pumps, bought fuel, and continued on their way. Gasoline fumes hung in the air and sounds from the nearby lube joint echoed off the pavement, reminding Mark of his father's garage. He'd spent most of his adult life trying to forget about that place, but right now it helped to remember it. He needed the right mix of rage and control and was surprised to learn that his dad's example was good for something.

Mark felt the anger pulsing through his veins. He was on the precipice again, looking out over the abyss. He was in danger of losing all those things he'd struggled to build for himself, all those things that made him differ-ent from his father, but he honestly didn't care. The only thing he cared about at this moment was Allison.

The phone sounded, and he snapped it to his ear.

"He's coming down the steps," Jonah said.

"North or east?"

"North. Crossing the street. Looks like he's headed my direction—whoa. Nix that. Think he spotted my vehicle. He's headed to you."

Mark scanned the sidewalk until the man came into view.

"Got him," Mark said, and hung up.

Damien Moss approached the gas station. His gait was sloppy, careless. He walked like a man who had nowhere to be and not much reason to make an effort.

Mark made his breathing even. He waited beside the ice machine with his arms loose at his sides. Damien reached for the door, and Mark stepped out. Recognition flickered in his eyes as Mark clamped a hand on the back of his neck.

"Picking up some smokes, Damien?"

"Hey, what the fuck? They just let me go."

Mark dug his fingers in like meat hooks and steered him around the corner of the building. "We're not done yet."

Damien glanced around and quickly registered they were alone. His gaze darted to Mark's gun. He decided to play it cool and slouched against the wall.

"You got questions, ask my lawyer."

"This one's for you." Mark stepped forward, forcing him to stand up straighter. "I'm looking for Edgar. Where is he?"

He stared back at Mark blankly.

"Damien?"

A shrug.

"I know you've seen him. And I know you lent him your boss's van last year."

He looked blank.

"Tell you something else, Damien. We've got a policewoman missing, and I think your brother knows where she is."

Another shrug.

"And I think *you* know where your brother is. See how this works? You help me, I help her."

The corner of his mouth curled up in a smile. "If Ed's got her, there's no help for her."

Mark gazed into those insolent blue eyes. Then he looked away at an empty parking lot. "Maybe you're right."

He jammed a knee into the man's gut. Damien crumpled forward, gripping his stomach. He swung out with a wild right hook—just as Mark had expected. He caught Damien's wrist and used his momentum to pull him into a solid blow. Damien howled and reached for his lip.

"Fuck, man!"

"One more time. Where is he?"

"I don't know!" he rasped.

Mark smashed his jaw with a brutal uppercut. He followed with a jab to the abdomen. Damien swung out, but Mark grabbed his fist and twisted his arm behind his back. He shoved his face against the brick and heard the *thunk* of a tooth.

"Listen close, Damien." He spoke right in his ear. "Patience isn't my strong suit. I want answers or your teeth are going to be all over this sidewalk." Mark increased the torque on his arm. "After that I haul you in for accessory to murder, and I will *personally* make sure you never see the light of day."

"Okay, okay." His words were muffled against the wall. "There's a house."

"Where?"

"Don't know. He lives with some girl."

Mark jerked his arm higher, until he was up on his tiptoes.

"*Shit, all right!* Route . . . Twelve. I swear, that's all I know!"

Mark released him and stepped back. The man slumped against the wall, wheezing. He spat blood onto the ground and glared up at him.

Mark crossed the street without a backward glance and slid into the waiting police unit.

"Route Twelve," Mark said, and Jonah peeled away. In seconds, they were back on the highway and racing toward the juncture.

Jonah cut a glance at him. "That's gonna bite you in the ass, you know."

Mark looked at his hand and flexed his fingers. He thought of Allison.

"Ask me if I give a damn."

Allison kneeled beside the pipe, frantically trying to loosen it from the wall. Her head throbbed. Her knees stung. Her fingertips were raw and slick, but still she fought with the metal. She'd done her best to ignore the darkness, the smells, the ominous silence. But she hadn't been able to ignore the growing certainty that the man up there planned to kill her.

He was Damien's brother. And David's. The realization had come to her, along with Mia's words, as she'd clawed and pulled at the pipe joint. *Full matches are one thing. Partials are a whole different ball game.* Allison had been so certain they had who they were looking for, she'd stopped looking. She'd *assumed*—they all had. It was an inexcusable mistake, and now she was going to suffer for it.

Allison twisted harder. If she could just get this pipe—

A loud creak as a door swung open. A yellow beam of light fell over some wooden stairs, and Allison blinked up at it. A man was silhouetted in the doorway, holding something in his left hand. Her Glock. Bile rose to the back of her mouth as she thought of being killed with her own weapon.

Those heavy boots clomped down the stairs.

CHAPTER 25

~~~

He crouched in front of her and reached for her head.
Allison winced as he tugged the rubber band from
her ponytail and her hair spilled over her shoulders.
He picked up a lock of it, and his gaze met hers as he
brushed it over his lips.

Allison jerked her head away. He smiled.

"Where's Erika?" she asked, and her voice sounded
rusty. The only advantage she had here was information,
and she couldn't waste any time using it.

"What do you care?"

So it *was* Erika.

"People are looking for her. An entire team of
investigators is on its way here right now."

He laughed. "I don't think so."

"You're wrong."

It was a gamble. He could turn around and shoot her
right now, get it over with. But she got the feeling he
wanted some foreplay. Mark was right. The man got off
on terror.

At the thought of Mark, her heart hiccupped. God,

why had she left this morning? Why hadn't she been brave enough to stay and tell him how she felt?

Moss sauntered across the room and switched on a lightbulb that dangled over a workbench. Allison's gaze went to the tools there—hammers, screwdrivers, a wooden mallet. Against the wall was a Peg-Board with hooks spaced evenly apart. Suspended between each pair of pegs was a hunting knife.

Moss smiled when he caught her looking at them. He pulled something from his belt and she noticed the sheath there. He held up a knife so that it caught the light. He walked over to a deep porcelain sink and started rinsing off the blood.

Fury welled in her chest. He'd already done it. Weeks and weeks of tireless effort, and none of it had mattered. He'd probably killed Erika, too. And maybe he'd kill her while he was at it.

He turned around and watched her as he wiped the blade dry on the leg of his jeans. She refused to look at his erection. She tried to keep her face blank, tried not to show fear. Sweat streamed down her spine. She bunched her hands into fists so he wouldn't see them shaking.

He turned his back on her and pulled a duffel bag out from the lower shelf of the workbench. One by one, he tossed the knives in, and she heard the blades clinking. He took a cardboard box from a shelf and started tossing things into it: a carton of latex gloves, a box of condoms. He reached above the knife rack and began untacking something from the wall. Newspaper clippings? Allison read one of the headlines as her heart thudded wildly. It was just like Mark had said—he followed his crimes in the media.

He pulled a set of keys from his pocket and crouched down in front of her.

"Time to go." He uncuffed her from the pipe, then smashed her wrists together and held them against his groin as he fastened the second bracelet. He smiled as he stood and yanked her roughly to her feet.

"Where are we—"

Smack! Pain exploded behind her cheekbone as he backhanded her. She blinked up at him, shocked. Her gaze went to the Glock in his hand, and she repressed the urge to kick him in the balls.

He grabbed her elbow and pulled her up the stairs. They stepped into a blindingly bright kitchen that smelled of beer. Something crunched beneath her boots. Shards of brown glass littered the floor. A chair lay on its side. Her gaze darted around the room, searching for Erika.

Moss jerked open a back door and hauled her through it. She stumbled to keep up with his long strides as he pulled her across the grass to the white van. The cargo door was open already and he shoved her inside. Through the dirty window, she watched him disappear into the house. The instant he was gone, she lunged for the door.

"Don't do it."

She turned to see Erika in the driver's seat. She had a swollen eye and a bloody lip. In her hand was a big black revolver.

Allison eased away from the door, re-calculating her odds. Moss was a giant, but this woman was nothing. Allison could take her on in a heartbeat, even handcuffed. All she needed was a distraction.

"Erika, give me the gun."

She didn't move.

"I'm a police officer. I can help you. My team is on their way—"

She raised the gun and cocked it. "Sit," she ordered, with surprising force.

Allison crouched lower in the back of the van, but still kept on the balls of her feet. She needed to be ready to move.

The cargo door opened again. Moss shoved a cardboard box into the back—the one with the gloves and news clippings in it. Allison noticed her jacket crumpled inside it, and on top was a dented can of turpentine. Moss slid a rusty shovel in next to the box and slammed the door again before returning to the house.

Allison's fingers itched for the shovel, but Erika was watching her, still pointing that gun. How did that skinny arm manage to hold it up? And why didn't she shoot the man who'd beaten the shit out of her? Clearly, she'd been brainwashed. Allison shuddered to think how long she'd been under his spell—how many years, how many women.

"Erika, think about this. I can help you."

She continued to look blank, and Allison felt a spurt of panic. He'd be back any second.

"Erika, *look* what he's doing." She nodded at the box. "He's packing, cleaning up loose ends. He's getting rid of evidence. Erika, he's going to *kill me* and he's going to kill you, too, if you don't do something about it." Allison glanced around frantically. She spotted a silver hatchback parked across the yard. He must have used it this morning.

She looked at Erika now. "He plans to ditch your van later, doesn't he?"

Something flickered in her eyes.

"He's moving on, don't you see? He's done it before. And you know what happened to his girlfriend in California? He killed her just before he left the state. Burned her up in a bonfire, along with a box full of evidence from all his crimes there." Allison could tell her crazy speech was making an impact, but she knew they didn't have much time. She eased forward. If she could just get within lunging distance . . .

"Erika, he's done with you—just like the van. You're no different from the rest of them. He'll kill you, too."

The hand holding the gun started to wobble. Allison eased closer.

The door swung open and Moss slid into the passenger seat. He deftly removed the revolver from Erika's fingers and handed her a set of keys.

"Drive," he ordered.

And she did.

Tires skidded as they hit the juncture for Route 12. Mark scanned the landscape as he argued with Ben over the phone.

"What about the call?" Mark demanded. "Can't you ping her phone?"

"I'm working on that."

Allison's cell-phone company should have been able to pinpoint her location using GPS, but forcing them to do it involved red tape.

"Best I've got right now is the location of the cell tower," Ben said. "But you're in a rural area, so the coverage zone encompasses about thirty square miles."

"Put it into your program," Mark ordered. "See what it spits out." He scanned the countryside dotted with farmhouses. Allison could be in any of them, or none of them. He looked at Jonah. "What do you have on hand in the way of firepower?"

"Twelve-gauge, Remington 700, couple of flashbangs."

Mark glanced over his shoulder toward the trunk. "You've got a rifle back there?"

"I'm on SWAT," Jonah said.

"Police sniper?"

"And hostage rescue."

It was some of the best news Mark had heard all day, but it didn't do them any good if they couldn't find Allison. The FBI's HR team was out of San Antonio, and Mark had them on standby, but the SAC—special agent in charge—of that office had made it clear he wouldn't deploy them until there was a confirmed hostage situation, which they didn't have right now.

"Okay, I'm bringing up a new map," Ben said over the phone. "Now I've got a high-probability stretch of highway about twenty miles south of the juncture."

Mark glanced around. He saw very little development— mostly outbuildings and fences.

A flash of white caught his eye.

"There!"

The car skidded to a halt. Jonah threw it in reverse, and Mark had already confirmed Allison's white pickup sticking out from a clump of trees. Jonah pulled up behind it. He and Mark jumped out, weapons drawn. Mark's chest tightened as he approached the driver's-side door and peered inside.

No Allison.

A set of keys dangled from the ignition, and he traded looks with Jonah.

"It's her granddad's truck." Jonah shook his head. "She wouldn't leave the keys in it unless she planned to be right back."

Mark reached into the police unit and used the key fob to pop the trunk. He grabbed the shotgun and a case of shells. Without a word, Jonah took out the rifle and a pair of binoculars. Mark loaded the gun with one hand while using the other to hang up on Ben and speed-dial the SAC. Mark's fingers shook. All his hopes that this was some misunderstanding were long gone, and the HR team was twenty minutes away, even by helicopter.

Mark heard boots on metal and glanced up to see Jonah climbing onto the roof of the pickup, the Remington slung across his back. He used the binoculars to scan the surrounding area.

"Shit, I see them," Jonah said.

"You see Allison?"

"White van, speeding across a field, 'bout two clicks southwest of here."

The SAC answered.

"I've got an abandoned police vehicle, officer not responding," Mark said. "We need that HR team, stat."

"Move," Moss ordered Erika. "We don't have all day."

Allison crouched in the back of the van, waiting for her moment. She'd narrowed it down to two options: lunge into the front and wrestle the gun from Moss's hand, or leap back and try to get the door open before Moss could react. Problem with the first option was that the gun might go off. Problem with the second option was that the door might be locked *and* the gun might go off.

"Where are we going, Ed?" Erika's shoulders hunched as she asked the question, and Allison thought he might hit her.

But he didn't respond. He glanced back at Allison and his gaze lingered on her hands, which were still cuffed in front of her.

Should have cuffed my feet, too, asshole. I can run like the wind.

"Eddie?" The question was meek, and it earned her a glare.

"Shut up and drive."

He glanced at Allison again. Did he notice she'd scooted toward the door? She'd decided going hand to hand with him was too risky. If Erika jumped in, it would be two on one.

Moss turned around to look at the road. "Up here, after the bridge," he commanded.

Allison scooted back again.

They lurched right suddenly, then left. Moss's voice bellowed through the van as it pitched forward. Allison thrust her arms out to catch herself. Her head smacked the side of the van. She saw stars and hurtled forward against the driver's seat as they slammed into a ditch. The driver's-side door popped open. Moss grabbed for Erika as she screamed and jumped out.

"Fucking *bitch*!"

He scrambled over the seat and jumped out after her. Allison dove into the front. Her head was still spinning as she tried to get her bearings. Keys still in the ignition.

But the front end of the van was crumpled against an embankment. She grabbed for the door handle and flung herself out the passenger side.

Shrieks and curses on the other side of the van. Allison scrambled to her feet and ran. A gunshot ripped through the air.

Mark heard the shots as he raced over the gravel road. He punched the gas.

"Shots fired," Jonah's voice said over the handheld radio.

"You see them?"

"Negative."

"Signal when you do."

Mark stepped on the gas, pushing the old pickup to fifty, fifty-five, sixty. His knuckles whitened on the steering wheel.

Please be okay.

Maybe she was. Maybe she was the one shooting. But Mark had never been an optimist.

Allison lifted her head from the ground. She listened. Across the road somewhere was the unmistakable sound of someone moving through the bushes. The sound was getting closer.

In the distance, a car.

Allison's heart skittered. The footsteps stopped. She remained motionless in the grass as the engine noise grew louder. The van door squeaked shut and she heard the cough and sputter of someone trying to start the engine. It wouldn't catch. The noise drew closer—it was a truck. *Her* truck. Allison would know that sound anywhere.

Another metallic squeak as the van door opened again. She waited a beat. Two. She lifted her head above the reeds and got a flash of Moss's dark hair as he disappeared into the brush, fleeing on foot.

Slowly, Allison stood up from the bushes where she'd lunged for cover at the sound of those gunshots. She felt dizzy. Her head throbbed. It took a moment to string her thoughts together.

Erika.

She ran back to the van. It sat at the north end of the low-water bridge, its grille smashed against the muddy embankment. The front doors hung open. Allison rushed to the driver's side. She pulled the keys from the ignition and fumbled with them until she found the handcuff key. She jabbed it at the lock and unfastened the bracelets, all the while darting her gaze around for any sign of Moss.

Instead, she saw Erika. She lay on her stomach beside the creek. Allison ran to her side and checked her pulse, even though the unblinking eyes and the hole in the center of her back told Allison she was dead.

The truck roared up behind her. Mark leaped from the cab, and for a moment she thought she was hallucinating.

"I thought you went to Quantico."

"You're bleeding!" His raced up to her and touched the side of her face.

"It's nothing. I—"

"What happened?"

"I hit my head." She batted his hand away and glanced around. "He went that way." She pointed to the creek as she jogged back to the van and yanked open the cargo door. She dumped the box out on the metal floor and rummaged through everything. Beneath her balled-up jacket were her binoculars, her phone, her empty holster.

Her Glock.

He'd probably planned to toss it in a river somewhere after he torched the rest. *Detective Allison Doyle, erased from existence.*

She snatched up the gun. No magazine. She rushed for her pickup.

"Allison, *stop.*"

She glanced back at Mark, who was on his phone with 911. She ignored him and yanked open the glove compartment. Two spare magazines. She shoved one in the gun and the other into her back pocket.

Mark was on the radio with someone now as he stalked across the road. "That's *west* of the low-water bridge." He looked at Allison. "Which side of the creek?"

"I don't know. North? The house is that way, but he'd risk running into our backup. Still, he needs a car."

"She thinks north. Okay, ten-four."

He dropped the radio in his pocket and took her by the shoulders.

"Allison, your head's bleeding. You need to sit down."

"He's getting away!"

"We're going after him." He glanced at the gun in her hand. "You need to sit down and wait for the ambulance."

"Like hell I will! He shot that woman in the *back*, Wolfe. Now he's armed and desperate. I'm not sitting anywhere until we bring him in!"

Mark gazed down at her. He had that intense hunter's look again, and she knew how it felt now.

"He's got a thirty-eight, and probably a knife." She shook off his hands and headed for the woods.

Mark fell in beside her. "I'll take the north side, you take south."

Allison agreed, even though she knew he was trying to use the creek to separate her from the fugitive. No time to waste bickering. She gripped her gun and jogged along the shore, looking for footprints.

"No tracks," Mark called across the water. "He must have veered into the woods."

They scaled the embankments and moved through the oaks and cypress trees lining the creek. The brush was thick. Mark signaled for her to be quiet as they pushed their way through it, trying to pick up the trail.

A rustle of branches in the distance, north side. Allison pointed toward it, and they ran faster.

A sudden pain as though she'd stepped on a live wire. *I'm hit.* She was on the ground. A weight crashed down on her. *Moss.* He flipped her onto her back and pressed a gun tight against her forehead.

"Got your girlfriend, Wolfe." Moss's nose was smashed and bleeding. Blood dripped onto Allison's cheek as he loomed over her.

"*Wolfe!* I shot her once, I'll do it again!"

"If you do, you're a dead man." The voice was surprisingly close, but still on the other side of the creek. Allison wanted to turn her head toward it, but the muzzle of that revolver was pressed against her skull.

Her leg was on fire. She'd been shot. She'd lost her

weapon. She processed those facts as she struggled to breathe under his weight. He had her arms pinned under his knees and the bulk of him rested squarely atop her lungs.

"What do you want, Ed?" It was even closer now. She pictured Mark, gun raised, easing steadily closer to his opponent.

"Throw the keys over. The ones to the pickup." Moss cocked the gun. "If they land in the water, she gets a bullet in the brain."

Allison's pulse roared in her ears. Her vision tunneled. All she could see was the monstrous face above her, dripping with blood.

A soft *thunk* as the keys landed beside her.

No, no, no! She squirmed. Pain shot up her leg.

"Now, put your weapon down and move ten steps back."

"No." Her voice was a croak. "Mark, *don't*!"

"I'm going to count to three, Wolfe. One."

"*No,* Mark! He can't shoot both of us!"

But even as she said it, she pictured him laying down his weapon and stepping away. She pictured Moss shooting him, then pointing the gun right back at her. It was a lose-lose, and Mark knew it, but she also knew he wouldn't trade her life for his.

"Two."

Allison knew he was going to do it.

An odd calm settled over her. The pain receded and she saw the leaves above her, felt the earth against her back. She heard the birds trilling. She pictured Mark nearby and felt a warm rush of love.

The monster's face lifted. He smiled.

"Good call, Wolfe. I knew you were smart."

Oh, God. She squeezed her eyes shut. *"Mark!"*

Crack.

Her eyes flew open.

Moss tipped over like a giant tree and crashed to the ground. She pushed his legs off of her and rolled away, as far as she could get before slumping against a rock and gasping air. She heard yelling, splashing. And then Mark was there.

"Jesus, you're hit!" Sweat beaded at his temples. He had dirt on his face, his clothes. He touched her leg and she cried out.

He snatched up a radio. "Officer down! Get that helo here *now*!" He dropped the radio and stripped off his shirt. His gaze met hers. "You're going to be okay."

She tried to sit up. "Moss—"

"He's dead." He pressed her shoulders down, forcing her to lie back. He wrapped his shirt around her thigh and pulled tight. She yelped in agony.

"Sorry." His hands moved quickly. He was pulling off his belt now, wrapping it around her thigh. "Jonah took him out. Sniper rifle."

"But how—?"

"The bird call. It was our signal." He glanced up at the sky, then at her. His face was taut with tension, but he tried to smile. "Hear that? That's your ride."

Allison heard the faint *whump-whump* of a helicopter. Pain pulsed up her leg, unlike anything she'd ever felt before.

"Mark."

"You're okay. You're going to be okay."

"It hurts."

"I know." He picked up her hand and kissed it.

"*Mark.*"

"Hold tight. I'm going to get you out of here."

CHAPTER 26

———◆◆◆———

She noticed the light first. It was soft and yellow and slanted in through the mini-blinds, making stripes across the bed.

She was in a bed. It wasn't hers.

Allison's gaze moved over a table, some coffee cups, a chair. A man sat there, silhouetted in the dimness, and she watched him for a moment, drinking in his familiar shape. She thought he was sleeping, but he leaned forward.

"Hey."

She tried to respond, but her lips didn't want to open. She ran her tongue over them, and her mouth was dry and cottony.

"Water," she rasped.

He reached for a cup sitting on the table. She tried to sit up, and a bolt of pain zinged up her leg.

"Easy." Mark brought the cup and pressed the straw to her lips to help her take a sip. The lukewarm water was like a salve on her parched throat. She wanted a gallon of it, but she started to feel dizzy. She rested her head back against the pillow and looked around.

"My leg."

He put the cup down and sat beside her on the bed, making it creak. She looked him over, taking in details for the first time. White shirt, rumpled and untucked. Sleeves rolled up. Dark stubble covered his jaw. Allison's gaze darted around the room and she realized there were paper coffee cups scattered over all of the tables.

"How long . . . ?"

"Three days."

Three *days*. It seemed impossible.

"My leg."

"It's broken. You also had a concussion, probably from the car crash." He paused. "Do you remember what happened?"

Images flashed through her mind—a van, a basement, a bloodred blade held up to the light.

She looked at his eyes. "Moss is dead."

"Yes."

She stared at him for a long moment as more images crowded her brain. She pictured that face hovering above her, bloody and contorted with hatred. She pictured the big black revolver pressing against her forehead.

"Your mom's here," Mark said. "She and your sister are in the cafeteria having some lunch. You want me to get them?"

Allison's head throbbed at the thought. Her mom would be fretful. Her sister would be dramatic.

"Not yet," she said. "Just . . ." *Just don't leave,* she wanted to say.

He picked her hand up and squeezed it, as if reading her thoughts.

Mark cleared his throat. "You had surgery on your

leg. Bullet shattered the bone in three places, but the surgeon said it should heal fine after a few months." He paused. "You're going to have to do some rehab, though. No running for a while."

Allison's chest squeezed. Hot tears filled her eyes, but she blinked them back.

"Guess it could have been worse, huh?"

"You going up against a serial killer?" His voice sounded uneven. "Yeah, I'd say that's an understatement. It could have been a lot worse."

She took a deep breath. Tried to loosen the knot in her chest. She remembered what Jordan had said. *People tell me I'm lucky. It's a shitty thing to say.* But she pictured Erika lying dead in that creek, and she *did* feel lucky.

She closed her eyes, and she wasn't sure how long they sat that way, holding hands in the dim little room. Her head started to ache. Three *days.*

"Have you been here all this time?" she asked quietly.

"Yes."

She squeezed his hand. "Thank you. When can I get out of here?"

He smiled down at her. "You just woke up."

"I know, but—"

"Maybe tomorrow. Doctor said everything should be fine now. You need to let the meds wear off, take it easy for a while."

"And when do you go back?" The knot was back in her chest as she asked the question. He didn't pretend not to know what she meant.

"Late tomorrow. I have some things I have to do. Things I can't put off."

He eased closer and rested his elbow on her pillow.

He reached over and moved a lock of hair out of her face. His brown eyes were somber.

"You scared me back there."

She didn't know what to say. He looked at her hair, not her eyes, and the soft way he was touching her took her mind off the pounding in her head. He smelled good. He smelled like himself, and she let her eyes drift shut and tried to think about him and nothing else.

"Do you remember what you said to me in the helicopter?"

She looked up. She remembered wind flying everywhere. Dust and leaves. She remembered a medic hovering over her and someone giving her a shot.

"I think they gave me something."

He smiled. "Morphine. You were in some pain."

She closed her eyes. "It's better now."

He pressed a kiss to her forehead. "I'm sorry I have to leave, but I'll be back."

"I know."

"I promise, Allison."

"I know," she said again, but it was hard to lie around the lump in her throat.

The elevator doors dinged open and Jordan braced herself against the antiseptic smell as she walked down the familiar corridor. She ignored the nurses behind the desk because she knew where she was going. She passed a waiting area with a television tuned to a local news station. Sheriff Denton was giving another "impromptu" news conference— his third in as many days—and Jordan ignored him, too. Maybe if she'd been raped during an election year, her case would have received more attention.

She took a deep breath and shook off the bitterness. It didn't help. And she'd recently resolved to allow less of it into her life.

A woman stepped out of a room down the hall, and Jordan looked her over. Short blond hair, sweater set, tailored slacks. She had pearls in her ears and a haggard, sleepless look about her, like a woman who might have jumped up from a bridge table to rush to the hospital—which, three days ago, she had.

"Mrs. Reichs?"

The woman snapped out of her daze.

"I'm Jordan. We spoke on the phone."

Worry flitted across her face. "Oh, well . . . I was going to get some tea. She's napping again." She cast a concerned look at the closed door.

"It's okay. I'll just sit." Jordan patted her shoulder bag and smiled. "I brought a crossword puzzle."

The woman nodded vaguely, and Jordan slipped into the room before she could change her mind.

It was dim. Cool. The bathroom door stood open, allowing a wedge of light to fall across an empty visitor's chair. An actual bedspread lay at the foot of the bed, neatly folded. Beside the sink was a vase filled with mums. On the bedside table was a framed photo of a yellow Labrador.

Jordan quietly crossed the room and lowered herself into the chair. Lauren's long blond hair was smooth against her shoulders, one of which was wrapped in bandages. Her wrist was in a cast. One of her eyes was packed in gauze while the other was black with bruises.

Jordan unwound the scarf from her neck as the eye fluttered open.

"Hi," she said softly.

The eye gazed out. "I don't want to talk right now."

"That's okay." Jordan nestled her purse at her feet and dropped her scarf into it. Lauren's gaze shifted to the purse. She looked at it for a moment, then up at Jordan's face.

"You're not with the police."

"No. My name's Jordan."

She looked suspicious. "Are you a reporter?"

"I'm not here to interview you. Don't talk to me at all if you don't feel like it." Jordan looked around the room so she wouldn't feel obligated to respond. "Tiny rooms, aren't they? I was in the one three doors down about a year ago. Worst two days of my life, actually. Swore I'd never come back."

Lauren's attention moved from the scar at Jordan's neck to her face. For what seemed like an eternity, she said nothing.

"Why did you?" Lauren asked.

Jordan held her gaze for a long moment, refusing to flinch at the swelling, or the bruises, or the black line of stitches that looked like whiskers across her throat.

Why did you?

"I'm not sure. I just thought, I don't know, that you might want a friend."

Salt crunched under Mark's feet as he walked up a neighborhood street in Baltimore. What had once been a good area was now in decline, and the thirties-era homes needed new roofs and new wiring and countless other repairs that residents hadn't been able to afford since the real-estate crash. It was a neighborhood where a

BPD cruiser parked in front of a house didn't warrant much attention. But two BPD cruisers, two unmarked units, and a white crime-scene van were enough to lure neighbors onto cold front porches to see what might be going on.

Mark walked up the sidewalk and mounted the steps leading to a one-story clapboard house with chipping blue paint. The door stood ajar and Mark used his elbow to push it open without leaving prints on the knob. He stepped over the threshold and found himself in a living room like others he'd seen before.

"That was quick," Donovan said from a doorway.

Mark nodded at him over a Ping-Pong table piled with newspapers and magazines. "Came from Clarksville," he explained, referring to the nearby town where less than an hour ago, Richard Gooding, forty-five, had ended a half-hour standoff with police by committing suicide. On the passenger seat of his Toyota, which had been pulled over for speeding, was a cell phone containing text messages from Hannah Eckert and Rita Romero. Insurance papers inside the vehicle had led FBI agents to this house in hopes of finding the women's missing daughters. Blood discovered in the trunk of that vehicle had dimmed those hopes, at least for Mark. But he was here to do his job anyway, and had already begun building a profile of the dead man to help investigators retrace his steps.

Gooding's home was squalid. Mark had been in many like it long before such places were brought to the public's attention by reality-TV shows. Mark stepped carefully around overstuffed boxes and milk crates and passed through a dining room crammed with trash and furniture. The place was an indoor junkyard, and Donovan stood in the kitchen, glancing around with dismay, as a woman in an FBI Windbreaker took photographs.

"Any other vehicles registered to this address?" Mark asked Donovan.

"No. Lady across the street says he lived alone."

Mark glanced at the back door as a camera flash outside caught his attention. He looked at Donovan.

"Wait till you see the back."

Mark stepped outside onto a cement stoop that led down to a lawn littered with all manner of debris. Two aluminum storage sheds sat at the back of the property along a high wooden fence. A blue tarp had been stretched between them, and several agents stood beneath it taking pictures of a rusted-out car carcass sitting up on cinder blocks. Mark recognized it as the hull of a '75 Corvette, similar to the one his father had once restored in his garage.

Mark noted the swags of wiring between the house and the sheds. He tromped down the stairs and glanced into the first one. Not seeing a light switch, he took out his mini flashlight and shined it around. Yard equipment, fertilizer, a pair of rusted wheelbarrows.

"Check this out."

Mark joined Donovan at the door to the second shed. A bare lightbulb dangled from a hook on the ceiling, illuminating a tarp covered in car parts. In the shed's corner was an overturned red wagon and a green plastic Big Wheel.

Donovan lifted his eyebrows at Mark.

"Have them printed," Mark said grimly, turning to survey the rest of the yard.

Mark's shoulders felt heavy. A familiar anger consumed him as he thought of the pair of missing girls. His thoughts went to a pair of toddlers in California who had never known their mother and a woman back in Texas who'd been scarred for life because of *his* mistake.

And he thought of Allison, fighting the same monsters he was fighting in her own little corner of the world. And now she was scarred, too. But she was going to get up each day and keep doing her job, investigating murders and bar brawls and domestic disturbances, because it needed to be done. She'd never stop, and Mark knew he never would, either, and for all their differences, it was an important thing they had in common.

Mark stood in the cold backyard and pictured Allison's smooth face, peaceful in sleep, and he knew he'd lost an important battle. For years he'd been struggling to live and work and exist while somehow remaining an island, so he'd never have to trade places with Sheryl Fanning's husband or Dara Langford's father.

But he'd failed. Because when he'd knelt on the banks of that creek with dirt and leaves swirling around him, he'd understood *loss* in a way he never had before. And he'd realized that losing Allison, the one bright spot in his life, would kill something inside of him, something he hadn't even known was still alive.

Hope. That's what she gave him. And lightness and laughter. And the possibility that maybe he wasn't destined to be alone.

"We done out here?" Donovan was watching him warily. "The computer guys got the password cracked. They're seeing what's on his laptop."

"I'll be there in a minute," Mark said as his gaze fell on a slat in the wooden fence. It stuck out from the others. He walked over and shined his flashlight on it and saw that it was two slats connected together, forming a narrow gate with a rusty hinge. Mark squeezed through and found himself in the yard of the neighbor's house, which he recalled had a FOR SALE sign out front. He glanced around the overgrown lawn, and his gaze zeroed in on a purple tricycle abandoned beside the back stoop.

Mark climbed the steps and peered through a dusty pane of glass. He shined his flashlight over the empty kitchen. On a hunch, he tried the door.

Unlocked.

Mark's pulse picked up as he stepped over the threshold. The air smelled musty. The kitchen was empty of all appliances, and even the faucet was missing from the sink. The only furniture was a gray metal folding chair. Cabinet doors hung open and the far wall was tagged with graffiti.

Mark listened to the silence. His skin prickled. He stepped through the doorway and shined his flashlight over an empty living room. In the corner, two metal folding chairs with a tattered quilt draped over them.

Mark approached slowly, holding his breath. He crouched down and lifted the corner of the blanket. A child lay curled on the floor, sucking her thumb, peering out at him with wide blue eyes.

Mark cleared the lump in his throat. "Hello, Kaylie."

She blinked at him, but didn't move.

"Your grandmother's looking for you."

No movement.

"Would you like to see her?"

A slight nod.

Slowly, Mark held out his hand.

Allison sat on the side of her bed and yanked off her white cotton blouse. Too virginal. She tossed it on the floor and thumbed through the pile of shirts she'd taken from her closet. She found a black scoop-neck T-shirt and pulled it on. Too low cut. Fuming, she yanked it over her head and threw it on the floor.

A knock sounded at the door. She glanced over her shoulder, panicked, then looked at the clock. *This* was what she got for being such a girl. Now he was here, and she hadn't even started anything.

Damn you, Wolfe. She grabbed the next thing she saw—a gray sweatshirt she'd worn all day yesterday and tossed over a chair. It wasn't virginal. It wasn't low cut. There wasn't a single appealing thing about it, and she pulled it over her head because tonight wasn't about sex. She grabbed her crutches and took one last look in the mirror before making her way to the door. She glanced through the peephole, and her heart did a little flip. She unlatched the door and pulled it open.

Two weeks since she'd seen him. Fourteen days. He stood on her doorstep now, and the sight of his broad, strong shoulders and his serious brown eyes put an ache in her chest. He wore one of his crisp white shirts, no tie, sleeves rolled up. His beautiful hands were tucked into his pockets.

"Hi," he said.

Why haven't you called me? she wanted to scream.

"You're early," she said instead.

"Sorry about that." He glanced down at her cast,

then leaned over and pecked her cheek. Allison's throat tightened. *Not* the greeting she'd been hoping for, but probably what she should have expected. She turned away. He stepped through the door and did her the favor of closing it as she adjusted her crutches under her arms.

She felt his gaze on her as she made her way into the kitchen with what had become a well-practiced lope.

She looked over her shoulder. "Drink?"

"I'm fine." He was smiling at her.

"What?"

"I've never seen you in a skirt before."

She glanced down at the faded denim mini she'd unearthed from the back of her closet. Until two weeks ago, she hadn't worn it since college.

"It's the easiest thing," she said. "Too cold for shorts, and I didn't want to cut up all my jeans."

"It looks good on you."

She cast a glance over her shoulder. That was a little better, but he had a long way to go.

"You sure you don't want a drink?"

"Maybe later." He leaned against the counter across from her, and for a moment they simply stared at each other. She tried to read his face, tried to figure out why after thirteen days of silence, he'd suddenly called to say he was in town and could he take her to dinner tomorrow?

She'd squashed her excitement at hearing his voice and told him she'd prefer to eat in. Damp weather, crutches, yada yada. The real reason was she felt fairly sure this conversation wasn't going to go well, and she didn't want to have it in public. Ever since Mia's phone call last week, in which she'd mentioned seeing Mark,

Allison had been in kind of a funk. The fact that he hadn't called her . . . well, there was nothing to say about it except that it *hurt*. She'd been dying to hear from him, assuming he must be busy with something important, but actually he'd come through town without even bothering to give her a call.

She watched him now, trying to calm her nerves. His gaze moved around her kitchen, and he seemed to notice the cans on the counter and the unopened package of spaghetti.

"The rain's let up," he said. "We could still go out."

"I'd rather stay in." She turned around and reached for a cabinet. She desperately needed something to do with her hands.

"How are you doing?" he asked.

She glanced up and saw the concern in his eyes.

"Good," she said as she filled a glass with water. "I mean, I'm piloting a desk right now. But that's only for six weeks. Everyone at work's been cool about it." She couldn't suppress a smile. "It's amazing what taking a bullet in the line of duty will do to your street cred. For the first time, I'm actually feeling some respect."

"You deserve it."

The sincerity in his voice both pleased and hurt her. She took a long sip of water.

"So," she said, turning to face him. "I had a chance to visit Moss again."

Mark's eyebrows shot up. Clearly, it was the last thing he'd expected her to say.

"When?" he choked.

"Sunday. Regular visiting room this time. We talked through Plexiglas."

He closed his eyes, looking pained. "Allison, *why*—"

"I needed some questions answered. The dates, for thing. Turns out they were birthdays—his and his mother's."

"I could have told you that."

"But you didn't." It came out sharper than she'd intended, and she knew she'd revealed how much his not calling had hurt her feelings.

"Anyway, I also needed to go for me," she said. "To show him I wasn't afraid. That he didn't win. He actually opened up to me, if you can believe it. Told me about his mother. She was pretty psychotic, it sounds like, especially when it came to Edgar. She used to scream at him about how he'd ruined her life, how she wished he'd never been born."

Mark's jaw hardened.

"Anyway, enough about him." Allison put the water glass down. "How are *you*? I saw on the news about those kidnappings. You guys rescued one of the little girls."

He nodded. "Only one, unfortunately. But it was good." He paused. "A better outcome than I'd expected."

"Congratulations."

"It was my last case."

Allison stared at him, not sure she'd heard him right. But the look in his eyes told her that she had. Her arms dropped to her sides.

"You mean—"

"I resigned last week."

She didn't know what to say. Her brain was spinning. She couldn't imagine him not being an FBI agent.

"But . . . but your *work*."

"I can still work without the Bureau." He looked at

her closely. "In fact, I seem to recall you pointing that out. Saying I should consider other options."

She gaped at him.

"Fact, I think what you *said* was if I continued on my current path, like some kind of robot, my cases were going to suffer just as much as my personal life."

Allison groped for words. "I'm just . . . I'm surprised. I didn't think you were listening."

"I was."

"So what will you do?"

He watched her face carefully. "I've been offered a job at the Delphi Center. They're starting up an online profiling team targeting child predators."

"*Delphi?*" Laughter bubbled up. "You'll be working for the Pub Scout?"

The side of his mouth curved up. "He'll be working for me."

Allison realized she was smiling. The fist that had been clenched around her heart had loosened and she could breathe again.

"I guess that explains why you came down last week and didn't call me."

He looked surprised.

"Mia saw you at the lab. She mentioned it." Tears came into her eyes, but she blinked them back. "I thought—" She paused. "Forget it."

He pushed away from the counter and stepped closer. "You thought I was dodging you."

"Yes."

He took her hand carefully in his. He gazed down at it and rubbed her knuckles.

"I was. I wanted to see if I could get the job first before

I came knocking on your door to tell you . . . what I wanted to tell you."

He lifted his gaze to hers, and once again it was hard to breathe because standing so close to him made her feel giddy. She'd *missed* him. And he hadn't been dodging her. And he wasn't here tonight to let her down easy and then walk away.

He reached up and tucked a lock of hair behind her ear. "Do you remember what you said to me in the helicopter?"

Her heart beat wildly in her chest, because she *did* remember. It had come back to her days after he'd left. It had twisted her up inside, made her a basket case. It was no wonder he'd run away.

"You said, 'I love you. Don't leave me. I love you. Don't leave me.'" He gazed down at her intently. "You said it over and over."

Her cheeks warmed and she looked down. He touched his hand to her face and gently tilted it up.

"Do you remember?"

She nodded.

His eyes were dark and serious. "If you feel that way, then I'm here, Allison. I'm not leaving."

She gazed up at him.

"I love you." He brushed his thumb over her cheek, and she realized she was crying. He leaned his head down and kissed her. It was a sweet kiss. A romantic kiss. The kind she wanted to have many more of with him.

"I love you, too," she whispered.

He smiled. "So it wasn't just the drugs talking?"

"Maybe a little." She laughed through her tears. "But the words were from my heart."

Turn the page for a sneak peek of

SCORCHED

the next heart-stopping Tracers novel from

Laura Griffin

Coming soon from Pocket Books

CHAPTER 1

Indian Ocean
East of Mombasa, Kenya
0300 hours

The Black Hawk flew well below the radar and Lieutenant Gage Brewer sensed more than saw the water below. Light cloud cover, no moon. Perfect conditions for an op like this, which was exactly what made him itchy. Gage and his teammates had trained long and hard to expect the unexpected, and there wasn't a SEAL among them who trusted an operation that got off to a perfect start.

"Going black," came the voice in Gage's headset. At his CO's order, the helicopter went dark except for the faint red glow of the control panel.

A ripple of movement as the eight men of Alpha Squad triple-checked gear and prepped for battle. Gage reviewed the mission. Tonight's landing zone was the size of a driveway—just small enough to make things interesting. He visualized the layout of the vessel they planned to fast-rope onto in a matter of minutes. The *Eclipse* was a handcrafted yacht, custom built in Maine specifically for this voyage—which had gone horribly wrong when Somali pirates seized the boat. Less than three hours after capturing the yacht, the pirates had used a satellite phone to call in an eight-figure ransom demand.

Gage pictured the captain, a man he was tasked with rescuing: fifty-two-year-old Brad Mason of Sunnyvale, California. The billionaire software mogul fancied himself an adventurer. According to the intel Gage's team had received, Mason was some kind of computer genius, who had made billions with his software company before taking a year off to sail around the globe with his family.

Gage didn't doubt that a man who'd made a freaking billion dollars off something he'd invented was smart. But his genius didn't extend to tactical matters, apparently, because the guy had put up a Facebook page that included weekly updates about his journey and details of his route, making him a prime target for the brazen and surprisingly high-tech pirates who roamed the seas just north of here. Not so smart, in Gage's humble opinion. But dumb-ass moves aside, the guy was an American citizen under attack on the high seas, and the SEALs had been ordered to get him out of harm's way.

Along with his daughter.

Gage pictured Avery Mason, seventeen, who'd taken a year off from high school to go along on the expedition. A copy of her varsity soccer photo had been passed around the briefing room a few hours ago. Avery was a blue-eyed, freckle-faced brunette, and one look at her had set the entire SEAL team's mood to extra grim.

Conspicuously absent from the rescue list was forty-eight-year-old Catherine Mason, who had been shot and thrown overboard yesterday, after the pirates' first deadline passed without a ransom drop. Mason's extended family had been allotted twenty-four more hours—of which three remained—to come up with the ransom, or else Avery would die.

No one doubted the pirates would make good on their threat. That was the bad news. The good news was, the seven Somalis on the yacht were lightly armed—only a half dozen AKs and some handguns among them, according to the intel the SEALs had received.

The helicopter swooped lower. Sweat trickled beneath Gage's flak jacket as he contemplated the battle plan. The sweat was from heat, not fear. After eight years in the teams, there wasn't much that rattled him anymore. Years of dodging bullets and IEDs and operating behind enemy lines had taught Gage to be cool under pressure, to take what life threw at him—be it bombs or bullets. And whatever shit came down, he and his team would deal with it, get the mission done, and get out, because failure was not an option.

Not usually.

A vision of Kelsey flashed through his mind, and Gage wondered where she was tonight. He shouldn't think about her now. But even as he commanded himself to focus, he was wishing for one more moment to tell her . . . what? There was nothing left to say. And yet before every single op, he felt a burning need to talk to her.

"Two minutes."

His CO's voice snapped him back to the task at hand. Joe Quinn sounded calm, resolute—the way he always did before an operation. There was a determination about him that steeled his team, no matter what the risks in front of them. Just the tone of his voice reminded them of the SEAL creed, which went with them everywhere.

If knocked down, I will get back up, every time. I will draw on every remaining ounce of strength to protect my teammates and accomplish our mission. I am never out of the fight.

On the horizon, the faint flicker of the target vessel. The helo dipped lower. As they neared it, the boat was just a lone white speck in the darkness. The pirates had switched off almost all the lights and kept belowdecks so as not to make themselves easy targets. Even the pirates on the mother vessel—a dilapidated shrimping boat being used as a communications headquarters—had kept a low profile. The Somalis had learned their lesson, apparently, when SEAL snipers had taken some of their comrades out a few years back.

"It's go time."

Quinn's words sent a jolt of adrenaline through him. Gage ditched his headset, stood up. Beside him, Derek Vaughn did the same. As the two largest men of Alpha Squad, Gage and the Texan would be working in tandem to get the hostages off the yacht and onto an inflatable boat that would take them to the destroyer that had been lurking nearby since the early hours of the crisis.

"Aces, man," Derek said over the din, his usual way of wishing Gage luck. Behind him, Mike Dietz slapped him on the back, while Gage traded insults with Luke Jones—another routine. SEALs were a superstitious bunch.

And that was it. They'd trained. They'd practiced. They were ready.

The door opened and the noise increased, making it difficult to communicate except by hand signal. The first man kicked the rope out. One by one, the commandos disappeared into the night. The pilot struggled not to suddenly gain altitude each time a three-hundred-pound load of man plus gear came off the rope. Gage waited for his cue, gripping the thick nylon in his gloved hands. Quinn signaled *go*. Gabe jumped out and slid down so fast that his gloves smoked.

The boat came alive with lights. Flashes of muzzle fire as one of the pirates hosed down the squad. Derek took out the shooter just as a bullet zinged past Gage's ear.

"Go, go, go!"

Gage's boots hit the deck. He sprinted for the hatch and slid down the ladder, planting a brutal kick in the face of a man at the base. The man went down like a stone, but he looked unarmed, and Gage swiftly zip-cuffed him as Derek leaped over them and kicked open the forward cabin.

"Cabin one clear!" Derek shouted.

Weapon raised, Gage kicked open one of the aft cabins. Pitch dark. He switched on the light attached to his helmet. On the bottom bunk was a bloodied man whose face was a nearly unrecognizable pulp. Looked like Brad Mason had been beaten with the butt of a machine gun.

"Hostage one secured," Gage said into his radio, as Mike—the team corpsman—quickly moved to check his pulse. Despite the thunder of boots and the *rat-tat-tat* of gunfire up on deck, the hostage hadn't moved.

"Alive," Mike announced, but Gage was already

kicking open the second aft cabin. He aimed his M-4 into the dimly lit space.

Empty bunk.

A low moan, and Gage turned his attention to a lump in the corner. Someone was curled in a fetal position. Gage crouched beside her and used his free hand to lift her face. Avery Mason's blue eyes drifted shut and her head lolled back.

"Hostage two secured," Gage reported. Her hair was matted with blood. He noted the blood on her shorts and thighs.

"Sitrep on the hostages," Quinn demanded over the radio.

"Alive, but injured. Girl's got a gash on her head and I think she's been drugged. Scratch the boat evac. We need the helo back here."

"Yo, Brewer, up and out."

He glanced up to see Derek in the doorway with Mason slung over his shoulder in a fireman's carry.

Gage scooped up the girl and positioned her limp body over his left shoulder. He moved for the ladder just as a man burst out from one of the cabinets.

Pop!

Pain tore through Gage's shoulder as he squeezed the trigger. The man dropped. Luke lunged around the corner and put a bullet in his chest, just to be sure.

Gage managed to hang on to his gun as he grabbed the rail with his free hand and hoisted himself up the ladder. On deck he did a quick head count. Three pirates dead, four cuffed—plus one casualty below.

Cursing their crappy intel, Gage eased Avery Mason

onto the deck beside Mike, who was briskly bandaging her father's leg injury.

"Knife?" Gage asked, looking at the nasty wound.

"We need that helo." Mike glanced up at him. "Shit, you're hit."

Gage looked at the patch of blood that was rapidly expanding on his right shoulder. Derek yelled something at him, but it was drowned out by the *whump-whump* of the approaching chopper. The rescue basket dangled from the hole.

Suddenly the helo lurched right, then left, doing evasive maneuvers. Gage swung around to face the shrimp boat, which was a dim shadow on the now-gray horizon.

"A fucking stinger!" Derek shouted.

Gage's pulse spiked as a trail of fire arced up from the distant boat. All eyes turned skyward as the pilot shot off tracers to fool the heat-seeking missile, but it was too late. The tail rotor exploded. The helo tipped sideways and cartwheeled into the water with a giant splash.

"*Joe!*" Gage dropped his gun and ripped off his flak jacket. His teammates frantically did the same. Water rained down as Gage sprinted across the deck and dove off the boat.

The ocean hit him with an icy slap.

The Philippines
Twenty-four hours later

Kelsey Quinn kneeled on the ground, tapping the sifting screen until the dirt disappeared and the tiny plastic object came into view.

"What is it?" Aaron asked over her shoulder.

Kelsey glanced up at her field assistant, who towered over the four Filipinos clustered around him.

"Tagapayapa," a woman muttered in Tagalog.

"What?" Aaron looked at her with puzzlement.

"Pacifier." Kelsey pulled an evidence bag from one of the pockets of her cargo pants and labeled it with a permanent marker. She dropped the pacifier inside and darted a concerned glance at the Filipino anthropologist whose face held a mix of sorrow and resignation.

The woman held out a slender brown hand. "May I?"

Kelsey gave her the bag and watched as she squared her petite shoulders and trekked across the campsite to the intake tent, where this latest bit of evidence would be labeled properly and entered into the computer. Kelsey sighed. As a forensic anthropologist, she had traveled the world unearthing tragedy, and it amazed her how the people who had seen the most suffering always seemed to have the capacity to deal with more.

Kelsey got to her feet and dusted off her kneepads. Her legs and shoulders ached from being on screen duty all morning.

"Ready for a break?" Aaron asked.

"Think I'll wait till noon." She checked her watch and realized her mental clock was about two hours behind.

"You're doing it again, doc." Aaron passed her his water bottle and watched reproachfully as she took a gulp.

"Can't be helped." Kelsey handed the bottle back and repositioned her San Diego Padres cap on her head. "We've only got five days left. There's no way we'll finish the second gravesite in that amount of time. What'd you hear about those klieg lights?"

"Nothing yet. I—"

"Dr. Quinn? Need your eyes over here."

Kelsey glanced across the campground to the doctor standing beside the radiography tent. It was a welcome interruption. She could tell Aaron was about to launch into one of his lectures about backing off the hours, and she was too tired to argue with him.

"Get me an update on those lights," Kelsey ordered, then remembered to smile. "Please." She jogged across the camp and ducked into the largest tent, which was blessedly cool because of the giant fan they used to keep the expensive equipment from overheating. Dr. Manny Villarreal, a short man who happened to be a giant in his field, was now seated at a computer with his usual bandanna tied over his bald head. Today's selection was army green, to match his scrubs.

Kelsey zipped the tent door shut. She tilted her head back and stood for a few moments, letting the decadent eighty-degree air swirl around her.

"When you're done slacking off . . . ?"

"Sorry. What's up?" Kelsey joined him at a computer, where the X-ray of a skull appeared on the screen.

"Victim thirty-two," Manny said. "She came out of intake this morning."

"She?"

He gave her a dark look. "Irene recovered a pink headband."

Kelsey glanced across the tent at Irene, whose unenviable job it was to painstakingly disentangle every set of bones from the clothing and personal items that came in with it. After being separated from the bones, each item had to be meticulously photographed and catalogued before being examined by investigators.

"You're the expert," Manny continued, "but I'm guessing the profile comes back as a four- to five-year-old female, about thirty-eight inches tall, based on the femur. In addition to the headband, Irene catalogued a pair of white sandals. What we didn't find were any bullets or signs of bone trauma."

"What about lead wipe?" Kelsey asked, referring to the opaque specks that typically showed up on an X-ray after a bullet crashed through a human skull.

"None," Manny replied. "And as I said, no broken bones. So no obvious cause of death." He leaned back in his chair and gazed up at Kelsey, and a bleak understanding passed between them.

If this child hadn't been marched to the edge of a pit and shot to death, like the rest of the people in the grave with her, then she'd died by other means. Most likely, she'd been buried alive and suffocated.

Kelsey's chest tightened and she looked away.

"I—Excuse me. I have to get some water."

With that completely see-through excuse she ducked out of the tent and stood in the blazing tropical sun. She felt light-headed suddenly. Her stomach churned, and she knew Aaron was right. She needed a break—a Coke, at least, or a PowerBar to get her energy up before she did something embarrassing like faint in the middle of camp.

Lead from the front, her uncle always said, and Kelsey knew he was right. Joe commanded Navy SEALs for a living, and he knew a thing or two about leadership. Kelsey needed to work hard, yes, but she also needed to set a good example for the six members of her task force, who had been toiling in the heat for weeks in the name of human rights. Kelsey was spearheading this mission on behalf of an international human rights group with backing from her home research lab—the prestigious Delphi Center in central Texas. She was young to be in charge of such a big job, and she knew more than a few people were expecting her to fail—maybe even hoping for it. She needed to prove them wrong. She needed to be sharp and in charge, not passed out from exhaustion.

Kelsey wiped the sweat from her brow with the back of her grimy arm. She traipsed across the camp and rummaged through a plastic food bin until she found a granola bar.

"Ma'am Kelsey?"

She turned to see one of her team members, Juan Ocampo, emerging from the jungle with his metal detector and his shaggy brown dog. Milo aspired to be a cadaver dog, but in reality he was simply a well-trained mutt who went everywhere with Juan. Kelsey didn't mind the pup. She liked him, in fact, and knew he was good for morale.

Juan stopped beside her. His blue *International Forensic Anthropology Foundation* T-shirt was soaked through with sweat and his face was dripping.

"You need to come with me," he said, and the low tone of his voice told her he didn't want the others to know about whatever he'd found.

Kelsey shoved the rest of her granola bar in her back pocket and followed him into the jungle. A route had been cut through the dense tangle of trees and vines, but the terrain was steep and uneven. Kelsey was glad for her sturdy hiking boots as she made her way down the path she and so many workers had traversed for weeks now. That's how long it had taken her team to recover the remains of a busload of civilians who had been hijacked by a death squad working for a local politician. Aboard the bus had been a rival politician's family on their way to file nominating papers for the upcoming election. Each member of the family had been bound, tortured, and shot. The other bus passengers had been mowed down with machine guns and left in a shallow grave.

Kelsey swatted at mosquitoes as she neared the first burial site, where a pair of local police officers stood guard over the workers. Like most policemen in the Philippines, they carried assault rifles rather than handguns—yet another cultural difference she'd found unnerving when she'd first arrived in this country.

To Kelsey's surprise, Juan walked right past the gravesite. He veered onto a barely visible path through the thicket of trees. Milo trotted out in front of him.

Kelsey's nerves fluttered as she tromped down the hill. He couldn't have found another pit. They'd recovered fifty-three victims already, the exact number of passengers that local townspeople believed had been on the bus that went missing during last year's election season. If there was another group of victims, surely her team would have heard something during their interviews with local families.

"You find gold in them thar hills?" Kelsey used her best John Wayne voice in a lame attempt to lighten the mood. Juan glanced back at her. He'd once told her he'd been named after the American actor and loved all his movies.

"I was out here this morning, ma'am, walking Milo." Juan's formal tone said this was no time for jokes.

Please not another death pit.

"I had the metal detector on, and it started beeping."

Kelsey glanced at the device in Juan's hand, which was one of their most useful pieces of equipment. It detected not only bullets and shell casings—which were valuable evidence—but also belt buckles, jewelry, and other personal objects.

"Look what I found." He stopped beside a ravine, and Milo stood beside him, wagging his tail. Juan shifted a branch and nodded at the ground.

Human remains, fully skeletonized. Kelsey crouched beside them, feeling a familiar mix of dread and curiosity.

"Male," she conjectured aloud. "Five-eleven, maybe six feet."

The height was unusual for a native Filipino. She studied the rotting clothing. Denim and synthetic fabrics withstood the elements better than soft tissue, and it looked as though this man had died wearing only a pair of jeans. She glanced around for shoes, but didn't see any.

"What'd you hit on?" She nodded at the metal detector.

"Something under his head. I think there is a bullet, but I did not want to move anything."

"Good call." She frowned down at the remains.

"Do you think he tried to run?"

"Different postmortem interval from the others, I'm almost sure of it." She glanced up at him. "He's been here longer."

Kelsey dug a latex glove from one of her pockets and pulled it on. She took out her digital camera and snapped a photograph before carefully moving a leafy branch away from the cranium. She stared down at the skull, and it took her a moment to realize what she was seeing.

"I'll be damned," she muttered, leaning closer.

On the road above them, the hum of a motorcycle. The noise grew louder, then halted, and she and Juan traded looks. Kelsey surveyed the trees lining the highway—the same highway the bus had been on when it was hijacked. Branches rustled. Kelsey stood and Juan reached for the pistol at his hip.

"Ma'am Kelsey!"

A boy stepped into view. Roberto. Kelsey breathed a sigh of relief and shoved her KA-BAR knife back in its sheath.

"Phone call, ma'am." He scrambled down the steep hillside and emerged, grinning, from a wall of leaves. Roberto had appointed himself the camp errand boy and spent his days zipping back and forth to town, fetching supplies for the workers in exchange for tips. He reached into his backpack and produced the satellite phone that usually lived in Manny's tent. The boy looked proud to be entrusted with such an important piece of equipment, and Kelsey handed him some pesos.

"Sir Manny said it's important," Roberto told her. "The call is from San Diego."

Kelsey's stomach dropped. *Oh, God, no.* She jerked the phone to her ear. "Hello?"

For an eternity, only static.

"Kelsey?"

Just the one syllable, and Kelsey knew. *Gage*. She'd been expecting this call for years. Her heart felt as if it was being squeezed by a fist, but she managed to make her voice work.

"Mom, what is it?"

Fantasy.
Temptation.
Adventure.

**Visit PocketAfterDark.com,
an all-new website just for Urban
Fantasy and Romance Readers!**

- Exclusive access to the hottest
  urban fantasy and romance titles!

- Read and share reviews on
  the latest books!

- Live chats with your favorite
  romance authors!

- Vote in online polls!

 www.PocketAfterDark.com

26119

"The perfect mix of suspense and romance."　　　—*Booklist*

UNSPEAKABLE

"Tight suspense with the sexiest of heroes and a protagonist seriously worth rooting for."　　　—*Romantic Times* (4½ stars)

"A page-turner until the last page, it's a fabulous read."
　　　　　　　　　　　　　　　　—Fresh Fiction

UNTRACEABLE
Winner of the 2010 Daphne du Maurier Award for Best Romantic Suspense

"Taut drama and constant action. . . . The suspense is high and the pace quick."　　　—*Publishers Weekly* (starred review)

"Fast pace, tight plotting, terrific mystery, sharp dialogue, fabulous characters."
　　　　　　—*New York Times* bestselling author Allison Brennan

"The characters are top-notch, and their gradual romance—entrenched in mystery and suspense—leaves readers sighing contentedly."　　　　—*Romantic Times* (4½ stars)

WHISPER OF WARNING
2010 RITA Award Winner for Best Romantic Suspense

"A perfectly woven and tense mystery with a . . . compelling love story."　　　　　　　　—*Romantic Times*

"Irresistible characters and a plot thick with danger . . . sexy and suspenseful."　　　　　—Romance Junkies

"Action, danger, and passion . . . a compellingly gripping story."　　　　　　　　　—Single Titles

THREAD OF FEAR

"Suspense and romance—right down to the last page."
—Publishers Weekly Online

"Catapults you from bone-chilling to heartwarming to too hot to handle." —*The Winter Haven* (FL) *News Chief*

"A tantalizing suspense-filled thriller. Enjoy, but lock your doors." —Romance Reviews Today

ONE WRONG STEP

"The twists and turns of the story leave the LeMans racetrack in the dust." —*The Winter Haven* (FL) *News Chief*

"Enjoyable, fast-paced romantic suspense."
—Publishers Weekly Online

ONE LAST BREATH

"Compelling characters, unexpected twists, and a gripping story." —Bestselling romantic suspense author Roxanne St. Claire

"Heart-stopping intrigue and red-hot love scenes . . . *One Last Breath* rocks!" —*The Winter Haven* (FL) *News Chief*

"An action-packed tale filled with passion and revenge."
—*Romantic Times*

"Fully fleshed characters, dry humor, and tight plotting make a fun read." —*Publishers Weekly*

"Mixes suspense and snappy humor with wonderful results."
—*Affaire de Coeur*

All of Laura Griffin's titles are also available as eBooks

Also by Laura Griffin